TEN BUCKS AND A WISH

JANINA GREY

Joyel,
sometimes the
wishes we dont make
are the ones that
come true.
love,
Janina
Grey
2024

SMP

SOUL MATE PUBLISHING

New York

TEN BUCKS AND A WISH

Copyright©2019

JANINA GREY

Cover Design by Ramona Lockwood

Published in the United States of America by

Soul Mate Publishing

P.O. Box 24

Macedon, New York, 14502

ISBN: 978-1-68291-938-5

www.SoulMatePublishing.com

The publisher does not have any control over and does not assume any responsibility for author or third-party websites or their content.

I dedicate this love story

to my hero, my best friend, and love of my life—

my husband, David Phillips.

A magic broom brought you into my life,

then cleared a pathway so that we could

continue our journey together.

But you, my love, are solely responsible

for sweeping me off my feet.

Acknowledgments

Thank you to the best short stories I've ever created—my children, Anthony and Alexandra—for your unwavering patience, and for always believing in me and cheering me on.

Many thanks to my Herkimer Diamonds Critique Group partners, Andrea Kaczor and Bill Blodgett. Your success and perseverance as authors kept me motived and focused on my goals. I will never forget the confidence and belief you had in me as we began this journey together.

Special thanks to Central New York Romance Writers and Romance Writers of America, for providing me with the tools, wisdom, and inspiration that aided me along this journey.

Thank you, Debby Gilbert, Publisher of Soul Mate Publishing, for taking me on and believing in my work through thick and thin.

Finally, I'd like to thank my grandma, Evaughn Jones. Thank you for sharing your romance novels with me during summer vacations on your Tennessee farm. And most importantly, thank you for teaching me to never stop believing in true love.

Chapter 1

Manhattan, Spring 2017

Two solid minutes passed before Deanna fully comprehended what Trish was trying to say in her most recent email. Deanna sat before her laptop, drumming her fingers against the smooth hardwood desk, reading and rereading her sister's brief but devastating news. When reality finally began to sink in, Deanna let out a shriek, slamming her hand down.

"You will never own my farm, Michael McCord. Never!" With that vow, Deanna shoved away from her oak desk and reached for her purse, digging blindly until she found the cool, sleek case of her cellphone. Her mind racing, her heart pounding, she struggled with the decision to call her sister until she knew *exactly* what she wanted to say. Yelling and screaming was not her forte, but right now she was so livid, nothing would hold her back.

Except, maybe, her inability to deal with conflict and confrontation.

Annoyed with her spineless self, Deanna collapsed into the hunter green plaid easy chair nestled in the corner of her living room. Her favorite chair. The one where she read her mail, read whatever good book she had borrowed from the library, and surfed the Net on her laptop. The safe place where she watched her favorite rom-com's or filled page after page in her leather-bound journal. She found solace in these arms. The only arms she felt comfortable enough to fall into at the end of the day since moving here nearly four years ago.

Her co-op faced the east, providing a glorious view over the East River. Of this she made sure while hunting for her new home in Manhattan. It was worth the exorbitant monthly payment of nearly two weeks' salary even though it was tiny, comparatively speaking. The living room/kitchenette combo with a bathroom and one bedroom would have fit neatly into the spacious living room of her parents' house back on Long Island.

However, Deanna had to admit it was money well spent. The place was clean—no cockroaches hiding in the cupboards or crack addicts hiding in the stairwells. And she did live in one of the safest neighborhoods this side of Central Park. Her building was close to the subway as well, making her commute to Courtney Davis Ad Ink a fraction of the time it took when she was living back home. In addition to all of this, she had a corner apartment which gave her extra windows, a terrace, and a glorious view of the sunrise each unclouded morning, even with the hazy blanket of pollution that appeared like smudges of pastel crayons across a nearly-finished canvas.

Her terrace was alive with plants year-round: ferns, peppermint, and all sorts of other herbs in the summer; marigolds and geraniums in the fall; and two potted fir trees that stayed green throughout the winter. Over the sliding glass doors leading from the living room there hung a plaque, DRAKE'S FARM. That sign was the only piece of home she brought with her when she left.

Although it was a tight squeeze, she had even managed to fit a chaise lounge between the budding tulips and the sweetest smelling irises.

With winter's cold grasp a faded memory, in a few weeks the warmer weather would soon allow her to sit out on her terrace every evening possible. Many a night was spent out there enjoying the evening air long after the skies were dark and an orange glow from the streetlights cast an ethereal haze about her.

The email still filled her laptop screen and it seemed to mock her from the shadowy corner where her desk sat. Raising a well-manicured hand to her mop of chestnut-brown curly hair, Deanna pushed a lock behind her ear and rested her cheek against her open palm thoughtfully. She frowned and pursed her lips, contemplating the mess her sister had presented to her in a few short paragraphs. Lost in thought, she turned her head slightly and stared out at the fragile blooms filling the wooden planters on the terrace.

What was she going to do? Go back home? To the farm? Trish and Pike's farm?

" . . . *i know reading this in an email is really crappy, but it felt weird calling you coz we never talk on the phone. well we never talk. sorry! But i wouldn't be asking if we didn't need help. Plz don't be pissed off at me or pike.*"

Trish's pleas seemed genuine enough. But, then again, they always did. Trish was always genuine when she needed something.

Well, there was always the smart thing to do. *Detach.* She could delete the email. Or she could respond and tell her no, she couldn't come home. Not even for a weekend, especially not for the week after Easter. Too much to do at work. A new ad campaign was recently assigned to her team. She couldn't leave them hanging.

But she couldn't leave her last living relative hanging either, could she?

"*you have it easy. it sucks out here with mom and dad gone. you are sooooo lucky.*"

Ha. She rolled her hazel eyes and tried to picture Trish miserable. As far as luck being her own reason for success, well. She wasn't lucky at all. She was a hard worker—like her mom. Everything Deanna had she owed to hard work. Everything Trish didn't have was the result of little effort on her part. That's how it always was and always had been.

"pike lost his job just before xmas. i'm workin at the salon but that barely pays the gas & electric."

Money. Trish never reached out to Deanna. But now that she needed money, apparently, emailing her big sis wasn't an issue. A foul taste filled her mouth. Her tongue poked the inside of her lower lip where she'd chewed and broken the skin. She closed the email program with a quick jab of her forefinger, then walked into the kitchen to pour herself a drink.

So, it's money my baby sister needs. Money. That's all.

They hadn't even exchanged Christmas cards this past year.

The nearly untouched bottle of Kahlua sat in the cabinet over the stove, dusty from neglect. She grabbed one of the crystal tumblers that had been resting bottoms up in the drainer by the stainless-steel sink, and held it beneath the ice maker on the outside of the refrigerator door, allowing two cubes to drop with a clink. She unscrewed the cap and poured the sweet-smelling coffee liquor into the glass, then set the bottle down and lifted the drink to her lips. She sipped at it gingerly, the word "money" echoing in her head.

Trish and Pike were going to lose the house. Her house. The house she loved and grew up in, played in, had sleepovers in. The house where she learned to ride her first bike, where she played with her first Barbie and

Ken dolls. The house where she brought her first and only boyfriend home. Where she got her first kiss. Her first broken heart.

Where her parents had died, and were buried, out in the old cemetery where her grandparents, great-grandparents, and their great-grandparents were buried. Where she always believed she would be laid to rest, in the family plot, beside her parents. Even if she'd never moved back, she knew her heart was there and that's where she wanted to end up at the end of her journey.

And now that lazy good-for-nothing brother-in-law of hers was going to ruin everything her ancestors, her parents, and even she as a young child and teen, had worked so damn hard to secure.

"Shoot!"

There was little she could do but help. Some sort of effort had to be made. She had to come up with at least some of the money, come hell or high water, she told herself as she grabbed her cell phone and hit the star key and the number three. After three rings, Deanna listened to Trish's voicemail message, then waited for the beep.

"Hi. It's me. I got your email." *No lectures. Breathe.* "I wish you'd let me known sooner. I can't come home, but I think I can get my hands on some money—"

"Dee? Is that you?" The woman's voice was breathless, delicate, and fragile.

"Trish?"

"Oh, Dee. I knew I could count on you. You're coming home?"

"No. I said I'd try to get you money." Deanna rolled her eyes and shook her head.

"Wait 'til Pike hears. He's gonna be so relieved. You don't know how horrible it's been. How worried we've been . . . Hold on."

Deanna started to speak, but Trish wasn't listening. "Pike. It's Dee. She's coming home." Then she continued breathlessly, "Hold on a minute, he's got the TV so loud he can't hear me." Deanna heard the phone clatter, followed by Trish's muffled voice. Deanna bit her lip, feeling her anger rise.

Trish's voice filtered once again through the line. "Pike wants to know when."

"I said I can't—" Deanna waved her hand at her empty apartment.

"You've got to. We need you here. It's not like you're two hundred miles away."

"I'm going to try to send you a check."

"A check? I don't think so. Besides, you've got to be here for the hearing. And, you've got to talk to Cord."

"Whoa. Hold on a minute. What hearing?"

"Didn't you read the email?"

"Yes, I read your email. All you said was that Cord was interested in the farm. You didn't say anything about a hearing."

"Oh. I thought I did? The town wants to change the zoning code and take away our farming rights. Cord and his dad want to buy the farm so Cord can develop it. They already offered me and Pike $450,000. As far as the mortgage goes . . ."

"Four-fifty? What mortgage? Patricia. That was paid off back in '97. What are you talking about?"

Silence crossed the phone lines momentarily, until Deanna prodded. "Trish?"

"Um. Well. Pike and Daddy took out a mortgage to do some repairs after Mom died. And so we could take a vacation and visit Pike's family in Pennsylvania. He hadn't seen them in years. And, well, to buy a new truck. Our old car wouldn't have made the trip. But we didn't expect Pike to get laid off."

"The taxes, Trish?" Deanna prompted. "Exactly how much do you owe?"

"Well. Pike told Daddy that he could go without paying the taxes for three years before the county would start proceedings. So, the year before Daddy died, Pike took the tax money and invested it."

"You *invested* it? How could you! What were you thinking? You weren't thinking, that's the problem!" She put a hand to her chest. Her heart felt as though it was going to explode from beating so hard and fast. Deanna shook her head again, knowing what was coming.

"Well. We lost it. We bought a handyman special in Lake Grove, but we couldn't sell it. And, well. The bank took that in January. It was a cold winter, worse than normal. All that snow and we couldn't work on it without heat!" Trish's voice trembled and cracked and dropped to a whisper.

"Geez." *Could it get any worse? Yes, it most definitely could.* "What about Cord? Why do I have to be the one to talk to him?"

"Well. Don't get mad."

"Patricia! I think it's a little too late for that!"

"Well. Okay. Cord's supporting the town board proposal to approve a revision in the zoning code. If it passes, all undeveloped farm land will be re-zoned to a multi-use category. Only if the farm is a working farm will it continue to be taxed as farmland. Otherwise, well, the taxes will increase because the land will increase in value . . . and, well . . ." Trish's voice trailed off with the worst unspoken.

"How could Cord support something like this knowing it's going to hurt you?" But knowing Cord, Deanna could guess the answer to that one.

"I told you. It'll increase in value. But then the taxes will go up. We can't afford them now as it is. We'll have no choice but to sell. And Cord offered to buy it. We could do a lot with $450,000, Dee."

"Shoot." Deanna swore softly and closed her eyes. "You're behind, what? Two years in taxes?"

Trish let lose a long sigh. "Well. More like three. I think it's three."

"How much, Trish?"

"A lot, Dee."

"What? Fifty, sixty thousand?" What could land out there go for in this depressed market? Besides, it was undeveloped farmland.

"Dee! Don't yell at me! I don't know! You know I'm bad with numbers!"

"I'm not yelling!" Deanna took a deep breath and repeated her words in a softer tone. "I'm not yelling. See?"

"It's not my fault. Pike can't handle business like Daddy used to."

"What's there to handle? I thought Dad was leasing the land?"

"In case you don't remember, Dad's dead."

"Don't you dare do that to me. You don't need Dad to continue leasing out the land. And it didn't take Dad dying to get things this messed up. Obviously, somebody's been screwing up longer than that. How could Daddy have listened to Pike?"

"Well, geez, Deanna! You took off for the city and haven't hardly ever come back home since Mom died! Now you're yelling at me because of some bad business moves Dad made? We needed you here and you ran off. It's not completely our fault."

There was no sense in arguing. It was always her fault. "I gotta go. I have some calls to make."

"Will you come home?"

"I don't know. I don't know. You need to let me know what you owe in the back taxes. $50,000? $100? I can't do anything without that number." She didn't have the heart to tell her baby sister that it might as well have been $100 million. There was no way she could get that kind of money.

"Dee? Please. I need you. It's bad. I don't know what to do." Trish's voice broke, and she sniffled softly on the other end of the line.

"C'mon, Trish. Don't cry. I don't know what to do. God. Why didn't you tell me sooner?" Deanna's voice cracked.

"We kept thinking things were gonna get better."

"Yeah, they'll get better for Cord. He's the only one to benefit from this whole mess. Typical!"

Trish remained silent for a minute, then offered a curt, "Uh-huh."

"Hey. I've got some friends in real estate. I'll see what I can do. When's Easter?" Deanna grabbed her purse and fumbled for her datebook.

"Two weeks."

"Shoot." There was no way she could take off.

"And the zoning hearing is the Tuesday after."

"Shoot," she said again, reviewing the appointments and notes highlighted throughout the next month. The biggest campaign proposal ever assigned to her team was due a week and a half after the holiday.

"Deanna. Please come home."

"I'll try." She'd only made it home once in the last three years. And that was for Dad's funeral, leaving straight from the church to come back to the city. She didn't even stay for the reading of the will.

"Even without all this mess," Trish said, sobbing, "I miss you."

"Stop crying! I can't think right now, Trish. I'll try to be there. I can't promise. Okay?" Deanna swallowed thickly and closed her datebook, slipping it back into her purse. "I'll call you on Sunday."

Deanna disconnected the call with a jab of her finger, her head nearly bursting with all she'd learned in the last half hour. The thought of losing the farm hurt, but not nearly as much as the realization that it was partially her fault for leaving Dad and Trish there with Pike, alone, after Mom died.

A vision of her mother's face floated before her now. Mom was still so young when she died, so pretty. Hard work suited her, filled her cheeks with color, and always left a twinkling in her eyes. She had been beautiful. Her best friend. She and Mom had been inseparable. Like two peas in a pod, Dad had always said. Trish had been like Dad. To the tee, Mom always said.

It was only natural that Trish would marry someone like Pike. She, Dad, and Pike—the three of them—were dreamers, foolish, *head in the cloud* optimists, who didn't have a lick of business sense combined.

Mom was the one who ran the business end of the farm, telling Dad what crops to plant, basing her decision on how the weather was down south and how planting season was faring in the rest of the nation. It was Mom who made sure Christmas trees were ordered by May for the following November, that apple pickers were hired by August. It was Mom who ran the farm stand, expanding it and expanding it until it was a tourist landmark throughout Olde Westfield, and then eventually the whole Town of Brookville. Drake's Farm.

Mom had made the astute decision to use the western acreage for boarding and training horses. Hayden's Horse Farm. Of course, the Drakes didn't have anything to do with the horse farm, they only leased the stables and land out to Billy and Barbara Hayden.

When did everything fall apart? Trish never said a word the whole two years before Dad died. It was crazy how he died exactly two years after Mom, to the day. January 20. It had snowed the day Mom died, and she fell walking home from the farm stand. She had spent the afternoon preparing to order for opening day, which would have been the week before Easter. At first, Dad wasn't too concerned about Mom when she didn't come home, thinking she was working late on orders.

By the time Deanna had come home from work Dad was frantic. Trish had been out with Pike and the weather had delayed Dee's train by two hours. Dad had been all alone, not knowing what to do except call the farm stand. He'd been trying 20 minutes when Deanna walked in the door, stomping the snow off her sneakers in the foyer. As soon as he blubbered to his eldest daughter that Mom wasn't answering the phone Deanna turned around and ran all the way to the farm stand.

But it was too late. She found her mother facedown, not twenty feet from the farm stand's front porch, eyes wide and vacant. Her nose and mouth were filled with snow.

Shortly thereafter, Pike moved in and Deanna moved out. Mom never liked Pike. Neither did Deanna, for that matter. It broke Deanna's heart knowing that her little sister was making the biggest mistake of her life—one Mom warned her about repeatedly.

About that time, Deanna got a promotion at the advertising agency in Manhattan, making her assistant to the vice president of social media marketing campaigns. With the salary increase and some of the inheritance money she received from Mom's life insurance policy, she put the deposit on the apartment she now called home.

With Mom gone and Pike in the house, Deanna found little reason to ever go back to Olde Westfield. It's not that she didn't love her father, but she was never his favorite, and she knew it. Like Trish had never been Mom's favorite.

When Dad passed, Deanna hadn't even asked Trish about Dad's will. She didn't want anything from him and didn't expect anything from him. Trish had offered Dee the chance to go through Mom's belongings they had stored in the attic after Pike moved in, but Dee never had the heart to do so. Now she had no choice but to clean out all the memories as soon as possible if they were truly about to lose the farm.

Easter time. It was time to go home.

She sighed now, a loud sigh, that started in her heart and worked its way up into her throat, sticking like a wad of over-chewed bubble gum, then spewed forth and burst from her lips in a choked sob. She raised a fist to her mouth and bit her knuckles to keep from crying. She couldn't lose it now. She had too much to do. Too many calls to make, too many arrangements to make. Too many decisions to make. She needed a clear head.

She dumped her half-emptied glass of Kahlua into the sink, the nearly melted ice cubes clinking softly against the stainless-steel drain. Once again she picked up her cellphone, this time punching in the phone number of one of her closest friends. Three rings, voicemail, *beep*. "Sal? It's Deanna. I need some advice on taxes and I was wondering if you knew anybody I could trust for some good legal advice. I'll be home all night. Talk to ya later."

~ ~ ~

Trish sat by the ancient, black, rotary-dial telephone for quite a while after hanging up with her older sister. She chewed her thumbnail so far down that she tore at the tender bed of skin below, causing droplets of blood to swell and flow. She should have been honest. But it was so hard with Deanna. She was always so critical, so judgmental. So right all the time.

But still, in her silence Trish knew she had betrayed Cord. He'd been trying so hard to help them out, guiding them, buying into a partnership with them. Now he was doing what he thought was best, what he thought was the only way to keep the farm out of strangers' hands.

The partnership that Dad, Pike, and Cord had formed should have been on Trish's list of things to explain to Deanna. How Cord had put up $200,000 while Dad and Pike had put up $20,000. Well, Dad had. Pike was supposed to work off his share. But that didn't happen. It wasn't that Pike was lazy. Trish lifted her head now and gazed through the kitchen doorway into the den where Pike sat in Dad's old recliner, snoring away.

For some reason, he didn't know how to stay motivated.

Cord had pretty much been a silent partner when the trio bought that handyman special. He'd fronted them the money and told Daddy and Pike that when they sold it to write him a check for $200,000 plus a third of the profit. And that was it. No questions asked.

Something happened to Dad the day he called Cord to come over to the house, a few days before Christmas, to tell him they'd lost his money. He grew quiet, depressed, stopped eating.

Trish sighed, remembering how Cord had handled the news, and for a moment she wished she'd married Cord instead of Pike. He took it like a man, saying nothing, clenching his teeth, that muscle in his jaw working overtime as it twitched away. He had pushed away from the table mumbling how sometimes things weren't meant to be and then left, much to Dad and Pike's relief. He never asked for a penny of his money back.

Then one month later, Dad died. Although Trish didn't know exactly when her father had made the changes to his Last Will and Testament, with his death he paid Cord back his money. Sort of. Trish and Deanna weren't the only beneficiaries of the Will. Cord was now a third owner of the farm. Not even Pike was listed as an owner. Only Trish and Deanna. And Cord.

That was how Trish found herself in the spot she was in now. She knew she should have listened to Cord. She knew she should sell it to him, support the zoning. But she couldn't do that to her sister, despite the rift that seemed unfixable. Besides, there was no way she was going to get Deanna to agree to sell the farm to Cord. Of all people.

Trish shook her head, imagining herself approaching her sister with that proposal. But as far as she could tell, it was either sell out to Cord to settle the debt, pay the back taxes and save the farm from scavengers and the auction block, or watch everything their ancestors ever worked for end up as a super center grocery store or indoor sports complex.

No. If anyone was going to develop this farm, it would have to be Cord. His ideas were good. His heart was in the right place. Deanna would have to be convinced. And for the moment Trish thought the best way to do it was to show Deanna how hopeless keeping the farm would be. But that wasn't going to be easy. Somehow, Deanna had to be convinced that selling was the only way.

And Michael McCord was the only one who could do it.

Chapter 2

She was crazy, Deanna thought, as she stepped off the Port Jeff Station Long Island Rail Road platform. The cool March night air slapped her across the face, and she shivered. It was so much cooler out here in the suburbs than it was in the city. Shaking off the cold, Deanna waved down one of the taxis waiting for business, then picked up her matching teal and peach tapestry overnight and garment bags and strode toward the dusty old white Caprice Classic that was parked and idling. The rear passenger door was wide open, inviting her to step in. She slid onto the cool, brown, well-worn vinyl back seat, setting her luggage on the floor beside her, then directed the driver to take her to Drake's Farm. Without a hitch, the driver sped off not even waiting for the address. Everyone knew Drake's Farm, Deanna thought with a smile.

Route 112, Nesconset Highway, Old Town Road. The scenery whizzed by, affording her little opportunity to note any major changes since she had last lived here. When she came home for Dad's funeral she hadn't noticed much of anything. She had arrived at the station at 9:25 a.m. Service was at 10 a.m. And she left on the noon train. She hadn't even gone back to the house.

Countless strip malls passed before her eyes unseen as Deanna thought briefly about her father's service. It was the most recent memory to hold on to, to compare things to, at this point in her life. Even then she felt like an outsider. A stranger. Yet at the same time, old acquaintances had treated her with a new respect. The hometown girl who made it in the big city. Even though "the big city" was only an hour or so away—with traffic.

Everyone acknowledged her, except Cord, even though he and his parents sat in the second pew, directly behind Deanna, Trish, and Pike. After the service, Mike and Jane had hugged her and her sister in a firm all-encompassing embrace, with Jane turning away to hide her tears, telling no one in particular, in a choked whisper, "He was a good man."

Deanna had nodded sadly, while Trish burst into tears and buried her face in Pike's faux leather jacket. A cool nod was all Cord offered Deanna, which she returned as an awkward silence fell between the two.

It had been difficult to keep her eyes off him, her first love. His navy-blue suit and gray tailored shirt fit him impeccably. Deanna hadn't thought that clothing could fit so perfectly for someone with shoulders as broad as his. But it did. It molded him, right down to his narrow waist. His snug slacks fit his muscular thighs perfectly, revealing that he was as active as he had been in his high school and college days.

And he was still as handsome. More, she had thought, if that were possible. No, not handsome. Knockdown drop-dead gorgeous. His eyes were bluer than the bluest summer sky, an azure blue, that lit fires in every girl's heart. Even hers. After all those years.

His hair, thick, light brown waves that he kept cropped close in front but a bit longer in the back so that it curled above his nape, hadn't started thinning yet. Or even graying, although his brother started graying before he turned thirty.

Wow, she thought, a bit surprised. Cord must be 30 by now, too. He graduated two years before her, and she was turning 28 in July. Deanna felt herself tremble, recalling a few birthdays that the two of them had celebrated together. Her musings brought forth a husky chuckle and another sigh.

The taxi driver glanced up at the sound, his eyes catching hers in the rearview mirror. Deanna blushed and turned her attention out the window.

After the service, Cord had offered to drive Deanna back to the station, but she declined. Being near him was so painful. He had seemed a bit relieved when she declined. But still, he accompanied her to the cab and bent over stiffly to offer her a brief embrace, telling her to take care.

That memory. The memory of his touch, his scent, his breath in her hair for the briefest moment jarred her back to reality. *That creep!* He must have been planning even then what he was going to do with the farm the minute Dad died. No. He hadn't changed at all. He cared only about himself, and wouldn't be satisfied until he'd taken everything from Deanna. He already had her heart, it was only natural he'd take everything else until she was left with nothing. Wait until she saw him this time.

Won't you be in for a surprise, Michael McCord!

"Could you turn down here first, and go around through town?" Deanna asked the driver. He nodded, never taking his eyes off the road.

There it was. Big. White. The McCord house was a beautiful, old Victorian, with a porch that wrapped clear around to the back. How many nights did she and Cord sit on that swing? she thought with a wistful smile.

"Not enough, apparently!" a voice in her head taunted.

The taxicab driver maneuvered along the main highway, passing the heavy equipment yard, the woods, the horse farm. Her dad's corn fields. The skeleton stalks

from last year's crop—or was it the year before?—
swayed in a subtle dance in the misty night air. The
fields. Untouched. The house. It sat all the way at the end
of a long, winding, gravel driveway. A white, two-story
farm house. Front porch. Nothing elaborate. Not like the
McCord's' place. But, obviously desirable. Obviously, if
Cord wanted to steal it from her family.

It was after 9 p.m. when the taxi rolled down Drake's
driveway. "You live here?" the man asked, tilting his
baseball cap up far enough to peer in the mirror once
more.

"Sort of." She fished twenty-five dollars out of
her leather wallet. "Keep the change," she mumbled,
suddenly uncomfortable. Then she opened the door,
tugged her luggage behind her, and headed toward the
house. Trish had left the front porchlight on. Pike's truck
was nowhere in sight. Good. The less she saw of him,
the better.

With each step, Deanna's heart beat faster, her
lungs grew tighter, and her throat muscles constricted.
She hadn't realized how hard this was going to be. She
should have stayed at a hotel, she thought, checking over
her shoulder. If the cab had still been there, she would
have turned around and climbed back in. But it wasn't.

Out near the highway, red taillights glowed faintly
in the distant darkness, one side flashing as it made a left
onto the main road. And then it was gone.

The front door was unlocked, and Deanna spotted
a note on the table below a mirror hanging on the wall
opposite the entrance. *Went out for pizza and beer down
at Graffiti's. Come down. T.*

No thanks, Deanna thought, taking a quick
assessment of her childhood home before opting for a
shower and bed. Climbing the stairs to the second floor,

she wondered if her room was still intact, or if Pike had turned it into a man cave.

Third door on the left, across from the bathroom. With her hand on the worn brass doorknob and her heart in her throat, Deanna pushed. The door squeaked, complaining of rusty hinges. The room smelled of Jean Nate, linens, and dust. She turned on the light switch by the door and smiled.

Thank you, Trish.

Nothing had changed. Her desk, her books. Her alarm clock. Even her old quilt. Deanna inched slowly over to the bed, passing a trembling hand over the patchwork design and chuckled, spying a note on the pillow.

Fresh sheets.

That brought back memories of when the two would sneak out after hours. Usually Trish would go off with her girlfriends to hang out at Graffiti's, then leave a note as to when she came home so their stories would be the same in the morning. Deanna would meet Cord on his back porch, and then the two of them would head off to the gazebo by the pool.

That damn lump formed in her throat again, making it hard for her to swallow or breathe. She closed her eyes and inhaled air into her lungs, then forced herself to swallow. When she felt steady, she opened her eyes and set her luggage down on the bed.

It took moments to unpack. She unwrapped the bottle of red wine she grabbed as a last-minute impulse and set it on the dresser. Her empty drawers hungrily welcomed the remaining meager offerings she took from the suitcase: undergarments, slippers, and her nightgown—a flannel old thing, with a tissue stuck in the pocket and a rip below the buttons. It was worn out enough to be discarded, but Deanna couldn't bear to throw the ratty old thing out. It was Mom's.

Once she emptied her overnight bag, she stuffed her jogging shorts, tee shirts, and jeans in the second drawer. She unzipped her garment bag and hung up her three blouses, the pale-yellow suit she planned on wearing to church on Easter, and the gray one she brought for the hearing Tuesday night. It was then she spotted a robe Trish had obviously washed and placed there in the closet that smelled of cedar, and again, Jean Nate afterbath splash.

Trish still had not returned home by the time Deanna had showered and slipped her mom's gown over her head. After giving her hair a good brushing, turning upside down to study her pale pink painted toenails while she gave her roots a good work over, she stepped softly toward her mother and father's old room, instead of heading back to her own. She paused before the closed door and squinted her eyes tightly shut, remembering.

The deep rumble of her father's snores, her mother's soft voice nudging him to turn over echoed through the years, settling in Deanna's memory. Other than this brief reflection, there was nothing but a soft, sleepy silence blanketing the hallway. An old clock tick-tocked somewhere downstairs.

Deanna made her way back to her room, closing the door behind her. She settled under the sheets, staring out the window. There were more streetlights and more store lights than there had been growing up. But not as many as she viewed from her apartment in the city. There was more traffic on the highway than she remembered. But again, nothing compared to Manhattan. No beeps, no screeching of tires. No sirens. No alarms going off. No loud laughter. No shouting. Again, nothing but silence.

~ ~ ~

Unlike the bedroom window in her apartment, Deanna's bedroom window in her old home offered a glorious view of the early morning dawn on Easter. Lavender, rose, and aquamarine ribbons laced across the horizon like splashes of Easter egg coloring dye, before the first crest of the morning star broke through a splash of clouds.

With a quick yawn and stretch of her arms, Deanna threw back the sheet and quilt and jumped from her bed. Within minutes she tiptoed out the front door, clad in shorts, tee shirt, and sneakers.

Pausing for a moment, she stood on the porch and took in the peeling paint, the threadbare lawn, and the shiny red pickup Deanna knew had to be Pike's. He'd had an old red pickup forever. Trish had said he bought a new truck.

A sense of familiarity crept into her body, but she still felt a bit alienated. She'd done this every morning throughout her high school days and throughout the year and a half she'd lived home after college. Even when she was sick with the flu, or had her period, she ran. Now she smiled broadly, eyeing two squirrels as they scurried across the drive.

It was still so much the same. Same buds peeping from the limbs of the oak trees that within a month would be shading the front lawn. Same gravel. Same tree stump with the flower box built around it. Same birdbath. Same crack in the bird bath where Dad dropped it the day he unloaded it from his truck. Mom had only chuckled, saying it gave the thing character.

Same view of the highway. The salon across the street where Trish said she worked. The gas station down on the corner, right next to the deli, where Pike *used to* work. The post office was now a pizza place, she noticed, wondering where they'd put the post office. She took a small hop down one step. Then another, another, and another, until she hit the gravel at a slow trot. Slow. Rhythmic. *Thut, thut, thut, thut.* Her breath came evenly, without effort. By the time she reached the highway, the blood was flowing through her legs. Her calves and thighs tingled with life.

Unconsciously, she made a right turn onto the highway, heading east, toward Cord's house. Again, the memories flowed like the blood through her veins. The pavement beneath her sneakers took her back to another time, when she was younger and in love. Every morning she and Cord ran together. Together until their bodies were soaked with sweat. Until their muscles and tendons quivered and flexed with unchecked energy.

The sun still had not risen completely above the horizon as Deanna jogged toward the light. With her hair caught up in a ponytail, little tendrils had started to escape, curling about her forehead and temples and down along her nape. She now brushed a lock of hair out of her eyes, blinking for a moment, refocusing on the image of another jogger heading toward her. Her heart skipped a beat or two as a feeling of *dèja vu* swept over her. She blinked.

Cord.

The next 30 seconds lasted an eternity as Deanna forced her legs to continue to move forward. She wanted to turn and run the other way. She wanted to cross the street, or run into the woods and take the old short cut home. But by the time she decided to do that, she was in front of the McCord Heavy Equipment lot, all fenced in and inaccessible to her.

They were close enough now for Deanna to see he was focused squarely on her, and she wanted to melt into the pavement. They would nod and continue their own ways, she decided. But maybe not, she thought, as he came closer and his lips slowly softened into an easy, wide grin.

"Figured I'd find you out here," Cord said as he greeted her with a huff and a smile. "Looking good, Drake." He slowed to stop, but when Deanna kept going, offering only "Hey," he made a sharp turn and came up behind her.

"Wait up, Dean."

"Getting slow in your old age, huh?" *Duh!*

"Hardly. Just better." A slow smile chiseled the lower part of his face, etching dimples in his cheeks. He laughed when a blush crept across her face. "Heard you were coming in."

"Yeah?"

"Yeah. Trish and Pike were at Graffiti's last night. She said you'd probably head down." They ran together, nearly but not quite matching strides.

"Got in late last night." The pair had reached his driveway now, and hesitated, both glancing beyond the house toward the gazebo in the backyard. Again, Deanna's face grew a warm pink with recollection.

"How's about a cup of coffee?" Cord offered this as they stood side by side, breathing hard from their run.

Deanna wiped her forehead with the back of her hand and shook her head, not trusting her voice.

"C'mon. Old time's sake?" He gave her that damn grin, the one that had always won every argument.

She raised an eyebrow and cocked her head. "Is your mom up?"

With a shrug, Cord grinned, and it reached his eyes that glittered with amusement. "Probably?"

"Well."

"Great." He turned and started a slow trot down the driveway, also layered with crushed stone. Only instead of the faded gray gravel that lined the Drake driveway, the

McCord's drive was blanketed with a layer of sparkling white rock, white as snow. Their sneakered feet made crunching sounds with each step.

When Cord trotted passed the walkway that led to the house, Deanna hesitated. He laughed and called over his sweaty shoulder, "This way, Drake."

Once again she followed him, curious as to where he was leading. *The gazebo?*

She paused a second time, and called his name when he turned toward the garage.

Turning with mock impatience, her ex-boyfriend-turned-rival chided her.

"Do you want that coffee or not? Come on."

"In the garage?" she answered, her voice filled with doubt. Nevertheless, she followed.

With a chuckle, he opened the door. Again, she followed and found herself facing a carpeted stairwell, one she didn't recall from their childhood days. She took the stairs two-by-two, guessing what was about to be confirmed within seconds. Sure enough, at the top of the stairs Deanna found herself in what could have been a very posh apartment somewhere in the heart of Manhattan. Cream-colored carpet and walls were accented by southwestern decor, terra cotta vases, a brown Italian leather sofa and love seat combo, and woven tapestries of orange, gold, red, and brown.

Deanna let out a low whistle of appreciation, but did not move from the landing. "Not bad." She watched him lean over the kitchen sink, splashing water on his face and sweat-dampened hair.

"Bathroom's in there," he said, pointing to a door to Deanna's left.

"I'll only be a minute." She slipped out of her grey Brooks running shoes and placed them beside Cord's on the tile floor at the top of the stairs.

Moments later, she emerged, smelling like Ivory Soap. The ponytail she wore moments earlier was now twisted into a knot at the crown of her head. Deanna watched as Cord turned around slowly, his hand resting by the coffeemaker on the tile countertop. She felt herself color as his gaze swept the length of her body, beginning with her cotton white anklets, moving up her slender— *and awfully pale*—legs, lingering at the expanse of her hips clad in running shorts.

A faint smile tugged at his lips before he continued his assessment, moving quickly over her trim waist, hesitating but a moment on the two slight peaks that protruded beneath her cotton Rolling Stones tee shirt, and ending, finally, on her flushed face and slightly parted lips.

Feeling thoroughly ravaged and totally consumed, Deanna responded in a steely, business-only voice, "Are you done?"

The thought of returning Cord's gesture by giving him as thorough a once over to put him in his place briefly crossed Deanna's mind. But in the end, she decided against it. There needed to be a clear and definitive line drawn, no blurring of motives, no misunderstandings. Definitely no flirting. Why would she even want to? She forced her legs to walk about the apartment, needing something other than her former lover to think about.

"For now."

A clay sculpture sat on a sofa table behind the couch, and Deanna forced herself not to throw it at his head. She recognized the signature as a popular artist who gave many an exhibit in the downtown galleries, and nodded her approval.

Cord's eyes, as crystal cool as the water he'd filled the coffee pot with, followed her every move. She noticed this as she stepped over to the glass dining room table, a budding cactus placed at its center. Six leather chairs that matched the sofas surrounded the table. She studied her reflection in the glass, as she did in the bathroom mirror moments earlier, and cursed herself for not putting a smidgen of makeup on.

"What was that?" Cord's voice brought her head up, which she shook with a slight side to side motion.

"Nothing. I'm surprised with what you've done to this old garage."

"We only added a second floor. It was easy," he said with a shrug.

"You did this?" Deanna asked, waving her hand.

"Yeah. Me, Dad, and Matt built it two years ago. Then Matt got married."

"Matt's married? Wow," Deanna said, laughing.

"Yeah," Cord chuckled. "He didn't have a choice."

"Oh. Oops." Deanna grinned. "Sorry."

Her response brought an out and out laugh from Cord, who offered, "Don't be. Terry's cool. And their little girl is something else." His chest puffed out a bit as he added, "I'm her godfather."

Amused at his reaction, she smiled and offered, "Congratulations."

He glanced over his shoulder, as the coffee finished dripping, and asked how she drank it.

"Black's fine."

"No milk?"

"Nope. I drink it black," she said as he handed her a mug before she even finished her answer.

"So what time did you get in last night?" he asked, fixing a cup for himself.

"After nine." She leaned over the bar dividing the kitchen from the dining area, her elbows supporting her as she sipped at the hot liquid. "Mm, good."

"So why didn't you come down?"

She shrugged and watched the steam rise from her mug, then answered simply, "I was tired."

"We were looking forward to seeing you," he said, his gaze never leaving her face.

"Well. You'll be seeing quite a bit of me for the next week, at least."

"I think I like the sound of that." He leaned across the bar also, their faces not even a foot apart. Deep blue eyes probed emerald-green ones. "What's the occasion?"

Choosing her words carefully, she stared him down, never blinking. "Seems they done called in the posse to fight off the bad guys," she replied in her best southern drawl.

He only frowned. "They? Who's they?"

"Trish," she said, her gaze unwavering.

"Really?"

His confusion was evident, and she didn't know how to process that.

"Dean?"

She raised her brows. "I know all about the hearing. The effort to re-zone the farm."

"Oh? And?" He cocked his head to one side.

"Yeah. I hate to ruin this lovely coffee klatch, but there's no sense in pretending. I'm not about to hide away in the city so you can put up some damn shopping center on my family's farm."

"Whoa," Cord said, raising both his hands to form a 'T'. "Time out."

"No. You think I'm going to stand by and see you take advantage of my sister and her husband and their bad luck?" She wagged a finger at him. "You are dead wrong. I'm fighting the zone change and I will not sell you the farm."

"Did you say you talked to Trish? Trish Jones?"

"Yes!" She snapped, annoyed with his amused arrogance.

"Patricia Jones, your sister?"

"Yes!"

"I don't think you know the whole story."

"I may not have the whole story, but I've got the whole picture," Deanna bit back, annoyed that he did not appear to be upset.

"Do you? Let's hear it." He threw her an amused grin and beckoned with his hands, urging her to fill him in.

"Um."

"I'm listening."

"I don't have to tell you anything."

"No, that you don't. But, I thought we were friends."

Friends? This fueled her anger even more.

"Friends? Friends don't take advantage of friends when they're down on their luck."

"I don't know what you're getting at."

"I better go," she said, straightening up. "I have to get ready for church."

"To pray for us sinners, huh?"

"You haven't changed a bit, have you?"

"You're angry with me. And it's not because of the farm. Hasn't enough time past that we can move beyond what happened? Haven't you punished me enough?"

Deanna swallowed the lump in her throat, and shook her head as she turned to make her way toward the stairs. Picking up her Brooks, she ran down the steps until she got to the door, then flung it open and slipped her running shoes on before taking off in a fast sprint.

She paused as she started down the driveway, glancing up over the garage to find Cord watching her. She turned without a nod and raced home.

Chapter 3

A sense of healing and strength filled Deanna as she stood waiting for the Easter Processional to exit the church. As Father John passed her, he smiled and nodded, then made his way to the entrance at the back of the building.

Lingering behind in the pew, Deanna waited with Trish and Pike until the entourage passed. As a child, she and her mother would spend the few moments after mass lighting candles in memory of loved ones who had passed on. She glanced over at the memorial area now, recalling how her mother would take her by the hand, help her light the tall, tapered candles, and kneel with her to pray. Now, it was her own mother and father who would be remembered. With a slight nod at her sister, Deanna gestured to the candles by the altar, where a small crowd waited. Trish nodded in understanding.

"We'll wait outside. C'mon, Pike," Trish said as she grabbed her husband's arm and led him through the exiting crowd, herding with the other churchgoers like sheep down the center aisle.

After making her way to the memorial, Deanna waited her turn in line to light her candles. She scanned the church, freshly painted for the Easter Vigil. The carpet was new, too, although it remained the deep burgundy she remembered it had always been.

This was the Roman Catholic church where she had been baptized, where she had made her Holy Communion, and where she had been confirmed. And, like her parents, grandparents, and their parents, she expected to have her funeral here and then be buried in the family plot on the farm, as was the Drake tradition. It never mattered where she lived; in the end, she always knew she'd be coming home to be with her ancestors. Now, if Cord got his way and she lost her family home, that might not be the case. A sigh hiccupped in her throat with the weight of it all, and she bit her lip to fight back the tears.

Resting on the padded leather kneeler before the statue of the Virgin Mary, Deanna tried to pray but words failed her. She thought about her parents, attempting to say something pious, but nothing came. She prayed for strength. When her rambling thoughts were finally reduced to bargaining with God along the lines of, "I'll go to church every Sunday if you let us keep the farm," she gave up.

A miracle was the only thing that could help her at this point, and right now she did not believe in miracles. In fact, there wasn't too much she did believe in, she realized, slowly walking out of the empty building.

As she entered the bright sunlight, Father John, a jovial, rotund man with a smiling face, greeted her at the door and hugged her hard, welcoming her home. "We've missed you, Deanna. We thought the big city swallowed you up," he said, patting her on the back.

With a shake of her head, she hugged her family priest and smiled wistfully. "No. I'm still alive. Been a little remiss I guess. I'll try to get home more."

"Please do. I miss our walks."

Nodding in agreement, she said softly, "Me too."

The smell and feel of springtime lifted the weight from her shoulders and sadness from her heart. She offered her upturned face to the sun, eyes closed, a smile widening beneath the warm rays.

"Dean!" The screech of her nickname brought her eyes open as she searched the crowd for the face to that familiar voice.

"Tammy?" she called out, squinting against the brightness of the morning.

"Over here!" The sea of people parted and a very pregnant young woman waddled toward her.

"Oh, my God. Tammy Reynolds!" Deanna's eyes widened in surprise as her one-time best friend came to stand beside her. "Check *you* out!"

"It's great, isn't it?" Tammy said, turning sideways as she smoothed her dress covering the huge expanse of her belly. "Any day now."

"And you're out walking around?" Deanna stared in amazement at the huge belly protruding from her otherwise tiny friend.

"Shoot, Dean. This is nothing. I'm still working at the dealership."

"Get out! You're kidding!"

"Nope. Dead serious. In fact, I think I see my boss now. Come on. I'll introduce you to him." Tammy clasped Deanna's hand, urging her to follow.

Trailing alongside her longtime friend, Deana scouted the crowd for a glimpse of Trish and Pike. The pair came into sight as Tammy tugged at her hand, and Deanna watched them head toward Pike's pickup.

"Dean? I'd like you to meet my boss, Frank Gordon." Tammy slipped her arms around the distinguished older man, pressing her lips lightly to his cheek. "And the father of my child. And my husband." She giggled. "Frank, honey. This is my bestie from high school I always talk about, Deanna Drake."

"Hello there." He tightened his embrace about his wife, placing a kiss on the top of her head. "Any friend of Tammy's is a friend of mine."

Deanna nodded and smiled at her friend's husband.

"Shame what's happened since your folks passed on. That was a big draw for the town," he said, shaking his head sadly.

"Yeah. Well. I'm going to see if I can fix that," Deanna offered slowly.

"That's wonderful to hear. You been talking with McCord, huh? He's got some good plans, that one does." He nodded to Deanna's right at the mention of Cord.

Deanna turned and spotted Cord, his parents, Trish, and Pike standing near the pickup.

Her voice was cool as she responded to Frank. "No. I haven't been talking with Mr. McCord. I got in too late last night."

"Mr. McCord, Deanna?" Tammy snorted and rolled her eyes. "I thought you two got passed all that. Since when is it Mr. McCord?" Tammy said with a giggle.

"Since I learned that he's trying to cheat my family." Deanna stopped talking and turned to follow Tammy and Frank's gaze. What was left of her family stood chatting with the three McCords, laughing at some story Cord was telling.

"Doesn't look like he's cheatin' anyone," Frank said, nodding toward the scene with a quick jerk of his head.

"Yes. I see that. Tammy, give me your cell number and we'll keep in touch, okay?" She rummaged through her purse until she found her cell.

"I'd love it. We need to catch up," Tammy said, then gave her friend her phone number. "You better text me. Now go save your family," Tammy said with a wink.

Cord was standing at the perfect angle, Deanna noticed, enabling him to watch her every move while she spoke with Tammy. He stared openly as she headed toward him and his parents, Trish, and Pike. She felt a bit more confident now, her hair done, makeup on. Although, she was sure she could have used a touch up of lipstick. She wet her lips with the thought, then pursed her lips tighter. He smiled as his gaze locked on her mouth.

As she approached the group, she called out to his parents and totally ignored him. "H'lo, Jane. Hiya, Mike."

"Why hello, young lady. I couldn't believe my eyes when I saw you sitting in front of us. I had to put my glasses on, didn't I, boys?" Jane said as she reached her arms out, welcoming Deanna into her embrace.

"She sure did." Cord smiled broadly, putting one arm around his mother's frail frame, and the other around Deanna.

"Trish was telling us you're in for the week?" Jane turned to Deanna for confirmation.

"Maybe?" Deanna offered a feeble smile and a shrug as she tried unsuccessfully to extricate herself from Cord's arm. He tightened his embrace ever so slightly and smiled down at her in an almost brotherly fashion. She wanted to kick him.

"You'll be by for a visit, won't you?" Jane's voice was stern as she offered an invitation that most definitely sounded like an order.

"Well, I'll try," Deanna said, shrugging her shoulders in another failed attempt to free herself from Cord's casual embrace.

"Of course you will." Jane smiled as Deanna and Cord fidgeted for control.

"Mom?" Cord asked. "Why don't we have them over after Easter dinner for dessert?"

"Why, Michael! That's a wonderful idea. What do you say, kids?"

"Oh, no. I mean, thank you, but—" Deanna tried to move away from Cord again, glaring openly at him.

"We'd love to," Trish said, and her response brought a gasp from Deanna that everyone ignored.

"Thank you, Jane, but we don't want to be an inconvenience on such a short notice," Deanna said. The thought of dessert with Cord turned her stomach.

"Mom's pleasure. You know how she likes a crowd on holidays. And with only Matt's family, and me and Dad here, she's a little lonely. Aren't you, Mom?"

As if the whole scene had been rehearsed, Jane nodded and immediately extended the invite from dessert to the full meal to all three of them. "Long Island Duck. Mint jelly. Sweet potato pie. Homemade corn bread."

Pike spoke for the first time all morning. "Sure beats Trish's turkey." That comment got him an elbow in his gut, a wave of chuckles from the crowd, all but Deanna, and then an awkward silence.

Standing there, on holy ground, Easter Sunday morning, Deanna tried once again to pray for that miracle. *No. Please, no dinner.* Dessert would be bad enough. But dinner? Seconds later, Deanna realized that God must have been busy making his own dinner plans.

"Fine, then. Dinner it is. How's three o'clock sound?" Jane beamed broadly at the two girls, then at her son.

Deanna slipped a side glance at Trish, but Trish only smiled and shrugged, her blond hair bouncing freely in the bright sun. "We'll bring the wine."

"Great. See you at three. Mom, Dad. Catch you later." Cord turned to Deanna, and for the first time she noticed he was wearing the suit he'd worn to Dad's funeral. She remembered because the thin pinstripe was the same color blue as his eyes.

"Can I give you a ride home?" The amusement had left his eyes, and he now held her gaze, as if he could will her to say yes.

Shoot. All he had to do was catch her eyes and she was putty in his hands. "I came with Trish and Pike," she said, without any real conviction.

"Oh, go on. We've got a few errands to run anyway. Don't we, Pike?"

"There you have it. What do you say, Dean?" His mouth twitched as that darn grin spread across his face.

Her glower came naturally by now, and she could care less who saw. "Trish, Pike. I'll be home soon. We'll talk later." She narrowed her eyes in warning, but Trish waved her off with a smile.

"Have fun, you two." Then Trish turned to Jane. "It's like old times, isn't it, Jane?"

"Sure is, honey," Jane replied, as Deanna watched her smile and wink at Trish.

Their voices faded in the distance as Cord placed a hand on Deanna's elbow and guided her to the next row of cars. They stopped at a green four-door SUV and her heart skipped a beat. Foolish girl, she chided, recalling how Cord had said he'd search high and low until he found a car that came in the same color green as her eyes. When he did, he'd buy it.

But, that was years ago. *Lifetimes ago.*

"You look great."

It was a simple statement, without any underlying tones. But it made Deanna tremble all the same. *Damn, how could he still do this to me?*

"You don't have to be nice to me now." She hardened her voice as she climbed into the truck, forcing herself not to compliment his vehicle. Or his suit. Or his hair, or his eyes, or his smile.

"I want to be nice to you, if you'd let me." Cord got behind the wheel and started the SUV.

She shook her head, then stared out the window and whispered, "I hate you."

"Yeah. I remember. So. Where do you want to go?"

"I thought you were giving me a ride home?" *Be still, oh traitorous heart.*

"Nah. You don't really want to go home, do you? You want to take a ride? Maybe head out east?" His grin was so broad his dimples were showing.

"If that means missing dinner, sure," she said, stealing a glance at him.

"Besides, I thought we had things to discuss." He cocked an eyebrow at her.

"Apparently, I have to talk to Trish."

"I thought you already did." Amusement filled his voice.

"So did I. But from what I've heard and seen this morning? Oh, hell. Never mind." Her mind was racing as quickly as her heart. Something was off. And only Trish could clear things up.

"So you want to hear my plans for the farm?"

"My farm? No thanks."

"So it's your farm, huh?"

"I spoke with a friend. He gave me advice on how to deal with the situation."

"Big city folk, huh? Us country folk ain't good 'nough fer the likes of a city slicker like you. Is that it?" He twanged at her, and a smile curved her lips despite her anger.

"I trust him."

"You don't trust me?" Cord's voice softened as he reached out, his strong, tanned fingers closing gently around her soft, slender hand resting in her lap. And it was as if he was making love to her right there and then, judging from the explosions in her heart and belly.

"Cord." Deanna didn't intend to whisper, but when she spoke she found that his nearness, his touch, the aloneness they shared, had stolen her breath away.

"Much better, Deanna. Much." His voice, too, was barely more than a whisper.

Deanna swallowed thickly, staring at his broad hand, dark and roughened from years of hard work under the sun. Hands that could rip through hours of hard physical labor, or caress her skin with a touch as soft as a spring breeze.

She glanced up to find the truck hadn't even left the parking lot yet. She wanted to be strong, to forget what it felt like to love him.

"It doesn't have to be like this." He removed his hand and placed it firmly on the steering wheel and spoke softly, his eyes never leaving her face.

Her skin cooled quickly with the absence of his touch. She shook her head and focused on the throng of parishioners mulling around socializing with one another, unsuccessfully trying to loosen the lump in her throat.

"I don't think you know the whole story. You don't know how hard it's been for me to not call you and warn you about what was going on." He emphasized each word softly, his voice filtering through the SUV. "This wouldn't be happening if we had been together this whole time."

"You blew it." She jutted her lower lip out in defiance and continued to stare out the window.

He shifted into drive and edged onto the highway. "Deanna. We've got two things to clear up between us. The past and the present. And the way I see it, once we settle these two problems it'll be smooth sailing from there. So, what do you say, huh? Can you retract your claws and try to work out our differences?"

He studied the road as she studied his profile. He was headed east, as he had suggested earlier. "I'll keep my claws to myself if you keep your . . . your paws . . . to yourself." Her deliberate hesitation emphasized the meaning of her words, and Cord slipped her a quick glance. Their eyes locked and for that moment everything was forgotten. They laughed, just like old times.

"Deal. When did you get so tough?"

"It's the city. It's quite empowering. Afraid?" she said in a teasing tone.

"Nah. I think it's kinda sexy," he offered, keeping his eyes on traffic. "So what about me?"

"You?" His question surprised her. There went her heart again.

"Yeah. How do you see me?"

"I don't know, really. I haven't thought about it."

"Bull."

She chuckled and glanced sideways at him from beneath lowered lashes. "You are so vain, Michael McCord."

"No. I'm being honest. Tell me you don't still feel it."

"God! Listen to yourself! I don't believe you!" She stared out the passenger window.

"Can't do it, can you?"

Chewing her lower lip kept her from saying something stupid. After a moment's thought, she responded. "What we had is over. Sure, I think of us sometimes. I'd be inhuman if I didn't. But what's past is past. It's over. Done. Forgotten."

"It may be over—for now. But it's not forgotten. If everything in the past was forgotten you and me would be together right now, working your dad's farm."

"And that is what this is all about, isn't it? The farm. You want to sweet talk me so I'll give the whole farm away for a song and a dance. You want it all, don't you?

You always did." She shook her head, her voice filled with disgust.

"And once again, you've got it all wrong, Dean. All I want—"

"All you want is everything. That's all you ever wanted."

"Are we talking about right now? Or are you gonna keep bringing up the past?"

"Don't you see? I'm not bringing up the past. It's here. It's now. Every time I see you. Your house. This damn truck!" She faced him, yelling, one hand braced on the cream-colored dash board, the other on the leather seat.

"So you do think of me."

Deanna groaned as she saw his chest swell ever so slightly.

"You, Michael McCord, are a jerk. Arrogant. Conceited—"

"Is this your idea of foreplay?" He glanced up at her, his lips half-cocked in the sexiest grin she'd ever seen on him, or anyone else for that matter.

"Where the hell did that come from?" She laughed in surprise.

"There you go. I figured talking about sex would lighten things up a bit." Then he held up a hand, seeing the fire flare in her eyes once again. "Sorry. No joking. Got it. My apologies."

She stifled a chuckle and turned away so he could not see how great an effect his charm had on her.

"But we do have to talk. Why do you think I took the chance of getting in a car with you all alone? This is dangerous stuff I'm doing here, Drake." Cord kept talking as he maneuvered through traffic.

"I've said everything I have to say." Deanna folded

her arms across her chest, crossed one leg over the other, and stared out the window.

"I can see you're going to be very open-minded for this conversation," he remarked dryly, shifting gears.

"Hey. You're the one who feels this great need to talk. Be my guest." She sliced an open palm through the air, extending the invitation to speak.

"Well. If we're going to come to any agreement on the farm, the way I see it—"

"Hold it." Deanna held up a hand. "I don't plan to come to any agreement on the farm."

"See? There you go again. You're being pigheaded."

"You're being money-hungry and greedy."

"You haven't even heard my proposal."

"I've heard enough."

"Ahh. But you haven't heard it at all. Are you gonna be quiet long enough to hear me out?"

Tightlipped, Deanna motioned for him to continue.

With a chuckle, he did, shifting gears once again. Traffic crawled around them as he slowed the truck for the yellow light up ahead.

"As I was saying, if we are going to come to any agreement—on anything—we've got a few closets to clean out."

"Cord! Don't bring it up again."

"You said you accepted my apology four years ago, damn it! But you haven't forgiven me, have you? What we had was good."

"Then why'd you go and blow it?"

"I said I was sorry. I never saw her again."

"I felt like the biggest jerk. I couldn't show my face for months. I still get embarrassed when I see any one we knew."

"I was the jerk. Everybody knew it then and nobody cares now. I stayed here. I didn't run off to the city. I've lived with it. Until Debbie had the damn kid and we had blood tests done, everyone thought I was the guy who got her pregnant. How do you think I felt? I ruined everything I had with you because I slept with her one—one, mind you—time. Once, Deanna. That was it."

"So you said."

"Are you so perfect that you can't forgive me for something that happened five years ago?" He slammed his fist on the steering wheel, causing Deanna to jump.

"Don't do that! And, don't yell at me."

"I'm sorry, but—" The light turned, and as his foot hit the gas pedal the truck lurched forward with a jerk, just before he made a quick right into the convenience store at the intersection. "I'll be right back."

Alone in the truck, Deanna took a deep breath and covered her face with her hands. She couldn't stop trembling, his words dredging up emotions she had worked so hard to bury. He actually wanted her to believe he still loved her. She knew that was his game plan. That would be the next log he'd toss on the fire. Get her to soften up to him and then *wham!* He'd take the farm, leaving her and her sister nothing but a clean tax bill and the clothes on their backs. His revenge for dumping him so long ago.

With a sigh, she dropped her hands and raised her gaze to peer inside the store. He was standing on line at the register, balancing two cups of coffee, the Sunday newspaper, and a box of her favorite chocolate chip cookies. He remembered, she thought with a reluctant smile. *I'm in trouble. He's bringing out the big guns.*

She watched him saunter away from the register, laughing as he called something out over his shoulder to the little blonde who gave him his change. He was too freaking handsome, she thought, watching him stroll toward her as if he owned the world.

"Hey, gorgeous," he said, slipping into the driver's seat.

"Hey, yourself," she answered, forcing herself to respond a bit lighter than she felt as she took the two coffees he handed her.

"You belong sitting right there in that seat."

She couldn't read his eyes as he flipped his shades off his head, so she focused on the coffees and tried to still her heart.

"Where to?" he asked, shifting the vehicle into reverse as he glanced over his shoulder.

"You're driving." She poked a peach-painted fingernail into the coffee cup lid, twisting the tab up and bending it backwards to reveal the steaming black coffee. "Want me to open yours?"

"Sure. Thanks." He maneuvered the car out of the parking lot after placing the cup she handed him between his legs.

They drove in silence until Cord turned south onto the parkway.

"You want to try Southaven Park?"

"What time is it?" She glanced at the dashboard for the answer. "It's already noon. I wanted to talk with Trish before I faced you and your father."

"What for? It's only Easter dinner."

"Yeah, right. And the subject of buying the farm won't be discussed at all?"

A deep laughed rumbled around her and she watched his dimples carve out two hollows against the smooth, tanned skin of his cheeks. "I didn't say that, did I?"

Shaking her head, Deanna mused aloud. "She sounded so upset on the phone. Now she's all but kissing your butt since I've been here. What gives?"

"Who, *Trish*?" Balancing his cup in the hand that

also held the steering wheel, Cord took a sip of the hot brew.

"Who else? What are you blackmailing her or something? Did you sleep with her, too?" Deanna knew full well even Cord would never do that, but still, she couldn't resist. She hid her smile as she took a swig of coffee.

Cord sputtered at Deanna's suggestion, his expression filled with disgust. "That would be like sleeping with my own sister!"

She smirked, then after a moment, she added, "Well? Did you?"

"God, no. I didn't. Wow."

Sipping her coffee, her smug smile stayed hidden behind the paper hot cup.

"So what do we do now?" Cord took a tentative taste of his brew before he nestled the cup between his legs once again, shifting gears. He cleared his throat and snickered as Deanna's gaze followed his action, resting on his coffee cup. "Hello?"

Her cheeks grew warm as she lifted her eyes up to meet his gaze, but she quipped lightly, "I wouldn't slam on the brakes or make any sudden movements if I were you."

He laughed out loud and raised the coffee cup to his lips again as if taking her advice. "Hey, get me a cookie, will you, Drake?"

"I can't believe you remembered these," she murmured as she slit open the box and grabbed two chocolate chip cookies.

He said nothing as she handed him one, and nibbled on the other. Neither spoke again until they reached the park.

The shade was cool and the air smelled damp and woodsy as Deanna and Cord strolled together beneath the lush canopy provided by the tall pines at Southaven Park. They headed toward the lake, the call of the geese giving them direction. It was quiet otherwise, and the air was sweet with the scent of pine. Each step was muffled by the soft bed of tawny pine needles carpeting the forest floor. They made it halfway through the dense forest before Cord wrapped his arm around her shoulders, drawing her closer to his side.

"For old times' sake," he almost pleaded, and in silent agreement she did not step away.

It was all Deanna could do to keep from grabbing his hand and entwining her slender fingers around his. But she didn't. It seemed like the thing to do. But, instead, they walked silently, the concept of rebuilding lingering between them, but neither knowing where to lay the first brick.

"What have you been up to lately?" Cord asked.

"Working mostly, at Courtney Davis," came Deanna's reply.

"Impressive. Good for you," Cord replied with a quick squeeze of her shoulders.

"How about you?" she asked.

"The same. The industry is finally picking up again. New housing starts are up over last year."

"That's good."

"Yeah." He focused on the ground, studying their footsteps.

"Too bad we didn't bring any bread. For the ducks."

"Yeah," he repeated.

Memory kicked in and they veered off to the left as they came to the horse stables.

They fell silent and she became lost in memory of the last time the two had come here. They had broken up.

Cord walked beside her until they neared the

clearing, and then finally he spoke. "If I could do it all over again, I would. No lie."

Instead of warming her, his words unleashed an anger from deep within. She wanted to scream, wanted to hit him, yell at him. Make him hurt. From the sound of his voice she didn't need to do anything to cause him pain.

"Deanna?"

They stood beside the lake, a murky green body of water filled with algae and grass and duck poo. "This is so sad. We used to swim in this water. Now look at this. What a mess." She shook her head in disgust, mesmerized by the slime and scum coating the shore water.

"Deanna."

She heard him gulp a swallow. Then exhale.

"You think they could do something to fix this," she continued, almost inaudibly. "To clean up this mess. They'd have to work at it though. It's probably too far gone."

"Deanna. Listen."

"Things never stay the same, do they? You know? *'Nothing Gold Can Stay?'* You wonder how the ducks can live in water this dirty?"

"Deanna, forget the water. Listen at me." He grabbed her by the shoulders and drew her close.

"Cord. I—"

"Can't you give me another chance? Us? Give us another chance. Life hasn't been the same without you. It will never be the same. I miss you. Damnit." The urgency filled his voice and pain glimmered in his eyes. "I need you. Don't you understand?"

For a moment, Deanna almost did. But only for a moment. Then the understanding was gone, replaced by wariness. "Need? You don't need me. You need the farm.

You think I'm that stupid? I can't believe you'd stoop this low!"

She jerked away, but not quickly enough. Firm and unyielding, his hand caught her upper arm. "That's not it, Deanna."

She yanked free from him not even bothering to glare, and headed back to the lot where she would find his green truck, her ride back to home, and her sanity.

Chapter 4

"Mom, can I get some potatoes over here?"

Jane handed the blue pottery bowl across the table to her son without a word. Cord was not his usual self this afternoon, she noted in distress. Out of both her boys she could always count on him for a laugh, whether he was in the mood or not.

"Pass the jelly, please." Jane grimaced and handed the jelly to a very sullen Deanna. This was not how she envisioned dinner turning out.

Trish peeked out from her lashes long enough to throw an apologetic smile Jane's way. Jane raised her eyebrows and shrugged.

"So Deanna, how's work going?" Mr. McCord made the first attempt to break the tension that had been hovering in the house since Deanna and Cord arrived moments before dinner was ready to be served.

Trish and Pike had come over earlier, with Trish going to the kitchen to help Jane, while Pike stayed in the living room and talked about cars with Mr. McCord. Matt cancelled by phone, apologizing because Jenna had come down with a fever during the night.

Not speaking a word, Cord and Deanna arrived shortly after Jane hung up with her eldest son. And that was how things stayed. This was not at all the way Mike and Jane expected things to be. Not at all.

"We're very busy. I'm swamped in fact. I shouldn't be taking off this week." Deanna glared quite obviously at Trish.

"We're all busy, Deanna. You aren't the only one who works." Cord shot back. "Potatoes?" He offered the bowl to Deanna, who ignored his comment, but accepted the potatoes. She silently took a scoop before handing the bowl back to Jane.

"Great jelly, Jane. Did you make it?" Deanna licked a splatter of potatoes off her thumb, offering a hesitant glimpse of a smile to Jane. "And the potatoes are awesome."

"Yes. That's the last of the jelly though." Jane let out a sigh of relief as the conversation softened.

"You gave us a batch of it. It was good. Pike loved it." Trish grabbed the jelly and dumped a spoonful on her plate.

"Yes, I'm glad you enjoyed it," Jane said, as the conversation lapsed into an uneasy silence.

After a moment Mr. McCord spoke. "How long you staying, Deanna?"

"I don't know. I should head back by Wednesday. It depends."

"On?" Cord asked as he scooped jelly onto his plate, then licked the spoon. His mother slapped his hand and yelled for him to go get another.

"C'mon, Mom. I can't help it." Nevertheless, he stood up and disappeared into the kitchen.

"Sometimes I wonder if he'll ever grow up." She shrugged in apology.

"I doubt it," Deanna answered, pursing her lips.

"I heard that." Cord yelled from the kitchen. "Now," he continued as he reappeared through the door waving the silver teaspoon, "you were saying?"

She stared as if he were speaking a different language.

"You're staying depends on?" Cord prompted, slipping the new spoon into the jelly.

After a second's hesitation, she answered him with a single word. "Work."

"Oh? What do you do, Deanna? I wondered about that." Mr. McCord spoke up.

"I work for Courtney Davis, and we're totally swamped with new projects. As it is, I left my team hanging so I could be here for the hearing. We were assigned a new client a few weeks ago. I got my part done, but there's . . . they were annoyed I had to take off."

Cord studied her for a moment, their eyes locked until she grabbed a dinner roll and lathered it with butter.

"That's impressive. Must be a lot of stress," Jane said slowly.

"A bit. But it's worth it. I really love my job, and my team. And it pays the bills," she added with a shrug.

"You'd have less stress if you moved back home," Cord said in a huff.

She smiled brightly and ignored his suggestion. "Could you pass me some more potatoes, Cord? Uh, and don't touch the spoon."

~ ~ ~

"That was the best duck I've eaten in a long time, Jane."

"Why thank you, Deanna. You are a sweetheart." Jane fished around the sink full of soapy water as she searched for the next plate to wash.

"No. Thank you for having us," Deanna said as she took the plate from Jane and rinsed it off before placing it on the drying rack.

"You set the table so pretty. I love that centerpiece," Trish offered as she towel-dried and stacked the dishes on the kitchen table. "And the duck wasn't greasy at all.

Any time I've ever made duck it came out chewy and greasy."

"Sounds like you're cooking it too long and on too low a setting." Jane wiped her hands on her apron, then picked up a stack of dishes and disappeared into the dining room, leaving Trish to wash the next round.

"You want to tell me what in hell is going on?" Deanna hissed under her breath as her sister came to stand beside her.

"With what?"

"You all are acting like it's old home week, which isn't exactly the picture you painted on the phone or in your email. Now, what's the real reason you brought me out here?"

"You want them to rezone the farm?" Trish waved her dishtowel at Deanna.

"Hell, no."

"You want to sell out to Cord?" She smiled sweetly and batted her eyelashes.

"Not if I don't have to."

"Have you come up with any of the money?"

"Hey, ladies." Cord appeared behind them from out of nowhere, placing an arm around each of their shoulders. "This sure beats a Maytag or Whirlpool."

"Cord, you pig." Trish slipped out from under his embrace and took a dishtowel and swiped Cord across his behind. "That's it. I quit. I don't have to take this abuse."

"Trish? We're not done," Deanna said, her voice sounding agitated and high-pitched.

"No sweat. I'll help you finish. Move over." He grabbed the dishtowel from Trish and tossed it on the counter.

"I've got it. I guess we were almost done after all." Deanna stiffened her shoulders as he moved behind her.

"Ridiculous. It's not every day I offer a hand in the kitchen." His voice was low, tinged with humor, and unbelievably sexy.

"Then why start now?"

"To show you what you're missing out on." He placed a hand on either side of her on the sink countertop and bent to whisper in her ear. "I'd be in the kitchen every night if you were there beside me."

She turned her head to escape the touch of his lips, but there was little space for her to move.

"Cross my heart," he whispered again, sending shivers throughout her body.

"Cord?" Deanna's attempted reply was barely audible.

"Um-hm." He nuzzled against her skin. "Wouldn't this be good? A man could get used to doing dishes like this."

Deanna rested her hands at the bottom of the sink full of soapy water, closed her eyes and swallowed thickly. "Th-Th-This is sexual harassment."

He sighed and straightened up as Jane spoke from the doorway.

"That was not what I planned on serving for dessert. But you young kids know best on how to keep the calories off, I suppose." Jane chuckled behind them. "It sure is good seeing you two get along again."

Deanna pushed away, her face flushed as she turned to face Jane. "Is that it for dishes?"

"Yes, dear. Why don't you two go inside. I'm done here except for wiping down the stove. Go on. In fact, Cord? You know that big fruit bowl I loaned you? Did you ever bring that back?"

"Don't think so. You want me to go get it?" Cord smiled at his mom and she smiled back. Deanna caught the exchange and immediately wizened up to them both.

"Yes, and Deanna why don't you go with him? Make sure he doesn't drop it, will you, dear?"

Deanna studied the pair and shook her head in defeat. "Jane, you are worse than your son."

"Yes, I am. Now, run along."

~ ~ ~

They stepped outside into the bright afternoon sun and Cord stretched wide, placing an arm around Deanna's shoulders. She shrugged it away and took a step to her right, groaning in mock frustration. "Don't you ever give up?"

"I did five years ago and I've been regretting it ever since."

Their steps nearly matched, with Cord struggling to keep his steps shorter and in time with Deanna's. She noticed this and for spite took shorter, slower steps until finally she couldn't bear to see him struggling, and burst out laughing as they reached his door. He held it open for her despite her behavior, but she shook her head.

"I'll wait out here."

"C'mon up. I'll only be a minute."

"Nah. I'll wait out here and enjoy the sun. I don't get this much nature living in the city."

"Suit yourself." He disappeared up the stairs without another word, and within moments, he returned.

"That was fast."

"Told ya." They headed back to the house.

"So you still jog every morning?" Deanna spoke first.

"Nope."

"Only on weekends?"

"Nope."

"Oh. Only on holidays?" Deanna started to smile.

"Only on Easter. Yes. It's become a religious experience for me. Every Easter Sunday. Crack o' dawn." He grinned down at her, the sun making his eyes dazzling pools of blue. "When Trish told me you were coming in I took a chance."

"Oh." Her smile broadened.

"You like that, eh?"

"Well. It is flattering to have a man get up at the crack of dawn hoping to run into you."

"Yeah. I'd do it every morning if I knew I was going to run into you."

"Cord."

"I know. You think I'm after you for your bucks."

Even that remark didn't erase Deanna's smile.

It was nearly 7 o'clock before Trish and Pike stood up to leave. They hugged the McCords goodnight, thanking them for a wonderful holiday. "I was dreading today. It's never been the same with Mom and Dad gone," Trish confided.

"I know, I know." Jane patted her on the back. "You call me when you need to talk, you hear?"

Trish nodded, her eyes brimming with tears.

When Deanna stood up to follow her sister, Jane touched her arm. "Don't go yet, dear. I'd like to talk with you, if you're not too tired."

Deanna narrowed her eyes and focused on the McCord matriarch. "When it comes to your boy, you've got no scruples, do you?" Without waiting for the woman to answer, Deanna told her sister, "Go on, guys. I'll be along in a bit."

As Pike and Trish left, Cord headed toward the kitchen, mumbling something about putting up another pot of coffee. Mr. McCord offered to help.

"What's up, Jane?" Deanna sat on the edge of the floral sofa, knees together, arms crossed over her chest.

"I thought we'd chat." Jane sat in a chair across the coffee table, smoothing her blue dress.

"About?" Deanna prodded, her gaze narrowed.

"Nothing." The older woman played with the fringe on a throw pillow. "In particular, that is."

"Okay?" Deanna cocked her head toward the kitchen, where laughter sounded with some joke between father and son.

"He's really a sweetheart, you know."

"Yes, you're lucky to have a husband who loves you. One that you can trust." Her body relaxed a bit and her crossed arms slipped to lightly cupped hands in her lap.

"I know it. He wasn't always that trusting though. We had to work hard to get where we are today. We both made some foolish mistakes in our younger days. But, I was talking about my son." The fringe took on the shape of mini braids as Jane spoke.

"When two people love each other as much as you two seem to, I'm sure it's worth the effort." She tried to smooth the edge off her words and ignored Jane's reference to Cord.

"Yes. Most definitely."

Deanna struggled for a change of topic, and settled on dinner. That was safe. "Great meal."

"Yes. I don't suppose you cook much . . . for only yourself?" Jane stopped playing with the fringe and stared Deanna in her eyes.

Suppressing a chuckle, Deanna answered the unasked question. "No. Never. Usually I make a salad. Or a peanut butter and jelly sandwich. Or cereal. No sense in cooking a whole meal only for me."

Jane smiled. "No. I suppose not."

"I think I enjoyed being with people even more than the food, no disrespect intended."

"None taken. It must be hard, with both your mom and your dad gone."

"Well." Deanna let out a sigh. "When Mom left, I split. You remember. I couldn't face waking up in that house every day without her. You know? And Dad. I can't believe he's gone, even though we never got along anyway. I mean. I loved him and I miss him. But, I hadn't seen him for almost two years." It was Deanna's turn to pick up a throw pillow, hugging the solid green square to her stomach.

A sympathetic smile passed over Jane's face as she nodded. "I'm so sorry, honey. I wanted to be there for you, you know, for your mom. But, with everything that was going on with you and Cord at the time, I felt like it would be pouring salt on an open wound."

Deanna nodded slowly. "It would have been. You did what was best. Your cards and letters were more than enough. When I first moved to the city they were what kept me going."

Jane stood up and came to sit beside Deanna. "I missed you so much. It was like losing my own daughter when you and Michael split up. And then when your mom died and you left. You were like the last ray of sunshine around here."

The two women embraced, with Deanna burying her face against Jane's shoulder.

"You smell like a mom," Deanna sobbed. "Like my mom. Pond's Cold Cream. And . . . " she sobbed again. "Johnson's Baby Powder." The tears started slowly, and Jane did the motherly thing to do. "There, there," she cooed into Deanna's ear, "you go right ahead and have a good cry. There's a girl."

"I'm s-s-sorry. I don't know w-what's come over me. I didn't e-even cry at her fu-funeral."

"Shh. It's okay, honey. It's okay." They rocked together, ever so gently, tears soon welling up and spilling onto Jane's own cheeks.

Moments passed before a still sniffling Deanna could collect herself, kissing the woman lightly on her cheek. "Thank you. I guess I needed that."

"Never you mind, young lady. You know, I've missed you. Please don't stay away so long again." With a pat of the young woman's hand, Jane stood up.

"I'll try not to. I promise." Deanna stood up, running her hands through her hair.

"Good. Now go wash up. I think I smell that coffee brewing."

~ ~ ~

"You and Mom have a good talk?" Cord sat on the front porch swing beside Deanna, their thighs close enough to share body heat without contact.

"Yeah. I've missed her." Her voice was quiet. Reflective.

"She misses you too. I caught hell for years for what I did. Shoot. It was like you were her daughter or something. I thought she was going to disown me." He chuckled softly now. "Not that that's funny."

Staring off into the yard, she smiled. "That's okay. She was always like my second mom. I'm glad we came today. It would have been hell at home. Thanks."

"No problem. I'm sorry if we got off to a bad start this morning." He shrugged, following her gaze. "And this afternoon."

"Yeah. Me too. Mean cup of coffee you make there, Cord."

"Thanks to Dad. Mine is usually too strong."

He cleared his throat and studied the traffic crawling slowly along the highway at the far end of the property.

"Well. It's good. And, thanks for not talking about the farm or the hearing."

"That's okay." As if her words broke a trance, Cord's voice became business-like as he smoothed his jeans and slapped his thighs with both palms. "Can we meet tomorrow? A business meeting. Strictly business. Say one o'clock. I'll summarize my proposal and you can discuss any reservations you have. Maybe we can find a common ground?"

"Cord?" She shook her head, turning toward him.

"I don't want to talk about it now and ruin the night. Tomorrow, one o'clock. Deal? If we're going to fight we'll do it then. Let's enjoy the rest of what's left of tonight."

"One o'clock. But you're not going to persuade me to sell—"

"Tomorrow. Hear me out first." He flashed that lopsided grin her way and smiled even wider as she relented.

"Fine, then."

"Want to walk?" He stood up and reached down a hand.

Ignoring his offer, she stretched, unfolding her legs and rising. "Sure. Which way?"

"How about the back?" He nodded toward the gazebo, and for a second she believed him. Then she laughed and offered the same old alternatives she'd give him over the years growing up.

"Field or driveway?"

"Field. Then we can check out the stars. Too many lights on the highway."

"Yeah. But at least you can still see some stars, even with all the lights. You can't even spot the Big Dipper from my apartment."

"That must suck." They started across the field toward Drake's Farm.

"Um-hm. But otherwise it's not so bad. I've got this terrace, you know. And I've got all these plants and trees and bushes out there. You should see it from the street. It's pretty cool. Almost like a jungle." She giggled. "I hung the old DRAKE'S FARM plaque by the door. No one who visits me gets it though. It's like a lost joke."

Cord was silent as she described her home. "Is it nice?"

"It's okay. Kinda small, but fine for me."

"Do you ever think about coming home? Back here, I mean."

Deanna shook her head, not trusting herself to speak, too confused to make any sense. This was her home, where she belonged. But the memories of everything— everyone—she had lost made it too difficult to come home for good. What if she hadn't left? Mom would still be gone. But Dad? On top of all this was the intense guilt she felt with the realization they were losing the farm because she had abandoned her father and Trish. And that she never got to say goodbye to her father.

"That bad, huh?"

A sob escaped her throat as she willed herself not to cry. The effort proved futile when Cord placed a comforting arm about her shoulders. The two stood still for a moment embraced in the middle of the field, a single silhouette beneath a topaz moon. Then, for the second time in three years, Deanna cried. For the loss of her mother, her father, and the loss of a love she'd counted as her one and only. A loss that she felt as dearly as the deaths of her parents.

"You don't know, Cord. You have no idea. First you. Then Mom." She sobbed, resting her face against his chest. He held her close, his face resting against her hair.

"Shh. Don't. I'm sorry. If I could go back, I would never have slept with Debbie. I swear. I was drunk. I know it was no excuse. But you were gone. And I thought we were going to break up from the letters you wrote."

"So what? You think it was easy for me?" She turned her gaze upward to search his face, still enveloped in his embrace. "God. I felt so stupid. And then to have to see her. I ran into her everywhere when I was home. And she always made it a point to say hi, patting her belly and smiling smugly. And she knew the whole time it wasn't yours."

"She slept with me when she already knew she was pregnant. I learned after the fact that the real father wanted no part of the baby. I was so stupid. I'm so sorry I hurt you. Can't you see that now? I can't believe we are here, together. I haven't been this happy in years. I've been miserable without you." His voice cracked with emotion.

"I don't know." She paused and laid her palms against his chest.

"All I'm asking is for another chance." His eyes bore into hers beneath the veil of night.

"I can't. I can't right now." She drew back, needing the cool night air to clear her head.

"Why not? Is there someone else?"

"No." This was happening way too fast.

"No, what? No, you don't want to try again? or no, there isn't someone else."

"Oh, Cord! Why do you have to push? Why? Why do you have to have everything your way? You haven't changed one bit. You want things your way and you want it yesterday! How do I know you're not going to—?"

"I won't. I'm older. I was a kid then."

"I should leave," she said, but stayed by his side.

"Fine."

Again, she didn't move. She wasn't ready for the night to end, but she didn't want it to go where she might not be ready to go. It was dark, but for the light of the moon.

She didn't want him to see how troubled she was, how unsure, and how nervous she was.

Whispering his name, she turned her face upward, searching his eyes, and finding his lips. His kiss came lightly at first, a soft fleeting caress. She shivered, straining her neck as Cord hesitated, waiting for her reaction.

He bent his head lower and captured her mouth in an all-consuming kiss. His lips molded to hers, probing, sucking, bruising. She responded, despite her vow, despite her unwillingness to trust him, to forgive him completely.

I need you. Her mind screamed, her body screamed, her heart screamed. *Damn you, I need you.*

Every cell of her body was blossoming like a moon flower at midnight. It was as if the last five years had not happened. They were young again, back when times were good, days were carefree, and love was theirs for the taking.

Arms wrapped around his neck, she held him close.

His mouth left hers, moving to kiss her cheeks, her chin, her throat. He cupped her face in his hands, guiding her toward his mouth again. He found her lips parted, waiting, inviting. He whispered her name, then kissed her as she responded by melting into him.

His hands moved over her, caressing her face, her hair, gliding over her shoulders, tracing the curve of her spine. They rested momentarily on the small of her back, bringing her even closer.

"Michael. Michael. Michael." She whispered his given name as his head dipped lower, nuzzling her neck, then lower, as he traced kisses along the opening of her blouse, down to where the lace of her chemise lay against the soft skin of her breasts. Deanna tilted her head back, delighting in the sensation of his mouth on her flesh, and opened her eyes, reveling in the stars, the moon, the coolness of the evening, the heat of his body wrapped around her own. She drew a quick breath and pulled away from him.

Regaining her composure, she laughed a bit self-consciously. "Whew. Where did that come from?" Her voice trembled and sounded strained.

"I don't know whether to apologize or thank you," he said, struggling to capture his breath. He kissed her temple, leaning his chin against her forehead.

She sighed softly and nodded in the darkness. "How about if you walk me home now before we both do something we may regret?"

"Huh. I wouldn't regret a thing. Well. Except for maybe location."

"That never bothered you before." They started walking and she welcomed the arm he placed around her shoulders as he drew her close. It had grown quite chilly in the last few moments.

"Is this an invitation?"

"Hardly. You'll know it when I extend an invitation."

"Maybe I should clear my schedule?"

Again, she chuckled. "Don't hold your breath."

He sighed forlornly and placed a hand on his chest. "Ahh. My heart."

They fell quiet, only the swishing of the grass beneath their feet could be heard.

When they reached the front porch, Cord turned to her and spoke. "Still on for tomorrow?"

"Don't you work?"

"Harder than you ever could imagine, Dean."

"Yeah, sure." She smiled at him, a genuine smile, one that reflected her gratitude, her peace of mind. "Thanks, Cord."

"My pleasure, ma'am. Glad t' be o' service." He tipped an imaginary hat and bowed low, grasping her hand and bringing it to his lips. "One o'clock?"

She nodded and watched him half-hop, half-skip down the steps as he headed toward their field. She sat down on the step as he faded then disappeared into the darkness. Her smile lasted as long as she heard his faint whistle, until it, too, faded into the night.

Chapter 5

Monday morning began with an uneventful jog down the main highway, which Deanna considered to be a good start since she didn't run into Cord. It gave her the chance to reflect with a clear head on all the events from the day before. If she truly wanted to be cynical, if not paranoid, the whole day could have been part of one big plot. From church in the morning to the walk home last night, everything could have been planned by the McCords, her sister, and brother-in-law.

Not that Jane would agree to be part of something so devious in a harmful sort of way. But, Deanna believed without a doubt that if Cord wanted the farm badly enough, he could easily convince his mother to do anything. She'd believe anything he told her. Including that he still loved Deanna and wanted her back.

But Cord had sounded so sincere. And his kiss. Oh, lord, his kiss. Deanna picked up speed and her feet pounded the pavement faster and harder, as if trying to escape that particular memory. She needed a clear head right now.

Lunch at one o'clock. Could she sit with him one-on-one again today? No. Not without succumbing to him completely. *Deanna Drake! Of course you could. You've weathered lunches under much worse circumstances.*

That was true. Deanna had now run well past the McCord property and turned around to head back home. The workout was turning out to be a good one. Running on this highway void of pedestrians racing off to work; of garbagemen throwing empty garbage pails; of dog walkers and bums sleeping across her path, was absolute heaven.

Glancing at her watch, she noticed she'd been running for nearly an hour. When she returned home it would be time to face Trish and Pike. Finally she would find out what was going on. Finally.

Pike's truck was gone by the time she jogged into the front yard, which was a surprise. She thought he was unemployed, and he really didn't strike her as being an early riser. She tried to recall if his truck had been there when she left this morning, but couldn't remember. Maybe he'd gone out last night and had not come home yet. Yes, that fit better with the picture she had of him. Ooh, she could be nasty sometimes, she thought with a grimace as she stretched her legs out against the porch steps.

Once inside, she listened for sounds of Trish then picked out music and running water filtering from the bathroom upstairs. Deanna climbed the steps two at a time and headed toward her old room, surprised with how good it felt to be living in her childhood home again.

Sure the wallpaper was frayed, the paint was faded. The rugs and hardwood floors were worn. She thought back to her apartment, how meticulously she kept it. Nothing out of place, no dust. It smelled like pine in the winter, jasmine in the summer, and cinnamon apples in the autumn, thanks to candles and incense.

While she waited for Trish to finish in the shower, Deanna made her bed and turned to the closet. There wasn't anything suitable for a business lunch, except the gray suit, and that was for the hearing. She thought about jeans, but figured she needed clothes that told Cord she meant business.

Deciding that a quick shopping trip was in order, Deanna grabbed fresh clothes and headed toward the bathroom.

Knocking first, she called out her sister's name, and when Trish hollered, she entered. "Hey," she called through the steam-filled bathroom, "save some hot water for me."

"Deanna. Get with the times. Pike and Dad put a new boiler and hot water heater in. I could stay in here for another hour and leave you plenty." Trish giggled. "Too bad I have to be to work in an hour."

"Work? You didn't take off?" Deanna stripped off her sweat-soaked clothes and threw them in a pile in the corner of the bathroom.

"Take off? And lose a day's pay?" Trish's hand slipped from behind the shower curtain and grabbed the towel off the nearby wall hook.

"Don't sound so shocked. I took off a whole week for you."

Trish frowned from behind the curtain. "No you didn't. You took vacation time, didn't you?"

"Well. Same thing."

"No, it's not, Deanna. I work at the shop across the street. They don't give vacation time. Or sick time, or benefits. I get paid for the time I put in. Minimum wage and tips. Period. If I want a day off I'd better be dead, then at least I won't have to worry about not having medical coverage."

Trish stepped out of the shower and wrapped her towel around her hair then grabbed another from a hook behind the door and began to rub her lithe body dry. Deanna stepped into the still running water.

"Sorry, Trish."

"It's okay. My choice. This is what I wanted. Despite

that, I'm happy. I love my work. I know everybody and everything in town. I couldn't ask for more."

"Are you, really? Happy, I mean?" Deanna called above the din of the rushing water.

"Yes." Trish poked her turban-wrapped head around the floral shower curtain. "Very."

"Good. I wondered about that."

"How about you? Are you happy?"

Deanna listened to the whir of the blow dryer for a moment before answering her. "Yeah."

"That's it? Are you seeing anybody? Do you have any friends? Do you like your work?"

"I love my work!" But even to her the words sounded forced, coming too quickly and too brightly for her own comfort.

"My apartment is beautiful." *Although I never get the chance to enjoy it.* She lathered her hair up and concentrated on that task as she spoke. "I travel a lot, so I don't have much of a social life. That's why I don't come home much."

The dryer stopped. "So I guess you're not married or anything?"

Ouch. She ignored that jab and rinsed her hair and her body. "How long have you been at the shop?"

"A year and a half."

"Oh. Where's Pike today?"

"Mr. McCord told him to get down to the town highway department by eight this morning for a job."

"The town?"

"Yeah. Told him to put in an application and use him as a reference. This'll beat the handyman jobs he's been struggling to find."

"You mean he's actually been working?"

"Well. I'll ignore that slam, Deanna," Trish said as she turned the dryer back on, raising her voice above the noise. "Pike's only missed four days of work from the factory since he got laid off. Once the unemployment was up, that is. He put signs up in the grocery stores and at the lumber stores and hardware stores and people have been calling him to do repairs and things. It's a cash thing, you know, off the books, so it helps, but . . ."

Trish's voice held a defiant note of pride. "He's a good worker. And, a good man. He's grown up a lot." She shut the dryer off. "I'm done. There's way too much hot air in here."

Trish slammed the door before Deanna could reply.

A little while later, with both sisters freshly scrubbed, a form of a truce was created as they drank coffee and ate Cheerio's at the same wood and Formica "Sears special" kitchen table they had eaten breakfast at throughout their childhood. It was a basic wooden style with four chairs, no leaf, pushed up against the well-worn, floral-papered wall.

"So what are you doing today?" Trish asked before mouthing a spoonful of O's.

She studied Trish and drew a deep breath, exhaling before beginning. "I've got a luncheon appointment at one."

"Mixing business with pleasure? Some things never change." Trish smiled brightly.

"Sort of." Her mouth grew dry, and she swallowed, now becoming nervous with the thought of seeing Cord again. "Cord."

"Ahhhh. Well, that's nice," Trish said nonchalantly.

"No, it's not. I mean to have it out with him." She eyed her younger sister, who was focused intently on her cereal.

"Oh?"

"So I need the truth, Patricia. What's going on?"

"I don't have time to argue with you. I've got to finish getting ready." She scooped up the last bits of cereal floating in the milk.

"No, you don't. I need some answers before I go to this lunch. Have you sold out already and aren't telling me? I mean, Pike's getting a job with the town, as per Mr. McCord. That whole dinner was a setup, if you ask me. Cord is coming on super sweet, and you're doing a mighty fine job of kissing his butt."

"If you can't beat 'em?" Trish offered a shrug and a sheepish grin.

"Excuse me?" Deanna's jaw dropped open.

"Dean. Do you realize how much debt we've got? Mortgage, back taxes, current taxes, estate taxes. We pretty much got no choice but to fold—"

"I don't buy that. Mom and Dad did fine all these years."

"But we're not Mom and Dad. And, hello? I don't understand a thing about the farm. As for Pike, he's learning, but farming isn't in his blood. He'd rather rebuild an engine than try to grow corn." She laid her spoon on the table and looked up at Deana. "Not to mention, there's no money in it!"

"But the opportunity is there! Lease everything out. You've got land out there that's being wasted, that could be used and profited from. I'm sure there are people out there willing to work? And farm stands are huge these days!"

"Then you do it, Deanna."

"Hey. I've got a job!"

"If you want to come here and get your hands dirty, and sweat with us to make it work, fine. But if you're gonna sit back in your big city apartment and tell us what we can and can't do and not claim any responsibility, then I don't think you're being fair. Besides. Farming on Long Island is dead unless you're hooked up with a major agro company. And you're wrong. Farm stands are way too common. No one's profiting from farm stands anymore."

"I'm trying to help you." Deanna waved her spoon at her sister.

"No, you're not. You're trying to hold on to a dream–a family legacy that's dead. And you're trying to carry out a personal vendetta with Cord." Trish waved a hand back in Deanna's face.

"I am not! Our ancestry isn't a dream. It's a reality. I don't want to let go of family tradition. I don't want everything Mom and Dad worked for to be paved over and turned into a superstore. I'm trying to get the money to bail you and Pike out so you can run the farm. But you can't do that without a plan! And exactly what vendetta are you talking about?"

"You don't want to see Cord take control of something you couldn't make work." Trish slapped her hand on the table for emphasis.

"I couldn't make work? Me? I didn't even know it wasn't working until two weeks ago!" Deanna mimicked her sister's action.

"Now you know. So do something about it!"

"I intend to."

"Then do it!" Trish picked up her imitation Coach handbag and headed toward the door.

"That's why I'm meeting with Cord! To see if I could get him to support us in our opposition of the re-zoning, for a start."

"Ha." Trish snorted. "Good luck. For your information Cord has plans for this land. And supporting that re-zoning is part of it."

"I don't get it." Deanna grabbed her handbag, a real leather Coach bag, she noted with a tug at her heart, and followed Trish out the door to wait on the porch for the cab she'd called.

"What's that?"

"Trish, why are you being so friendly with him if he wants to do this to us?"

"Because we want out. Unless you can think of a way to salvage this old place. I'm tired of being poor."

"You asked me to help. I'm trying to get you the money to save this place. But you've already sold out to him, haven't you? You're willing to give up everything? All our memories? Mom? Dad?"

"Memories don't put food on the table. But then again, you don't have to worry about that, do you, City Slicker?"

"Thanks, Trish." Deanna watched the cab turn off the highway on to their driveway.

"Have a nice lunch," Trish called out as she trudged off down the driveway, waving a greeting at the cabbie heading her way.

Chapter 6

It was 12:50. Deanna had been home for half an hour, rushed through a second shower, blew her hair dry, dressed, and now sat by the front window, waiting to hear from Cord. He hadn't left a message on the machine while she was gone, and he hadn't called her cell phone at all.

Did he forget?

Had he been toying with her yesterday?

Did something else come up?

Were her palms ever going to stop sweating?

She stood before the hall mirror, assessing her reflection once again. Cool, calm, and collected—like that old baby powder commercial. Confident. Not too professional. The skirt and blazer were navy blue, the silk shell a cool white. Around her neck rested a blue and white choker of glass beads to match. She'd french braided her hair, curling it into a knot at her nape. Blue and white glass-beaded earrings dangled from her lobes, accenting the line of her neck.

Her makeup had been applied with the utmost care, almost as much care as she'd taken in picking out the matching pumps and purse. Now she hesitated, and wondered if she should have chosen a more feminine style. More seductive. No. She was going to beat him with her brains. And she was going to enjoy every minute of it. She bent forward, seeing a mark on her cheek and panicked at the thought of getting a zit. Not now! But as she peered closer she realized it was a smudge on the mirror.

"Hey, gorgeous," Cord called from the porch, where he had pressed his nose up against the screen door and was busy studying Deanna study herself in the mirror.

She jumped at the sound of his voice, yelling at him for startling her.

"Ready?" He held open the door with a gallant sweep and ignored her chastisement.

Grabbing her purse, she turned to follow him, telling herself she was not disappointed when he didn't ask her for a kiss hello.

Not that he would have gotten one.

With a wave of his hand he moved away from the wooden screen door, inviting her to follow him. But as he turned to her once again he paused, his eyes hinting at his appreciation and the smile his mouth refused to offer.

With great difficulty, she forced herself to walk toward his green SUV, refusing to acknowledge him, even though he had unabashedly savored every inch of her. She watched his eyes travel up her body, as if she were a straw and he was taking a long cool drink. Slowly he studied her, from her new pumps (the bottoms hadn't even been scuffed) to the navy blue skirt and jacket (a power color, according to all those self-help books) to the twist of her hair, where oddly his gaze lingered. She felt her cheeks blush a soft pink under his scrutiny and she sucked in a deep breath, clinging to his promise that this would be a strictly business lunch.

He held her door as she climbed into his SUV, then swung it shut and sauntered around to the other side. Only now she covertly took a moment to check him out; the way his suit molded to his body, the crisp whiteness of his shirt against his tanned skin. Her heart fluttered.

"Mom loved having you guys over yesterday," he said as he focused on maneuvering around the driveway with a three-point turn.

"I enjoyed seeing her. Your dad too." She stared out the window, her hands twisting in her lap.

"What about me?"

She wasn't ready to deal with his charm or flirting. And he knew it. She could hear his amusement in his voice. "What about you?"

"*Touché.*" He smiled warmly as he turned onto the highway.

"So where're we going?" She half-heartedly expected him to suggest a motel.

"I thought we'd head down to Port Jeff."

"Cool." She gazed out the window again, not willing to give him the satisfaction of seeing her curiosity.

"Sleep well?"

"Fine. And you?" Her voice was polite and strained.

"Nope. Not a wink."

"Dad's coffee?"

He shook his head. "Nah. Don't know what, but something kept me up all night."

She blushed again, wondering if he meant what she thought he meant. She heard him chuckle, realized she was correct, and continued her interrogation. "Did you run this morning?"

"Nope. Told you. Only on Easter morning."

"You were serious? I thought you were joking."

"Besides, I had to get to the office early this morning, so I could leave early."

"You took the day for a luncheon? And the boss let you?" It dawned on her that aside from wanting to develop her farm, she had no idea what he did for a living.

"You could say that."

"Nice guy."

"He's great."

"What exactly do you do? I thought you worked with your dad?"

"Hell, no. I mean, I help him out when he needs it, but heavy equipment sales, landscaping equipment, that's not for me."

"So? What exactly do you do?" she asked a second time, her curiosity piqued.

"I'm involved in real estate."

"Sales? Development?"

"Yeah, sorta." She watched him study the red light, apparently impatient with the delay as he began drumming his fingertips on the steering wheel.

"I figured it was something like that, considering you're trying to steal the farm out from under Trish and Pike's feet." She lifted her chin and averted her gaze out the window.

"So, d'ya run this morning?" He slid a knowing glance her way.

"Of course."

"Of course. How was your day?"

"Fine. I did some shopping. I don't get the chance to shop for fun much at all. It was nice."

"Pick out anything good?"

"A few things." She felt herself color lightly again. If he only knew how many times she'd picked out a sweater that reminded her of the blueness of his eyes. Or found a shirt, or tie, or jogging suit, or even sneakers she thought he'd like.

"Thought so. Nice shoes. And, power suit." He chuckled.

She felt her blush deepen. "This old thing?" she offered, and received a burst of laughter as a response.

In no time Cord was turning into Danbury's parking lot.

"Danbury's?" Her voice was tinged with dismay, as he maneuvered into a parking spot near the ferry parking.

"Got a problem with it?"

"Nope," she said, dismissing memories of many a date night they shared here. If prices had kept up with the times, it would be a bit pricey for her lunch budget. She made a good salary, sure. But most of her paycheck went into her housing and transportation. That was her choice. She didn't go out much, didn't travel for fun. She worked, and when she wasn't working she stayed home for the most part. Yes. She would go out occasionally with friends from work. But she budgeted for these things.

Yes. Technically she had the money to pay for her lunch today, which she would insist on. But she hadn't intended to go to lunch with Cord. And she didn't think about where they would be going or her allotted budget for this trip or else she would have never gone shopping this morning. She could pay for it with her card, but that was not normally how she paid for food. Then again, how bad could it be? She lived and ate in Manhattan of all places.

"Hello?" Cord's voice interrupted her train of thought. His eyes were so tender and brimming with warmth. She never thought she'd see that again. It set her heart beating wildly beneath her crisp, new suit.

"What?" And as suddenly as it happened, the moment was over and his eyes once again held that ever-present amusement.

"Are we going to sit here or do you want to go in?" He nodded toward the restaurant.

"Isn't this a little fancy for lunch?" she asked,

clutching her purse as she unfastened her seatbelt. "And pricey?"

"Nah. They'll put it on my tab. Business expense," he offered with a flash of a grin and a wink.

She hopped out of the car and followed him across the lot and up the stairs, questioning him further. "Tab? So you come here often?"

He laughed outright and chided her. "See what you've been missing?" Cord reached for her hand, and when she bristled he released it with a chuckle, slipping his fist into his pants pocket. "This way, Ms. Drake." He gave her a lopsided grin and shook his head.

Moments later, her surprise was evident once again when the *maître d'* greeted him by name and ushered Cord to *his* table. It turned out to be a table for four, located in what had to be the best spot in the two-story restaurant, facing the water from the second level in the atrium section of the building. Exotic plants shielded them from the rest of the dining room, which was only sparsely filled with tables. Ceiling fans whirred quietly above them.

After their waiter filled their glasses, took a drink order, informed them of the day's specials, offered menus, and then left, Deanna spoke. "So do you come here often?"

"A bit." He studied the menu briefly before snapping it shut.

"How do you afford it on a salesman's salary?"

"Good commissions." He sipped his water.

"I guess so." She studied her menu. "What are you getting?"

"Maybe the surf and turf."

"For lunch? Isn't that a lot? Of food, I mean?"

"I always get it. I don't eat breakfast and I usually don't eat dinner until eight or nine o'clock." He shrugged.

Deanna thought about her bowl of Cheerio's and her stomach growled. "Oh."

"What are you getting?"

"I don't know. I think I'm okay with an appetizer. I'm really not hungry." She swallowed hard as her stomach growled again.

"The portions aren't that big."

"For this money?"

"What I'm saying is go ahead and order anything. You'll probably be able to finish it." He studied her, amusement sparkling in his blue eyes once again and twisting his smile ever so slightly. The waiter came with their drinks. Cord had ordered a martini, dry, two olives. Deanna, a white wine spritzer.

"Are you ready to order, Mr. McCord?"

Cord smiled at Deanna, who gave a slight shake of her head and widened her eyes before studying the menu once again. "Give us another minute, would you, Peter?"

"It's a whole new selection since we last came here," Deanna explained as she studied the menu without seeing the words.

When the young man left, Cord leaned over and took the menu from her hands. "Let me order for you."

"Don't be ridiculous. I'm a big girl." She made a grab for the menu, but he took it from her and placed it out of her reach.

"Listen. I eat here all the time. I know what's good and what isn't. What would you like? Fish, chicken, beef?"

Deciding to choose her battles today, she let him take the lead. "Fish, I guess."

"Good choice." He raised a hand and waved for Peter.

"We'll start with baked clams. Two salads. The house

dressing will be fine. Two cups of your seafood bisque. Stuffed filet of sole for Ms. Drake and I'll have—"

"The surf and turf," Peter finished.

"You got it." Cord smiled and handed him the menus.

"Your soup will be right out."

"That was a waste. I won't be able to eat all that. You don't need to show off," she said, not comfortable with what this lunch was going to cost.

Cord shrugged and leaned back in his chair. "Are we having a good time yet?"

"I didn't come here to have a good time," Deanna said pointedly, leaning forward and keeping her voice low. She did *not* want to be beholden to him.

"You need to relax, Deanna."

"I came to discuss business with you. And don't think for a moment I'm going to go easy because you're throwing money at me. I didn't realize how hard up you were for the farm."

"Hard up?" Cord leaned forward, his face drawn into a comical mask of shock. "I'm not after your farm because I'm hard up. Believe me."

"I'd like to, but I can't. Not after last night, yesterday. I am not stupid. You set me up. That whole thing was planned to get me on your good side. So I'll sell you the farm at rock-bottom price. A big enough offer to blindside Trish and Pike, who would be happy with any crumbs you throw their way. Don't think for one moment I don't see what's going on."

He chuckled and nodded at Peter as he approached with two bowls of the bisque. They each tasted the steaming, creamy bisque gingerly before deciding to let them cool for a moment. "So. You see exactly what's goin' on, huh?"

When she nodded, Cord urged, "Go on, then."

Eying him carefully, Deanna sipped her bisque. "You aim to buy low, wait out the zone change. Hold on to it maybe a couple of years, maybe longer. Maybe try to make a go of it, but nothing serious. Claim it as a business loss. Sell it down the road and make a nice nest egg."

Cord nodded, saying nothing for a full minute, as he watched her sip at her soup.

"Suppose you're right?" he finally offered.

"Suppose I am?" Deanna set her spoon down, confident she had pegged him.

"What would you say today that might make me change my mind?"

"All I could do is plead to your emotional side. As a friend of the family."

"Your former lover."

My only lover. She blinked slowly to clear her thoughts. "That's beside the point."

"Pleading to my emotional side has no place at a business lunch. Your mixing apples and oranges." He also bent now to taste his bisque, their remaining conversation weaving its way around the rest of their meal.

"Having us to dinner yesterday while all along you plan on stripping us clean wasn't though?"

"Where do you get this idea that I plan to strip you clean?"

"Isn't it obvious?"

"Only to you. I have the support of practically the whole town."

"Maybe you should tell me what your plans are, then."

"Finally. I keep trying and you constantly cut me off." Throughout the meal Cord unfolded his proposal to save a good portion of the farm. Yes, he wanted to buy the farm, but not all of it. Yes, he supported the zone change. They were living in the 21st century, they needed to prepare for the future. No, he didn't plan on selling it. Yes, he planned to develop it down the road. Yes, he intended on making money off the deal, of course. Eventually.

"Eventually is the key word here, Deanna." He cut his steak with precision, speared a morsel with his knife, and waved it at her as he spoke.

"So this means you're not going to support me on opposing the zone change?" She toyed with the stuffed filet that lay uneaten on her plate.

"Not completely. No."

"Damn you, Cord." Deanna threw down her napkin with a vengeance. "If that zone change is approved we have no choice but to sell. We can't afford the taxes now. As it is my sister and her dumb husband don't know what to do with the farm to keep it going anyway."

"So come home and you take over."

"It's not that easy."

"Sure it is. I'll help you."

"Yeah, sure. Mr. High Society Salesman? When? In between your business luncheons?" She pushed her plate away.

"Are you finished? Eating, I mean?" Cord had also put down his napkin and was now motioning for the waiter, who had been eyeing them from behind a potted umbrella plant. Peter came over, the bill sticking out of a small leather portfolio. Cord opened it, glanced down briefly, picked up the pen, and signed. He then handed it back to Peter and nodded. The young man bowed slightly, grinned broadly, and wished him a good day.

"Come on. Let's get out of here." Cord stood up and walked over to Deanna's chair, extended a hand, which she refused, and rolled his eyes as he followed her to the stairs and down, then to the main exit.

Once outside the two squinted at one another in the late afternoon sun. Deanna rummaged through her purse for her sunglasses while Cord slipped a pair out of his breast pocket. "Is our business lunch over yet?"

She shrugged. "I guess."

"Feel like walking?"

"No," she said, her voice sullen as she kept her gaze toward the sidewalk.

Cord smiled down at her. "You're so grown up in that suit of yours," he offered.

"Can you say 'condescending'?" she snorted.

"No. Not when you get all pouty like when you were 16," he said, putting an arm around her waist as they walked.

"Pouty? Pfft. The sun is in my eyes. And—" She uncoiled his arm from about her body as she reminded him, "You promised."

He quickly pointed out that she had moments earlier confirmed the business lunch had come to an end.

"Then I guess you'd better take me home."

"Why's that?" He studied her pout, as if mesmerized.

"No fraternizing with the enemy."

"Come on. In a week you'll be back to the old grind, forgetting all about this place. Face it. If you cared—you know, more than a sense of responsibility—you wouldn't have stayed away so long."

"That's not true."

"Chalk it up as a loss. Forget it. Life goes on." His voice was chiding, but his gaze was warm and searching.

"It's not that easy." Their eyes locked for a moment, and then she turned her sight to the wooden slats of the dock they walked, and the water, lapping and choppy with the wake of a boat chugging in a bit more quickly than the 5 m.p.h. inner harbor speed limit. She took a deep breath of the salty, misty air, imprinting it in her mind for when she returned back to the city later in the week.

"Sure it is. Trish and Pike will be fine. Besides, the farm was bound to change eventually. Your dad never had a boy to hand the family name down to."

She bristled. "It's been in my family since Long Island was first settled. And it doesn't need a 'boy' to keep it alive."

"First, that was nearly four hundred years ago. Second, I don't see any sons picking up the slack."

"How can you be so *blasé* about it? Imagine if it were your family, your home, your property? How would you feel?"

"Honestly?"

"Yes."

They stepped slowly down the dock, glancing every now and then at the few boats already tied off for the season. "I'd do everything in my power to make sure the farm didn't fail. And if I couldn't do it, I'd make damn sure I sold it to someone I trusted."

"So you think I should sell out?" She stopped by a boat with the name 'With or Without you,' scrawled in script across the stern, and turned to face him in the bright afternoon sun. "I don't believe you."

"I didn't say that."

"Yes, you did. You said you would sell." She searched his eyes, but all she could see was the harbor water reflecting in the bright sunlight.

"You're not listening."

"Yes, I am."

"No. I said I'd first try to make a go of it. That doesn't even seem to be an option with you."

"You'd give up your job?"

"If I had to."

"Well, I guess we are too different after all."

He sighed, stood on the end of the dock for a moment, the frothy blue and gray waters churning in chaos below them, then turned around to leave, pausing only until she turned and followed.

Chapter 7

"And in conclusion, the proposed PUD would eliminate the over-commercialization of a still relatively rural area while at the same time providing a basis for the long-term planning of future residential housing and business needs." The Commissioner of Planning stood up from the desk and microphone from where he addressed the Brookville Town Board and walked over to the blueprint drawings set up on easels. He turned them around so the people crowding the auditorium could view them, then proceeded to his seat.

"All right then. Thanks for a great presentation, Marv." Supervisor Joseph LaScala spoke into his microphone from the center seat of the dais. He glanced down to a pile of index cards in his hands, then covered the microphone and said something to the town attorney sitting at his side.

"We will now begin the public hearing session. Please be reminded that there are many people who wish to speak, so promptness and originality are requested. First we'll hear from those in favor of the proposal."

This is nuts. Deanna watched the circus unfold from her seat in the third row, as she picked at the cuticle around her thumbnail and listened to the arguments supporting the proposal given by all the bigwigs dressed in their nearly identical power suits. Chamber of Commerce . . . School District . . . Long Island Business Association. One after another, representatives came in total support of destroying her family legacy without one flipping thought to everything Drake's Farm represented, past, present, and future.

Cord spoke last. As he walked from the back of the auditorium where he had been standing, he paused by Deanna's aisle seat and patted her briefly on her shoulder. She seethed up at him as he passed, but if he noticed he did not react.

"Good evening, Supervisor LaScala, members of the town board. My name is Michael McCord, I reside at 2100 Olde Town Highway, Olde Westfield, the heart of this PUD rezoning being considered. I come before you in support of this proposal, as both a lifelong resident and a business owner.

"The plan shows common sense when dealing with future population increases. It also provides for current landowners to reap a nice financial profit from their investment and considers the necessity of open space in this growing area." Cord's voice flowed throughout the auditorium, neither too harsh, nor too muffled. Perfectly, as if he'd done this every day of his life. It flowed melodiously through the room, deep and lyrical to Deanna's ears. Reluctantly, her heart stirred with a flutter of pride.

"The mixed-use zoning you are proposing will not only provide developers with an outline to base all future plans on, but will also provide the community with the security that over-development will not threaten their quality of life. I support the approval of the Olde Westfield PUD whole heartedly. Thank you for your time." Cord proceeded to rise, but then hesitated as one of the councilmen spoke.

"Hey, Mike, I have one question."

"Councilman Murry?"

"When am I going to get a re-match on our last golf game?"

Cord laughed. "I guess I couldn't make that a consideration for the approval, huh?"

The audience, all but Deanna, laughed at the humorous exchange, as did the board. "No. But if you go easy on me we might be able to work something out." The senior council member again drew a ripple of laughter from the crowd.

"I'll keep that in mind."

"Thank you for your support." This came from Supervisor LaScala. "Is your dad here tonight?" LaScala scanned the crowd.

"No. He left this up to me."

"Give him my regards."

"Yessir. Thank you."

Again, Cord made the effort to acknowledge Deanna as he walked to the rear of the auditorium. He paused near her seat, touching her shoulder and winked at her. She clenched her teeth and ignored him and the flutter his touch invoked deep within her belly.

"He was good," Trish whispered in Deanna's ear as the supervisor now turned the meeting over to the opposition.

First the Olde Westfield Citizen Association spoke, followed by the Olde Westfield Historic Society, the Civic's for Open Space Council, and the Long Island Farming Association. The list went on and on, until finally Deanna heard the supervisor read her name from the card she had filled out prior to the meeting. Her heart missed a beat as she walked to the microphone.

"Good evening, Supervisor LaScala, members of the town board. My name is Deanna Drake. I reside at 5102 First Ave, Apartment 12 B, Terrace Tower in Manhattan. Drake's Farm has been in my family since this town was first founded more than 300 years ago. Drake's Farm has been an integral part of Long Island's, particularly this town's, history, as previous speakers so eloquently stated."

Deanna turned at that point to address the audience. "Thank you for the tribute, by the way. I've always known how popular Drake's Farm is with tourists and consumers, but to actually hear complete strangers stand up and fight on behalf of my family—well, this has been quite an emotional evening," she said to the civic leaders who spoke previously before turning back to the board.

"I grew up on Drake's Farm, which was recently handed over to my sister and myself with the passing on of my father two years ago." She paused for a moment, the impact of her words hitting her squarely on the chest. Her voice was soft, barely audible throughout the auditorium, which had grown deafeningly quiet.

"I oppose the re-zoning and the development of this PUD because I fear it will lead to the destruction of the quality of life the community has enjoyed because of Drake's Farm, as well as all the other reasons stated prior."

Applause sounded behind her, from more than half of the audience, and she smiled down at her hands. However, her satisfaction faded and was replaced by anger after viewing the board.

Only three of the seven members were paying attention—which had been the norm since the opposition took the floor. Supervisor LaScala had gotten up from his seat, obviously while she spoke, and was nowhere to be seen. Two of the other board members had leaned away from their microphones and were talking, while the third board member was studying a document.

"Excuse me?" Deanna's voice became clear and concise, her dissatisfaction apparent in those two words.

"Councilman Murry? Councilman Jones? Councilman Peters?"

The three councilman raised their heads, boredom etched across their faces.

"Is it wrong for me to expect the same respect and attention you have given the other speakers?" Her direct question caused the three who had been paying attention to break out in grins, with one of the councilwomen raising her eyebrows at her counterparts who were being reprimanded.

"Not at all, Ms. Drake. I apologize." Councilman Murry wore a grin also, and did not appear apologetic in the least, which further irked Deanna.

"You know. I may not play golf with any of you, but I think that my point of view should be considered with as much attention and respect as Mr. McCord's." The auditorium, which began humming with Deanna's admonishment of the board, now stilled completely.

"So noted, Ms. Drake." Councilman Murry gave a slight nod in her direction.

Supervisor LaScala approached the dais, coming from somewhere in the audience seated behind Deanna, and after taking his seat he directed his attention to her. "May I ask you a few questions, Ms. Drake?"

"By all means, Mr. Supervisor." Her tone was curt and disapproving.

"How do you intend to ensure that your farm will continue to provide this quality of life, now that your father has passed on? Which, by the way, we were very sorry to hear about. He was a good man."

"Thank you," Deanna sniffed with indifference, not believing him. "Well. My sister and her husband are living there presently."

"Is the farm operating?"

"Partially."

"Do you intend on keeping it a working farm?"

"We would like to see that."

"If you can maintain it in the same fashion your parents and ancestors did, which is a working farm that contributed to the community and did not detract from our quality of life, then your position is warranted and your property may be protected under the grandfather clause.

"However. If you or your sister have no knowledge of how to continue the operation of this farm—or no desire to do so—I don't understand how you could oppose the proposal."

"This is my farm. I believe I have a right to take part in determining how it will be developed in years to come."

"Yes. But don't you also have a responsibility to the community, and any descendants that might be burdened with the responsibility of maintaining a farm?"

"What are you implying, Supervisor LaScala?" Deanna fought the urge to pick at her cuticle.

"You gave your address as Manhattan? You're here to fight for the preservation of the farm, but this is no longer your main residence?"

She paused as anger, embarrassment, and frustration balled up in her throat. "Yes, sir."

"Is it a summer home, perhaps?"

"No, sir."

"I see."

"Well I'm glad you do, because I surely don't. I'm not the one on trial here."

"Are you planning on returning to work the farm?"

"Not any time soon. No, sir."

"Have you ever taken part in the operation of the farm?"

"Yes, of course I have. What does that matter? As I said, *I am not on trial here*. Your proposed Planned Urban Development is. I resent your questioning of my motives and—"

"I'm not questioning your motives. I don't understand where you are coming from?"

"It's obvious where she's coming from!" a man yelled from the audience behind her. "She doesn't want your stupid PUD and neither do we!"

Applause and cheering sounded. Deanna drew a deep breath of relief.

"Silence, please. I want quiet!" the supervisor called from his seat. "Quiet down or I will have you removed!" When the audience hushed in response to his threat, Supervisor LaScala continued. "I expect you all to remain peaceful and respectful as each speaker presents their viewpoints. If I have to say this again I will close the hearing."

The auditorium grew quiet, and Deanna leaned into the microphone, her voice wavering with her emotion. "I oppose the proposed PUD because it will destroy one of the few remaining farms in this county. With *McMansions* and strip malls polluting every last quarter-acre parcel, this much acreage still intact should be respected and preserved, not mown down and developed. Your PUD would provide changes of zone that would destroy the last remaining piece of beauty in this town. And it would erase the history of the property. History created by my parents, grandparents, and my great-grandparents. How can you replace centuries of tradition with a superstore or strip mall?"

Her silence was met with a roar of applause, whistles and cheers, and Deanna felt her cheeks flame with emotion. She bit her lower lip, nodded toward the public officials, and stood.

"Thank you for your time, Mr. Supervisor." Deanna made her way back to her seat as the applause continued. Behind her, the supervisor asked if anyone else was interested in speaking, if not, the hearing would be closed.

Deanna sat beside her sister now, trying to concentrate on the last two speakers. One was a woman who was attending the meeting for another reason, but had been moved by Deanna's speech and wanted to offer her support in opposing the PUD. The second was a gentleman whom brought his invalid mother and a folk guitar and sang about the vices of strip malls. Obviously he was a regular, because the board humored him for approximately five minutes, and then nodded for one of the security guards to usher them back to their seats. Deanna pictured herself up there with a guitar in 40 years or so and snorted in disgust. It might as well have been her now, considering the lack of respect she received from the town's elected officials.

At that point Deanna picked up her purse, stood up and addressed Trish and Pike, shaking her head. "You want to leave?" They nodded, with Trish raising her eyebrows and offering a sympathetic smile.

"You didn't do too bad."

"He is an arrogant, pompous—"

"Hey, sis. Voices carry in here." Pike grinned as he warned his overzealous sister-in-law. "You sure know how to start a riot."

Deanna searched the crowd for Cord as she and her family turned to leave, but could not find him anywhere. He didn't even have the decency to stay and at least listen to her. She shook her head in dismay.

The three of them walked outside together, for the first time in years, sharing some sort of camaraderie.

Once outside in the cool night air, Pike spoke again. "What say we head down to Graffiti's? I think this calls for a celebration."

"A celebration? Of what? How I made an ass out of myself?" Deanna asked sullenly.

Trish hugged her sister and said optimistically, "I think you did fine. And I agree with Pike. Let's go sink a few. It'll make you feel better. We'll play some pool and cool off a bit. It's only 8 p.m."

"Don't you guys have to work tomorrow?"

"Yeah. But you need some cheering up. Doesn't she, Pike?"

"I'd say so." They had reached the truck by this point and Pike opened the door and waited for Trish, then Deanna, to slide onto the bench seat.

The parking lot at Graffiti's was not even half full, Deanna noted as she searched for Cord's SUV. A sigh mixed with disappointment and relief escaped her lips seeing its absence, and she slumped back against the seat's vinyl upholstery until Pike parked his truck.

Her disappointment faded quickly, however, as the trio stepped into the dimly lit bar. There, bent over the pool table, was Cord. Deanna bristled as she watched him line up a shot, ease the cue stick back and forth along the curve of his fingers, and shoot. She didn't even need to follow the ball as she heard the telltale *click, click,* and *clunk* as it found a home in the corner pocket.

"Cord's here," Trish whispered in Deanna's ear with a giggle.

Cord straightened up to view his audience, the cue stick slung over his shoulder like a rifle, its thick rounded end resting in an upturned palm. The suit jacket he'd worn at the hearing was now casually slung over a bar stool, and the sleeves of his still crisp white shirt had been rolled up as far as his muscular forearms would allow.

Damn, she hated him, or at least wanted to. How could one person have everything going for him? It wasn't fair.

"You made it! Great!" He sauntered over to the group casually, greeting Deanna specifically with a "Hey, darlin'" and attempted a quick peck on her forehead.

She drew back and avoided his contact, with a grimace.

"Hey, Cord! You were great tonight," Trish gushed, despite an icy glare from Deanna. Pike and Cord shook hands as Cord offered to buy the first round. "What'll it be?"

"Rum and Coke." Trish threw her coat on a bench and turned to rack up the balls.

"Gimme a beer." Pike also laid his jacket down next to Trish's and picked up a stick.

"Dean?" Cord's amusement read like a road map across his features. "Can ya give me a hand?"

"I don't want anything." She started to walk toward the juke box, but Cord slipped an arm around her shoulders and steered her toward the bar.

"Come on now. Don't be a sore loser," he chided, his voice came low, a hairsbreadth above her ear. "Have a drink, but no wine spritzers."

She shook loose his grip and glared. "Now you think you can tell me what to drink?"

"Dean. You think you can get a wine spritzer here?"

"Of course not. But you automatically assumed I was going to order one. You don't know me at all anymore."

"You made me make you wine spritzers at dinner and you ordered one at lunch. I figured you've turned into a wine spritzer kinda gal."

"I'll have a wine spritzer."

"Hey, Sam. Can we get some service over here? What, are you on break again?" Cord's voice bellowed good-naturedly down the bar to where Sam was watching a *Friends'* repeat on the far corner flat screen. A Mets game played on the screen down at the other end of the bar, and CNN played on the one by the pool table.

"Hold your horses. You want the world and you want it yesterday, don't you, Cord?"

"That's right, Sam."

"Hmph. Funny I was saying the exact same thing about you yesterday." Deanna scowled up at Cord, stepping away from the arm he laid casually across her shoulders.

Sam sauntered up to them dishtowel in hand, eyeing Deanna up and down. "Is that you, Deanna Drake?" He let out a low whistle. "When did you get all grown up?"

"About an hour ago, I believe."

"Well it suits you, sweetheart. Good to see you back. We missed you." Sam smiled warmly at her and dipped his head.

Blushing brightly she turned back to Sam. "You're not going to proof me now, are you, Sam?"

He laughed. "I should, as payback. Deanna, lemme tell you something. You were the master of fake IDs. Everyone knew to go to you. But hey, you all lived close enough that you were walking home anyway. I kept my eye on you, young lady. You didn't fool me for a minute."

"Tell me about it. Now that I think about it, you made us pay full price for flavored fruit juice, didn't you?" She laughed, as did Cord, at their childhood shenanigans.

"Hey. You thought it was the real thing back then. You were happy, I was happy, and the cops were happy. Yessir. Never had one drunk driving accident on my conscience. It's good to see you again, honey." Sam winked at her then turned to Cord.

"How'd you get so lucky? I thought she dumped you years ago?"

Cord grinned broadly and shrugged.

"He's not as lucky as you think Sam. He's still dumped."

"Ahhh. But the night is young," Cord said, laughing so hard Deanna could only attempt to suppress her grin and shake her head in response.

"You've got your work cut out, Cord. Maybe if you're lucky, she'll take you back one of these years. Now. What can I do for you?" Sam's laugh was hearty as he threw his dishtowel down on the bar.

"Two Jacks, on the rocks. One rum and Coke and a Bud, tap will do."

"I said I wanted a wine spritzer," Deanna interjected.

Sam paused for a moment to assess the situation, then laughed at the couple. "Honey, we don't do wine spritzers."

When Sam shuffled off to fill their order, Cord sat on one of the wooden bar stools, elbows on the lacquered bar before him, chin resting on the knuckles of his folded fists. He studied Deanna's reflection in the mirror behind the bar, flanked between a dusty bottle of vermouth and newly opened bottle of sloe gin.

"You were good tonight." He nodded at her reflection.

"How would you know? You left."

"Only after the golf comment. I didn't appreciate the slam. And I stood in the back by the exit until you finished."

Deanna snorted at his comment. "Yeah, right. You left."

"You did well."

"Yeah. So well that LaScala didn't even stick around to hear what I had to say." She climbed up on a stool beside him, responding to his reflection.

"Wrong. He thought you were good too. In fact, I had to tell him hands off. He thought you were real good," he said, raising his brow to emphasize his drift.

"When did he say that?" She scoffed in disbelief.

"When you were talking. That's where he disappeared to. He wanted to know where you'd been hiding all of your adult life."

"So not only is he corrupt, but he's a pig too?"

"He can look, but he better not touch." His dimples showed as he grinned wide.

"Cord. You're getting senile in your old age. He was downright rude to me."

"He's pretty conservative, in fact, about as conservative as Rush. And he was highly annoyed that someone as pretty as you could be so eloquent, intelligent, *and* young and beautiful."

"Now that thought makes me sick." Deanna shook her head in disgust.

"He came back to ask me if I knew you. He said a couple of things that I would've hit another guy for saying, so I, you know, corrected him."

Unable to decide if he were teasing her or not, Deanna studied him with veiled eyes. "Really?"

"Scout's honor."

"You'd hit a man over me?"

"In a heartbeat. Don't you remember Billy Creek in ninth grade?"

"Hmph, I'd forgotten about poor Billy." Deanna turned away from Cord as Sam approached them with their order. "Cord. I don't do Jack's anymore."

"Sure you do." He offered a lazy wink.

"Seriously, Cord. I can't drink like I used to."

"Don't worry about it. Here. Take yours, and here's Trish's rum and Coke. I've got Pike's. We've got some balls to sink."

~ ~ ~

It was 11:30 when Cord and Deanna racked 'em up one last time after knocking Trish and Pike out of the running. "Well." Trish yawned from behind Deanna as she jumped off her stool. "We're gonna head home. We'll leave the porch light on and the door unlocked." She fished in the front pocket of her jeans for a five-dollar bill. "Here. Put this in the pot and call it even. Pike, pay up. God, I forgot you two were ruthless."

Pike laid out a five and hit Cord on the back. "Good luck, buddy."

"Thanks . . . I'll . . . need it . . . " Cord aimed and shot, sinking the six ball off the side and into the far right pocket. He stood up, kissed Trish on the cheek and gave Pike a manhug, each of them giving two quick but hearty pats on the back before releasing their hold.

"Wait up, guys. We'll be done in a bit." Deanna stood up a little too quickly, and her sister swayed before her. "Don't go, Trish."

"Dean. I gotta work tomorrow. Pike too." Trish kissed her on the cheek and cocked her head. "You gonna be all right? Don't drink anymore. I don't want to hear you ralphing in the john all night."

"C'mon, Pike. We gotta celebrate your new job." Deanna hiccupped and giggled. "Oops. Sorry."

"I won't have a new job if I stay out and get up late," he said as he winked at his sister-in-law. "You should drink more, sis. You're almost likeable."

Trish elbowed him, but he continued, laughing. "She actually called me bro tonight."

"Hold up, I'm coming with you," Deanna said, pleading with her sister as the two headed for the door.

"Relax. I'll get you home safe and sound, I promise." Cord picked up his drink and drained the glass, the ice cubes clinking as he set it back down on the table.

The front door closed behind her sister and brother-in-law, and Deanna stood there staring at it, chewing her lip. She watched them get into the truck and blaze out of the lot, heading home.

"Hey. Ten bucks and a wish says I can drink you under the table," Cord said, his eyes trained on her as he waited for her to respond.

Immobilized with the memory of a much younger Dean and Cord in this very bar, laughing and in love, playing pool on Thursday nights when the place was empty and all theirs, Deanna could only lock eyes with him and blink. And remember. Neither had classes on Friday morning, so Thursday nights started their weekend. And they usually started it with that very wish and bet.

"Hey," Cord said again, bringing her back to reality. "Whattaya say?"

With a scowl, she shook her head in dismissal, aimed, then hit too quickly. She missed, concentrating more on how he made her heart race, her body flush, her resolve tremble, than she was on her game.

"Keep it up and you'll have to grant me that wish, Drake." Cord made it a point to walk around her slowly, close enough for her to feel his body heat. "You wanna know what my wish is?"

"No. Go, Cord," she snapped, as she sidestepped in search of a new circumference of personal space. "And if you want to try to drink me under the table, I'll win. I switched to water." She waved at Sam and called out for another bottled water.

By 12:15 Cord had beaten her soundly, and leaned casually against the pool table, offering a very confident, lopsided grin. His eyes crinkled with laughter as he reminded her, "Time to pay up, woman."

"I'm not granting you any wish," she mumbled as she turned to the bar stool where she'd laid her jacket and purse.

"My purse!" Deanna whirled around in a panic, holding only her jacket in her hands.

His deep laugh echoed in the otherwise nearly empty bar, as he offered, "I'll forgo the cash in lieu of the wish."

"Cord. I'm serious. It's gone." Deanna searched the room, but only two men were here, the same fellows that had been here when she came in.

"You sure you brought it in?" Cord walked over to the stool and lifted his jacket to check.

Deanna thought for a second, chewing her lower lip. She shook her head. "No. I'm not. I think I left it in Pike's truck."

"You think or are you sure? You know, I don't remember seeing it."

"I'm almost sure it's in the truck, now that I think about it," Deanna said, squinting in recollection.

"Well, then. I guess you'll have to settle your debts in trade." Cord slipped his paisley tie around his neck, leaving his top shirt button unfastened and the tie untied. He unrolled his sleeves, buttoned the cuffs, and threw his jacket on.

Deanna had also put her jacket back on and was murmuring something about checking the truck as soon as she got home as she headed toward the door.

"How about a cup of coffee?"

Deanna shook her head. "It's past midnight."

"The night is young."

"I have to go home. I gotta make sure I left my purse in the truck."

"They probably brought it in by now."

"Trish would have called."

"All right. We'll swing by. But then we're going for a cup of coffee. Besides. You owe me a wish."

Her heart pummeled against her ribs at the sound of his words, but it wasn't from fear or apprehension, and she hated her traitorous body for that.

By this time, they had crossed the paved blacktop and came to stand beside a sleek black sports car. Deanna checked it with a soft "Wow," then glanced up at Cord in confusion. Cord lifted his key fob and the alarm sounded a quick *bleep-bleep*. The locks flipped open, the lights flickered, and the engine turned over and started purring. He walked over to the passenger side, leaned down, and opened the door with a wave for her to slip in.

Deanna ran her hands along the leather seats and wood-grain dashboard as he closed the door behind her. The driver's side door opened and shut before Deanna could speak. "It's gorgeous," she finally offered.

"You're gorgeous." He shifted the car into gear and it purred effortlessly onto the highway.

Chapter 8

Cord's car slipped quietly through the sleepy hamlet of Olde Westfield, with no other vehicles sharing the two-lane highway. Nothing was said as he turned into Drake's Farm, while Deanna contemplated silently exactly what sort of payment Cord expected when collecting his debt.

She stole a glance his way, and felt a rush of butterflies in her tummy as the moonlight caught his chiseled profile. *How much did he think ten bucks in trade could get him, anyway?* When he slowed to a stop and put the car in park, she hopped out and ran over to Pike's truck, tugging open the door. The seat was empty, as were the floor and dashboard. Her shoulders slumped as she shook her head in despair.

"Well?" Cord stuck his head out the window, and sighed when she shook her head. "C'mon, let's go."

"I want to go to bed."

"Not yet you don't. Don't worry about your purse. Trish probably brought it inside. Let's go get a cup of coffee."

"I'm pretty beat." She stayed by the truck, her hand resting on the door after slamming it shut.

"C'mon, Dean. I'll call the town first thing tomorrow. If someone found it, they would have turned it in. There wasn't anyone at the bar who would have taken it. You'll get it back." He waved her over, and as if she were a marionette and he was controlling strings attached to her legs, she slowly moved toward the car and climbed back in.

"I can't believe I could be so careless. I'm usually so good."

"I bet Trish took it inside. You'll find it later. You don't need it now, so don't worry about it." When she didn't respond, he prodded. "You weren't carrying a lot of cash, were you?"

"Nah. Twenty bucks. But my charge cards, my bank card, my license . . ." She paused and felt her pocket, confirming she had her cell phone before continuing.

"It'll turn up. And as for the twenty bucks, half of that is mine anyway, so you really only lost ten." He chuckled as he turned the car around and headed down the driveway toward the highway. "I guess I'm gonna have to put this coffee on your tab as well." Then, in his worst Godfather impersonation, he added, "And you-ah knowah whatta happens iffa you donta pay uppa. I hate ta hafta breaka you legs."

"That was bad." She groaned and suppressed a grin, and he laughed in reply.

Eyes closed, she rested her head back against the seat, and asked, "So where are you takin' me, Mr. Corleone?"

"Where do you want to go?"

She lifted her head up and stared at him, and tried to ignore the double meaning. "What are the options this late at night? Is there any place open? Besides a Dunkin Donuts or 7/11?"

"Now that you mention it. Friendly's closes at 11. The diner down the street went out of business last summer. You got the Hi-lite Diner in Port Jeff or my place. Your call."

Her heart hammered wildly and with a deep breath she tried to slow the beat before replying. "Your place, huh? I'll bet the price for coffee is pretty steep there."

"I make a mean cup of cappuccino."

She swallowed thickly. "Well, then. That's an offer I can't refuse, isn't it?" Her voice was weak and she knew if she had been standing at this very moment her legs would have buckled beneath her and she would have collapsed into a puddle of mush. *This is not good.*

Tires spun on the gravel driveway as he turned onto the road and headed toward the McCord farm. When they pulled down the private roadway that turned into his driveway they passed his SUV parked outside the garage. "So tell me, how do you afford these kinds of toys on a salesman's salary?"

"Great budgeting skills."

"I think you are lying to me."

"Hey, I don't pay $3,000 a month in rent, either."

"How do you know what I pay in rent?" She stared at him.

"Good guess?" He shrugged.

Seconds later, the door to the garage gaped open then closed again, swallowing them into its darkened belly.

Neither said anything for a moment, and Deanna was sure he could hear her gulp a deep breath within the thick silence of the sports car.

"Wait here and I'll get the light," he instructed, slipping out of the car, inching his way through the darkness. Her eyes adjusted quickly and she followed, not listening to his direction.

"Some things never change, do they?"

"Nope, they don't," she started to reply, bumping into him as he stopped short at the doorway.

Within moments they were climbing the stairs to his apartment. "Aren't you afraid of fumes leaking up here?"

"Fumes? Nah. We built over the roof and added a double floor and insulation. Don't worry. You're safe."

He flicked the light on at the top of the stairs where she slipped her pumps off to follow him stocking-footed across the entranceway and living room. She hugged her upper body to ward off a shiver, and sat herself down on the soft, chocolate-brown Italian leather couch.

"Cold?" he asked, as he picked up a remote and clicked the gas fireplace on. Without waiting for a comment, he turned, then walked into his bedroom. "Hey, Dean, put the kettle on, would ya?"

"Sure thing," she mumbled, heading for the galley kitchen, wondering how this was even happening or why she was allowing it. "Where do you keep your cups?" she asked after filling the kettle and setting it back down on the flame.

"To the left of the sink."

She reached up, opened the cabinet, selected two mocha-colored ceramic coffee mugs, and placed them on the counter. Then she correctly guessed which drawer of three held flatware and reached and took out two teaspoons. With a curious smile, she realized that if this had been her place this is exactly where she would have put the cups and spoons.

"Still cold?" Deanna jumped at the nearness of his voice and whirled around to find herself face-to-face with him, her back to the countertop.

She forced a laugh, annoyed when it sounded husky, and tried to move around him. "Did you forget to put heat in this place when you built it?"

"Well, go sit by the fire. Or if you prefer, I can warm you up." He didn't move to touch her, but he may as well have by the heat simmering in his eyes.

"Um." Her eyes settled on his tee shirt-clad chest, as she attempted to move around him. The thin cotton was taut across his torso as he held out his arms offering a hug. "Don't go there."

"I thought you were cold."

He was too close. She couldn't deal with him when he was this close to her. She pushed past him and headed for the fireplace.

"Sorry. Again."

Head bowed, she stood by the fire place and let out a long deep breath as she focused on regaining her control. The gas-fed flames crackled brilliantly, mesmerizing her. Then she raised her head and called over her shoulder, "No problem, Cord."

With control regained, she watched as he reached into the pantry and produced two packets of instant cappuccino.

"That's your mean cappuccino? You coerced me up here for that?"

"Not exactly coerced. But if I told you what I wanted you up here for, you wouldn't have come. Would you?" He offered a lopsided twist of his lips as an apology.

"Definitely not." She grinned back at him and shook her head.

"Now about this debt you owe me." He poured a packet into each mug.

"Yeah. About that debt. What are you doing hard-nosing me for a measly ten bucks when you've got that little beauty hiding in your garage? Have you no decency?"

"What I could take out in trade for that ten bucks is worth far more than any old car." He finished dumping the instant coffee into the cups and now stared at the teapot, as if willing the water to boil.

"Oh. I don't think so."

"Then you're wrong again." His eyes twinkled, and his dimples cut deep into his cheeks as he grinned broadly. "As usual."

"When am I ever wrong?" She crossed back over to

the kitchen, feeling a bit safer. He was less threatening out of his suit, wearing an old tee shirt and sweat pants.

"You're wrong about me, about my motives for buying the farm. About my motives as far as you're concerned."

"Don't make this evening any worse than it is."

"I'm not. You should at least try to consider my offer."

"Oh yeah. An offer I can't refuse." Her attempt to beat his earlier impression failed as miserably as he had.

"That's the only thing you've been right about so far." He snickered good naturedly at her.

"You are so conceited."

"No, I'm not." He reached over and picked the kettle off the burner as it let out a full-blown whistle. "I know what I want and how to get it."

"And you want the farm. And you think bringing me up here is how you intend to get it?"

"Hell, no. I'll get it without you coming up here. One has nothing to do with the other."

"Sure it does."

He rolled his eyes and carried their cappuccinos to the living room. "I can't wait to hear this one."

Grinning at his back, she followed. "Okay. You want the farm. I've got the farm. Part of it anyway. You already beat me bad at pool, right? Put that on my tab. Then you've got that lunch I owe you for. Now the cappuccinos. Do you charge for rides in your toys? The way I see it, Mr. Entrepreneur, is that you intend to keep racking up my debts until I have no choice but to hand the farm over to you." She grinned with how idiotic her theory sounded, but it kept conversation flowing, and filled the awkward moments of silence the voices in her head liked to invade.

Cord studied her for a moment, then said, "You pegged me. I guess it's over."

With a shake of her head, Deanna eyed him suspiciously. "That was way too easy."

He shrugged, sipped his coffee, and studied her, his scrutiny causing her to fidget with her hair, the spoon, her shirt.

"What?" was all she could think of to say.

"Nothing." He offered a slow smile, his eyes blazing.

"Obviously, you're lying. Again. What are you thinking?" She turned toward him, arguing with herself to stop playing this game and get home.

"You don't want to hear."

"Yes, I do."

"You sure?"

"I'm an adult. I can handle it." She rolled her eyes and shrugged her shoulders. "Come on. Spit it out."

"Well. I was contemplating throwing you over my shoulder and whisking you off to my bedroom."

"Okay. We're done here." Deanna set down her cup and stood up, but Cord tugged her hand and nudged her to sit back down.

"You asked. If you didn't want to hear, you shouldn't have asked."

"Fair enough. But that ain't happening." She laughed and picked up her cappuccino again. The frothy liquid was hot, thick, and sweet and filled her belly, warming her toes and fingers. She then set the mug down again and turned toward the man who sat ever so still beside her. "I don't know what to say about any of this, to be honest. Seriously."

"We're not kids anymore, you know." He leaned into her, his gaze trained on her mouth, and she scooted away, putting a couch cushion's length between them.

"Please." She held up her hand and they locked eyes.

A moment passed before Cord spoke. "You can't tell me you don't feel this," he said, motioning at the space between them. A straggled sound escaped from deep within his throat and he raked a hand roughly through his hair. Leaning over, he picked up the two mugs of cappuccino, handing Deanna hers while he took a swig from his. He watched her sip at the liquid gingerly, passion alight in his eyes.

"You've got milk on your upper lip." He reached up and brushed it away with his thumb.

"Thanks."

"Now. Where were we?"

"I do," she offered simply.

"You do?"

"Feel it." Her breath caught as she spoke.

"Then why are we fighting it?"

"Is this what you want? You want to avoid everything that needs to be fixed, so you can get laid?"

"First of all, I don't need to 'get laid.' Secondly, making love would be the start of fixing everything that's wrong."

"Ohh nooo. *That* would complicate things. Making love to you isn't going to change anything."

"I disagree. I think it would be very . . . healing." His voice was soft, and the passion still burned in his eyes as she searched his face for some tell that he was playing with her. She saw nothing but desire and tenderness.

She looked down, placing her mug on the table, then closed her eyes and swallowed thickly. God, she wanted him so badly. When did this happen? One minute she was angry with him, the next minute she was jumping in his bed, on his couch, to be more exact. What if he was right? What if making love started a healing process? It had been so long since she allowed herself to feel passion. To feel it again with him . . . Wouldn't that be healing?

Biting her lower lip, Deanna scooted back to sit beside him, her heart pounding so hard she felt faint. Her hands came up to rest on his shoulders, nudging him to turn toward her.

"Help me," she said, her eyes locked on his gaze, and as he reached for her hand she guided it to rest against his cheek.

Cord hesitated for a moment, moving his gaze to her lips, then back to her eyes. "Is this what you want?" Everything about him was tender, yet burning with passion. Every muscle in his face was tensed, as if he was fighting to keep from consuming her with all his might.

She placed a hand on either side of his face and drew him down toward her. "More than I ever imagined," she whispered as she claimed his lips with a bruising intensity.

Her invitation was all he needed. His lips claimed hers, his hands tangling in her hair.

The years faded away beneath their passionate kiss. She moved into the hard contours of his body, and he molded perfectly into hers. He ran his hands down her shoulders, her arms, resting on her hips, as they both struggled to get closer to one another.

He paused momentarily, his breath ragged as he searched her gaze. She followed his lead, and inhaled slowly, struggling to regain her sanity.

"I guess we still got it," she offered with a half-smile, straightening up, adjusting her skirt, focusing on tugging the hem over her thighs.

"At least we know now." He leaned forward, resting his elbows on his knees, clasping his hands together.

"So, why did we stop?" She bit her lip, not believing the words coming out of her mouth.

"You'll never know how difficult it is for me to do this. I want you more than anything in the world right now." His voice cracked as he spoke, but he still did not look at her. "We've both been drinking and I don't want us waking up in the morning wondering if we did this because of the alcohol or because it was the right thing to do. Itwouldn't be fair to you. To me. To us."

Tears of humiliation and frustration filled her eyes and she nodded, unable to speak.

"We've been through too much already. I don't ever want to hurt you again. Do you understand?"

She nodded silently.

"We can do this. We *will* do this. But not right now. It wouldn't be right."

"I feel so stupid." She shook her head.

"So do I." He held her close, hugging her tightly as her cheek rested against his chest. She smiled to herself as she listened to the untamed pummeling of his heart.

"How could I want this when I'm still so angry at you?" She pushed away from him, but stared into his crystal blue eyes.

"It must be the car. I knew that would get you." He winked, and exhaled loudly.

She offered a feeble laugh as she commanded her body to cool down. "I think I just wanted to pay up that debt and get it over with. This was about ten bucks' worth, wouldn't you say?"

"Hell, no. You didn't even put a dent in it."

"You saying I'm cheap?"

"No. I'm frugal. I've learned to get my money's worth, that's all."

She continued to lean back, studying him long and hard. "So, I guess my business is finished here."

"No. I'm not done with you yet."

Deanna felt her eyes widen as, damn, her cheeks heated yet again.

"We've got business to discuss, Ms. Drake. And I mean to settle this once and for all."

"I'll hear you out, but I'm not signing anything or making any decisions tonight. I think I've had too much to drink."

"I want you to promise me you'll hear me out with an open, even slightly drunk mind."

"Okay, Cord. Give it your best shot."

"Work with me. Trust me. We can do this together."

"We can fight the zoning."

"You can't pay the taxes now as it is."

"I'm working on that. I'll file for Chapter 11. We'll reorganize. I'll lease the farm out again."

He shook his head. "You couldn't if you wanted to. I was talking to your dad about this the December before he passed. He lost his renters that last season because he was asking for too much. It wasn't profitable anymore."

"There's got to be another way."

"The entire strip is developed. We've got the last bit of land. It can't stay like this forever. Don't you see? In ten years from now it's going to be paved over whether you fight the zoning now or not. Let me buy you out. I'll pay the back taxes, give you the going rate on all but twenty acres. You guys can keep that, ten for you and ten for Trish."

"It isn't that easy."

"Come on, Deanna! You don't even live here! You wouldn't even be here now if Trish hadn't called you. How hard can it be?"

"This is my family's land! How easy can it be to take something that has been in your family for centuries—

centuries!—and sell it? It would be like snuffing out another life."

"You'll keep the house and the surrounding twenty acres. You can work with me hand in hand on any plans. God. Deanna. I won't even be doing anything with it for at least a few years!"

"I can't fathom letting it go."

"You think I would do anything to hurt you?"

"Do you want me to answer that honestly?"

"Fairly, if not honestly. If I wanted to hurt you we wouldn't be talking right now, believe me." He stood up and paced around the room. "You think I would do anything to destroy the last bit of open space right next door to my own house?"

"You'll develop my piece, make a bundle, and move far away, so you'd never have to see it again."

"You're being childish. You're not listening to reason. And you obviously don't know me. This is my home. I'd never abandon Olde Westfield." The accusation hung hard and cold.

"I think I'd better go." She stood up, but Cord came to stand beside her and then nudged her lightly back onto the couch. "Not yet."

Deanna peered up at him, his face a mask of grim determination.

"You're not leaving here angry. Or misled about what I intend to do with the farm."

"My farm."

"Don't you even care that you're about to lose it?"

"I thought we had three years."

"Your father hasn't paid the taxes since the year after your mom died. You've got until the end of this year and that's it."

"Trish told me that, but I didn't want to believe her."

"There's no way—no way—you could save that farm. Let me help you. Work with me." He sat beside her and held her gaze.

"No," was all she could whisper.

"I didn't want it to be like this. Let me help you."

She shook her head slowly. "Why didn't they tell me?"

"Your dad didn't think you would forgive him. He was ashamed. I helped him the first year. But after that I had to turn him away. I'm sorry." Cord leaned over her trembling body, encircling her with both his arms.

"So we owe you already, don't we?"

"Forget I said that."

"Forget it? What are we talking about? Twenty dollars or twenty thousand? Or two hundred thousand? My god. Here I am making snide remarks about how you're trying to get rich off me."

"Didn't Trish tell you about the will?"

Deanna rubbed her eyes with the backs of her hands and shook her head. "No. Go ahead. What about the will."

"I was executor."

"Executor? You? What the—?"

"Yes." He nodded.

"And?"

"And. And now I'm one-third owner of Drake's Farm."

"This is bullshit!" She jumped up and stalked away from him angrily. "Why are you even talking to me then? Go ahead and do whatever you want. You've got Trish on your side already. I know it."

"Deanna!"

"You've been making a fool out of me all along. Why? Why let me speak? Why make me believe I had a chance?"

"I never led you to believe anything."

"Trish did!"

"Trish did what she had to do to get you out here, I guess. I don't know why she lied. I would've told you straight out, but I never got the chance."

"You could've said something on Easter–or our so-called business lunch!"

"Easter? And ruin my mom's day? No."

"Lunch then. Don't give me this crap, Cord. You've been stringing me along this whole time. God. I am so stupid."

"No you're not. You're doing what you think is best. But you're wrong."

"I'll fight you. Whatever it is you want to do I will fight you. I will not stand by and watch you ruin everything my family has worked for. I won't let you make a fool out of me—or my family. Ever again!"

He shook his head. "You won't get anywhere by fighting me. All you will do is lose the farm."

Deanna wasn't listening anymore. She walked over to her shoes and picked them up. "By supporting you I will lose all self-respect. I cannot in good conscience sit back and watch you ridicule me and my family. Executor!"

There was nothing left to say, so Cord stood up and walked into the bedroom. Emerging with sneakers and keys in hand he turned to Deanna. "I'll drive you home."

"No thanks. I owe you enough already." She descended the stairs quickly, slamming the door behind her.

Chapter 9

The smell of leather, cappuccino, and Cord kept Deanna tossing and turning all night. The lack of sleep, the sound of rain tap-tapping on her bedroom window—the rain soaked morning in general—made her long for the familiarity of her apartment in the city. Resisting the urge to sleep in even longer, she dragged herself out of bed by 7 a.m., an hour and a half later than she normally rose, threw on her shorts, sweatshirt, and sneakers and headed downstairs. She passed Trish who was on her way to the bathroom, but she couldn't even find the voice to respond as Trish slipped a devilish smile at her and called out, "Hey! Your purse is on the kitchen table!" A glare was all Trish received in return.

Outside big drops fell steadily from the sky, creating a maze of puddles down the driveway that Deanna had to pick her way through. She breathed deep the sweetness of the rain, the fresh smell of the water mixing with the earth. She lifted her face to feel the cool droplets fall against her feverish cheeks and sleep-filled eyes, then sighed.

The rain felt good, despite the grayness. Despite the heaviness in her heart. When she reached the road her legs guided her automatically toward Cord's. Some things were imprinted into her core and there was no changing it. She realized that last night.

She knew there would be no chance of seeing him this morning. Her heart ached with the thought of him. With what she had almost allowed last night. Damn! She had been so stupid. He had let her rattle off time and time again how she thought he was going to steal the farm, and here he owned a third of it. No matter how she fought him, with Trish on his side he'd be able to do whatever he wanted. They didn't need her approval for anything. And what did it matter? She didn't live here anymore anyway. She was an outsider. He reminded her quite clearly. And often.

So lost in thought, Deanna didn't see the nose of the hunter green SUV drive up between the columns lining the McCord driveway until she was upon it. And then it was too late to do anything except glance his way to see if he saw her. She blushed in part as the image she surely presented flashed in her mind. A drowned rat. But that didn't seem to matter to Cord, who took her in head to toe. Every raindrop that trickled down her skin had been accounted for in that sweeping assessment. She knew this as surely as she knew it was raining. She could feel it.

He nodded at her, any expression in his eyes veiled by half-closed lids. His lips lay unmoving, neither in a grimace nor a smile, nor a smirk. She jogged past the truck, not acknowledging his nod, and kept her head down, her entire body blushing once again as she felt his gaze never leave her. In fact, she had been quite a distance down the road before she heard him turn off and head in the other direction. And there hadn't been any traffic coming from either way. Not one car.

Soaked and chilled to the bone by the time she climbed the steps to her house, Deanna was greeted by the cuckoo clock in the foyer as it chimed eight times. Trish was standing in the hall, lunch bag, umbrella, purse, and raincoat in hand.

"Kate's called in sick so I've got to open," she murmured apologetically, avoiding her sister's accusatory eye. "I can't believe you're so dedicated that you'd run in this weather. It's disgusting outside."

Slipping out of her soggy running shoes, she watched Trish rummage through the hall closet, but still, Deanna said nothing.

"So." Trish's voice was bright, though muffled. "How was last night? Or do I not want to know?"

"Informative."

Trish sighed heavily, finding the umbrella, but continued to rummage anyway. "Oh? Really?"

"Really." Raindrops dripped off Deanna's body, forming puddles on the wooden floor of the foyer. "I won't agree to any sale, Trish. I'm telling you right now." She watched her words still Trish's fumbling as she straightened her body and whirled around.

"So Cord told you?"

"I would have rather heard it from you."

"I was afraid. You're so, so—"

"So what? I'm your sister, damn it. You dragged me out here as part of some crazy scheme the three of you cooked up. You don't give a shit about me, you never have!"

"That's not true. I love you so much. I just don't know you anymore!" Trish flailed her arms wildly in protest.

"Bullshit. You and Pike figured out how to get me out here. You knew there was no chance in hell of getting me to agree to sell over the phone. The only chance you had was in person. And you enlisted Cord to do it. Huh." Deanna shook her head, recalling the tactics he'd used on her last night at his apartment. "Cappuccino, my foot," she muttered as she turned toward the stairs.

"Cap–? Dean. Wait."

"I got a train to catch."

"No!" Trish grabbed Deanna's hand as she placed it on the wooden banister. "Deanna. Please don't go. I-I have to go to work. But I don't want you to leave angry. Please. One more night. Give me tonight. Please?"

Deanna squinted at her sister, unsettled by her tearful pleadings. She jerked her hand. "You betrayed me. You know how Cord hurt me and yet you were going to use him to get me to agree—"

"That's not how it was at all! I swear. Please, Deanna. I have to go to work. Please!" A sob escaped her lips. "Don't leave me. You're all I've got left."

"What about Pike? Doesn't he count? And Cord? You don't need me." Her voice was hard as she started to climb the stairs. "All you need is my signature."

"Deanna!" Trish called from the bottom of the stairs, but her sister ignored her. As Deanna entered her bedroom she heard the front door shut softly. From her window she watched as Trish's red umbrella bobbed down the puddle-filled driveway toward the highway.

The morning passed quickly, but the rain stayed, wrapping the Drake household in a dark gray velvet cocoon. Deanna showered and dressed, dusted her bedroom, the living room, vacuumed and swept the downstairs. She hadn't planned on leaving, she had been speaking in anger and now she regretted hurting her sister. The pain had been real, Deanna realized, recalling Trish's sobs, the tears in her eyes.

Absolutely nothing had changed in the house since she'd lived there, she thought, roaming from room to room. The same carpets, although a bit threadbare; the same furniture, cushions sagging and tables, scuffed; even the same pictures and mirrors decorated the walls. Deanna felt a bit guilty, recalling her newly furnished apartment, and wondered if Trish kept it this way out of respect, or out of a lack of funding. Knowing Trish,

Deanna guessed the second reason was more accurate, and that increased her guilt even more.

By 11:30, Deanna had made coffee and called the office. After learning the proposal had gone well and the contract was in the bag, Deanna hung up and rummaged through the cabinets and refrigerator scavenging for something to eat. She settled on some store-bought scones, recalling that these were always a staple when Mom was alive, only Mom had made them from scratch. She spread the two halves with butter and stuck them in the microwave that now seemed ancient compared to the compact model Deanna had in her own kitchen. As if riding a bike, her fingers automatically pushed the correct buttons to set the machine whirring noisily as the bread warmed. She drummed her fingers, recalling the first day Dad had brought this thing home.

Mom had wrinkled her nose in distaste, chastising him for his foolery. "What in the world will I do with that thing? Take it back."

But Dad insisted on keeping it, his two daughters coming readily to his defense. Mom swore she'd never use it, but within days she was defrosting and heating up leftovers without a second thought.

Deanna finally settled down at the table with her coffee and biscuit and the morning's *Newsday* when the front doorbell rang. Her heart leaped as Cord came to mind, and the hair on her neck bristled as she prepared to do battle. She rose and walked slowly to the door, her surprise evident as she glanced through the screen.

"Delivery, ma'am." A young pimply-faced youth greeted Deanna with a smile as he held out an iPad with a signature page displayed. "Sign here."

Youth. The "kid" had to be at least 18 or 20. *Man, I'm getting old.* Deanna signed and took the long white box tied with a satin red ribbon and bow. She raised her brow as her glance fell to her name on the card. She thanked him, then watched as he turned and ran, dodging raindrops, toward the van marked Olde Westfield Florist. Her heart thudded as she walked toward the living room, laying the box on the well-worn couch. She sat down next to the package and gently detached the envelope and card from the ribbon.

D-Here's to your fame and success. You won the media-that's half the battle. Cord.

Deanna frowned at the cryptic note, unable to resist the urge to smile as she recognized Cord's familiar scrawl. He'd ordered these in person. She untied the bow and lifted the top off the box, the heavenly sweet scent escaping before she'd even parted the white tissue paper. A dozen long-stemmed blood red roses lay before her, dark green ferns and sprigs of baby's breath nestled amongst the thorn-free stems.

"Oh, Cord." She half-whispered his name as she lifted a bud from the box and brought it to her nose. Her heart skipped as her anger dissolved, her breathing quickened, and she swallowed thickly. She still didn't understand his message, and as she studied the note once again, the telephone rang. She jumped with the sound of the shrill bell and ran to the kitchen before it rang again. "Hello?"

"Deanna Drake?"

"Who's this?" Surprised at hearing her name, she wondered who the unfamiliar voice belonged to, and how they knew she was here.

"This is Barry Devon, from the *Evening Times.*"

"Yes?"

"I'm calling in reference to last night's meeting? I understand you spoke against the zoning proposal."

"Yes."

"Well. I wasn't at the meeting, so I was wondering if I could have a word with you?"

"How did you know I spoke if you weren't at the—"

"*Newsday*. Didn't you see the paper yet?"

"No. As a matter of fact, I haven't." Deanna leaned over the table and grabbed the newspaper as the voice on the end of the line continued.

"Page thirty-six. Nice shot."

Deanna flipped through to the local section and came face to face with a very mournful, soulful picture of herself. It was indeed a nice shot, as Barry Devon had suggested. So this is what Cord's message was all about. The headline read "Drake Heiress Pleads With Board."

"Oh my goodness."

Devon was silent as Deanna quickly scanned the article, which seemed a bit slanted, reading between the lines. Nevertheless, it was balanced, presenting her view first, then Cord's, which had been tied in only because the reporter had noticed that "although Drake's opinion differed from an earlier speaker, Developer Michael McCord, the two exchanged endearments before and after McCord presented his testimony."

She snorted. Endearments? He had patted her on the shoulder and she had tried to kill him with a staredown.

"Miss Drake?"

"Ms."

"Ms. Can you comment?"

Deanna spent the next ten minutes answering Barry Devon's questions while scanning the article.

Two more reporters called before Deanna had the good sense to unplug the vintage 1980s rotary phone from the wall. By then her coffee and scone had grown cold and frankly, she'd lost her appetite. Where the flowers had begun to chip away at her anger with Cord, the reporters' inquisition had re-ignited the feud, in her own mind anyway. It was well after one o'clock before Deanna found herself climbing the stairs to the attic, intending to rummage through her mother's belongings. She had put it off for three years. It couldn't wait any longer.

It was cold on the third floor of the house, where only two small round windows, each placed on either side of the attic, let in light through their dust and grime-caked panes. She reached overhead and tugged the chain for the single bulb that hung in the middle of the angled eaves. At once, a yellow comforting glow was cast about the piles of boxes and old furniture, bric a brac, and junk.

Deanna stood at the top of the stairs, reading the black marker labels scrawled across the boxes. *Trish/wedding . . . Trish/books . . . Trish/knick-knacks . . . Trish/childhood memories . . . Deanna/college . . . Deanna/Childhood Mem . . . Deanna/high school.*

Resting on top of that box was an old bootbox that she recalled lovingly covering with contact paper. It was now bound closed with twine, which she also recalled not-so-lovingly doing. It wasn't labeled, but she knew what lay within. It was a makeshift coffin for her and Cord's relationship, filled with letters, photos, and mementos of Cord. *Cord.* She walked over to that one and picked it up, hugging it close. She then turned back to the stairs, placing it at the landing to be brought down when she was through peeking about. Her search began again and soon ended when she found nearly one dozen boxes piled in the far right corner all labeled *Mom.*

It was time consuming, going through all of the boxes that contained her mother's entire life—her clothing, purses, makeup bag and cosmetics, shoes, and her more personal items like her undergarments and lingerie. All of her costume jewelry, still in her velvet-lined cedar jewelry box, and accessories had been placed in one box, along with scarfs and handkerchiefs.

Another box held all of the black and white, and some color, photos from Mom's childhood—including pictures of some relatives Deanna now only faintly recalled. She named them absentmindedly as she shuffled through the old white-bordered, slightly faded, black and white pictures. She did a quick intake of her breath when she found the collection of photos from when Mom and Dad were first married—before Deanna and Trish were even a glimmer in their eyes. Photos Mom had always wanted to put into albums, but had never gotten around to do. Deanna picked through these now, choosing childhood shots of her mother, school pictures, never before seen wedding photos that hadn't made the final cut for their wedding album.

Deanna laid these beside a pile of jewelry—a cameo pin, a flower-shaped rhinestone pin, a string of pearls, a gold crucifix, Mom's wedding band and engagement ring, and an emerald bracelet. She sighed deeply when she came upon a box of letters her parents had exchanged while her father had been in the service and on tour overseas. Deanna didn't even open the box, marked *Do Not Read*, in red ink, in her mother's handwriting. Let their memories stay buried, she thought with a wistful smile.

It was late afternoon, and still raining when Deanna climbed down the stairs with her own box of memories and the photos, jewelry, her babybook, and a few other treasures she had selected. Once in her bedroom, she placed them on her bed, then turned to go downstairs to the kitchen. That wine she brought would come in handy right now. It would give her the strength she needed to get through the rest of the afternoon. Red. Room temperature. No spritzer.

After she filled the dollar store stemmed glass with her wine, Deanna studied the antiquated telephone and realized this was Trish's only way to contact her if she needed her. Deanna, guilt-ridden, plugged it back into the phone jack. Immediately the phone rang.

"Hello?"

"Is this where I can reach Deanna—"

Deanna didn't even wait for the person to finish. "Wrong number," she said before placing the receiver on the hook, then lifting it off and laying it on the table. She shook her head and went back upstairs to her bedroom.

The glass of wine and the uncorked bottle remained like a faithful old friend on the night stand beside her bed while Deanna sat cross-legged on the bed sifting through the memories of her and Cord's relationship. Movie ticket stubs, concert stubs, the dried corsage's (in plastic pre-Ziplock sandwich bags) from all four of the junior and senior proms they'd gone to together. Her yearbook. His class ring. Letters. More letters.

Cord was very good at writing letters, she recalled draining the glass and feeling a rush as she tilted her head back to do so. She poured another glassful before mulling through a bundle of letters from her last year away at school, trying to read between the lines for some indication that he'd been cheating on her. Nothing. The only difference she found was in the frequency he wrote, with the last one dated one month before they broke up. Deanna remembered *that* date clearly, as well as the date she lost her virginity and the dates Mom and Dad died.

Dad. She tried to remember the funeral, but it was blurry and rushed. All she wanted to do was get there, pay her respects, and leave. Would things have been different if she'd stayed a few days and mended things then? If she'd stayed for the reading of the will? Her heart clenched with the thought that Cord had been made executor. Not that she had expected to be named such. That right probably belonged to Trish. How had Trish taken it? Cord as executor and part owner of her family's legacy. And now he wanted to develop it.

She sighed, wanting to cry but not finding the energy to do so. She leaned her head back against her headboard, Cord's last letter clutched to her chest, and closed her eyes.

~ ~ ~

And this was how Cord found her sleeping nearly half an hour later. He'd gotten a frantic call from Trish, who had been unable to leave the shop since no one was there to watch it for her or take care of the customers who were lined up until closing. She hadn't been able to get through to Deanna all day. No taxi had picked Deanna up as far as she could see. Deanna hadn't left—she had no car.

Cord had no need for the key he'd picked up from Trish on his way over since he found the screen door unlocked and the front door opened. He called out Deanna's name and rapped twice then entered when he got no response. Immediately he walked to the kitchen, following the sound of the taped recording coming over the telephone. "If you wish to make a call, please hang up and redial your number." He hung up the receiver and scanned the room for any signs of trouble. "Deanna?" His voice echoed in the silence.

He glanced in the living room before heading upstairs, feeling strange walking through the house that appeared unchanged since his youth. Memories flooded back to him, causing him to smile with recollection at the good times he and Deanna had shared within these walls. He made his way down the floral-papered hallway, his footsteps muffled as he stepped along the well-worn, brown shag carpet. Her bedroom door was opened and as Cord was about to step foot over the threshold he stopped—the sight of Deanna sleeping stealing his breath and his nerve away completely.

He watched her for a few moments, taking in the wine bottle, before he decided to leave her be. Back down in the kitchen, he called Trish to let her know everything was okay. After hanging up the old black rotary phone receiver, he headed for the front door, noting that the roses he had sent still lay in their box on the couch. He smiled, wondering what her reaction had been.

With that thought he walked over and picked up a bloom, bringing the fragrant flower to his nose while inhaling deeply. He chuckled aloud as he decided there was one more thing to do before leaving. He took the stairs swiftly two at a time then headed toward her bedroom, bloom in hand.

Fast asleep and curled on her side, papers held protectively against her chest, she seemed so angelic, so peaceful. He laid the rose on the pillow beside her face and reached over to unfold the quilt that lay at the foot of the bed. After covering her he bent over, unable to suppress the urge, and placed a soft kiss on her forehead. She smiled and snuggled under the blanket as he started to straighten up.

Then his eye fell on the papers in her hand, recognizing his own handwriting on the faded page, and he froze. Cocking his head he read a line or two, unable to recall writing them. A glance in the box beside her bed revealed more letters, some dead flowers, scraps of paper. A bunch of old stuff. He peered a little closer and saw an 8 x 10 of their last prom picture taken. Deanna's prom. She had worn this slinky green thing that made her eyes glow like cat's eyes. He'd worn a white tux. They had been great together, he recalled, picking up the photograph yellowed with time so he could study it. He chuckled and laid the photo on the bed beside the flower. Breathing deeply, he closed his eyes and fought the urge to crawl under the blanket with her. He didn't know how she'd take to waking up with the flower and photograph beside her. He knew exactly how she'd react to waking up and finding him beside her. Hell hath no fury like Deanna had, that's for sure.

Studying her face once more, Cord noticed that her eyelids twitched and he wondered if he filled her dreams like she did his. He denied the impulse to kiss her once more, figuring he shouldn't press his luck, and reluctantly left her bedside.

One more urge did overtake him as he made his way downstairs. The comforting quiet of the house, and the sound of the rhythm of the rain and how it continually fell in a torrential downpour at the moment, led Cord to albeit impulsively, rearrange the rest of his schedule. He called Trish at the shop and asked what time she and Pike were heading home, and learned that neither would be home until later in the evening.

"I'm working until eight and then Pike's picking me up and we're going bowling. League night," Trish had informed him.

Cord decided he'd stick around and catch the hell he deserved from Deanna in person.

Off came his London Fog raincoat which he laid on the stairway banister. Off came his Dingo cowboy boots, which he set by the front door. Off came his navy blue tie, which he laid over his rain coat. He unfastened the top button of his light blue shirt, rolled the sleeves up to his elbows, and headed toward the long-stems still resting in their box on the couch. Moments later he placed the thornless buds in a vase he found under the kitchen sink after rummaging through a few cabinets. He set the vase and flowers in the center of the dining room table, then walked over to the hutch and found two very dusty plates. After a quick inspection he decided to give them a quick rinse, along with two soup and salad bowls, then set them in the olive green dish drainer to drip dry.

After calling the Jade House and placing an order to be delivered, he sauntered into the living room to the very stereo and albums that still occupied the shelf they sat on when he and Deanna were younger. He hummed softly to himself as he flipped through the dust-covered jackets, all arranged alphabetically. He selected the album that included Deanna's senior prom theme, which played while he sat cross-legged on the floor, reading album cover backs and recalling memories so many of the tunes brought to mind. The first side of the first album had only finished playing when the doorbell rang.

After flipping the album over, he glanced out the window and spotted a Toyota minivan idling in the driveway with the Jade House name and logo emblazoned on its side doors. Cord paid the delivery girl and brought the package into the kitchen. The soft strains of "I Will Remember You" by Sarah McGloughlin drifted into the kitchen as he dumped beef with broccoli, shrimp fried rice, shrimp in lobster sauce, wonton soup, and spare ribs all into separate bowls to be heated when dinner was served. Proud of himself he turned around, only to find now it was he who had the audience.

"Great! You're up!" He grinned at Deanna, who

stood in the doorway, arms folded across her chest, disheveled, angry and confused, and as beautiful as ever. "Have a nice nap?"

"What are you doing here?" she snapped at him, not moving from her stance. "I thought I told you I never wanted to see you again?"

"You never said those words to me." He shrugged. "Besides, I was worried about your purse. Did you ever find it?"

"Don't change the subject! What are you doing here?"

"I brought dinner. Trish and Pike are going out tonight."

"Out?"

"Bowling. Every Wednesday. They belong to a league. You want to go sit inside? This will only take a few minutes to heat up. You want a beer?" She watched him open the refrigerator and bend down searching for a beer.

She shook her head, still looking very confused. "For people who keep complaining about being poor, they go out more than I do."

He stood up, a brown bottle in hand. "Yes? No?"

"No!"

"That's right. This is a red wine kinda day," he said, nodding to the floor above, dimples flashing. He bent down again and came up with a fruity white wine spritzer. "For the lady." He tossed it at her and Deanna caught the bottle with both hands. "Nice catch, Drake."

"This isn't going to work," she said, setting the wine cooler on the table. "I don't want to see you."

"Sure you do." He led her to the couch, nudged her to sit and took the spot next to her, then handed her the wine cooler he had picked up from the table.

Deanna reached up to turn the brass lamp beside the couch on but Cord spoke softly as he twisted open his beer, his voice stilling her actions. "Please don't."

"It's getting dark."

"I can still see you."

Deanna twisted off the cap of her own bottle, placing it on the table. Cord handed her the cap he twisted off his longneck bottle and she placed it next to hers, then turned to study him in the dusky darkness.

~ ~ ~

"So if you're not here to change my mind then what are you doing here? And," she added with an accusatory tone, "what the hell were you doing in my bedroom?"

He laughed softly and she hit him in the leg with an open palm.

It had only taken her seconds after waking to realize someone had been in her room, with the rose and photo giving her an idea as to who the intruder had been. And when she came down stairs, still half a sleep, Sarah McGloughlin playing softly while Cord whistled away in the kitchen, Deanna had been amazed, stunned, and totally bewildered.

He grabbed her hand as she slapped his thigh, placing his over hers as it rested on his leg. She studied him as he stared at his leg, her hand, his hand. "This is how it's supposed to be." His voice cracked as he spoke.

With a slight cough and a clearing of her throat, Deanna leaned away from Cord, turning to face him again as she proceeded to interrogate him on his motives. "Well? You can't deny it. What were you doing in my room?"

Her eyes narrowed, her brow furrowed sternly. Cord laughed out loud. "Not near as much as I wanted to Deanna. Believe me."

Ignoring that remark she raised an eyebrow and prodded further. "Did you snoop?"

"Would I do something so horrible as that?"

Deanna studied him for a moment. "I was reading your letters."

They locked gazes, crystal blue meeting forest green. "I know. I recognized my scribble. I didn't touch anything. Except the picture. I promise."

She bit her lip to still the trembling and studied her jean-clad knee, which now relaxed against his trouser clad thigh. "I hadn't thought of those since . . . I'm glad I didn't throw them out or burn them like I wanted to."

"Yeah?" His eyes crinkled as they studied her in the fading light. "How come?"

She hesitated, then swallowed thickly. "I had forgotten. All I could remember was the pain. Everything else was a blur."

Cord smiled with her honesty and let loose a deep breath. "Yeah, well. It was pretty good, wasn't it?"

"As good as it was, that's how bad it got."

"I know I've told you this already. I know you don't believe me. I was a jerk. I admit it. But that was five years ago, number one. And number two, it hurt like hell losing you. I swear I'll never get over you."

"Good. I wanted you to hurt. I wanted to hurt you as badly as you hurt me."

"Will you ever forgive me? Will this ever end?"

"We can't go back."

"I don't want to go back. We've got the rest of our lives to live. I only want to go forward."

She shook her head and stood up. "You've caught me in a bad way, Cord. I can't talk about this now."

He grabbed the belt loop at the back of her pants and tugged her down to sit beside him. "Why not?"

She squared her shoulders. "Because I've had to spend the afternoon laying my mother's memory to rest and bringing yours back to life. I am emotionally drained, physically exhausted, and unable to decipher what the hell I'm really feeling inside."

"But, Dean—"

"No." She held a hand up, her fingers trembling. "Let me finish here. Furthermore." She took a deep breath. "Furthermore. I don't want to trust you. I don't even want to like you right now. I sure as hell don't want to sell the farm to you. And I cannot believe my father made you—YOU—executor of my family legacy! I'm pissed as all hell at Patricia, and you, for dragging me out here on a wild goose chase. For not being honest."

She turned to him now, a quirky grin twisting her lips into a wry smile. "But."

He relaxed with the sight of her grin. "But?"

"I loved the roses. And I'm starving. Correction. I'm famished. I have no pride when it comes to my stomach."

"Well, let's go then." He stood up and offered her his hand. Raising her eyes, she studied him in the darkness as she accepted. "I'll put this on your tab too."

"I'd better get out my check book soon or I'll have to declare bankruptcy."

"Checkbook? Does that mean you found your missing purse?"

Deanna nodded as they walked into the kitchen, all signs of tension stemming from anger or desire or mistrust gone completely for now. "Trisha brought it in."

"Well, that's good news, except for one small problem."

"What now?"

"I don't take personal checks."

Chapter 10

Packing leftover shrimp in lobster sauce into the orange and brown Tupperware bowls her mother had bought the week before Deanna's sixteenth birthday should not feel so normal a task, Deanna thought, licking a drop of sauce off her thumb after sealing the container tight. Especially with Cord by her side, washing and drying the last of the dishes.

"Remember that, Cord?" Deanna chuckled softly as she recited the memory. "I cried and cried when I came home from the library and saw all Mom's friends here."

"Yeah, how can I forget? You ran all the way to my house bawling your eyes out and scared me to death." He hung the cloth dishtowel on the crow-shaped wall peg by the sink. "All because you thought the Tupperware party was a ruse and you honestly thought you were going to your birthday party."

"Not *any* birthday party. My sweet sixteen—"

"Which you had the following week," Cord reminded her. "If it hadn't been for that Tupperware party we would have never gotten together."

"Hmm. Sweet sixteen and never been kissed." The memory of her first kiss, delivered by the man here with her now, left her feeling dreamy, but made this entire moment even more surreal.

"Mark Drummond always bragged how he was the first boy you ever let kiss you." Cord followed Deanna into the living room.

"Well. Then Mark Drummond lied. You were my first." Deanna knelt on the floor beside her parents' and her old record collection, still contained in the red plastic milk crate she had used as a teenager.

"But will I be the last? Now that is the million-dollar question."

Rummaging through her old record albums took all of her attention and left him without an answer. "Well?"

"Wouldn't you like to know?" She found the frayed Meatloaf album that had been all the rage when her parents were young.

Cord knelt beside her and caught her gaze. "Yes. I would, as a matter of fact."

She twirled around on her knees searching for a bit of personal space between them and shook her head. "That'll never happen."

"Why not?"

"Cord. Don't go poking through my closets. You're liable to find something that doesn't fit." She continued flipping through the albums.

His hand came up to caress her cheek, her chin fitting nicely in his palm. "I'm not. I was wondering if you've been seeing anyone lately."

"It's none of your business, Cord. You lost that right." Her voice was soft, void of malice, anger. It was weary, trembling, threatening tears.

His face came close to hers. "I want to make it my business again, Deanna." He leaned forward, rubbing the tip of her nose with his, prompting a smile from her.

"Cord." Her voice came in a husky whisper. He chuckled softly in answer and closed his eyes, tilting his head ever so slightly, while his hand nudged her face upward, gently positioning her mouth at just . . . the right . . . angle.

At first contact of lips against lips Deanna made the most quiet little mewl as she melted into him. He held her close, his thumb caressing her cheek, his mouth searching, seeking, beckoning her to answer his demands.

His tongue lightly flicked her bottom lip tasting and testing before kissing her slowly. He kissed her lower lip softly at first, then more fully, until she responded, seeking and probing as completely as he. She raised her arms, wrapping her body around him, bringing him closer.

Both of his hands came around to settle on the small of her back, caressing at first, then massaging, rubbing, bringing her nearer to his body. She shifted to kneel between his thighs and he growled hungrily. He molded her to him, wrapping both his arms completely around her, nearly crushing her in his embrace.

Trembling, Deanna clung to him. And although she had never forgotten his touch, time had lessened the memory of the overwhelming effect he had on her. She started slightly when his hands slipped beneath her shirt and settled on the smooth curve of her lower back, caressing her skin, his fingers tracing up her spine. She froze for a brief second when he found the clasp of her bra, unhooking it with a mere snap and a twist. A soft moan sounded from deep within her as his hand slipped around to cup the soft underside of her breast. She inhaled sharply, every muscle in her body twitching with restraint. His musky, heady scent filled her being, and she became mesmerized by the harmonies of their breathing, heated by his touch.

His hand, so rough against her softness, caressed and coaxed her to make love with him. She felt her skin tingle as he created magic within her, making her want to sing, to laugh, to love. She eased backward and lay down on the rug, bringing him with her, their bodies never losing contact, their lips never parting. The living room swirled around them as she closed her eyes, unconscious to all but this man and the feelings he aroused in her body. Even with her eyes closed, she saw him above her, straddling her. The thick muscles of his thighs molded against the soft curves of her hips.

It was her turn to explore his mouth with her own kiss now, hesitantly at first, then bolder as his free hand came up to unbutton her jeans. Her knees drew up in reflex, parting slightly with his probing. Heaven. Pure heaven to be in his arms again, she thought, dazed.

Her name escaped his lips in a breathless whisper as Cord buried his face in Deanna's neck, inhaling her essence. "It's been so long," he whispered. "I want you so bad."

Those words stilled her, and she paused to study his face. Passion glittered in his eyes, turning them a deep, deep blue. She saw his desire. And with it she recognized her own. Her own passion, her own vulnerability. Could she take a chance on him again? Could she let him into her heart? A voice within her head screamed for her to wake up before it was too late. And the love that had so briefly flickered within was immediately replaced by doubt, fear, and then anger. Her gaze went vacant and wide. "I can't do this."

"You can't do this?" Cord exhaled deeply, shaking off the confusion. "What happened?"

Deanna pushed away from him, then sat up and lifted her shoulders, forcing a light shrug as she straightened her shirt. "What happened is I woke up."

"Woke up?" His disbelief was evident as he raked a hand through his hair, hair that had been tousled into an unruly heap moments before by Deanna's wandering hands.

"So is this how you're going to pay me back? Denying yourself to get even with me?" His frustration sounded thick in his words.

"I'm doing no such thing." She shrugged again, fighting to appear unaffected.

He stood up, his desire obvious by the strained material of his slacks stretched below his waist. "Why are you doing this?"

She shook her head and averted her gaze. "I'm not—"

"Deanna! I'm not stupid!"

"Don't yell at me because *you* can't control your lustful urges. I'm not some animal that's going to-to screw around because my body wants me to!"

He stared at her in surprise, her phrasing leaving him speechless, as it did her. And that was how Pike and Trish found them seconds later.

"Hey, you two. What have you been up to?" Trish asked innocently, oblivious of the turmoil the couple had experienced seconds earlier.

However Pike sensed the tension immediately and hit Trish on the back. "Let's go make some coffee. You guys want coffee?"

"No. I'm going to bed." As her sister and brother headed for the kitchen Deanna struggled to reclasp her bra.

Cord shook his head. "You can't run away from us. We aren't over."

"How about you, Cord?" Pike called from the kitchen.

"No. I've got to get going." He turned from Deanna and walked to where he had left his coat and boots earlier. "Thanks, anyway."

"On second thought, maybe I will have a cup, Pike. Thanks," Deanna called into the kitchen as she stood up and walked toward Cord.

"We still have to talk," he reminded her, slipping into his coat and boots. "I'll call you tomorrow."

"My Lord. Where'd these come from? Pike? How come you never bring me flowers?" Trish's voice echoed from the dining room.

"Don't bother. I'm going home tomorrow." Deanna whispered.

"Home? This is home, Deanna." Cord whispered back.

"Not if you get your way, it won't be. Goodbye, Cord. Happy developing." She turned toward the kitchen. "Oh. And by the way. Consider that little exchange as payment rendered in full. Therefore, I believe my debt is satisfied."

"And I consider that your first installment. See you next month." He shoved his tie in his pocket and turned and left without another word.

Chapter 11

Deanna ached. Her arms ached. Her belly ached. Her head ached. But most of all, her heart ached. It ached like hell, she thought as the taxi cab arrived curbside in front of her apartment. It was raining again. And Manhattan rain was not nearly as rejuvenating an experience as Olde Westfield storms. Deanna's expression was sour as she stepped ankle high in a puddle by the curb. Even giving the driver a hefty tip didn't budge him from the warm comfort of his seat to help her with her luggage.

She awkwardly balanced her pocketbook, garment bag, overnight bag, and two shopping bags full of her attic treasures as she gingerly stepped around the puddles lining the walkway that led to her apartment building. Every now and then she would nod to one of her still nameless neighbors, and they would greet her similarly, but no one offered to help her.

Her apartment was cold. The answering machine was blinking full of calls. She dumped her packages in the middle of the floor of her living room and walked over to the sliding glass doors that led to her porch. She drew back the blinds, sat cross-legged at the window, and stared at the little green shoots pushing up through the black soil. Life. A promise of something to come, of something good, of life. Deanna leaned her forehead against the cold glass and closed her eyes, trying to remember what had happened to make her feel so miserable.

The farm. Yes, that was definitely cause for a headache. Going through her mom's things wasn't the best cure all for her loneliness. Cord's kisses. His touch. Now, that was truly the root of all her problems. She sighed loudly and shook her head to clear the memory of her former lover. They almost made love last night. And the night before.

And with that he would have gotten the farm. All of it. And then he would have dumped her. Like she had dumped him years ago. Deanna lifted a finger to the window and traced the path of a raindrop downward, downward, snaking along an invisible course until finally it ran itself dry, ending its journey midway down the door.

~ ~ ~

Trish called later that night to make sure Deanna had returned home safely. Trish also asked if Cord had called, then told Deanna that he had rang the shop asking about her.

"So call him, okay?"

"No thanks. I have nothing to say to him."

"Ask him what he wanted."

"Trish. I said no. I can't."

"Why not?"

Deanna was silent.

"Well?"

"I don't know." Deanna couldn't confide in Trish, not when she knew Trish would run back to Cord and repeat every word. "I gotta go. I have to get up early for work in the morning."

"I thought you took the week off?"

"Yeah, but I'm going in anyway. There's no sense in staying here." Suddenly what used to be Deanna's haven from her problems now seemed like a prison. She wanted to feel the gravel beneath her feet, the grass between her toes. She wanted to hear the katydids outside her window, smell freshly mown grass, and the morning dew. Cord's words echoed in her mind. *"This is your home."*

"When are you coming home again?"

"I don't know, Trish. It's so hectic out here."

"I'll let you know if anything comes up with the zoning."

"Have you decided what you're going to do with the farm?"

The silence over the telephone wire gave Deanna her answer.

"Never mind."

"Deanna. We're going to have to talk about this sooner or later. I didn't want to do it over the phone."

"Trish. I told you and Pike where I stood on selling last night. I don't want to sell. But now that Cord told me he was executor and part owner, I guess what I want doesn't matter."

"About that." Trish started to speak but Deanna cut her off.

"Yeah, about that. How could you keep that from me?"

"That doesn't matter now anyway. I'm sorry. What's done is done. Fact is, we're going to lose the farm if we don't listen to Cord. And then we won't have nothing except bills, bills, and more bills! I'm tired of being poor, Deanna!"

"You don't get it, do you? If I sell out that's it. If you sell out I won't have anything except this dumb apartment."

"If we do it together we'll still have each other."

"Yeah, right. What will keep you on the island? You work in a salon and Pike could be laid off with a change in the administration. Real stable future."

Trish was silent for a moment, then said, "I know. Pike's talking about moving to Pennsylvania if Cord buys us out."

"See?"

"You're in the city, what do you care? I've got to do what's best for me and Pike."

"And I've got to do what's best for me."

"Well, then. I guess this is it."

"I guess it is."

"Well."

"I'll call you soon. Okay?" Deanna fought to keep her voice steady.

"Yeah. Whatever." Trish sounded disgusted.

~ ~ ~

Deanna had thought that going to work would be the cure for all her ills. But she was wrong. She couldn't concentrate, she snapped at everyone, and messed up the final copy she'd written for an ad campaign earlier in the month so badly that she had to start from scratch and begin again.

The following week wasn't any better. She couldn't even feel relief by Friday because the thought of returning to her empty apartment for a whole weekend intensified her depression.

Late nights at the office, happy hours with her co-workers, and business trips filled her weeks and kept her busy, but as summer rolled in, Deanna realized she had to stop running.

It was the first Friday in June, and the promise of summer in the city had the streets bustling with friends and lovers enjoying the warming temperatures and longer days. Deanna wove her way through the throng, accompanied only by a personal pizza and six-pack of longnecks, and made her way home to face reality. She was alone.

She could have gone out with the crowd from work again, but her misery spoke before her desire to be happy could, and she declined. She could have swallowed her pride and called her sister, maybe even hopped the train and surprised her. Deanna knew Trish would welcome her with open arms.

But she couldn't do that either. Not with Cord there. Hovering, waiting to pounce on her every time she let her guard down. It was too dangerous. She was too vulnerable, too weak where he was concerned. God. How could she still love him after all this time? Didn't it ever stop? Wouldn't the pain ever go away? She downed the last of her beer and proceeded to pop open her fourth in one and a half hours when the telephone rang. Again. Every half hour since she'd gotten home it had rung.

Deanna stared at it for a long while, counting the rings that seemed to never end. She had shut her answering machine off last night, not wanting to deal with the media trying to keep the McCord/Drake feud alive for a good story. The phone grew silent and the apartment became deafeningly quiet. She laid her head on her forearm, her fourth beer half finished before her. And she didn't move until the doorbell rang the next morning.

At the sound of the buzzer, Deanna jumped. In her semi-conscious state she thought it was her cellphone and she grabbed it quick from its resting spot by her head. There was no call coming in and this confused her, but when the intercom buzzer continued without relief Deanna realized someone wanted to come up. She walked over to the intercom system, asking for identification, but no one answered.

Damn kids, she thought, heading for the bathroom in search of aspirin for her pounding headache. Moments later, Deanna heard another pounding, this time coming from her door. Her heart skipped a beat in fear. No one ever came to visit her. Ever. She tiptoed to the door, not wanting to let the person on the other side hear her approach in case she chose not to answer.

Deanna peered through the peephole and gasped.

Upon hearing the click of the peephole's shutter, Cord called out her name. "Deanna? Open up."

"Go away," she called. Be strong, she told herself. *Be strong.* She tried, but failed, to ignore the fluttering butterflies in her stomach.

"I'm not going away. It took me two and a half hours to drive here. I got stuck in traffic because of a broken down charter bus and rubberneckers, and then I drove for ten minutes because I couldn't find a parking spot. I am not leaving. Open up." His voice was calm, almost coaxing.

"No. I-I'm not dressed."

"Well. Get dressed and open the door. I didn't get up at the crack of dawn to stand in your hallway and argue." Cord sighed loudly enough for Deanna to hear it through the door. "Come on now. Please?"

When she did not reply he rapped lightly but steadily on the door with his fist. "Deanna, come on."

"Stop it. I've got a blasted headache and you're not making it any better."

"I'll sit here all weekend if I have to. I want to talk with you and I'm not leaving until I do." Again, his voice sounded unbelievably calm.

Deanna giggled nervously.

"It's not funny," he added.

"I'm not laughing." She giggled again. He'd come all the way out here to see her. "You must want that farm pretty bad to sit in traffic two and a half hours. And to search for a parking spot for, how long? Ten whole minutes? What's the matter, Mr. Developer? Run out of trees to chop down?"

"Please. Open. The. Door."

"You should have saved yourself the trouble and called."

"I tried. Both numbers. You don't answer your phones."

She bit her lip for a moment, trying to control the peals of laughter that were about to burst forth any second. Nerves, no doubt.

"Open the door."

"How about 'please,' asshole?"

Silence slipped beneath the door, and Deanna's eyes widened as she thanked God for the thickness of the wood that separated her from Cord. She grinned broadly, imagining what shade of purple his face was turning right about now.

When he spoke his voice remained calm, void of any emotion. "All right. You win. Please, asshole?"

Deanna chuckled and opened the door, coming face to face with the man who had tormented her every waking and sleeping moment.

"What do you want?"

Relief played across his handsome features. His voice was soft. "Why don't you answer your phone?"

"I always keep it on silent."

He shook his head at her, asking, "Well. Are you going to let me in?"

"Is it safe?"

"I come bearing gifts."

He lifted numerous packages toward her. In one hand was a leather Pierre Cardin overnight case. In his other fist he held two large shopping bags. She bit her lip and feigned indecision for a moment, before she squinted and said, "All right, I guess."

"Finally."

"Come on in then." Deanna turned around and stepped into her living room, Cord following as he elbowed the door closed behind him.

"I thought you said you weren't dressed. I'm disappointed."

Deanna blushed with the thought that she was still wearing her clothes from yesterday. She hadn't even taken her makeup off or brushed her teeth before she passed out last night. "Oh. Yeah. I am."

"You look like hell."

"Thanks. You can put your stuff over there." Deanna eyed the suitcase, wondering if he actually had the gall to think he was staying here.

He noticed the direction of her glance, and shrugged. "What time do you cook breakfast in this joint? Unless you've already had." He nodded toward the empty beer bottles lined up on the kitchen table, tugged his arms out of his leather jacket, and threw it over the green-checked easy chair.

She walked into the bathroom and turned the shower on. "If you're smart enough to find the kitchen without getting lost, you can cook whatever you want. But give me ten minutes before you put my eggs on. I like them over medium. I'll be right out."

Again Cord shook his head and chuckled at her, his dimples cutting into his lean face as his grin broadened.

~ ~ ~

"Doesn't it seem like all we do is eat together?" Deanna asked as she shoved a piece of whole wheat toast in her mouth.

"Yeah. You think we'd be able to come up with something a little less fattening." He quirked an eyebrow at her, throwing a boyish grin in her direction.

She chewed thoughtfully, not sure what kind of comeback could squelch a remark like that. So she said nothing, sitting in the ladder back kitchen chair as she fed the rest of the toast into her mouth.

"But . . . unfortunately, that's not why I'm here. Not right now, anyway." He stood up and placed his plate in the sink. "More coffee?"

She nodded. "Good eggs."

"I thought so." He emptied the last of the brew into their cups then set the empty pot in the sink. "Done?" He motioned to her nearly emptied plate.

"Yeah. Here." She handed him her plate and stretched, wrapping her flannel robe about her body. "I am exhausted."

"Rough night?" They walked into the living room, and she moved his jacket choosing to sit a safe distance from him, in her favorite chair. Cord settled into the loveseat.

"Yeah. I didn't get to bed at all, as a matter of fact. And drank too much on top of it. I thought I was going to toss my cookies in the shower." She grinned sheepishly, embarrassed with her own admission.

"What did you do?" he asked.

"Nothing special."

"Anyone in particular?"

"No."

"Well. You want to sleep for a while? I can keep busy."

"Nope. You came out here to talk. So talk." Deanna curled her legs up underneath her, giving Cord her complete attention.

"Yeah. I had my attorney prepare a proposal. Wait," he said, and lifted a hand when she started to protest. "Hear me out. Take it, read it at your leisure. If you want to make a counter offer, fine. If you want to decline, that's fine too."

"I don't want to sell. I told you." She hugged her knees close, curling up protectively.

"I know you don't. Please. Read the proposal." He waved the document at her.

"You won't change my mind."

"If you haven't been told yet, I'm probably going to buy out Trish and Pike. Unless you can beat my offer."

A frown was her only answer to that suggestion.

"I want to give you the same opportunity I'm giving them." He shrugged and shook his head.

"Michael McCord. You are so annoying."

"Deanna Drake. You are so stubborn. You're thinking with your heart. You're not using your head. We have to be logical about this."

"Well that was a bit of implied sexism, not to mention insulting. If you mean I'm thinking like a woman, that is what I do best. Unlike thinking like a man, which means destroy everything you see," she snapped, totally on guard now.

"You're not being logical."

"Wow. Even more insulting. Keep going, this is getting good." She shook her head and rolled her eyes.

"This is business we're talking about here."

"That's where you are wrong again, Cord. This is not business. This is my childhood. My family. A part of me."

Cord was stilled by her words, then blurted out, "Maybe that's why I want it so bad."

Deanna stared at him momentarily and then studied her hands, not sure she'd heard him correctly.

Cord shook his head, rubbing his chin. "Deanna. We have to put our differences behind us or that farm won't belong to either one of us." He laid the manila envelope on the table. "Read it when you get the chance. I'm not in any hurry. We have until November to notify the banks of our decision. I paid some of the back taxes and that bought us some time."

"Why didn't you tell me who you were? Who you became?" She narrowed her gaze at him.

"Who am I?" he asked, running a hand through his hair.

"That *Newsday* article referred to you as 'Developer Michael McCord.' Is there anything they failed to mention?"

"Deanna. I've made a few good investments. I've bought some land, made some good deals. You knew I was studying architecture. You knew what I wanted to do."

"And you got what you wanted."

"Yes. I did. And so did you."

"Yes. I did, didn't I?"

He studied her a moment, leaning back and laying his arms along the back of the couch. "Are you happy?"

"Yes."

"You sure?" He nodded to the empty beer bottles that now rested in the drainer by the kitchen sink, rinsed and ready to be returned.

"Um-hm. Are you?"

"Very."

She nodded. "Good for you."

"So will you read it?"

"Um-hm. But I won't promise you anything. I'm working on something. A way to raise the taxes."

"Deanna. It's not the taxes. I paid part of them already. It's the operation of the farm. It's the day to day maintenance. It's becoming an eyesore. The leasing. The lack of use. It's sitting there. Doing nothing."

"Doing nothing when it could be making money."

"Exactly. I'll buy the whole thing—everything but the twenty acres which I'll leave for you and Trish. And I could even make more with your ten little acres than you could working every inch of that damn farm."

"But my house—"

"It's not your house. It's Trish and Pike's house. If you lived in it then you could say it was yours. But you don't. This is your home." He pointed to the plaque hanging over the sliding doors.

Silence settled between them and Deanna took that as a welcome cue to change the subject. "So what other gifts did you bring me?" She leaned over to peer into the bags. As she reached into one, Cord slapped her hand away.

"Uh, uh, uh. Patience, my dear. Here." He lifted a bulky package wrapped in tinfoil. "Mom's power cookies."

"She remembered?" Jane always made Deanna her famous oatmeal, raisin, carob chip, and wheat germ cookies when Deanna was training for a track meet.

"A bottle of white wine and a bottle of seltzer." He snorted as he set these on the coffee table.

"A bottle of Jacks."

Deanna wrinkled her nose, but said nothing.

"A bottle of Moet."

"What's that for?"

"Just in case—"

"You're a little too cocky, Mr. McCord."

"—you agree to my proposal." He smiled.

"Which proposal is this, now?"

"Deanna. I'm trying to behave." He winked.

"Behave? You brought three different types of liquor for two days?"

"So you're inviting me to stay?"

Her cheeks grew warm and she sighed. "Come on. What else have you got in there?"

He paused for a minute, then breathed deeply. "Well. Here goes. I dug these up for you. I thought you might want to complete the set."

Deanna watched on in confusion as he cradled a frayed plastic bag, which he unwrapped from around a shoebox. Inside the shoebox were all the letters she had ever written him. "You kept them?" she whispered, her voice choking and her eyes blurring with tears.

He nodded, staring at the box. "Here." He offered the mementos, his gaze unwavering.

"Thanks. I'll give them back when I'm done." She searched his face, silently pleading for him to lift his eyes so she could see what he was thinking.

"You can hold on to them. I know where to find you now." He did look up then, and he smiled at her. "I thought you'd enjoy them."

"I-I don't know what to say. Thank you?" She hugged the box close.

"You're very welcome," he responded, before adding, "but I do want them back."

"Deal." She kept her head bent, clasping the treasure close to her heart.

"So?" Cord broke her train of thought.

"So?" She stared at him, at a loss for words.

"You wanna show me the big city or what?"

"Why not? They say it's a helluva town."

"Yes, so it's been said. Come on, let's get outside."

"All right, all right. Have it your way." She stood up slowly. "Let me change my clothes and we'll head out."

"Need any help?"

Deanna chuckled at his request as she headed toward her bedroom, his letters still cradled close to her body.

"Seriously. Thank you. You've almost restored my faith in you."

"Anytime, Drake. Anytime."

Chapter 12

Sunday afternoon came quickly, too quickly for Deanna. She and Cord had spent Saturday touring Manhattan, taking subways and buses, eating hot dogs from a street vendor, feeding pigeons in Central Park.

They ate lunch at the Hard Rock Cafe and dinner at the original TGIF's and by the time they got back to Deanna's apartment it was 9:30. She could barely keep her eyes open as she shoved her key in the lock and pushed open the door. She groaned and collapsed on the couch without even removing her sneakers or jacket.

"We should have taken the truck," Cord said as he settled at the opposite end of the couch, pushing her feet aside and then repositioning them on his lap.

"What? And miss the true New York experience? You wimp." Her feet ached, but it was a good pain.

"I don't know about you, but I'm exhausted. This city living is not for me. I'll take suburban sprawl any day. Foot rub?" He grabbed her foot and she yanked it away.

"No! But thanks. You don't need to be touching my smelly feet," she said, laughing. "Wow. I don't think I could move right now if you told me the president was at the door."

"I don't think that would get me to move even if I wasn't tired."

"Tell me about it. Now there's something we can agree on, at least." She placed a forearm over her eyes and yawned.

When she felt a tug at her shoe lace she smiled, but lay still. He slipped a sneaker off, then unlaced her other one and slipped that off too. When he placed a thumb at her arch she attempted to move away from his touch. "They stink."

"No, they don't."

"They're all sweaty."

"Stop struggling. Relax. They're not sweaty. They're hot."

"Perv."

"Deanna. Consider this a thank-you for a great day."

"It does feel good." She yawned once more.

"See? Close your eyes and relax. There you go."

And that was the end of Saturday as far as Deanna could recall.

~ ~ ~

Sunday morning, Deanna awoke at her usual time, right around six o'clock, to find herself curled up on the couch alone, with only an afghan to keep her warm. She pushed herself up and searched for Cord, wondering if he'd left. She stretched and yawned loudly, figuring out exactly where he was. In her bed. *Oh, god.*

After her shower, she slipped on her robe, realizing for the first time this weekend she hadn't jogged in two whole days. Even though she probably burned more calories yesterday than both missed jogs, guilt still filled her as she walked into the kitchen. A quick estimate of all the calories and grams of fat consumed since Cord showed up yesterday morning made her cringe. She was standing at the counter waiting for the water to boil, tallying all this up, when she heard the bathroom door close. Deanna sighed. *I could get used to this.*

Since she figured it was her turn to fix breakfast, Deanna chose whole wheat pancakes, which were ready by the time Cord came to stand beside her. A glance in his direction showed him to be fully dressed in khaki trousers and an olive-green polo shirt.

"You look good standing there." He reached up and grabbed two mugs from the cabinet where he'd watched Deanna take them from the morning before.

"Was that a compliment or a sexist remark?" She arched an eyebrow at him.

"Of course." He grinned back.

"So I guess I should thank you."

"Something like that."

With a shrug, she scooped coffee into her coffee press, then poured the water in and set the strainer on top, waiting for the grinds to steep. It was unsettling how good this whole thing felt. Not fighting. Not even making love. Just being together. "Can you get the butter out?"

He turned to the refrigerator, reached for the milk with one hand and the butter with his other, asking casually, "So what are we doing today?"

Deanna snorted. "Don't you have a life?"

When he didn't answer, she asked, "That bad, huh?" She gave him a grin along with the plate of pancakes.

"You've no idea, Drake."

"You work too hard."

He sat down and pried the cap off the syrup. "How would you know?"

"Birds of a feather, I guess?"

"Yeah, well. Hey," he said, after taking a bite, "these are great."

"Thanks. So. You seeing anybody?" So much for beating around the bush.

His fork paused midair for a moment with the question, then reached its destination as he answered her with a silent shake of his head. "You?"

"No." Deanna toyed with her two pancakes, wishing she hadn't brought up the subject. By doing so she was letting him know she was interested. That she was ready to give up her heart again.

"So. What *are* we going to do today?" he asked again slowly.

"Don't you have to go home?"

He shrugged. "I'll go home later. Unless you have something to do?"

"Nope. I usually run, read the paper. Sometimes I go to church. Sometimes I veg out. I usually clean on Saturdays, but I'll have to do that today because *someone* kept me busy yesterday."

"So we'll clean today. After church."

"We don't have to go to church."

"I want to."

"We don't have to clean."

"I don't mind."

"Well. No. Don't be stupid. I'm sure this is not how you want to spend your Sunday."

"Dean. I made the offer, I'm not gonna argue. If you want to we will. If you don't, we won't. That's all. More coffee?"

~ ~ ~

So, that was how they spent Sunday. Now it was nearly four o'clock and again they were both exhausted from their efforts. Cord had gotten stuck scrubbing the bathroom while Deanna vacuumed and dusted. Right now, a chicken was roasting in the oven as they were preparing once again to eat together.

"You're a hard taskmaster." He laid out two burgundy linen placemats on the table, then folded two napkins and set them down beside two plates Deanna had handed him.

"Take it or leave it. Besides. You owe me for getting the bed last night. Some gentleman you turned out to be, leaving me on the couch." She withdrew two wineglasses from the cabinet over the refrigerator.

"I was willing to share. You just didn't wake up." He walked around to the counter where he had stored the unopened bottle of wine yesterday.

"Good point." Deanna handed him the corkscrew, not knowing what else to say. "I sleep on the couch all the time."

"Yeah. A bed that big must get pretty lonely."

"Not funny." She made a face at him as he uncorked the wine with a loud pop.

Dinner passed as quickly as the whole weekend had, Deanna thought a short while later, savoring the moments she and Cord worked side by side while cleaning up. She washed, he dried and stacked everything on the table. He now sat silently, watching her every move as she put away the glasses, flatware, plates, and bowls.

When she was finished, Deanna came to sit across from him, folding her hands neatly before her. "Well?" Her green eyes were filled with warmth.

"I guess I'd better be going," he said, not moving.

"How about more coffee? One for the road?" she asked quickly.

"That would be great," he answered before she even finished her question.

She spoke again only after she stood at the counter, her back to him. "Cord, I'm sorry I left things like I did when I was home."

"Don't apologize, Deanna. You were right. We've got a lot of things to work out before we . . . get involved again."

"If," she said as she turned to face him.

"*If* we get involved again," he agreed with a slight nod.

Once the coffee had brewed and their mugs had been filled, Deanna joined him at the table. "So what happens now?"

He shrugged. "What do you want to happen?"

"That's not fair."

"Why not? The ball is in your court. You've got the proposal. Read it. See where I'm coming from as far as business goes. As far as me and you. Well. If you can't figure out where I stand after this weekend, then . . . I don't know what to say."

"I see. So, what happens now?" She repeated this as her lips twitched into a grin.

"Are you asking me to stay and make love to you all night?"

Her face flamed, but she did not reject the offer.

He laughed at her and took a gulp of coffee. "I guess I go home and you can call me after you've read the proposal. We'll take it from there."

"Meaning you're not interested in speaking with me until after I've read this proposal of yours." Her eyes narrowed at him as her heart tightened.

"Meaning I want to get this out of the way and done with so we can begin to move forward."

"I get the feeling that if I don't agree to this proposal, that's it. It's done with? We're through before we even started?"

"Hell, no. But to be honest, I'll do whatever I must do to save the farm, and I seriously doubt you'll want to hook up once I've started procedures."

She stared at him, shocked that he could be so forthright with his assessment. "I see. That's all it would be? A hook-up? Friends with bennies?"

"I didn't mean it that way. You know what I meant."

Deanna shook her head. "No. I don't. I get the feeling that I'm being played with. Like all you want is that damn farm and my body."

"Well at least you're starting to up the ante. First, it was only the farm. Now you've thrown your body into the proposal." He smiled at her, laughter lighting his eyes and softening his words.

"That's not what I meant."

"No?" He reached for her hand but she pulled away.

"There you go again. You did this the last time we saw each other. Stop trying to confuse me." She clasped both hands safely around her coffee mug.

"What? I'm trying not to confuse you. It's going to be okay. Everything will work out. I promise." He took a final swig of his coffee and swallowed hard, never taking his eyes from her.

"How can you sit there and laugh at me?" She slammed her hand down on the table, eyes glittering angrily.

"There *you* go again. You're fighting with me so you don't have to deal with us. *You did this when you were home*. I'm not engaging." He stood up and walked to the cabinet. "You got any cookies?"

"You're nuts." Deanna pushed away from the table, her efforts to leave the kitchen thwarted when Cord reached out and touched her shoulder.

"Don't do this. There's no reason to fight." His fingers closed gently around the soft skin of her upper arm.

"Don't boss me around. Let go of me." She stepped away from him.

Squaring off, he pleaded, "You can't walk away or tell me to leave every time we talk about us."

"It hurts."

"We get so close to getting past it," he said. "We can do this. It's been five years. It's time to move forward, forget the past."

She shook her head, unable to find the words to speak.

"Every time we start feeling good again you do this." He spread his hands palms up, motioning between them.

"That's when it hurts most, Cord."

"Let it go, Deanna. I'll never make that mistake again, I promised." His blue eyes were clear and honest as he gazed into hers. His sincerity burned with an intensity Deanna found most unsettling.

She shook her head. "You told me we have nothing if I don't agree to your proposal."

"No, I didn't."

"You said—"

"What I said and what you think I said are two different things. But that's not the problem here, is it? Is it?" He dipped his head and caught her gaze with a soft smile.

"No. I guess not."

"The only way you're ever going to get over what happened in the past is to let me prove to you it won't happen again. Right?" When she nodded, he continued. "How am I supposed to do that if you never give me the chance?"

"This is so difficult." She shook her head in defeat, her voice broken, eyes filling with tears.

"Deanna." Cord took a step closer, filling the space between them, both hands reaching out to her. "Come here."

Every nerve in her body tingled. Every muscle ached to move at his command. But still she stood firm and unmoving. He leaned over, softly touching her lips with the briefest kiss. "Let's go sit inside. I'm not leaving with things like this. Come on."

He clasped her hand in his own and led her gently to the living room, tugging her behind him as he walked. They sat together on the couch, his arm about her shoulders, keeping her close to his side. "Does this hurt?" he asked.

She shook her head, all her energy directed to trying to still her wildly pounding heart.

"I'm here because I want to be with you. Not because I want the farm. Do you understand me?"

Deanna exhaled slowly and nodded.

"I'm probably going to want to do this again, and I hope you will too. Whether we move forward with the plans or not. Understand?"

"Yes." Deanna rested her head on his shoulder. She was tired of fighting. And this felt so good.

"I will still want to pursue the acquisition of the farm. That's why I want you to read the proposal. There is too much for me to explain. I don't want to waste any more time with you talking business. We've wasted too much time already."

"True."

"Now. If I do go ahead with my plans to acquire the farm and it's against your wishes, can you honestly see us sitting like this?"

"The farm means more to you than I do." She was trying to process, but couldn't bring herself to trust him completely. This was too fast. *But it feels so good.*

"The farm means a lot to both of us."

She straightened up and squared off. "But it's my farm!"

"You have to trust me. But, yes. It is your farm. But it's also one-third mine. I've sunk a lot of money into it—into your family—and I'm not about to lose my investment to a bank. You've got to understand where I'm coming from."

She was silent as she digested his words. For once she could not find a reason to argue.

"If I sell out to you, that's it. It won't be Drake's Farm anymore." Her voice broke with the realization that soon all traces of her family would be gone. And Cord was right. This was going to happen whether he bought it or whether she lost it to the bank.

"If you support me on this—if we do this together—it will stay Drake's Farm. It will always be Drake's Farm if we own it. If the bank takes it, or if someone else swoops in and steals it, it won't be Drake's Farm. The entire property will be condos or a supercenter or a gated community."

"I'll read your proposal."

"Thank you. And you'll call me?"

She sighed and rolled her eyes.

"That's all I ask."

Deanna bit her lip and forced a smile at Cord. A sudden sadness washed over her, filling her with the realization that things were changing, she was growing older and life as she knew it would never be the same. A soft sob escaped her lips and she bent her head.

In response, he sighed deeply. He nudged her against his chest, kissing the top of her head and holding her until her sobs became sniffles, with those subsiding moments later.

"I've got to get going." Cord spoke against her hair, his breath warm and comforting.

"Thanks, Cord. I'll help you get your stuff together."

He stood up and stretched. "When are you coming home again?"

"I don't know. I didn't really think about it."

"Well, how's your schedule the rest of the month?"

"Swamped." She frowned and wrinkled her nose.

"You can't find any time for me?" He crooked an eyebrow.

"I don't know. I guess that depends on what your proposal says."

"Would you mind some company?"

Deanna smiled, her heart soared and her pulse raced. "Business or pleasure?"

"I guess that depends on what you interpret my proposal says?" He shrugged and smiled at her.

"We can always work out the agenda when you get here."

Cord slipped into his coat, bent over and gave Deanna a full kiss on her lips. He chuckled at her bewildered gaze. "Thanks for a great weekend. You can text me if you want. I don't want to hound you."

"Yeah. Okay. I got it. Go. Safe home." She ushered him out the door, shutting it and snapping the deadbolt into place only after she watched the elevator doors close behind him.

Deanna watched from her window as his SUV turned the corner, then she picked up her cell phone and hurriedly dialed Sal's number. Three rings and Sal's familiar voice instructed her to wait for the beep before leaving a message. "It's Dean. Please call me. I need to see you."

~ ~ ~

"So, what do you think?" It was only a short 24 hours later, as Deanna dished out a bowl full of linguine and tomato sauce and placed it before her friend.

"Smells great."

"I meant about the proposal, Sal." Deanna sighed

with exasperation as she sat down and watched her company's attorney study the document.

"Well. He's thorough. He wrote this himself?" Sal paused, pushing his wire-rimmed glasses up the bridge of his nose. Admiration was visible in his eyes.

"Probably not. I think he's got enough money to pay . . . you, even, if he wanted, to write his legal stuff. I doubt he did it himself."

Sal wound a fork full of linguine and brought it to his lips. "Not bad."

"Well. What does it say?"

"I thought you read this?"

"I did. But, you know. It's like reading another language to me. All that party of the second part and designated purchaser stuff throws me for a loop."

"Well. He's prepared to offer you big bucks. Or he's willing to fight you if you decline his offer. The way I read it if you contest his acquisition, which from what I understand he already has your sister's signature, you could end up with nothing in your pocket but fair market value of your share if the court rules in his favor."

"So that son of a bitch would take me to court."

"Yeah. Says so right here. That son of a bitch, as you put it, sounds determined."

"What do you think I should do?"

"What do you want to do?"

"What I want to do and what I'm able to do are two different things."

"Try me."

I want to spend the rest of my life with that son of a bitch.

"I would love to move back home, work the farm, and pay off the back taxes. Unfortunately, that is a pie in the sky dream. What I'm able to do is absolutely nothing. Nada. I can't come up with that kind of money. The only person with that kind of money is Cord. And he won't lend us another penny. He's already sunk—"

"At least $450,000 cash into your family and the farm, according to this." Sal waved his fork at the proposal resting on the table by his glass of wine.

"Holy crap!" She pressed a fist against her lips as a sob caught in her throat.

"I can't blame the guy. Hey, you got any cheese?"

Deanna stood up and reached for the block of Pecorino Romano she kept in the refrigerator door. She grabbed the grater from the utensil drawer and placed both on the table in a daze.

"I get the feeling you'd do anything to keep this guy from buying you out."

"Short of selling my soul, yes."

"A regular bank wouldn't give you a loan for the taxes."

"No."

"But . . . Nah."

"Nah, what?" Deanna straightened up, intent on gleaning the information from Sal. "Tell me, Sal."

"Nah. I couldn't do that to you."

"Why don't you let me decide what you can and can't do for me?"

"Well. I got a cousin. No. Deanna. Forget it."

"A personal loan?"

"Sort of."

"What's the matter? You think I'm a bad investment?"

"No. More wine?" Sal refilled his glass then topped off Deana's.

Deanna groaned. "What then?" she asked, lifting her glass and taking a sip.

"Luigi is, how do I say? I don't tell too many people this."

"What?"

"He's from the old country."

"He's old? What are you afraid he'll die before I pay him back?" Deanna snorted.

Sal laughed. "He's not old. He's from Italy. Sicily, to be exact."

"So?"

"You heard of the Franzetti family?"

"The Franzetti Family?"

"Yeah. The same." Sal looked injured with the tone of voice Deanna used. "They're not lepers you know."

"No. They're murderers and drug peddlers. And money launderers. And human traffickers and . . ."

"They're not that bad."

"Right. I said I'd do anything but sell my soul. I consider taking a loan from them if not selling my soul than at least—the very least—leasing it."

"Well, I tried."

"Thanks. I guess I have no choice, do I?"

"Not really. But you know what I can do? I can write up a counter proposal. I'll throw in a few extra provisions to make it meatier. You two can start with that."

"Great. When can you have it ready?"

"When do you need it by?"

"Tomorrow."

Sal laughed heartily, taking half a meatball and shoving it into his mouth. "Good meatballs."

"Can you do it?"

"It'll cost you."

Deanna noted the gleam in his eye. "I'm willing to pay."

"You haven't even heard my fee."

"Sal. I don't want to sell out. And if I must, if I don't have a choice, I want to do it on my terms. I want you to write up the most appealing but beneficial to me counteroffer you can."

"You know you might end up pissing him off." He stuck the other half a meatball in his mouth and chewed.

"That's nothing new. Besides, I owe him one. A big one."

"Oh. I get it. What's he been harassing your family for a while? A Mr. Scrooge type a guy?"

"Oh. No. Not at all. Worse. Much worse. My family loves him. They treat him better than they treat me."

"Who the hell is this guy then?"

Deanna grinned without shame. "My first lover."

Sal swallowed thickly. "Shit, Deanna. Warn me first, okay? Geez, here I thought you were a virgin."

"Oh, stop it." Deanna giggled then sighed and rolled her eyes. "I might as well be." She and Sal had met her junior year in college, but only because they were in the same English classes. They dated once after graduation, but after Deanna wouldn't sleep with him they cooled it. Then Deanna was hired on by Courtney Davis Ad Ink. A few months later the two bumped into each other at a social event. Her agency needed an in-house attorney and Sal nailed the position with the help of Deanna's recommendation. Their friendship grew, but immediately boundaries were set. Although he tried awfully hard for a while to break those boundaries, he eventually settled for BFF status. Every now and then Sal still haggled to get Deanna to go out on a date. But by now she was used to it.

"Hell, now that I know who the son of a bitch is, you can bet I'll do my best and do it fast. I'd like to meet this guy face to face." Sal drummed his fingers on the table.

"Why's that?"

"I don't know if I want to punch his lights out, congratulate him, or ask him for pointers."

"You men are all pigs. Have I ever told you that?"

"Several times." He belched loudly, which was followed by an immediate "Oops. 'Scuse me. How about an espresso?"

"Sorry, pal. You've got work to do. You better get home." Deanna walked into the living room and grabbed his coat. "Here. Don't forget. I need it ASAP."

"Slave driver." He grabbed his coat, barely getting it on before she dragged him to the door.

"Thanks. I owe you one," Deanna called as she slammed the door behind him.

"Yes!" She cheered to no one in particular, her fist raised in a victorious salute.

Chapter 13

"Come on up! Door's unlocked," Deanna called into the intercom Friday night when Cord buzzed a few minutes before nine o'clock. After unlocking the door she half-ran, half-skipped back into the bedroom to get dressed. She shed her robe and threw it on the bed, her heart working as fast as her body was moving. She grinned at the sudden change of events and thought this was much better than going to bed early.

As she was buttoning up her flannel shirt, Deanna heard Cord call her name from the living room. "I'll be right out."

Her heart missed a beat or two. In fact, it just about did a tap dance when she saw him standing in her kitchen. He must have come straight from work as he still wore a suit she noticed, remembering how broad his shoulders were. "Want a drink?"

"Sure," she answered, speaking to his back from across the room. "Did you eat?"

"I stopped on the way. Thanks." He still hadn't turned around, but was now pouring Jack Daniel's over ice in two glasses he'd taken from the drain.

"I thought you'd come out tomorrow. I didn't realize you'd be here tonight." Why was she so nervous? Her voice sounded breathless. *Relax, Dean. Chill out.*

"Did I interrupt something?" Cord pivoted slowly, his eyes scanning the empty living room. When his gaze settled on her, he offered a crooked half-smile. "You wear flannel well."

"If I'd known we were having a power meeting I would have dressed more appropriately." She rubbed the cuff of her sleeve between her thumb and forefinger.

He drained his glass, then poured another shot. "Did you read the proposal?"

"I told you I would. Don't you believe me?"

"I don't know. That's why I asked. You didn't call."

"You don't have to get huffy." She walked over to the counter and picked up her drink. "I was busy." Fact was, Sal hadn't come up with a counter proposal until this morning and Deanna didn't want to face Cord without it—either on the phone or in person.

"So you didn't read it."

"Of course I read it. I did better than that. I'm even ready to respond."

"You're willing to consider? Honestly?" Cord eyed her suspiciously. "This is too easy."

"I read your proposal, Mr. McCord. And let me tell you, it was interesting, but . . . I don't know. You're gonna have to sweeten the pot if you want me to bite."

He laughed, a loud belly laugh. "I think I'm afraid of your bite."

She raised her eyebrows and shrugged.

After studying her a moment, he scratched his chin and asked, "So. Who've you been talking to?"

"If you must know, my attorney," Deanna answered airily with her nose tilted upward ever so slightly.

"Oh. I get it. Let me guess. You've got a counter proposal all ready. And, let me guess again. You like my offer, but you want forty acres, as opposed to twenty all together. And you want triple what I'm offering. And you want to retain rights if I decide to use any part of the Drake's Farm name." He paused for her reaction and when she nodded he completed his thoughts. "And you want a clause regarding open space surrounding the acreage we do agree on—say two acres all around—fully vegetated."

Deanna suppressed a grin. "Very close. Except for one thing. House improvements."

"What?"

"If you're going to be building big beautiful homes around my house then it's going to make my home look like Olde Westfield Slums. I want you to renovate it."

"I was correct?" He narrowed his gaze and tilted his head.

"Basically. Give or take a few acres, a few dollars." Deanna nodded, draining her glass and holding it out for a refill.

"You said 'big, beautiful homes.' You didn't read it."

"Yes, I did."

"Dean, I don't want to build big beautiful homes."

"Condos, then. And your Main Street thingy. Yeah. I know, I know. I read it, Cord. I didn't understand most of it with all that stupid legalese you had your dumb lawyer put in."

"Dumb lawyer?"

"Yes. Dumb lawyer."

"Is that why you got a lawyer? Because you think I've got one?"

"Well. Yeah. I mean. You threatened to take me to court."

"I wrote the proposal, for the most part. My lawyer advised against it, but I knew he'd try to screw you."

"Huh. Sal thought it was great."

"Sal? Who's Sal?"

Deanna smiled brightly. "My lawyer."

"Sal?"

"Yeah. He came over the other night and read it and interpreted it for me."

"Sal was here?" Cord glanced around the apartment. "With you? Alone?"

"Oh, don't worry. He's just a friend."

Cord studied her for a moment, then picked up his glass and walked inside.

"So where's this offer?"

"Aren't you going to take your jacket off? Your shoes?" Deanna held her glass in her hands and followed.

"That depends. I don't want to intrude on anything. You sure Sal isn't coming over?"

"No. I called and cancelled our plans after you rang the buzzer. He was a little disappointed, but he'll get over it."

He eyed her again, from where he stood in the center of the living room, completely missing her joke.

Something was off, but Deanna couldn't place her finger on it. She felt vulnerable, like she was going to battle without a weapon. "Do we have to do this now? I mean. I don't know about you, but I'm really beat. I don't feel up to arguing with you tonight. Truth was, Cord, I was getting ready for bed when you buzzed." She flopped down in her chair, hugging a throw pillow to her body.

"Bed? Are you feeling all right?" He still hadn't sat, and now he came to stand beside her. This wasn't how Deanna wanted to start this weekend off.

"Yeah. I'm fine. A bit tired." *And not at all emotionally ready to face you.*

Cord let out a sigh and put his glass down on the table. Then he slipped off his jacket and threw it on the arm of the couch, loosening his tie as he took a seat; his gaze never leaving Deanna, who fidgeted nervously until he spoke her name.

She watched him unbutton the top two buttons of his gray dress shirt, but said nothing.

"I'm sorry I didn't call or text first. But I thought we planned on me coming out again." When she didn't reply, he continued. "Besides, you never texted me."

"I told you. I was super busy. And I wanted to wait until Sal drafted a proposal, so I'd have something to give you back to consider." She didn't like being put on the defensive.

"I see. You left me hanging. I didn't know what to think."

"You're here, aren't you?"

"Does that bother you?"

"No." That came too quickly.

"If it bothers you, tell me. I'll leave."

"I don't want you to leave. But I wish you'd have let me know."

"You knew I was coming. I told you last weekend."

True. "I know. I guess I would have liked you to call and tell me you were on your way, coming tonight, instead of tomorrow."

"Like I wanted you to call to tell me you read the proposal."

Deanna blinked slowly then nodded. "You're absolutely right. I guess I should have called."

"This is pretty awkward as it is. If we don't give each other something to hold on to, some guidelines and if we don't follow them there's going to be a lot of crossed signals, a lot of misconceptions. Deanna. I do this for a living. This is my job. I don't want to ruin something we might have personally—together—over this. Do you understand?"

This was Cord talking. His voice was earnest, that hardened glaze in his eye had disappeared. The cynical tone and aloofness had slipped away, shed along with his jacket and tie. Was that his armor? His weapon to battle with? Deanna thought, nodding to herself with this realization. She smiled, knowing she'd learned something very important about this man.

"Good," Cord answered, acknowledging her nod. "You said you were going to bed. I'll be fine. I've got some work to finish up anyway."

"No. I'll stay up with you a while."

"I'd like that. How was your week?" He slipped his shoes off and put his feet up on the coffee table. She watched him as he finally started to truly relax. And, it felt real good.

"Horrible. I couldn't come up with one original idea this week. I coasted while my team did all the work. It was like, I don't know. My brain stopped working." Deanna rolled her eyes in exasperation.

"Yeah. I hear you. I hear you. Work sucked. Today was bad. A deal fell through and now I've got to sue to get my deposit back. On top of that, I missed the filing date for an application yesterday. My general contractor on another project fell and broke his leg, so I've got to find a replacement until he gets back."

The list went on and on, and while Cord lamented Deanna sat there silently, sipping her drink and shaking her head in dismay. *And on top of it all, I didn't text you.*

"Enough of that. Thanks. I needed to vent." He smiled ruefully at her and ran a hand through his hair. "So what have you got planned for the weekend?"

"Planned?" Wide-eyed, Deanna stared at him. She hadn't given it a thought. In fact, she had avoided thinking about seeing him because it made her so nervous. Besides that, there were too many other memories in her brain, leaving no room for any other thoughts.

"Yeah. Reorganizing closets? Cleaning the fridge?" He chuckled and stood up, walking into the kitchen. "Shampooing the rugs, maybe?"

"No. I had my new maid clean for me last weekend." She curled her feet up under her, watching from where she sat as he refilled his glass.

This was his third, she counted mentally. He truly must have had a hard day. "You sure you don't want me to fix you something to eat?"

"I stopped at the deli and got a hero before I headed out. I'm fine, Dean." He walked back to his spot on the couch and sat down again, studying his drink. "So tell me about Sal."

"Sal?"

"Yeah. Your lawyer boyfriend."

"Trust me. He's my friend. That's it." She closed her eyes and shook her head with a soft snort.

"A friend, huh? A good friend? An acquaintance? How good a friend, Deanna?"

"*Just* a friend." Deanna dipped her head and frowned. "Pretty good, I guess. Now that you mention it, he reviewed your proposal and wrote mine for free." Deanna motioned to her proposal sitting on the coffee table near his drink.

"Free?"

"Yeah . . . and . . . well, you know. Basically free."

"What is basically free?"

"You know. A dinner here, a dinner there type of thing."

Cord nodded with a frown. "And?"

"And, what?" A mischievous twinkle lit her eyes.

"You said 'and' before. I was wondering what other services he provides you with?"

"Well. He was going to help me get the money to pay off the rest of the taxes and—"

"What?" This news made Cord sit up straight.

"Don't worry. I told him no. I couldn't do that to him. What if the farm failed?"

"I get it. You'd do it to me though. You were willing to let me lose a couple a hundred thou—" He waved his hand at her in agitation, a grimace marring his face.

"Cord?" Deanna stood up and sauntered over to him slowly, never losing eye contact with him. "Jealous?"

"Hell, no." His dark eyes burned into hers.

She tilted her head to one side, an impish gleam burned in her eyes. "Not even a little?"

"No. Of course not. What you do is your business."

"I think you're lying." Deanna whispered as she knelt beside him, taking his glass from his hand. She lifted his hand up, pressed his palm against her lips and planted a long full kiss in its center.

"No."

Deanna studied his palm for a moment, then lifted her gaze to his eyes, as she brought his hand to her mouth once more. "No as in no, don't do this?" She trailed her lips along the outline of his hand, planting brief little kisses on each of his fingers until she reached his thumb. She smiled devilishly at him, biting the ball of his thumb gently, then sucked and rubbed her teeth against the calloused appendage. "Or no, as in, no you are not jealous?"

He stared at her, surprise, confusion, and desire burning in his eyes. His breath quickened and the pulse in his throat beat visibly. "Deanna?"

"Shhh . . ." Deanna moved his palm against her jaw, her chin, directing it down toward her neck. When she released her hold on his hand he lifted his other, resting it gently against her throat. He leaned down, capturing her lips in a deep, all-consuming kiss. He released her and the two stared breathlessly at one another, hesitation hanging thickly between them.

"Deanna?"

"Um-hm . . ." She tried unsuccessfully to complete her mission.

"You're fully aware of the message you're giving me?"

"Do I have to give you a written proposal?" She chuckled, a husky sound coming from deep within her throat.

A low growl sounded as he called out her name and pulled her close, running his hands down her back, then up inside her flannel shirt. She squirmed closer to him when his hands moved across her back, then under her arms to brush against her breasts. He captured her lips again, practically devouring her with his intensity. He brought his hands down, slipping them beneath her jean-clad buttocks. She moaned softly as she nibbled his earlobe, pushing against him in her desire.

He bent down, placing a full kiss on her lips. And when he released her, he whispered, "Good night, Drake."

"Good night?" Deanna called out in confusion as he untangled their bodies from one another. "Cord!"

"Yes?" He ran his hands over his face, his frustration and restraint evident in his eyes.

"Is something wrong?" Deanna sat up, spreading her hands before her.

"Hell, no. Everything was too right. Except the timing. Let's get some sleep and I'll take a rain check. I promise."

"This is ridiculous. We are two adults. If we both feel it now, then the timing is right. I can't believe I even have to argue this point."

"Trust me. I get it. I've waited so long for us. I want it to be perfect. For you. For me. For us. Please trust me on this one." He said in earnest, and she sighed.

"Fine, but I think this is ridiculous."

"Me too," he said, dipping his head to kiss her firmly on the lips. "Good night."

~ ~ ~

He watched Deanna walk to her bedroom, closing the door loudly behind her. *My god,* he thought, exhaling a long deep breath.

First thing tomorrow morning, business would be taken care of and out of the way. Then and only then would he be able to devote his full attention to making love to Deanna. And as he sank back into the couch, Cord knew that letting Deanna sleep alone in that bed was the second hardest thing he ever had to do. Sleeping on this couch, feet away, was the first.

~ ~ ~

It was raining when Deanna awoke. But the sun had been shining in her dreams. She and Cord had been sunning themselves on the roof, completely naked, with the hot sun beating down, baking their skin a soft, warm, golden color. Cord had nudged her over and was massaging tanning oil all over her body, her back, her arms, her behind. His hands had slipped lower, and were massaging the backs of her thighs when she awoke in a sweat, her heart palpitating, her most womanly parts aching and throbbing. *Going to bed horny made for the most interesting dreams.*

"Deanna!" Cord's voice sounded through the door. "Coffee's on. Time to get up."

"Be right there." Her heart sang with the realization that he was here. That part hadn't been a dream. The evening before came flooding back to her now and she felt her body crimson with embarrassment at her recollection. How could she face him? What was happening to her?

"Deanna? Are you all right?"

"I'm fine. I'll be out in a minute."

"Hurry up."

You and me both, buddy.

~ ~ ~

"Well?" Deanna came out of the bathroom wearing her robe, her face flushed from the steam and hot water of her shower. Cord sat at the kitchen table studying her counter proposal, a calculator at his fingertips. "Are you finished with it?"

"Hm?" Cord continued reading and Deanna grew uneasy recalling some of the provisions as she stared at the top of his head. His hair was thick, a golden honey chestnut brown when the light shone the right way.

"My proposal? Aren't you finished yet?" She grabbed a mug and poured a cup of coffee.

"Yeah." He turned his attention to her, that same vacant expression he'd worn last night masking any emotion. "I read it last night. I'm going over a few things."

"And?"

"I'm working on something. I think I've found a common middle ground."

"So you're not going to go for my stipulations?" Deanna grinned slightly, knowing full well his answer.

Cord shook his head absentmindedly as he stared at her. His eyes took a leisurely stroll across her face, down her throat to where her peach terrycloth robe formed a vee between her breasts, then down to where her feet with their peach-painted toenails peeked out from beneath the hem. When he looked up, his face was also flushed and there was a fire smoldering in the depths of his blue eyes.

Deanna shrugged and grinned, at a loss for words as Cord placed an elbow on the table and settled his chin in his palm. A smile that bespoke his satisfaction spread across his unshaven face. Her heart somersaulted as she sat down across from him, grinning like a lovestruck fool.

"Good morning, gorgeous."

"So you chose my proposal over me last night? I think I'm highly insulted."

"Don't be. Trust me." Cord held out his hand to her across the table and without hesitation she responded to his unspoken request. Her hand trembled as his fingers folded around her, squeezing her in reassurance.

"About last night." Deanna felt her face grow warm again as she recalled her behavior. When Cord remained silent her embarrassment grew even stronger. "I-I feel like a total jerk."

She stared at him, growing more uncomfortable as his smile spread wider, revealing his perfectly even white teeth.

"And I want to apologize for what I guess was a pretty awkward situation. I mean. I don't know what came over me. I'm not used to drinking Jack's and with you here and all. I guess I was tired. Rough day and it was good to be with somebody instead of being alone. I got carried away. I'm not used to seeing you so much and I guess I kinda thought things were gonna fall back into the way we used to be and—"

"Deanna. Will you be quiet for a minute? Do you always talk so much in the morning?"

"I was rambling, wasn't I? I thought—"

"Stop thinking."

"But last night—"

"Forget last night."

"Cord. You're not making this any easier."

With that remark he burst out in laughter. "What am I not making any easier?"

"This. Me and you. Spending time together. I don't know what's going on. I don't know what to think or do anymore. I feel like I'm back in school again. I feel like a bumbling idiot. Do we slip back into the old Deanna and Cord relationship thing? Can I trust you? Do I even want to? I don't know. I don't know what I want. I can't even think straight anymore. You are driving me nuts! And stop laughing at me!"

"I'm not laughing at you. I think you're cute."

"Cute? I'm nearing thirty and you think I'm cute?" Hands on her hips, she rolled her eyes at him in disbelief.

"Would you rather me describe you as old and haggard?"

Deanna chuckled. "I guess not."

"Good. Because I know I couldn't lie that convincingly."

"Nice pick up line. Thanks, I think."

He sat there smiling at her.

"So tell me, what's this middle ground?"

"Nah. I want to hold off on that until I'm positive."

"Well. What did you think of my proposal?"

"I thought your suggestions were outrageous and unthinkable." That came with a dismissive wave of his hand.

"I thought that's what you'd think." She cast her eyes downward and bit her lower lip as she tried not to laugh. She was beside herself with joy and Deanna for once in her life couldn't get a grip on herself or the situation. This man was about to steal her family legacy away from her and she was throwing herself at him like a teenaged, lovesick fool. What was she thinking?

"So what's planned for today?" Cord stacked the proposals one on top of the other, placing both and the calculator and pad he was writing numbers on into his briefcase.

"It's raining out, so I guess we'll just have to find something to do inside." Deanna spoke softly, suggestively, blushing at her boldness.

"Great. Let's go to the museum. Or no. The Met. I haven't been there in ages."

"The Met?" Deanna's mouth dropped open in surprise, or was it disappointment. "Cord?"

But he didn't answer her for he was already in the living room, bending over his suitcase as he selected his clothes for the day. She stared at him from the kitchen as he stripped off his sweat pants and stepped into his jeans, turning away from her as he zipped his fly. "Go get dressed," he said over his shoulder as he pulled off his tee shirt, revealing a broad tanned back void of fat, rippling with muscles. "C'mon, slowpoke! Let's go!" he called again when he didn't hear her respond.

"I'm going, I'm going," she answered, her voice sullen and filled with disappointment at his rejection.

~ ~ ~

"I think these will frame nicely, don't you?" Cord was holding up two van Gogh prints—"Wheat field With Rising Sun" and "Starry Night."

"It depends on the frame and matting, I would think. And where you're going to hang them." She didn't have the heart to tell him she didn't think they'd go very well with his decor.

"Do you like them, though? I can't decide?"

"Do I like them? That goes without saying. Those two are my absolute favorites. Vincent van Gogh is one of those people I wish I could have met."

"So you said." Cord studied the prints once more. "What kind of frame would you think?"

"It depends on the room you'll be putting them in."

"I don't know where I'll be putting them yet, to be honest. I just like them." He rummaged through the racks finding two undamaged, rolled up prints still in their wrapping. "Anything else?" He glanced around the gift shop.

When Deanna shook her head, Cord grabbed at her hand and led her to the register.

Chapter 14

It was hours before Deanna and Cord were back in the warmth of the apartment and dressed in dry clothes. Life right now felt as surreal as some of the art they had admired today. And, had anyone told her a year ago that Michael McCord would be sitting with her in her apartment she would have told them they were nuts. But here he was, and at the moment it was so much easier to forget everything outside this apartment, outside Manhattan, then fight or worry. She was tired of fighting. At least for right now.

Words were few as they sat side by side, his arm about her shoulders, unmoving until the shadows turned to darkness, enjoying being together. It was nearly seven o'clock before Deanna stood up and stretched, her hunger prodding her into action.

"You sure do eat a lot," Cord teased her moments later as he washed leaves of romaine lettuce under cold tap water. "It's a good thing you run every morning."

She chopped tomatoes, he peeled cucumbers. She shredded the lettuce, he grated cheddar cheese. He sliced olives, she cubed a piece of ham and a chunk of turkey breast they'd picked up from the local butcher on their way home.

When they were done eating, they washed the dishes and flatware, a routine they seemed to be developing without effort. It was after dinner, as Deanna reached up to place the plates on the second shelf of the cabinet over the sink that Cord came up behind her, his hands encircling the narrow expanse of her waist. He leaned his head down and placed a kiss on her crown, sighing deeply.

Deanna lowered her eyes for a moment, savoring his touch. And even when she turned to gaze at him he still kept his hands at her waist. Nothing more, nothing less.

"This has been a great day." His gaze was sincere and peaceful.

She smiled up at him. "Yes, it has."

Leaning into her, Cord placed a lingering kiss on her lips. Time stilled for a moment, then with a heavy sigh, Cord turned to make a fresh pot of coffee. "So tell me about working at the ad agency. That must be fun."

Her answer came as they waited for the coffee to brew. "It's loads of fun, but in the end it's a job. A salary. It pays for my apartment mostly."

"How long you been there?"

"A few years," she answered, wondering where this was going.

"You like it?"

"Actually, yeah. It lets me be creative. It's challenging. I get to travel." As she spoke her face lit up, her voice livened.

He nodded absentmindedly.

"How about you?" she asked as the pot finished dripping and she fixed her coffee. "I thought you wanted to be an architect. What happened?"

"It wasn't hands on enough for me. I like taking a bad investment and making it good again. I like the hard labor. I like pounding the nails, the smell of sawdust."

Deanna nodded as they walked into the living room and settled side by side on the couch. "That sounds like you. You were always good with your hands."

Blue eyes met green eyes, then he smiled at her, his smile turning quickly to a chuckle as he shook his head, then laughter, causing Deanna to color a bright red. "You do have a way with words, don't you?"

"I meant—"

"I know exactly what you meant." He leaned down to place a kiss on the side of her neck, and didn't move until she spoke.

"What are you doing?" Deanna cocked her head to see his face.

"Savoring this moment," he replied. "You."

She turned to kiss him but his words stilled her. "Cord?"

"I can't accept your counteroffer in its entirety," he said, holding her firmly.

"Shouldn't we be dressed and facing each other across a conference table or something?" She tilted her head to one side.

"This is fine for me. Unless you want, uh, your attorney present."

"Do I need him present?"

"I should hope not."

"If you can't accept my counteroffer, and I didn't like your original proposal the way it was, what's left?"

"We have a few options."

"Such as?"

"Us. The future."

"You make it sound so together."

"It can be. Or we can continue negotiations. We can wait and see what the town board does. I can let you lose the farm and then buy it at the next county auction. I'd have to check into that."

As he spoke, Deanna stiffened beneath his embrace.

"This sounds like I should call my attorney."

"Why don't you let me finish listing our choices?"

"Oh, you're going to give me an actual choice in the matter?" She started to get up, but Cord tugged her back down onto the couch.

"Relax, Deanna. Let me finish before you start planning my death."

"The more you talk the more tortuous my plans become."

He laughed and the sound made Deanna frown. It wasn't a mean laugh, or victorious. It was a warm sound. She twisted her head around and frowned even harder in confusion at what she saw. The laughter she'd heard was evident in the warm sparkle his eyes held. "How can you laugh?" The words stuck in her throat.

"Sometimes you are too serious, Dean." He bent down and placed the softest of kisses on her lips then lifted his gaze to study her befuddled face once more. "Don't you want to hear my last alternative?"

"I don't think so." Her voice was hardly more than a forced whisper.

He bent his head again, capturing her lips this time, in a possessive though brief caress. "Are you sure you don't want me to continue?"

"I-I don't know."

He chuckled, a husky, throaty chuckle as he lowered his lids and his lips at the same time. Only when she responded and his tongue met hers did he break contact.

Deanna opened her eyes, her gaze dulled with passion, her brow knit in confusion. "Spill. Get it over with, Cord." She bowed her head in defeat, waiting to hear the words that once uttered would destroy her heritage and any chance of a future she and Cord might have together. What horrible, devious plan could he have concocted to ensure his ownership of the farm? How low would he stoop to get his way? What on earth could he—

"We could get married."

Complete silence enveloped the two as they each sat motionless on the sofa. Deanna was completely immobile, disbelieving what she thought she had heard him suggest. "Married?"

"Yes. Would that be so bad?" He breathed finally, expelling air in a long sigh of relief.

"Married?" Her green eyes turned to study him, wide with disbelief.

"Yes. Married. As in 'until death do us part.' Married. Husband and wife."

"Me and you?"

"I don't see anyone else in the room?"

She shook her head, trying to clear her thoughts. "Are you nuts?"

"No. This is the sanest thought I've had in the longest time."

"I think you'd better check the definition of sane." She stood up, needing to get away from him, needing some air to think straight.

"Is that your answer?"

"Yes. No. I-I don't know." She was pacing now, to the window, to the kitchen counter, to the window. "Why do you want to marry me? What would that accomplish? Wouldn't that complicate things?" She wrung her hands in frustration at him.

"I don't see how. I want you. You want me. We have a lot in common. Our past, our future. The farm."

"The farm. You'll do anything for this farm, won't you, Michael? Even marry someone you dumped years ago." Or say you'll marry . . . She studied him now from the window, hands on her hips. He stood and walked over to her.

"I didn't dump you. You dumped me. And that was five years ago. Let it go. Let's work through this. Yes, I won't lie. I would like to develop the farm and save it from someone else's plans. But I already own a third of it. It's more than the farm. I want you in my life. I want to take care of you. I don't want to hurt you. Ever again."

"But you will hurt me, if you have to, if I stand in your way. So the only way to get me out of the way is to own me."

"Don't twist this."

"I marry you and become Mrs. Michael McCord, housewife and mother. No more ad agency. No more apartment. No more jogging through Central Park. No more friends, parties. Business trips."

"We could work out an arrangement. If you want to work, I'd let you. You wouldn't even have to take the train. I'd hire a limo."

"Let me? Limo? I'm not going to let you chauffeur me around like your whore."

"Whore? Come on, Deanna. You'd be my wife!"

"Ha! You'd let me. Let? You think you can come in here and take away everything I've become so you can have the damn farm?"

"Oh, my God! Deanna! You are totally turning this around!" He waved his hands at her in frustration.

"You asked me to marry you because you want my farm!" She stomped her foot as she yelled at him.

"You don't want me to buy you out. You're willing to lose it. I'm giving you the chance to hold on to it forever. If you'd only meet me halfway."

"Halfway? You want halfway? You want me to give up everything, Michael. Everything. My life, my independence. So you can have the farm to do what you want with it. How is that halfway?"

"You're going to lose it if I don't take it over. I've done everything I could to help your family when you weren't around. I'm trying to save your family's legacy and recoup my losses!"

"And I'm supposed to jump at the chance to marry you to show you my appreciation?" She scoffed in disbelief, her hands on her hips.

"To show your appreciation?" Cord threw his hands up and scowled. "You won't move back and work it. You don't want me to handle it. What else is there? You'd rather lose the farm than be my wife?"

"Listen to yourself!" she shouted. "When I get married, it's going to be for love. Not for some business deal."

He took a deep breath, ran his fingers through his hair, and studied her for a moment before speaking. "Fine. Then how about this. Why don't we get engaged? We'll do a trial run for a few months. Get to know each other again. We'll set a date, say, for six months from now. If you still don't want to get married, we'll cancel it. But in the meantime you and I will work to come up with a proposal for the farm we're both happy with. By the end of six months if the wedding's off, we can start legal proceedings for finalizing the deal. A deal we both approve. If you still want to get married, that's even better. We'll get married."

"You make it sound so cold."

"It wasn't meant to be cold. You can stand there and tell me you don't feel what we have? What we never lost?"

"Why should I have to give up my life?" In all honesty, she wouldn't mind 'giving up' her New York City lifestyle, if it were for the right reasons. Love and a family would suit her fine. These last few weekends made her hopeful that she and Cord could work through their differences. That she might actually be brave enough to let him into her heart again. This might even be something acceptable if she believed Cord's proposal might be based on love, not some business arrangements made up by him and his lawyer.

He sighed and raked his hand again through his hair in exasperation. "Damn you, Deanna. We'll keep the apartment. You can keep your damn job. Is that what you want? A marriage in name only?"

"Name only? What is this the Middle Ages? Is that what you want?"

"No. I want to make us work."

"Of course you do. It would be financially beneficial for you to make it work."

"You don't get it, do you?"

"Obviously not."

"Do I have to give you a written proposal?"

"You already did. And I countered. And you rejected, so you think now I'm going to jump at the chance to marry you to save my farm."

With a loud growl, he tilted his head back and studied her through half-closed lids, one eyebrow arched. "I meant a written proposal outlining what I'm suggesting."

This didn't seem real. Was he only suggesting they get married so he could have the farm? How far would he go? She tested him, calling his bluff. "Like a pre-nup? Maybe. But for now, a verbal one would have been sufficient."

He cocked his head up and narrowed his gaze. "Verbal?"

"Yeah. You know. Bended knee type of thing."

"You'll marry me if I get on my knee and ask you?"

She shook her head. "I didn't say that. But it would seem a little more meaningful, a little less cold. I mean, but if it's going to be in name only, for appearances' sake. I don't know. I guess it doesn't matter then. If you're going to *let me* keep the apartment. My job . . . I mean, six months should be long enough to, to arrange, to prepare a wedding. No?"

"You will say yes if I propose to you?" he repeated.

"This is crazy." Her heart hammered in her chest. Silence hung between them with this turn of events.

Cord grinned widely. "I hear you."

"We must be nuts."

"That depends on what your definition of nuts is."

"So?" Deanna stared at him, wide-eyed, her heart pounding.

"So what?"

"Do I get a verbal, real, honest-to-gosh proposal?"

"I don't know. You're asking an awful lot here. You want to keep the apartment *and* get a bended-knee proposal?" He walked back to the couch and sat down, shaking his head. "We've got to have guidelines here. This is either going to be a business proposition, a marriage in name only. Or it's going to be a full blown deal. Bended knee, marital rights—"

"Marital rights?" Deanna laughed.

"Yeah. If I'm going to propose, give you a ring, make an investment in this deal, I think I deserve—"

"A tumble here and there?" She twisted her mouth into a wry smile.

"More there than here, preferably . . . and . . . "

"And?"

"No more Sal."

"No more Sal? Sal's my best friend. You can't tell me who I can and can't be friends with." She walked back over to the couch where he sat and jabbed a finger at him.

"I don't care about friends. It's the lovers I'm concerned with."

"God! You're so thick! He's not my lover!" She breathed deeply before speaking. "You know . . . Part of our issue we need to work on is trust. I'm going to have to learn to trust you, and you're going to have to learn to trust me. Or the deal is off."

"He means that much to you?" He scowled at her and shook his head.

"Yes. He does. But your trust means more." She sat beside him, took both his hands in hers, and searched his eyes.

They studied one another silently, then Cord said simply, "You're right. It does. As does yours." He leaned in for the briefest of kisses, as if to seal the deal, and then stood up. "I got to get going. I have a lot of work to do. I got to meet with Howie."

"Howie?"

"My attorney."

"Ah, the proposal." Reality sunk in once more.

"Well." He bent over the couch and collected the sheets. "Where do you want me to put these?"

"I'll fold them. That is, if you think you'll be back again." She bent over the couch, repositioning the cushions and throw pillows.

"Deanna?" He spoke her name so softly she almost didn't hear him.

Something in his tone kept her from responding.

"Deanna?" He said once more, and this time she turned to him. "The next time I come out here I don't plan on sleeping on the couch."

Her hands stilled with his words, but her heart raced with their implication. "I see. Well. Then I guess I'll throw them in the hamper."

"That sounds like a good plan."

He straightened up after stuffing his papers into his briefcase. "I'll call you during the week."

"Okay." She stared at him, not knowing what to do next.

He made the decision for her, leaned over and planted the briefest kiss on her forehead. "Text me, okay?"

~ ~ ~

It was only after she watched his truck drive away from the curb did Deanna sit down to consider the full impact of the agreement the two had discussed. Married? Could she really marry *Michael McCord*?

Had this moment taken place five years ago the answer would have been obvious. But now. Now? She considered his proposal. Engagement for six months. Plans for a wedding. Finalize the purchase or plans for the farm. What if he got his way with the farm, then backed out of the wedding? Even if he lost all of his deposits for the hall, limos. Whatever else a wedding required. He'd still make out on the deal. He'd still have the farm. What would *she* have? An engagement ring? The humiliation of being left at the altar?

No farm. No Cord.

What if he was sincere? What if he was going to follow through and marry her? Could she handle being *Mrs. Michael McCord*? Honestly? Could she give up everything she worked for to make a go of this marriage?

She wouldn't have to, of course. Cord said so. She could live here, he could live there. A marriage in name only. Would that mean he could see other women? Would she be allowed to see other men? A marriage made to satisfy both of their financial and business concerns. She wouldn't lose the farm, he would get to build his dream community. She would have his money to fall back on. He would have her land.

What about children? What if he fell in love with someone down the road? What if he wanted to divorce her?

What if she fell in love with him all over again? It was happening already. She was behaving like a fool. Thinking like a completely gullible, naïve bimbo, willing to give up everything for a man?

Oh, god. That was too much to even consider. Deanna had barely survived the first time he broke her heart, why was she even thinking about getting involved with him again?

The answer came then, as clear as day, in a rush with the force of a wave crashing on the shore at Smith's Point Beach. It smacked her head-on and washed coldly over her body, causing her to shudder and tremble with the reality.

Because, she told herself, it was too late. She had already fallen head over heels back in love with Michael McCord. And there was nothing on earth anyone could do to stop it.

Chapter 15

One dozen red roses placed perfectly amidst clouds of baby's breath and luscious green ferns stretching lovingly from a crystal vase greeted Deanna on her desk Monday morning. Her eyes widened, and her face colored a more becoming shade of red than the velvet buds before her. Cheers, whistles, chuckles, and a few raised eyebrows greeted her as she reached for the card.

Her name was scrawled across the envelope, but curiously, when she removed the card there was only a name written inside. *Will.*

"Who the hell is Will?" she asked aloud, to no one in particular, disappointment evident in her voice.

"A client, maybe?" Barb overheard her question and stepped to her side, glancing at the card.

Deanna shrugged and tossed it onto the pile of unreturned telephone messages. "He'll call when I don't respond."

Work was uneventful in that Deanna did not hear from Cord, although she half-expected, half-wished he would call. Neither did this guy Will. And by five o'clock Deanna had given up caring who Will was or that he had given her the blossoms. It was probably an incorrect delivery and no doubt the florist would be reaching out when they were alerted.

No messages from Cord waited for her at home and her apartment suddenly seemed so quiet. She checked her cell phone, remembering he had asked her to text him. She had been too busy all day. And now it felt weird. *He could have texted me.*

No calls. No texts. No Cord. Only her and her apartment, which felt way too big. And way too empty.

~ ~ ~

Tuesday, a second floral arrangement adorned her desk when she arrived. This time it was a bouquet of orchids, violets, and sprigs of lilacs arranged in a Lenox vase. This card also contained a single word. *You.* Deanna grinned with a strange thought, considered texting Cord and sending him a photo of the two vases filled with flowers, then changed her mind. Wait it out, she decided. *Wait it out.*

~ ~ ~

Wednesday's now-expected bouquet—this one arranged in various hues of yellow carnations, day lilies, and daisies—brought a third card with a single word on it. And Deanna knew even before she ripped open the envelope what that word would be. *Marry*

She laid the three cards out on her desk blotter, *Will. You. Marry.* And even though she now knew what her answer would be, Deanna could not call Cord. Not until she got the final card. She hugged herself hard and tried to focus on work. And struggled desperately to not text him.

~ ~ ~

The final card came Thursday, accompanying a white arrangement of roses, carnations, daisies and azalea's. The note said . . . *Me? Think on it. C.* Deanna swallowed thickly as she studied the cards before her, wondering how she could answer him in as interesting a way. She sent him the text he requested, but all she included was a red heart emoji.

~ ~ ~

It was Friday afternoon when one more surprise presented itself. Sal was waiting to go to lunch with Deanna as he stood by her desk, when another package delivered by special courier arrived. A rectangular box, nearly eight inches long, wrapped in green velvet and tied with a white satin bow was delivered to her desk as she was putting her laptop to sleep. Only when the display was void and the motor quiet did Deanna sit within the informal circle of her colleagues, who gawked and gaped as she held the box in her trembling hands.

"Aren't you going to open it?" Barb asked softly, a smile forming on her lips.

"If you don't want it, I'll take it, whatever it is," Cara called from where she sat perched on the edge of her desk.

"If you don't open it soon I'm going to call this guy myself and tell him you didn't like it. Then ask him if he's picky or will he be willing to settle for me." Chelsey guffawed loudly as she popped her chewing gum.

"Maybe she wants to be alone." Sal's words silenced everyone momentarily.

She shook her head as she gently tugged the ribbon free. It fell away and she unwrapped the green cloth, revealing a crystal translucent box, the bottom half of which was also lined with green velvet. Deanna watched her fingers tremble, feeling like a spectator herself as she opened the box.

There, lying on the bed of velvet, was nestled the most dazzling heart-shaped emerald pendant, cradled by three of the most brilliant diamonds Deanna had ever,

ever seen. Tears blurred her vision and her heart dropped as she thought of Cord shopping for this for her. The small crowd "oohed and ahhed" as she lifted it from the box and held it up to the light.

As she moved to clasp the gold chain around her neck, she wished Cord was here to do it for her. Once the heart was nestled against her skin, Deanna picked up the box, and it was then she noticed the slip of paper folded and stuffed into the cover.

She opened it slowly, her friends ceasing their murmuring as they watched her actions.

This is only the beginning. How about grabbing a bite to eat? C.

Deanna laughed aloud, realizing her wish had come true. No sooner had she stood up and rushed to the door then it opened and in walked Cord, grinning ear-to-ear.

"You are nuts, aren't you?" Deanna asked him as she flung herself into his open embrace.

"About you, yes." He kissed her gently before he set her aside. "Do you like it?"

"Like it? Like it? I love it!" She flung herself at him again, kissing him soundly on the lips.

"So does this mean I've got a date?" He pried her arms from about his body, laughing as he untangled himself from her grasp.

"Yes!" She laughed as she wrapped herself around him once more.

"Can you leave now?" He asked her as he scanned the crowd surrounding his bride-to-be.

"Sure. I think the boss might understand. But first, I gotta do something. I hope you don't mind." Deanna turned around sniffling, wiping her eyes with the back of her hand. Her co-workers had been standing there waiting for an introduction. "Guys. This is him. This is Cord."

Cord nodded, his face flaming slightly under the attention of the crowd. A few waved at him before wandering off, satisfied having met the mystery man. Only Sal lingered, walking toward the couple when Deanna beckoned him over.

She left Cord's side and put an arm around the dark-haired man, dressed in a well-fitted gray suit and Mickey Mouse tie. "Sal, I want you to meet Cord. Cord, this is Sal."

"Sal, huh?" Cord studied him for a second, then extended his hand although his face remained emotionless.

"McCord." The two stood there, hands joined for the briefest moment before Sal drew back. "Congratulations."

"Thank you."

"Nice work," Sal muttered under his breath as he walked away.

"Ready?" Deanna smiled brightly, ignoring Sal's jibe, as she slipped the box into her jacket pocket. "Let me get my bag and tell my boss I'm out of here. I'll be right back."

Cord smiled easily and leaned back against the wall, watching Deanna as she bopped across the office searching for her boss.

~ ~ ~

"I thought we'd go back to your place, change, and catch an early dinner." Cord spoke as he maneuvered his car through the late afternoon traffic, passing cyclists and taxis with ease. Without hesitation, he wove around buses that moved like weary elephants as they paused at every corner with a groan and a sigh to pick up and drop off passengers. Deanna kept one hand on the dash board as he darted like a silver fish in and out of the schools of cars.

"Cord, I'm convinced there are only two things that motivate you in this world. Food and my farm."

He chuckled and shook his head, then cast a quick glance—one dark eyebrow raised cockily—in her direction. She blushed as she read his mind and directed her gaze out the window.

"Where are we going? Chinese? Italian?"

"It's a surprise."

She waited for him to continue, but he said nothing more. And when Deanna prompted him, Cord only shook his head, keeping his thoughts to himself.

~ ~ ~

It was only after Deanna emerged from her shower, taken after Cord, did she begin to sense something very special was in the works. She stepped out of the steamy bathroom to find him in her bedroom, before the mirror, cursing at the bow tie he was unable to straighten properly.

Deanna froze for a minute, mesmerized by the sight of him in formal attire. *Breathtakingly beautiful* came to mind. She stood in the doorway, her hair concealed in its customary post-shower towel-turban and her body wrapped in her robe, studying him from head to toe. His brown hair was slicked back, still damp, his blue eyes dark with concentration as he ripped out the bow tie and attempted to retie it. His broad shoulders almost strained against the black material of his jacket, that narrowed perfectly to reflect his trim waist. Although his muscular legs were hidden beneath the trousers, Deanna got a sense of their slim lines, as she well knew every other woman who studied him throughout the night would. She sighed, and catching his attention, he paused from his task.

"That wasn't disappointment I heard, was it?" he

asked her reflection in the mirror, his fingers pausing for a moment.

She smiled softly, and her eyes told him what he needed to know. She turned toward her closet, swallowing thickly to find her voice. When she spoke, her words were barely more than a whisper. "I wish you had warned me, I brought all my evening gowns to the cleaners." It was meant to be a joke, but in all actuality, Deanna had little occasion to buy such formal evening wear.

Her mind assessed the formal dresses hanging in the back of her closet. A red sequined thing she'd worn to a Christmas party two years ago. A black chiffon purchased for a night at the opera with a client last fall. A forest green silk dress she'd bought on a whim after visiting a client on Fifth Avenue. The purchase had nearly equaled one whole paycheck, but then it had included gloves, a light cape and shoes. She'd never worn it, had all but forgotten about it, and now questioned the forces of fate. She pulled it from the closet and whirled around to face Cord. "Are you going to tell me what in the world you're planning or not?"

"No."

"You're in a tux. You're not even going to give me a clue?"

"Don't wear jeans."

"Don't wear jeans. That's helpful. Now out. Out of my room! Now!" She turned to him, fighting to conceal her grin. He faced her, showing no signs of intimidation with her threat. His bow tie, she noticed, was as perfect as the rest of him. "You are so handsome."

"I know," he called over his shoulder with a wink as he sauntered out of her bedroom.

~ ~ ~

Deanna gulped when they arrived at a very elite Greenwich Village restaurant nestled on Barrow Street.

"You don't approve? We can go somewhere else."

"Don't we need reservations?"

"Yep. Ready?" He eased into the parking garage, got out, then strode around to her side and opened her door. "If you don't hurry we're going to miss the opening act. We've only got two hours."

"Opening act?" Deanna allowed herself to be led out of the car and down the walkway.

"Yes. I've got tickets to a show. Come on, Deanna. Quit dragging your feet. I told you I was hungry."

~ ~ ~

"I feel like I'm dreaming," she told him later as they sipped espresso from tiny demitasse cups.

"I feel like I won't have to eat again for a week."

"Me too. I must have gained five pounds with this meal alone."

"I don't see where you could have hidden it." He flashed her a wicked grin as his gaze turned downwards toward the low dip of her neckline, below where the emerald pendant rested. "Have I told you how beautiful you are?"

"Only about fifty times."

"Then I've been neglecting you."

She chuckled, her eyes shining brightly. "Thanks."

"Don't mention it." He lifted an arm and motioned for a waiter. Seconds later, he handed his gold card to the young man who had catered to their every wish for the last hour and a half.

~ ~ ~

It was nearly ten o'clock when the pair stepped out of the Ambassador Theater, humming a tune from the musical *Chicago*. Deanna shivered in the chill night air and Cord wrapped an arm about her shoulders. "Do you want my jacket?"

"No, thanks. I'm fine." Her voice was dreamy, as she rested her head against his shoulder.

"Tired?"

"A little." Yawn.

"Want to stop for a cup of coffee?"

Deanna shook her head. "Haven't you spent enough money on me for one night?"

"Deanna. A cup of coffee isn't going to break me."

"No. I guess not. But wouldn't you enjoy it more if you could lay back on the couch and sip it with your shoes off?"

"Sold." The alarm beeped as Cord unlocked the car and opened the passenger side door for Deanna.

~ ~ ~

Within forty minutes, the two were sitting side-by-side on Deanna's couch, drinking Swiss Almond Mocha coffees from two ceramic mugs.

"I had a great time. Thank you." She yawned and set her cup down on the coffee table, then crossed a stockinged foot over her knee to rub the arch.

"So did I. Thank *you*." He loosened his tie from around his neck.

"Did you notice that guy taking our picture?"

"No. Can't say I did." Cord took a gulp of the brew, then wiped his mouth with the back of his hand.

"I wonder why?" Another yawn escaped Deanna's lips as she laid her head against the back of the couch.

"I wouldn't worry about it." He slipped an arm about her shoulders.

"You think he thought we were somebody famous?" She closed her eyes.

"Who knows."

"Umm."

"Deanna."

"Umm."

"Deanna." He called her name again and tickled the bottom of her foot that was still crossed over her right knee. Eyes closed, she uncrossed her legs and smiled, stretching and yawning before curling up beside him like a kitten. Cord brought his hand up to cradle the softness of her cheek and her dimpled chin, his thumb lightly brushing over her bottom lip. Immediately her eyes flew open, green pools of surprise.

"You startled me."

"Sorry. I couldn't resist." He turned toward her, resting his head against the couch, as she did, so that their faces were inches apart.

"Thank you so much for a wonderful evening." A sleepy smile curved her lips.

"It was my pleasure."

"And the necklace is beautiful."

"It matches your eyes."

"I figured that's what you had in mind. Oh. And the flowers. I forgot to thank you for the flowers, didn't I?"

Cord suppressed a grin, dimples cutting into the lean contours of his face. "No. You thanked me for the flowers."

"They were gorgeous. I think I'm the most envied woman in the office." She closed her eyes and smiled.

"Well?" he asked, raising his eyebrows in question.

"Well, what?"

"Have you had time to think on it?"

"It? Oh. It. Yes, I have." Deanna studied her stockinged feet resting on the coffee table. Her gaze settled on Cord's hands, well-formed, tanned, roughened by hard work, yet meticulously manicured.

Cord moved now, slipping off the couch to balance on one bended knee. "Deanna?" He took her hands in both of his, resting them in her lap.

She grinned, now completely awake, knowing full well what he was going to say. "Yes, Michael."

"Deanna. Will you marry me?"

Chapter 16

Although she expected this, after all the effort he had gone through with the planning of this whole week, this evening, Deanna was still at a loss as she gazed down at him on his bended knee.

"Will you be my wife, not in name only, but in every true sense of the word?"

"Every true sense, Cord?"

"Every true sense."

"For better and worse?"

He nodded. "Richer and poorer?"

"Is that why you did all this? Dinner, show . . . this?" Deanna lifted the pendant resting against her skin. "Trying to bribe me?"

"No. I was courting you."

"Courting me? Since when were you so old-fashioned?"

"Since I realized I've been given a second chance at something I should have never taken for granted in the first place."

That quick turn to such seriousness caught Deanna off guard. She frowned, then squinted, as if trying to conjure up the courage to speak. "I'm scared."

"Me too."

"You? Why are you afraid? You have nothing to lose."

"I have you to lose."

She nodded, too choked to speak.

"I'll be a good husband. I promise. I won't beat you. I'll keep food on the table, a roof over your head."

"Cord. I'm serious. What happens—what if you decide this isn't right? What if you meet someone?"

"Deanna. Let it go. What went wrong between us happened years ago. There isn't anyone else for me. Only you."

"And my farm."

"The farm is important, but do you really think I'd marry someone to take their land? Seriously? I'm doing this because I can't live without you. I haven't been living these last few years. I've been existing. I want you to be a part of my days, my nights. My winters and summers."

"I see."

"That's it? What else do you want me to say? I want you to marry me. I will provide for you, take care of you until we draw our last breaths. I will never hurt you. Will you marry me?"

What about love? her heart screamed at him. *How could you marry me without love being the motivation?* Maybe in time. Deanna knew the sex would be great. She knew she'd never want for any material thing. He even said he'd *let* her work. Maybe in time he would grow to love her?

She'd taken so long to answer that Cord started to withdraw his hand. She tightened her hold, stilling his actions.

"What about the farm?" She caught his eyes and stared unblinking.

"I don't think now is the right time to discuss this."

"Cord. What about the farm?"

"We buy out Trish and Pike. And, as partners, we start the change of zone and site planning process on all but the twenty acres surrounding the main house. That remains as is. Yours. You can do whatever you want with it."

"I see." She paused for a moment, studying the grooves in his knuckles and on the back of his hand. "All right then." Caution kept her from putting her whole heart into her answer. Without love it seemed like one more contract to be squared away. Another deal to close. Trish wasn't the only one being bought out.

Deanna thought she saw a flicker of sadness fill his eyes before he closed them and leaned over to kiss her lips, an act that sealed their bargain. When he straightened, he produced a small package from his inside pocket. "I didn't know when I should give this to you. I guess it's now or never." He handed the package to her and straightened out to sit beside her again, his eyes never leaving her.

The box was nearly identical to the one she'd received this afternoon, except that it was a ring box, square and deep. Deanna lifted the lid off, gasping softly at her discovery of its contents.

"Cord!" She whispered breathlessly, gazing down at the heart-shaped diamond similar to the emerald she had received earlier in the day. And like the pendant, this one was also surrounded by a cluster of stones, only these weren't diamonds, but emeralds.

"Do you like it?" He chuckled softly as he lifted the ring from its resting place and took the box from Deanna's trembling hands.

"Like it? It's beautiful." She held out her left hand and allowed him to slip the ring on her third finger. She suddenly felt shy, and didn't know what to do next. The intense passion burning deep in his eyes told her she was about to find out.

Deanna forgot to breathe as she watched Cord dip his head lower, his lips seeking hers out. It was only after he kissed her that she remembered how to work her lungs, and exhaled a deep, contented sigh. The refrain of an old classic song came to mind and she smiled. "You take my breath away," she murmured.

"Well maybe I should give it back." He bent his head again, capturing her lips in a kiss so fierce, so demanding that Deanna swooned and would have fallen had she not been sitting on the sofa. His lips prodded and parted hers with his kiss, his tongue ravishing and exploring, coaxing her to respond.

Never, never had Deanna been kissed like this. By Cord or by any one. She grew dizzy. Her heart raced and her temples pounded. Her body came afire with the response he sought. Cord's hands came up behind her, catching the zipper of her delicate dress, his movement baring her back to reveal she wore nothing but panties and stockings beneath. He moaned softly, his hands moving to brush the spaghetti straps of her dress off her shoulders, baring the creamy white skin of her breasts. His lips traced lightly over her skin, moving from her mouth to her jaw and chin, kissing lower, nuzzling her neck, her shoulders, then lower still, to capture the rosy tip of one breast.

The feel of his lips, his teeth, his tongue nibbling and kissing sent shards of fire through her belly, down to the tips of her toes. Deanna inhaled sharply and arched against him, her hands framing his face. She felt his fingers gently working the fabric of her gown, slipping it down the length of her body. She shivered, entwining her fingers in his hair as his tongue traced a path across her belly. It was only when he stood up and began unbuttoning his shirt that she realized he had stripped her completely, leaving her erotically vulnerable.

His shirt was off, as well as his tee shirt. He slipped out of his slacks, his movements slow and deliberate as he caught and held her gaze. Deanna's cheeks flamed and her heart quickened. It had been years since she'd seen him, any man for that matter, so undressed—and so ready—to make love.

"Cord," she whispered, reaching her hand out to him, beckoning him to come to her.

He joined her, desire smoldering in the depth of his blue eyes.

What if he's doing this for the farm? What if he has no intention of marrying me? What if he's playing me for a fool? Her fears were soon forgotten as he kissed her thoughts and her sanity away, replacing all worries with a heady, unchecked desire.

Like the young lovers they once were, Cord and Deanna kissed and caressed, explored and enticed one another on the sofa as they learned and relearned the curves and contours of one another's body.

He lifted his head, searching her eyes with an unspoken question. Her answer came in one last breathless kiss as she stood, bringing him along with her, making her way into the bedroom. Cord moved behind her, folded back the bed covers, then slid between the sheets, waiting for her to join him. Fighting the last of her fears, Deanna knelt on the edge of the bed, feeling like a virgin, telling herself that this was right, it was only natural she make love with Michael McCord—her fiancé.

After she had been burned by him so long ago she vowed never to sleep with another man until after they were married. And as innocent and childish as that vow sounded, Deanna had abided by it easily since no man had ever stirred her desires as this man had.

"Smile, will you?" Cord laughed as she slipped under the covers. "You haven't been sentenced to death, you know."

Forcing a smile, she confessed in a soft whisper. "I'm a little nervous I guess." As she spoke, his lips came down to caress her neck and she tilted her head to the side as she felt his breath whisper against her skin.

"Do I do that to you? Do I make you nervous?" His voice was deep as he nuzzled her neck softly. He caressed the smooth contour of her belly and Deanna jumped involuntarily at his touch, nodding.

At her reaction, he raised his head, a quizzical frown marring his handsome face. "You aren't kidding, are you?"

She shook her head, her eyes wide.

"It's not like it's your first time. I can vouch for that," he joked. The memory made Deanna laugh too. They'd both been so nervous they were going to get caught by his parents that it felt more like a chore than the beautiful experience they had hoped it would be.

Blushing, Deanna spoke. "It feels like it."

He eyed her suspiciously, a quirk of a smile settling on his lips. He studied her unwavering gaze and whispered softly, "Relax." Then he nudged her over onto her belly and placed his hands on her shoulders, the balls of his thumbs rubbing away the knot of tension at the top of her spine. Deanna felt her eyes grow hypnotically heavy, his touch soothing, comforting, guiding her to do as told—to relax. He concentrated on her upper body, working especially on her shoulders and around her shoulder blades, before allowing his hands to travel lower, down the trail of her spine to the tip, taking time to caress each and every rib, every vertebra, every muscle.

Although Cord's hands never strayed from Deanna's back during the massage, she felt his touch change from therapeutic to sensual as if he had caressed every part of her body, from her toes to the top of her head. She hugged her pillow tightly, reveling in the sensations coursing through her blood he elicited so easily.

She attempted to turn over as soon as Deanna felt Cord hesitate, but he stopped her by placing his flattened palms down on her naked, trembling body. "Let me do this," he whispered. "I want to memorize every bit of you, in case this is all a dream."

His hands worked their magic along the length of her body, down to her feet, rubbing away all tension and stress. Then he slowly traced his fingers along her legs, coaxing them apart with his knees as he came to kneel between them. By the time his hands reached Deanna's thighs she felt surely she would explode. Her body was on fire, craving sweet release with his every caress, every kiss.

His hands came to rest on the soft curve of her butt, once again, where he changed his course of action and redirected his fingers downward, searching gently between her thighs. He growled a lusty moan, and she responded similarly as he penetrated the soft folds of her womanhood with his fingers. She moved in sync with the rhythm he played within her body, burning with his touch. Shivers swept along her spine as he alternately kissed and softly bit at the skin on her back, her shoulders. Lost in this sea of sensation, Deanna whispered his name when he withdrew from her, only to be silenced with a kiss as he turned her over onto her back. His body lay along the length of hers and instantly she felt the hardness of his sex straining, pressing against her, searching for the path his hands had journeyed moments earlier.

Deanna moved against him as he readjusted himself so that he was now laying on his side, beside her, half covering her body with his own. Gently he guided the rosy tip of her breast to his mouth, where he paid homage to her nakedness until Deanna's world burst into bits of light and song and heat. Cued by her soft whispers, Cord moved to cover her, and she welcomed him into her.

He found her, driving surely into the place of refuge he'd lost the privilege to enter so many years ago. He filled her with his being, his heart, his soul, and his body. His hands came up beneath her, moving her close to him. Hot kisses rained down upon her neck, her breasts, her chin and cheeks and eyes.

And then he kissed her fiercely on her mouth, as they joined together in their timeless dance of love. He called out her name in a cry of surrender as his liquid heat exploded into her womb. Her cries mingled as if in answering echo to his call and her body trembled and pulsated, matching his desire with her own.

What seemed like an eternity later, a bliss-filled exhausting eternity later, Cord eased away from her, settling down onto the bed beside her. She opened her eyes for a second, then closed them again as she realized the bedroom lights were still on and had been on the entire time, and that he was watching her as she fought to control her breathing, while trying to hold on to the glorious sensations he awakened in her.

She glanced up at him again as she turned to bury her face in his chest and saw him leaning on his crooked arm beneath his head, smiling down at her. As she burrowed against him he chuckled softly, leaned backward to shut the light off that was glowing brightly on the table beside the bed. Once the two were embraced by darkness, save for the neon and street lights filtering through the curtained window, Cord brought the quilt and sheet up around their shoulders. His arm curled around her waist beneath the covers and her body trembled like the aftershocks of an earthquake.

"Whew. That was amazing." Her whisper was barely

audible as she nuzzled against him, her lips tracing kisses along his chest.

"Is. It is amazing. You are amazing. We are amazing."

"Well. If the farm doesn't keep us together, hopefully the good sex will," she said, attempting but failing miserably to joke.

His tone was somber with his reply. "That's not all we have," he started.

"I was joking. I'm sorry. Bad timing," she said as she hugged him hard.

"Well, you are wrong. And I'll show you. We don't have only good sex going for us," he began.

Biting her lip, she waited for the words that should accompany a lovemaking session with your new fiancé. The words that would ease the doubt in her heart. She waited for a few moments for him to continue, then asked, "What else do we have?"

A light snore was his only reply.

~ ~ ~

Deanna awoke and snuggled deeper into the crook of his arm as she listened to the rain splatter against the fire escape outside her window. She had been dreaming of Debbie, of Cord leaving her without a place to live, of Cord laughing at her as he drove by in a gold sports car while she cried on the corner, standing in a pure white wedding gown. Curled safely within his embrace, she dozed again, only to have another unsettling dream, one in which her parents were standing by the side of the bed, holding an infant swaddled in white.

"No!" Deanna sat upright in bed, her chest heaving as she gasped for air.

"It's all right. Come here." Cord was awake, and apparently had been watching her while she slept. "It was only a dream."

Deanna shook her head as she fell into his arms. "My mom. And dad. They were standing right here."

"It was a dream."

Again, she shook her head. "A baby."

"What about a baby?"

"They handed us a baby."

Cord laughed out loud and sat up, then threw his legs over the side of the bed. "God forbid, Dean," he called as he walked to the bathroom. Moments later, he returned and climbed back in beside her. "You are on the pill, right?"

"Of course not."

"You're not?! Ah, geez." Cord swore softly with her revelation. "Why not? I thought all women were on the pill."

Deanna's face flamed—angry with herself for feeling defensive. Angry with him thinking safe sex was her responsibility alone. And very angry that they both had been so careless.

"Hey, I was only kidding." He ruffled her already mussed hair, then nudged her onto her side so they lay like spoons, her back against his chest.

"You better be kidding. You were here too, you know. Haven't you heard of safe sex?" Deanna squirmed as she felt his desire growing, but his arm lay possessively around her waist, pinning her to him.

His lips found that sensitive spot on her neck, right behind her ear. "Safe is not the word I would use to describe sex with us," he whispered.

Deanna sighed and closed her eyes as she felt his hand travel upward, capturing an already tautened nipple between thumb and forefinger. Turning over to face him she chuckled seductively and threatened in a low voice. "Safe is definitely not the word you're going to use when

I get through with you." She laughed as he raised an eyebrow at her. "This time I get on top."

Surprised laughter escaped his lips as he fell onto his back and raised his hands in surrender. "Anything you say, Drake. Anything you say."

Chapter 17

"So you said yes, huh?" Sal shook his head in disbelief, his voice low so their co-workers in nearby cubicles could not hear their conversation. "Are you sure you want to do this?"

"I think so?" She hesitated, her words tinged with a hint of confusion.

The two were sitting at her desk Tuesday afternoon, eating fruit salads from the corner gourmet food shop. Sal had taken Monday off, and Deanna had nearly burst not being able to talk to him until lunch break today.

"Do you trust him? Believe him?" Sal questioned, shaking his head at her, surprise echoing in his words.

"Why do you say that?"

He speared a pineapple chunk and studied it carefully before speaking, his words came measured and slow. "The proverbial carrot. McCord could be dangling this marriage proposal before you to get you to sign. Once he has your signature, that's it. He can say you've changed, he's changed. That your differences are too great."

"Yeah, I know. I thought of that too." Deanna's admission came reluctantly with a weighted sigh.

"So, he's not trustworthy." It was more a statement of fact than a question.

"No. He is. I think. I don't know." She shook her head again, studying the confusion etched across her friend's face. "It's complicated. I haven't slept in two days. I don't know what to do anymore. I want to save the farm. I don't want to lose it. But I can't go out there and work it. I like my job, my life here. I think. Oh, Sal. What am I going to do?"

He drew his well-shaped black brows together in a frown and threw the now emptied plastic container, lid, and fork in the trash can by Deanna's desk. "Does he love you?"

"Love?"

"Yeah. You know. That's the traditional reason people usually tie the knot."

Deanna stared unblinking into his coal black eyes. "I don't know. Maybe he really only wants the farm." She sounded as miserable as she felt. Her fruit salad—barely touched—followed the same path Sal's container had taken moments before.

"Sounds like he doesn't need to do something as drastic as marry you to get the farm. He is a third owner, after all."

"Cord isn't satisfied until he has everything. He knows I'd never sell out like Trish. And he knows I'd die fighting him and his stupid plans. I guess by marrying me he would not only get the farm, but salvage his pride as far as what happened to us before. He won't be happy until he owns everything—me as well as the farm."

"Listen to yourself. I think the answer is evident. Don't do it, Dee."

Deanna's telephone buzzed twice, the in-house signal from the receptionist. "Deanna Drake speaking," she answered automatically.

"Sal's secretary is on line eight."

"Thanks, Mindy. I'll tell him." She hung up, repeating the message as she pushed away from her desk. "You can use my phone. I gotta go to the bathroom."

"Great. Listen. I gotta book anyway. Dinner tomorrow night. You need to get out."

Deanna started to protest, but Sal wouldn't take no for an answer.

"I'll be out all day tomorrow. So be ready by six. I'll pick you up."

"Thanks."

~ ~ ~

Wednesday night dinner was postponed until Thursday night, with Sal calling her at work seconds before she left. By Thursday night Deanna needed an evening out badly. Work had been so very stressful this week, partially due to new accounts, but mostly because she could think of nothing, no one else, but Cord. And even though she didn't see Sal those two days, his comments regarding Cord played over repeatedly in her mind.

To make matters worse, she and Cord kept missing each other's calls, and spent the last three days playing telephone tag. The texts they shared were basic. *Good morning. How's your day going? Can't stop thinking of you.* But other than that, little or no substance. No *I love you.* Not one.

By six o'clock Thursday evening, Deanna was starting to believe that Sal had been right, that marrying Cord would be the biggest mistake of her life. All she could think of was Cord, the way his eyes glittered blue when he was laughing, like sapphires, or like onyx when angry or burning with desire. As she sat on the crowded subway home she thought a man sitting toward the end of the car was Cord. Her heart raced erratically and then plummeted when she realized she was wrong.

She thought she saw him again, as she walked up to her apartment building. Every green SUV made her heart skip a beat.

In the shower, with the water beating down hot and hard against her back, she thought back to their college days, when his hands knew every inch of her flesh, when she knew every bump and bruise on his body. When she thought she knew him so well. But didn't.

She rested her forehead against the cool tiles of the shower, letting the hot water traverse down her back as she relived the most recent memories of their love making, and she cried. It had been good sex—no great sex—that was all. Who was she kidding? Great sex and his insatiable desire to develop her damn farm.

The cellphone rang as she toweled dry and Deanna jumped, knowing it was Cord. She hesitated one, two, three rings, then picked it up and engaged the call quickly before it went to voicemail.

"Hello?"

"Deanna?"

"Cord?"

"Finally! Crazy week!"

"Uh. Yeah, totally." She wrapped the furry red towel about her body.

"You've been busy."

"So have you. What's up."

"Nothing. I'm working late and I can't get you out of my mind."

"Huh. Tell me about it."

"That didn't sound very enthusiastic," he joked, but when she did not reply, he asked, "You there?"

"Yes." She tucked her towel back under her arm, biting her lip.

"Something wrong?"

"No. Not at all."

"You still want me to come out?"

Silence. "Sure. Why not?"

Silence. "Are you sure everything's—" Someone spoke in the background. "Damn! Deanna? Give me ten minutes. A call I've been waiting for all day is on the other line. Okay? I'll call you right back. Bye."

Deanna placed her cellphone on the counter and went back to drying her hair and getting ready for dinner with Sal. When the door buzzer sounded, she swore softly, racing to the intercom to let her friend up, annoyed that he was a half hour early.

Within fifteen minutes she was dressed in a slinky rust-colored pant set, a wide gold loop belt cinched at her waste, gold hoop earrings and matching necklace adorning her ears and throat. Deanna blushed accordingly when Sal whistled at her, following her out her door.

The elevator doors closed behind them at precisely the same moment Deanna's cellphone—forgotten where she left it on her bedroom dresser—rang before going to voicemail.

"Dean?" He hesitated, then almost as if it were background noise, the sensitive microphone picked up his very colorful expletive as he disconnected the call.

~ ~ ~

Her cellphone screen indicated that Cord had called seven times and left messages each time, since they last spoke. It was midnight as she and Sal arrived at her apartment. She directed him to make coffee and put on some tunes as she grabbed her forgotten cellphone and headed straight to her bedroom to change. As Deanna traded her pants set for a pair of jogging shorts and U-2 tee shirt she checked her messages, her heart skipping when she saw Cord's missed calls and voicemails.

At least three messages had been left by Cord, with nothing more—after the first message which ended in him cursing as he hung up—than her name being called.

Then there were four calls from her newly claimed fiancé that ended in abrupt hang-ups, no messages at all.

She hadn't intended on forgetting her cellphone when she and Sal left. But Cord had been so rude, hanging up like that, and with everything she was feeling, she wasn't thinking clearly. To make matters worse, he had also texted her twice, telling her to call when she had time.

What, did he think she was going to wait around all night for him to call or text?

No. He expected her to.

Like he expected her to marry him.

Like he expected her to allow him to develop the farm.

Deanna sighed, stood up, and wondered why the apartment was silent.

Stepping out of her room, the reason quickly became apparent.

The reason was Cord.

"Wh-What are you doing here?" Deanna asked as she saw not one, but two suited men awaiting her in the living room.

He narrowed his eyes at her, then nodded to Sal. "I might ask you the same question about him."

"We-We just got home." *Quit stuttering, you dope.*

"Obviously," he answered dryly.

"I'd better go." Sal picked up his tie he'd slipped off and thrown over the arm of the couch. "I'll see you tomorrow."

"You don't have to go, Sal." Deanna's voice was hard and cold, but Sal waved her off with a grunt.

"See ya tomorrow, Dee." As he slammed the door behind him Deanna whirled around pointing a finger in accusation at Cord.

"You had no right!"

"Spare me." Cord shrugged out of his jacket and walked into the kitchen where the coffee Sal had made had finished brewing.

"Who the hell do you think you are coming in here like you own me!"

"You've been drinking. He was drunk. I'm not going to fight with you tonight. You can explain yourself in the morning." He kept his back to her, but as she studied him she noticed his hands were shaking as he poured one cup of coffee.

"I am not drunk. And if you think—"

"I don't know what to think right now, so drop it. I'm so angry right now. And you've been drinking. That doesn't make good company for either of us."

"You're right. I don't have to explain anything to you." She stormed out of the kitchen and into her bedroom before he had a chance to turn around. Slamming the door she let out a half-groan half-scream of frustration and anger. Then she opened the door and yelled, "Lock the door on your way out, if you don't mind." She slammed the door again and stomped over to her bed.

He opened it seconds later. "I'm not leaving, I told you."

"I don't recall inviting you."

"Then you're drunker than I thought."

"Stop saying that! I'm fine! And how could I have invited you? I didn't even know you were coming."

"That was obvious. So tell me, Deanna? Where'd you go, huh? Dinner? Was he going to spend the night?" Cord put his coffee cup on her bureau and walked over to her bed and sat down.

"How dare you?"

"Don't get so indignant. I knew something was up. I heard it in your voice. God. I thought you'd been kidnapped or something."

"Oh, come off it. Don't tell me you came all the way out here because you thought I was kidnapped. I wasn't born yes—"

"I had a meeting in Manhattan, eight o'clock. That's why I was calling, to see if I could crash here a day early. I didn't think you'd mind. In fact, I thought you'd be excited. Obviously, I was mistaken." He stared her down, his eyes dark and glittering in the dim light of the lamp beside her bed.

"What I do with my life is my business."

"Wrong. That is where you are mistaken, Deanna. I'm marrying you *so you have become my* business. And I'm your business. That guy, Sal? This is it. You tell him tomorrow it's over. Got it? Over. I should have known." He shook his head and stood up.

"Known what? He took me to dinner, for cripes' sake. Dinner. Got it?"

"Pretty long dinner, it's after midnight."

"We went out for drinks after."

"So it was dinner and drinks, then?"

Deanna almost found his jealousy comical. Almost. Maybe it was the wine, maybe it was the fact that she'd had a similar conversation with him, only in reverse, what seemed like a hundred years ago.

"We settled this before. I told you. He's *my friend,* damn it. That's all."

"It's after midnight!" Cord slapped an open palm on her bureau, rattling the perfumes on the tray beside her jewelry box.

"So what?" She sprung on him now, jabbing him in his chest with her manicured pointer finger nail. "We're not married! We haven't even set a date yet! Now I don't even know if I *want* to marry you! Is the farm worth all this? You're behaving like a total jerk!"

Her words intended to slash at him like a steel dagger, and she hoped they cut him to the quick. He shook his head softly and whispered, "After what passed between us last weekend, right here in this bedroom, you can still have doubts?" He shoved his hands in his pants pockets and stared down at the top of her head as she avoided his glance by studying his black leather shoes.

"I'm sorry." Her whisper echoed around them.

"Sorry for what? That we made love as if our lives depended on it? Or that you're back to questioning my motives?"

"I was a little more vicious than I intended." She squinted her eyes shut for a moment to clear her head. "But you can't barge in here like you own the place. You may own half of the Town of Brookville, but this here place is mine."

Her words stopped him in his tracks. "You're absolutely right. I'm sorry. I never—" He turned and left the bedroom without a word.

And she followed.

~ ~ ~

"I'm sorry I stopped by unannounced. I thought you'd be happy," he said moments later as they sat facing each other across her kitchen table.

"I might have been if you didn't act like such an ass."

"That was nothing. I really wanted to hit him."

"Cord!"

"It's true." He paused a moment, then gave a short laugh. "Okay so that sounded way too Neanderthal. Sorry."

Deanna laughed with him, but the sound wasn't exactly filled with humor. "You don't get it, do you?"

"I'm trying. I truly am." He studied the woman

across the table. Even in a tee shirt and shorts she turned him on.

"The problem, Cord, is . . . is . . . I like Sal. He's my best friend. Shoot, if I could, I'd ask him to be my maid of honor."

A scowl marred Cord's face as he shook his head in disagreement. "I can't allow that. Besides, Trish would be devastated."

"*Allow*?"

"Call me old-fashioned, Deanna. Don't expect me to sit here and tell you that I support your need to work and live here during the week, or even occasionally. Not if I'm going to have to sit at home wondering if you're here fu—"

"Hey! Watch it! He is *my friend*, damn you. If I haven't been with him by now I don't think I ever will."

"Don't give me that crap, Deanna." Cord pushed away from the table. "I see how he looks at you. I feel it when he shakes my hand and stares me down. He'd love to take a swing at me."

"Only because he knows what an idiot you can be sometimes."

"I don't think I'm acting like an idiot now. Coming into my woman's apartment at two a.m. and getting angry at finding another man with her is not idiotic. Don't you get it?"

Slowly she shook her head. "Midnight. Not two a.m. And, no, I don't get it. Don't you get it?"

He paused and frowned at her, sensing what was coming.

"I don't think—"

"Don't say it." He held up his hand as if to ward off her words. She kept her eyes averted as she started to speak. His heart froze and his limbs felt numb.

It only took a moment before reality began to unravel.

"I can't marry you." Deanna slipped off the ring he had placed on her finger last week. She held it out to him with a trembling hand.

He ignored her. "You don't know what you're saying."

"I know exactly what I'm saying."

"Are you going to give me a reason?" He rubbed his jaw with his thumb before leaning back in his chair and folding his arms over his chest.

"I guess you deserve that much, don't you?" She put the ring down on the table.

"I would say so." When she glared at him, Cord exploded. "Damn it, Deanna! This isn't a game!"

"You can't have my trust if you don't trust me. You can't have it all," was all she could whisper before she pushed away from the table and ran into her bedroom. "You can't own me," she finished as she slammed the door shut.

How was he going to get her to realize this was about so much more than the farm? All she thought he wanted was the farm. He closed his eyes in an effort to keep from following her into the bedroom and proving her wrong. But he couldn't. He wouldn't play her game. Not this one. Deanna wanted his heart on a platter, but she wasn't getting her way this time. The proposal for marriage had already left him vulnerable, and look what she had done! Not even a week after they'd made love for the first time in years she was sleeping with this guy Sal. He thought he'd learned his lesson about the games women play. He thought he'd learned to keep his heart out of his affairs—both business and pleasure. God, she made him look like such a fool. She played him well, and probably couldn't wait to pay him back for what happened with Debbie.

She did not wait long to play her hand.

Cord forced himself to finish his coffee, the bitter liquid tasting sweet compared to the taste in his mouth left by Deanna's rejection. Then when he was done, in his efficient organized way he stood up, walked to the sink and washed his mug, placing it upside down in the drain to dry.

Then he let himself out, locking the door and pulling it to as Deanna had ordered. The engagement ring still sat in the middle of the kitchen table. Just in case.

His steps were slow but determined as he headed for his car, parked half a block away. The ride home was going to be a long one. If she called before he got back to Olde Westfield, maybe he would change his mind. But if not, he had a number of serious decisions to make.

Chapter 18

Deanna slept little that night, dreaming only of Cord; making love to him, their now cancelled wedding, riding in his truck with the wind blowing her hair. She cried steadily, waking in the morning with a damp pillow and puffy red eyes. She hadn't heard him leave last night, and half expected, half hoped to find him on the couch. Her discovery—nothing but a washed coffee mug in the drain, and her engagement ring on the table—brought a fresh onslaught of tears, and the decision to stay home from work.

~ ~ ~

Cord didn't sleep at all. Not a wink. He didn't even try. He drove straight to the office, getting there by 4:30 in the morning, which was only two hours earlier than normal. He worked hard on an outline for his next plan, for his next proposal, next development.

It was time to forge ahead with his original plans to develop the farm. By 8:30 a.m., he had drafted the rough details of his letter to Deanna. In it he explained the process regarding his takeover of the farm. He didn't even wait for Janice to take her coat off before he called out to her through his open door.

His gray-haired office manager, who he had known from the time he was a young boy and who had worked for him since he opened his firm three years ago, popped her head into his office. "You're here early."

"I'm going to need you first thing. When Lisa comes in, get your pad and pen and let's get to it." He kept his attention on the papers before him.

"Must be something big. You look like you've slept in your clothes." Janice raised her eyebrows and clucked her tongue.

"Drake's." He raised his head and acknowledged his lifelong confidant. He was tired, worn out, and frustrated. He ran a hand through his already mussed hair, then rubbed his stubbly face in agitation, sighing deeply.

"Would you like me to make a pot of coffee before we get started and we can have a little chat?"

He pushed away from his cherry wood desk. "Nah. But thanks. I gotta clear my head. I'll walk down to the deli. Want anything?"

Janice shook her head. "No. I'm fine. It's you I'm worried about. Are you okay?"

As he walked to the door, he faltered. "No, I'm not." The door slammed behind him.

~ ~ ~

It was nearly 12 o'clock noon when Cord ended his dictations with one final request of Janice to read back the final version of his letter to Deanna.

She followed his order, ending with, "'And in closing, I regret, Ms. Drake, that we were unable to find suitable arrangements that met with both of our goals. However, I know my proposal is the only and best alternative left for our holdings. I trust you will adhere to my knowledge and expertise in matters such as these, and come to terms with my final offer. Respectfully, Michael McCord.'"

"Sounds great. Can you type that, along with the formal offer to Trish, the contract and letters to the town board, planning and zoning boards, and have them ready to mail when I leave? I want it postmarked today. All of it." The finality in his voice sounded as hard as steel.

Janice, a mother of three and grandmother of eight, waved the letter addressed to Deanna at him. "You sure you don't want to think on this one?" she asked, adding, "At least until Monday?"

"No. What's done is done." That was the one thing about living in this town he hated most—everybody knew everybody else's business. He stood up and walked to the door, opening it and calling for Lisa. Janice slipped by him rolling her eyes as her co-worker jumped up at their boss's beckoning.

Lisa was a young thing, working here for less than a year, straight out of the local community college. As hard as he tried to be nice to her, she acted like a frightened deer every time he addressed her.

"Did I get any calls?"

"Oh. Yes. I'll-I'll get them." Lisa gulped a deep breath to steady her nerves as she turned toward the outer office with Cord following close behind her. He drummed his fingers impatiently on her Formica desk as she gathered at least a dozen pink message slips together in a messy pile.

He frowned as he shuffled through them, placing the ones he intended on calling first on top and those that would have to wait on the bottom of the pile. None had Deanna's name on them. "What did Sergio want?"

"AID's Awareness ball tonight. You sent your regrets? Remember?" Lisa's eyes shimmered with awe. "Billy Joel is going to be there."

"You should go, Michael." Janice spoke from behind. "I believe you need to let loose and get your mind off of, uh, work."

He turned to walk back into his office, wanting to

call no one but Deanna, wishing she had called him. But she hadn't. She hadn't and that had been the deciding factor. He was mailing the letters. He was going ahead with the takeover of the farm.

He dialed Sergio's number to tell him yes, he'd changed his mind and he'd be coming. "Which sister needs the date?" he asked without even bothering with a "hello."

The man on the other end chuckled. "Sophina. How's it going, darling?"

"Business is great. Sophina? The blonde?"

"Yes. The model. She is so gorgeous, I hate her. Why couldn't Mama have given me her looks? I'd make a divine blond, especially with *my* eyes, wouldn't I?"

Cord smiled into the phone, forgetting his problems for a moment. Sergio always had that effect on him. "Paparazzi?"

Sergio sighed. "Michael, you know the answer already. What's a party without pictures? And press? I know how you value your privacy, but darling, this is for a good cause. Please don't change your mind."

"On one condition."

"Yes?"

"Make some calls and be sure I get at least one good shot with your sister. And I want it in the Sunday social column. This Sunday."

"Well. Considering that coverage of my bash is going to hit every paper, I doubt that will be hard. Sophina's going to be so excited to hear you changed your mind. Want me to pass any message on or do you want to call her?"

"You can tell her I'll meet her there. Oh, and tell her to wear the sexiest, slinkiest dress she's got." Now all Deanna had to do was buy a Sunday newspaper.

"Michael? This isn't like you at all. Want to fill me in? I'm very good at keeping secrets."

"No secret, Sergio. It's like I told you. Tell Sophina I'll meet her there by nine."

~ ~ ~

Deanna slept all day Friday, battling what must have been the flu. She hoped she'd given it to Cord and that he was suffering as badly as she. Sal called by 10 o'clock, worried about why she hadn't called or shown up at work. Other than that the telephone remained silent for the rest of the day, afternoon, and evening.

Half a box of nighttime cold medicine later, Deanna found herself wide awake and watching a late-late show on some obscure cable channel. It was after one in the morning and she'd discovered she slept herself out all day. Now she couldn't catch a wink if she said the alphabet backward while standing on her head. Cord monopolized her every thought. She wondered if he'd gotten home safely the night before. If he was very angry at her. Would he call ever again? Would he give her a second chance? Did he love her? Should she call him?

When her musings took on that vein she shook her head to make them vanish and focused on reality. He didn't love her. He didn't trust her. He thought she and Sal were lovers. That thought made her laugh aloud. He could give it but he couldn't take it, hm? Well. She'd done the giving Thursday night, well Friday morning, actually. And where had it gotten her? He thought she cheated on him.

That thought made her sigh, the tears coming once again. Was she ever going to dry out, she thought, grabbing a handful of Kleenex. She picked up the remote and flipped through a sea of infomercials until she found a rerun of *Get Smart*. This was good, she thought. This would make her laugh. But it didn't.

~ ~ ~

It was nearly noon on Saturday when Deanna heard the buzzer ring, waking her from a dead sleep. She'd finally fallen asleep right before dawn and probably would have slept all day if her visitor hadn't shown up. Cord! Deanna thought suddenly, springing from her bed. She would show him. She'd tell him a thing or two. Her anger cut through the fog brought on by the cold meds and she rose, running to the door before he had a chance to leave. "Come on up," she said, then waited for him to arrive.

She nearly burst into tears seeing the Federal Express man standing with an envelope at the door. "Sign here," was all he said as he handed her the clipboard and envelope while taking in her disheveled appearance.

~ ~ ~

Deanna didn't know what a good cry was until she read halfway through the special delivery letter Cord had sent, which he had apparently written yesterday, addressing her as Ms. Drake throughout its entirety. He was going through with his plan, buying the two of them out, or at least buying Trish out, and he was going to develop the farm. All but 20 acres. And owning two-thirds gave him power to obtain a court order to have her comply. Damn him! He hadn't even had the decency to wait until their relationship was cold before burying it!

The battle against her tears and self-pity was lost before she finished the letter. Grabbing a box of Oreo cookies in one hand, the letter in the other, she went back to bed to nurture her grief. He hadn't even written the letter himself. It was typed, the lower left hand corner giving evidence that he had composed it, with the familiar secretarial notation MM/js. Deanna ran the ball of her thumb over his initials, a fresh torrent of tears bursting from her very soul.

Now she lost everything. Trish, the farm, and Cord. But had she ever had any of them?

No, she answered. Realistically, she had no one.

Chapter 19

The 120-foot yacht glittered like a jewel resting on a bed of black velvet. To the west, the September evening sky was tinged a deep orange and red, fading to deep lavender as the eye traveled eastward, melting into a royal blue, then black sky even further to east, where the first stars danced against a black satin sky. Deanna gasped aloud as her gaze settled on the yacht moored at the yacht club in Hempstead Harbor, causing Sal to chuckle as he backed the rental car into a reserved parking spot.

"You like?"

"My God. I feel like I'm in a fairy tale."

"You'd make the perfect princess." His voice was thick with admiration.

Deanna slipped a sly glance toward him. "You're the best, you know."

He groaned and reached for the door handle. "Let's go. It's nearly seven-thirty and Randall expects his guests to be punctual."

~ ~ ~

There had to be close to one hundred people on board. And there was still room left over. Deanna had gotten a private tour from Randall's sister Penny, who seemed to take a liking to her immediately. Deanna warmed to her as well, but knew a friendship would never flourish between them after this evening. Although they were the same age, the two women were worlds apart. Penny had gone to private schools her whole life, vacationed abroad in the UK, Switzerland, Italy, and Australia, to name a few of her more recent jaunts. Deanna never even left Long Island until she attended college.

Penny received her master's degree from one of the most influential schools in the nation, while Deanna never got past her bachelor's degree in communications.

Penny worked on Wall Street. Deanna worked further up town.

Penny was married and divorced and involved with a married man, 20 years her senior.

Deanna hadn't even been kissed in two months.

"Here's the master bedroom. Isn't it grand? Oh, Deanna, even after all these years this boat still takes my breath away." Penny's eyes shone in wonderment. Her childlike honesty made Deanna realize how much she truly liked Penny. She wasn't pretentious, she didn't put on airs. She was real and down to earth, despite her socialite status.

"Little sister. How many times do I have to tell you, it's not a boat." A smooth, melodiously deep voice sounded from behind the two women, causing each to whirl around. Penny laughed aloud at her brother's admonishment. Deanna smiled politely and tried not to gawk at the Adonis who entered the room.

"Who's this friend you're bedazzling now, little sister?" The Greek God flashed a smile, brighter than any of the stars out tonight, at Deanna.

She gulped and concentrated on not dropping her drink.

"Randy, stop calling me that. You know I hate it when you patronize me. This is Deanna. Drake?" She ended with a question and turned to Deanna for confirmation, who nodded silently.

"Hello, Deanna Drake." He smiled at her and she returned the gesture, still unable to find her voice. His warm brown gaze cascaded over her body, not resting anywhere indecent, just assessing. Nevertheless his attention made her blush from head to toe. He turned his sun-bleached, platinum-blond head toward his sister once again.

"So, where's Todd?" He eyed the room as if he expected this 'Todd' to materialize from the 14-karat, gold-laced wallpaper.

"Granddaughter's birthday." She grimaced. "Duty calls," she added on a bored note.

"As expected." His voice sharpened, belying his disapproval, but nothing more was said. To Deanna he asked, "Are you enjoying yourself?"

"Yes. Thank you. You have a beautiful—" She smiled as she almost said "boat" and finished carefully, "yacht."

"Dad's pretty generous with his toys. Lucky for us he likes to share."

"Lucky for you," Deanna said, smiling. *My god, it's getting warm in here*. She wondered if he had bikini lines, or if he was naturally that bronzed.

"Penny. Sal was asking about you."

"Sal? Salvatore?" Deanna's eyes widened once again in amazement.

"Yeah. He's my attorney. You know him?"

"I came with him." Deanna watched Penny's expression falter, then added, "We work together."

"Oh. I was wondering who you were with," Randall said slowly. He glanced at his sister then back to Deanna.

"Sal and I are friends, that's all," Penny offered quickly.

Shrugging her bared shoulders, Deanna chuckled.

"So are we. I mean, like, just friends. That's all, Penny. Go find Sal. I'll catch up with you guys later."

Penny smiled apologetically, murmuring something as she fled out the door, leaving Randall and Deanna alone. Alone in the master bedroom, Deanna noted wryly, *Control yourself, you wanton little . . .*

"Well. If you're interested, I can spare a few more minutes from my duties as host. Want to see the rest of *the boat*?" His eyes twinkled as he held out a hand.

"I'd love it. Is that really gold spun into the wallpaper?" she asked as she joined him, taking the hand he offered as if it were the easiest thing she'd ever done.

"Yeah. Mom had that stuff put in years ago." He answered leading her out into the hall. "I think it's a bit too much if you ask me. I prefer wood."

He paused and stared at her pointedly, and when she did not reply, he added, "Hard wood, actually."

~ ~ ~

Cord stood on the upper deck, watching the crowd mill about on the level below him. He spotted Sal, talking with Penny Eldred. Sal, that son of a bitch Deanna had been sleeping with the whole time she was leading Cord on. The grip on his glass turned his knuckles white as he gritted his teeth together.

"Hey, handsome. Why so glum?" Sophina slipped an arm about his waist, resting her chin on his shoulder.

"See that guy down there in the tux?"

"Michael. They're all wearing tuxes," she replied and stifled a bored yawn.

He scowled. "The one with Penny."

"Um-hm. Oh, yes. The yummy one."

"His name is Sal. And he's a real slime bag."

"Oh, really now? Since when are you jealous of

Penny?" Sophina arched an eyebrow as she studied the man by her side.

"Penny? Nah."

"Oh, then. I get it. Was that the Sal with what's her name? Deanna?"

"That's the one."

"Michael. I'm offended. I haven't made you forget her yet?"

"Funny," Cord said and turned toward the blonde as he draped an arm casually across the small of her back.

"So what's he doing with Penny, if he was so hot for Deanna?" Sophina leaned over and whispered in his ear.

A choked gasp sounded from behind the couple, and then a strangled voice whispered his name. "Cord?"

Slowly Cord lifted his head at the sound of that all too familiar voice. It had taken every ounce of strength he possessed not to jump away like a bumbling teenager snagged by a disapproving parent. He focused on Deanna through veiled eyes, working overtime on his poker face. "Hello, Deanna."

He watched her visibly stiffen at the sound of her name. She was standing with Randall, the host of the party and Penny's brother.

"What are you doing here?" He grimaced at the tight hold his host had on his former lover. First Sal, now Randall. She was learning fast, wasn't she?

Before Deanna had a chance to respond, Randall came to her rescue. "She's with me, Mike."

"I figured Sal—" He glanced over his shoulder toward the lower deck.

"Sal brought her, but he's with Penny. Must be my lucky night." He smiled broadly and wrapped an arm around her waist. "So you know each other?" Randall glanced down at Deanna, but her gaze was locked on Cord.

"Yeah." Deanna found her voice. "We're old, uh, acquaintances. We went to school together."

"Small world, isn't it? Hey, Sophina."

"Hey yourself, Randy." The blonde left Cord's side and walked over to Randy to give him a sweet kiss hello right on the lips. "How about you buy me a drink and let these two lovebirds catch up?"

~ ~ ~

Deanna took a deep breath and straightened up slightly, realizing she was out of her league here as Randall's arm tightened around her waist, preventing her from stepping back even while he kissed Sophina. One glance at Cord made her even more confused, as she noted the wry grin twisting his lips. What kind of life did Cord lead, anyway, associating with these people? A developer turned playboy, she thought, recalling that photo caption she had read the weekend they split up. At that moment she put two and two together, realizing the woman kissing Randall was the same woman who had been at Cord's side in the photograph. At the time she had Googled him and found similar pictures with various women. There was even a photo of her with Cord, the night he proposed to her. She shook her head clear of that tainted memory and focused on Randall and Sophina.

The kiss deepened and did not appear to be letting up any time soon, but still, Randall kept his hold securely about Deanna, who was so mortified she was caught in the middle of this that she could do nothing but cough, softly hoping to remind the two she was still there. Her face flamed as she heard Cord chuckle from where he stood watching the whole scene with his arms crossed over his chest.

Randall shifted away from Sophina then gazed down at Deanna, bringing her even closer. The look in his eye invited Deanna to join in, and as Deanna tried unsuccessfully to extricate her body from Randall's hold, Sophina finally acknowledged her, smiling down at her as if she were a little girl. "So you're Deanna Drake. How wonderful to meet you after all this time."

Deanna stared at her for a moment, trying to figure out if she was being sarcastic or if she was coming onto her. Her second thought proved to be correct when Sophina leaned over as if she were going to capture Deanna in her next full-lipped kiss. Deanna froze, completely ignorant as to how to remove herself from this whole mess, when Cord, wonderful horrible Cord, rescued her.

"Well, Ms. Drake, what say we get a drink and catch up on old times?" Cord reached for Deanna's hand, and drew her close. She shivered and burned all at once with his touch as he eased her out from the middle of Randall and Sophina's embrace.

"Michael. You are no fun anymore." Sophina pouted prettily with the words.

"That's what you keep telling yourself." Cord laughed, his arm securely locked about Deanna's waist.

"How do you know the little lady wants to go with you?" Randall eyed Deanna hungrily, even as he pulled Sophina against his body.

Again Cord laughed. "She probably doesn't, but I don't care at this point. Don't be greedy, Randall. It doesn't suit you."

"Have fun," Sophina singsonged over her shoulder as Randall led her back down the stairs that came directly from the master bedroom. "I'll finish your tour later, Deanna," Randall offered over his shoulder.

"Take your time," Deanna murmured softly, from the comfort of Cord's embrace. "Holy cow," she whispered as she leaned into him.

Even after everything they had been through these last few months, it seemed the right thing to do to seek refuge in his embrace. He enwrapped her in the soft haven of his arms. "Nothing you didn't want would have happened. They're good people. You know the old saying, 'Consent is sexy. Enthusiastic consent is sexier.'"

"Ha. Never heard that one. I felt so stupid. I thought I was imagining it."

"You weren't imagining a thing, Deanna. That's their life. They work hard and play hard."

"That's crazy!"

"Hey, take it as a compliment. I guess they figured if you were here you must play the game too."

Deanna leaned away, surprised that Cord—straight-laced, serious Cord—was so comfortable with this lifestyle. *Developer turned playboy.*

"Well," she started stiffly, "maybe I'm keeping you from playing too?"

"Nope, not at all." He turned around with her still attached to his side, to stare out over the railing at the water. The full moon hung low over the black horizon, its golden reflection shimmering in the water. "I'm not the one they invited. Randall's not into that scene."

"Would you have gone?" Her voice was meek, trembling as she questioned him softly.

"You think you know me so well. Decide for yourself."

Deanna was silent as she considered his words. She decided she would rather not learn his answer. Some things were better left unsaid. A loud sigh escaped her lips.

"Bored?"

"No, not at all." The answer to his question came too quickly for her satisfaction.

"So what are you doing here? You came with Sal?" His voice was bitter.

"Yes."

"Is he good to you?"

"Very."

"You love him." It was more a statement than a question.

"You think you know me so well. You decide." She answered with a raised brow and sardonic twist of a grin.

"You look beautiful tonight," he offered, training his sight on the water, while ignoring her jab.

"Not as beautiful as Sophina."

"No. But few women are. It's her job to be the most beautiful woman anywhere she goes."

"You two have been seeing each other a while, huh?"

"We go way back."

"Does she make you happy?"

"As happy as Sal makes you, I'm sure."

"I see," she said, when she didn't see at all. "You come to a lot of these things?"

"When I have to. Sophina likes to come to them."

"Does that"—Deanna jerked her head toward the stairs and the master bedroom—"happen often?"

"Not as often as they'd like. But it does happen. As long as it's between consenting adults, and they're careful, it's harmless. It's their release. They've got really stressful careers."

She shook her head and shivered. "I guess I don't work hard enough then."

"Me neither."

A lump formed in her throat as she searched for something to say to his implication. "Thanks."

"You're welcome."

They stood there until the moon traveled high in the

midnight black sky, until Deanna's shivering signaled that she was cold. "Why don't we go inside?"

"Inside?" she asked meekly.

"Yeah. I don't know about you, but I'm starved. And I came here to drink. Unlimited bar and buffet. Five hundred dollars a head and I'll be damned if I don't get my fill."

"Five hundred?" She gulped in the cool night air.

"Oh, I get it. Sal doesn't let you in on the finances, huh?"

"Sal? He said he got them for free. He's Randy's attorney."

"So in essence, I'm paying for your dinner."

"It seems to me, Mr. McCord, that I'm forever in your debt." Deanna smiled at him in the moonlight.

"I love when you smile." His voice was thick and low, causing Deanna's stomach to flutter as she gazed up at him, her eyes pools of liquid onyx in the night.

She went to bend her head to avoid his gaze, but Cord's hand caught her chin, coaxing her to look up at him once more. She licked her lips and swallowed, closing her eyes in that ageless invitation. A soft groan escaped from Cord as he lowered his mouth to hers, prodding her to part her lips beneath his query. She yielded eagerly and a flood of desire burst forth, consuming her, setting her body on fire.

His hands trailed across her back, her waist, and as they made their way over the curve of her bottom, she caught her breath and struggled to gain control of her senses. "Please, don't," was all she could muster.

"You're right. I'm sorry." They locked eyes beneath the moonlight, neither moving. And then, on impulse, Deanna leaned against him, resting her cheek against his chest as she wrapped her arms around his body.

He smelled like fresh air, sea spray, faintly of cologne, but mostly, he smelled like Cord. She stayed like that, listening to his heart beat and memorizing his scent, until he leaned down and kissed her on her forehead, suggesting they go inside and grab a drink and some food.

Chapter 20

Stuffed filet of sole. Shrimp scampi. Bright red mountains of lobster tails. Oysters on the half shell. Sushi. Alaskan King Crab legs. Mounds of caviar. And, for the landlubber, the selections offered included slabs of roast beef, stuffed Cornish game hens, quiche, asparagus in butter sauce, Caesar salad, and loaves of warm freshly baked bread.

Cord piled Deanna's plate with one of everything he took two of—which was just about everything—despite her protests. They found a table by a window, opting to stay inside as it had grown cool on deck. Deanna picked at her food while Cord ate ravenously, as if he'd not eaten in a month.

"What's wrong?" he asked in-between mouthfuls.

"You gave me way too much food," she pointed out as she watched him pop another shrimp into his mouth.

"I have to get my money's worth, since you didn't pay for your ticket, and it doesn't appear Sophina's going to be coming down for food—or up for air for that matter." He chuckled and took a gulp of his beer.

Deanna shook her head at the ease with which he referred to his date's escapades. "Aren't you jealous?"

"No. Should I be?" He speared a piece of Deanna's uneaten shrimp and ate that one too.

"Wait a minute. Let me get this right. Sophina can openly sleep around with any man—or woman, for that matter—that she wants, and that's okay with you?"

Deanna's cheeks crimsoned with the thought, and as she drained her glass, a waiter hovering nearby replaced it with a full one. She dipped her head in gratitude and turned to stare at Cord, who had now finished both their shrimp and was picking at his crab legs.

He nodded as he sucked on a piece of the white meat he'd dipped in butter.

"But I go out for dinner and drinks with a friend and am immediately branded with a scarlet letter?" She raised her brows in quiet confusion.

Cord stopped chewing as she made her point. After a moment, he wiped his lips with the cloth napkin laying in his lap which he then placed on the table neatly beside his plate. "That was different." He spoke after considering her words for a solid minute.

A scowl marred Deanna's usually smooth features. "How so?"

"We had an agreement."

Her shoulders slumped and she blinked as she nodded slowly. "That's right. The farm."

"No. The marriage. We agreed—"

"What we agreed on was to get married so you could develop my parent's farm. How could I have been so stupid? That would have been worse than a prison sentence!" Deanna pushed away from the table and dove into the crowd.

~ ~ ~

Cord groaned in frustration and rolled his eyes as he stood up to follow her. Fate threw them together tonight. He couldn't blow it again. He took his beer and her champagne and headed for the deck, where he found Penny standing alone among the crowd. He went to her. "Hey, Pen."

She responded with an accusatory frown. "Hello, Michael."

"I guess by that greeting, Deanna was here." He grimaced and looked around the crowd. "Well. I know she couldn't have gone home. Where is she?"

"Sal took her for a walk." Then she nodded discretely beyond him.

"She's in the bathroom. Now leave her the hell alone," Sal said, approaching from behind, his face contorted in anger. "Why do you get off hurting her so much?"

Cord stared at him through narrowed eyes, his teeth clenched and the muscle in his cheek twitching overtime.

"I'll go check on her," Penny said quietly, leaving the two men alone.

"Get lost, McCord."

"You should learn to mind your own business."

"She doesn't love you. She doesn't want you. And she doesn't want anything to do with your stupid proposal." Sal turned from him, not waiting for a response, and walked toward the bar.

Each point Sal made stabbed Cord in the heart and hurt worse than the one before. He knew Deanna didn't love him, but he thought in time he could change that. To think that she didn't want him anymore, when seeing her again made him ache with his need for her in his life. That hurt bad. And the proposal. He also knew she wanted nothing to do with the proposal. But to hear the words, to know that something so important to him—preserving her family legacy in any way possible—meant nothing to someone so important to him? Now, *that* was agony.

~ ~ ~

"You all right?" Penny called into the ladies' room and was answered with the flush of a toilet. "Deanna?"

"Sorry." Deanna opened the stall, with hardly a sign she had been weeping. "All better." Her smile was overly bright.

"Thought I should check on you. Michael's outside. He's pretty upset."

Deanna barely knew this woman, but the keen sense of friendship overwhelmed her. "How well do you know Cord?"

"Pretty well." Penny nodded. "Small world, huh?"

"I wonder how it is that Randall knows them both so well and yet neither Cord nor Sal have ever run into each other before," Deanna mused aloud.

Penny snorted. "That's simple. Michael's never accepted an invitation to this kind of party before. He usually comes to the smaller socials Randy throws. He's not into any of this." She wrinkled her nose in distaste. "Neither am I," she added as an afterthought.

Deanna's eyebrows shot up in surprise. "You're not? Then what are you doing here?"

"A favor to Randall. Fundraiser for one of his friends running for congress. And, I was kind of hoping to meet up with Sal, sorry." Penny blushed, something Deanna was sure she didn't do very often.

"But what about Todd?"

"I think that's pretty much over. Besides, I've carried the torch for Sal for years. Only every time I'm available he's not. And vice versa." She took a step toward the door.

"And now?"

"Well. He's acting available." Again, she blushed. "Is he?"

Deanna chuckled at her bluntness. "Very."

"Then you wouldn't mind if we . . .?"

"As long as you don't expect me to join in." Deanna

laughed when she recalled her earlier initiation into the wild life.

"Ohhh. Did Randall?" Penny's eyes widened in horror. "He's a little free-spirited like that. But he's harmless."

"He's gorgeous. I'm sure he could do anything he wants with most women and get away with it."

"You pegged that one right. Now that we've talked about every other man we know, care to fill me in?"

"Cord."

"Yes. Cord. Sal gave me the lowdown, but it was entirely from his point of view, which is clouded by your point of view and especially, his fondness for you. It didn't sound at all like the Michael I know."

"Yes. I suppose it wouldn't." Deanna sighed and smiled sadly at Penny's reflection in the mirror as she washed her hands and checked her makeup. "Cord and I go way back. I've known him all my life. We grew up next door to each other. He was my first love."

Penny's smile was sympathetic as she leaned back against the sink and listened.

Fifteen minutes later, a pounding on the door ended Deanna's recap, which was nearly concluded anyway. Penny went and unlocked the door only to find Cord standing impatiently before them.

"Are you okay?" He focused exclusively on Deanna, not even acknowledging Penny.

"Excuse me. I've got to go find Sal. See ya!" Penny shot a grin at Deanna and slipped past Cord in a flash.

"Are you going to run from me all night?"

She stared at him for a moment, took a deep breath, then exhaled slowly. "No."

"No?"

"Is there an echo in here?" Deanna walked toward

him, suddenly finding peace in his presence. "I guess you didn't bring my drink."

He studied her warily for a moment, confusion marring his face. "I tossed it. Champagne isn't very good warm. There's a whole bar, but they won't serve you in the bathroom." He scanned the pink room before focusing on Deanna once again. "You staying in here all night or are we going to do some serious drinking?"

She shrugged. "I guess we're gonna do some serious drinking. Sal drove so . . ."

Offering a hesitant smile, Cord threw out their old challenge. "Ten bucks and a wish says I can drink you under the table."

"You're on. *Ten bucks and a wish* says you can't. But no champagne. I want a wine spritzer."

He laughed. "No wine spritzers. You're forgetting the rules. What you're drinking is your weapon."

"Well, that's not fair. I never drink champagne," she whined as she followed him to the bar.

"Then I'll drink champagne too. Fair enough?" He stopped at the outside bar and stuffed a ten-dollar bill in the crystal glass tip jar. "Freddie? Got a bottle of Moet we can snag?"

Freddie the bartender, dressed in a starched white shirt and black bow tie and slacks, grinned broadly at Cord before glancing at Deanna. "Thanks. Have fun." He popped a cork from a chilled bottle of Moet and handed it, along with two crystal fluted glasses, to Cord.

He propelled her to the stairway leading to the upper deck. From there Cord led her to a glass-enclosed lounge area, where a piano played softly and couples were immersed in conversation while seated on plush love seats placed throughout the room. Deanna breathed deeply as she admired the décor—teakwood paneling, teal wallpaper, cream carpeting.

"Nice, huh?"

"Can you imagine? I can't imagine having this much money. My whole apartment would fit in this room." Deanna shook her head in amazement as Cord found an empty couch in a softly lit corner by a window. He eased onto the sofa and placed the bottle and glasses on the table. While he poured, Deanna sat beside him still soaking in her surroundings.

"Here's to mending fences." He lifted their glasses now filled with the bubbly topaz liquid.

She smiled and clinked her glass against his, then tipped it to her lips and sipped.

"You can do better than that."

"I'm trying to drink you under the table, not pass out in a half an hour."

"No, no. Passing out is unacceptable." He took another swig. "So. Is this a truce?"

"I guess. For tonight anyway."

"I guess I should apologize."

"No. We both have too many things we probably regret. Let's start over," she said quietly before her second sip.

"From the very beginning?" He refilled his glass and leaned back.

"I guess." She gazed at him through her lashes, a tentative smile on her lips as she continued to sip her champagne. "But to do that, we have a lot to let go of and fix."

"Like?" He picked up the bottle and attempted to top off her glass.

"Like this." She covered her glass with her hand.

"You're conceding?" He laughed, but squinted in confusion.

"No. Seriously. Trust me enough to know that I decide how much champagne I want, and when I want it. Don't force me to do things your way, when you want them."

"I only want to take care of you. Why won't you let me take care of you?" He bent his head and studied their hands.

"There's taking care of me, and then there's . . ." she gently squeezed his hand as she struggled for the words. "I know you mean well, but you have to trust me in that I know how to live my life and make my own decisions. Sometimes you come off a bit . . . dominating. And controlling. And I can't live like that." She bit her lip and searched his eyes.

Silence filled the space between them, until he leaned in and stopped short of kissing her. "I get it now. I'm sorry."

Cord lightly cupped her hands in his, staring out the window at the moonlight reflecting off the calm waters of the Long Island Sound.

~ ~ ~

Two hours and two bottles of bubbly later and Deanna found that she could not stop giggling. In fact, she was laughing so hard tears were puddling her eyes.

"Mom never skied after that." Cord chuckled as he finished his story. "You should have seen her." He raised his hand and the waiter who hovered at a respectful distance responded immediately. "Another bottle, please, Paul."

"Oh, no," Deanna protested. "That will be our third!"

"You feeling sick?" He eyed her with a triumphant arch of one eyebrow.

"No. Not yet."

"You ready to concede?"

Deanna laughed as he puffed out his chest in pride. "It's not fair. You can hold more than I can."

Cord laughed heartily as Deanna burst into a peal of giggles.

"I haven't . . . laughed . . . this hard . . . in . . . years," she gasped, wiping her eyes with the back of her hand.

The grin on Cord's faced echoed her sentiments. "Me either."

"Deanna?" Sal's voice cut through the fog surrounding the two. "Are you okay?" He studied her tear-streaked face.

"I'm . . . fine!" Deanna burst out laughing before she could explain.

"You're drunk." Sal's tone was accusatory as he assessed the situation.

"No. She's happy, for once. Leave her alone."

"Well. We're getting ready to dock. I was going to ask you if you could get a ride home? Penny and I . . ."

"Penny?" Deanna queried, suddenly serious.

"Do you mind?" Sal hesitated.

"Of course not, you goose. But, uh, I'm not sure—"

"I'll take you home."

Not even acknowledging Cord, Sal turned back to Deanna. "Is that all right with you?"

"I guess." Could she trust herself, trust Cord, once they got back to her apartment?

"Well then, it's settled. I'll call you tomorrow." He nodded curtly at Cord and turned. "Be careful. And thanks," he called over his shoulder as he took off to meet up with Penny.

Cord waited until they docked, until Randall called over the speaker that the midnight run was about to begin, and then turned to Deanna. "Sal's worse than your father ever was."

Deanna watched through the window as the majority of the passengers disembarked. Motioning to them she suggested to Cord, "Maybe we should go. It's getting late."

"We could stay. They have plenty accommodations, and it's better than getting a DWI." Cord poured two more glasses of Moet, and handed Deanna her glass as the yacht lurched away from the dock.

"How long do you think this tour will last?"

"I don't know. I guess as long as Randall wants." He smiled devilishly at her. "Sometimes I hear they run all night."

"All night?" Deanna sputtered on her drink. She tried to stand but Cord placed a hand on her thigh and nudged her to stay seated. "It's too late. They won't turn this thing around. Besides, I've got an apology to make and I'm not ready to do it." He chuckled again, anticipating her anger once she realized what he had done.

"I thought we put our past behind us?" Her back stiffened as she sensed something was up.

"I did. And on that note. Here's to our past, the future . . . and tonight." He took Deanna's glass and raised it against his own, signaling her to join in his toast. When she hesitated, he questioned, "Conceding?"

"Here, here," Deanna murmured, her green eyes locked on Cord's glittering sapphire gaze. Then she tipped her head back and swallowed.

~ ~ ~

"Deanna? You're not falling asleep on me, are you?"

"Uh-uh," she offered, eyes closed as she snuggled beneath his arm that rested along the back of the sofa. She smiled as he kissed her temple.

Easing closer to her, he coaxed, "Wake up, sleepyhead. We've got another bottle to finish."

"No more. You win."

Cord gazed down at the woman sleeping beside him, wondering why God had given him a third chance. He sighed and waved over to Paul who responded immediately.

"Another bottle, sir?"

"No. We never even got through the fourth. Lightweight." He laughed softly and nodded toward Deanna who was snoring ever so daintily against his chest.

"Could you bring two coffees? Both black."

"Yes, sir."

Cord leaned over after Paul departed and kissed Deanna soundly on her lips. She was out cold. Damn. Cord hadn't thought she'd be so stubborn. He thought she'd concede before the third bottle was emptied.

Well, whatever. A bet was a bet. But with her out cold, there was no way he'd be collecting his winnings now. When Paul returned with the coffees, Cord questioned him on Randall's plans.

"I believe he's decided to anchor off shore for the evening, sir."

"Any rooms available?"

"I believe so, sir. Only three other couples stayed on. And they've already retired."

Cord glanced at his watch. Two-thirty. "Thanks a lot, Paul."

"My pleasure, sir."

Cord waved a cup of coffee under Deanna's nose, and prodded her. "Deanna. Wake up. Here. I got you some coffee. Come on, now. Atta girl. Sit up."

"Are we home yet?"

"Not quite yet. Come on. Here. Drink."

"No." She stretched and yawned as she slowly came to life. Disoriented, she stared about her.

"Where is everybody? Are we docked?"

"No. Anchored." Cord stirred sugar into his cup of coffee.

"Anchored?!"

"Yeah. Randall decided to anchor off shore."

"Cord! I can't stay here the night!"

"Why not?" He sipped the hot brew gingerly as he suppressed his laughter.

She ignored him. "I . . . I can't. I don't have a toothbrush."

"Randall keeps a full supply of all toiletries."

"I don't have anything to sleep in."

He said nothing and quirked an eyebrow in her direction.

"Cord."

"Grab your coffee and let's go on deck. I think the crew is waiting for us so they can clean up and call it a night."

"I think I'll call it a night then too." She stood up and stretched once more. "G'night."

"Wait up a sec and I'll get someone to show us to our room." He grabbed Deanna's hand and started for the dining room.

They passed through the dining area, where Cord waved to an attendant who led them to their room.

"Where the hell are we?" Deanna asked, sounding miffed.

"You'll see." They came to another carpeted hallway, lined with four narrow wooden doors to the left and four to the right. The attendant walked to the third door on the right, knocked lightly, then tried the brass handle which turned easily. He waved the couple into their room and bowed before departing.

The room was completely pitch dark until Cord flicked on the wall switch, flooding the room in a soft, amber light, revealing a décor of muted honey yellows and earthy browns. Very warm. Very comforting. Cord watched Deanna take in her surroundings as she swayed unsteadily. Two easy chairs, two night tables, a television, and a bed. "Ten bucks and a wish," she murmured.

Cord secured the door behind her and motioned to the far wall. "That's probably a closet. I'm sure there's at least two robes in there." He cracked open the other door and peered in, finding the bathroom. "And here's the shower. You want to go first?"

~ ~ ~

A short while later, relaxed by her shower and now safely snuggled under the sheets and blanket, Deanna attempted to force herself to sleep while Cord occupied the bathroom. She'd rushed through her own, afraid if she lingered he'd take that as an invitation. When she emerged scrubbed and carefully ensconced in the thick folds of the white chenille robe found in the closet, Cord chuckled at her.

"That was fast," he noted dryly as he closed the bathroom door behind him.

Now she prayed for sleep as the shower water drummed against the wall. But sleep eluded her for all her efforts. Wide-awake and sober, Deanna couldn't think for her heart was beating so wildly.

Moments later, he slipped between the covers, shut the light, and rolled over to embrace her trembling form.

And it felt good. And right. And she wondered for a moment if she had lost the bet, or were they both about to win?

"Cord?" Her voice squeaked as his lips found the smooth skin of her neck.

"Um-hm." He brought his bared leg up to cover hers. His hand fumbled beneath her robe and found her flat belly.

She tried to breath. "Do you think this is a good idea?"

"Um-hm."

"You're not listening to me."

Cord stopped for a moment and leaned back, staring at her in the darkness. "You're not reneging, are you?"

"Of course not." She tried to sound indignant.

"A bet's a bet."

"Of course it is." She tried to sound confident.

"Well?"

"What?" An awkward silence ensued in the darkness.

"Good night." He rolled over quickly, leaving Deanna facing the warm naked skin of his back.

"Cord?"

He replied with a sigh, "Go to sleep. We'll talk in the morning."

"But?" She reached out, placing a hand gently on his shoulder. His skin was warm and smooth. And he smelled so good.

"Deanna," Cord started. "It's late. I'm not going to force you to have sex with me. Go to sleep."

"Well. Thank you for not wanting to have sex with me. I mean. Not thank you. After all, a bet is a bet and you did win it. Although technically it wasn't fair to begin with because I never drink champagne. That was good champagne though, wasn't it? But still. I fell asleep, so I guess you can say you won."

Cord rolled over and sat up and laughed. "You guess? I won. You lost. You passed out."

"I fell asleep."

"You passed out cold. You were snoring." He chuckled as she shrieked in horror.

"I was not snoring!"

"Yep." He bent his head and found her nose, kissing the tip lightly. "Now go to sleep, get some rest, and let's try this in the morning when we are both a bit more clear-headed."

"But," she started as he laid back down and welcomed her into his arms, kissing her softly on her head.

~ ~ ~

Sunlight seeped through the two panels where the blackout curtains met, but for the most part, the room remained dark. Deanna eased quietly out of bed, went to the bathroom, brushed her teeth, then climbed back in beside her former lover—her ex-fiancé—before he woke up and found her missing.

"Good morning," he whispered as he rolled over. His minty fresh breath made her giggle.

"Great minds think alike?" she offered.

He kissed her softly, murmuring in agreement. She kissed him back, matching his passion and desire. He left a trail of kisses along her jaw, down her neck, and she lifted her chin unconsciously and groaned softly. Running her hands along his arms, his back, his waist, she moved closer, their legs entwining.

The rhythm of the water made the moment even more sensual, as the yacht swayed gently in the early morning light. Deanna found her body responding with an unconscious volition as Cord explored her contours and curves, dipping his head to nuzzle her breasts before circling a peak with his tongue. She moaned softly, sure that she was indeed the winner of last night's bet.

"You taste so sweet," he whispered against her softness. "You feel so good."

She molded against the length of his body, his flesh warm and firm and smooth. As skin touched skin, soft touched hard, she yielded, arching against him, bringing her arms up and around his neck. It was his turn to groan and he did so as he claimed her lips. An aching, longing sound rumbled from deep within his throat. "My God, Deanna. I want you."

"Me too. I know. So do I." Her words and the truth she spoke frightened her. Her hands roved over his back, down to the firm muscles of his bottom as she drew him closer, aching to feel him inside her, pushing, finding release, giving her satisfaction. "I want you too."

The morning was theirs, and this time there was no rush to explore one another's bodies. Two months was a long time, and for them both, this reunion was way overdue. He teased and tempted her as his tongue trailed sensuous paths along her smooth skin.

She tested and tasted him, wanting to know every inch of his flesh before this beautiful morning ended. He explored her as well, as if memorizing every sacred cell of her body. Her body was his temple, and he worshipped her by bringing her wave after wave of ecstasy, coaxing her release time and again. And when he brought her sweet release, she cried out uncontrollably, "I love you."

He groaned, crushing her lips with a kiss so consuming it stole her breath away, he nudged her onto her back, and followed her, parting her legs with his thick, muscled thigh. His hips pressed her into the bed, urging her to respond. She did, rising up to meet his every move. He took her then. One thrust and she was his.

They lay still for a moment, the realization of what they were doing now hitting them full force. Unable to turn back Cord cried out her name and moved deeply. Deanna responded as forcefully, raking her fingernails down the length of his back, raising her hips to join him in that timeless love dance. Skin against skin, lips against lips, passion meeting passion. They rose and fell like the ebb and flow of the Long Island Sound, until their desires culminated in a tidal wave of sensation washing over them, like the tide washes over the beach.

The room was silent but for the whispered, erratic pace of their breathing.

Cord kissed her tousled head. "Well, I guess this changes everything."

Deanna didn't answer him as she rested her cheek against his chest, the sound of his heartbeat lulling her back to sleep.

~ ~ ~

It was nearly noon when Cord unceremoniously jerked the covers from her body, jarring her awake as he stood up. Grabbing her hand, he urged, "C'mon, sleepyhead. Boat's gonna dock and I want a shower."

"I'm so tired!" She needed to sleep. Maybe when she awoke she would find that this had all been a dream. A wonderful, horrible dream.

"Up. Let's shower."

"We showered already," she argued as he tugged her to sit up, then nudged her from the bed. She unraveled the white cotton blanket from the heap of covers at the foot of the bed, and wrapped it around her for protection from the cool morning air.

"Sleep is for the weak," he called over his shoulder as he set the water.

"You're crazy." Deanna eyed him warily as he turned to face her, naked and obviously ready to make love again. She suppressed a smile.

"No. I'm determined. How often does a guy get a third chance?"

Deanna shook her head at him, and forced a little laugh, suddenly uneasy with his words. This was too casual for her, and though it meant something to her, she knew this was probably normal for Cord. Her heart ached, but so did her body. And she knew in her heart that he was right. Enjoy the moment now. Worry about it all tomorrow. After all, how often did a girl get a third chance?

He stepped into the shower and bent his head around the translucent curtain.

Stifling a smile, she groaned in mock defeat, dropping the blanket to let it pool about her bared feet as she reached for his outstretched hand.

As she stepped into the shower stall he moved aside to share the pulsing hot water stream with her. "See? This isn't so bad?" He bent his head to gently lap the river of shower water cascading over her shoulder.

"That feels delicious," she purred, then added, "but we don't have time."

He laughed and brushed her skin lightly with his teeth. He squeezed her hard, then let her go as he reached for the bar of soap and washcloth. "Wanna bet?"

"I don't think so. Haven't I lost enough bets?" Deanna closed her eyes as she felt his lathered hands slide the length of her spine, beginning at her shoulders and moving downward.

"Now you're learning, Drake. That's a girl." His voice was melodious and low, and as he whispered into her ear Deanna felt his hands slip around her waist then come up to cup her breasts. She shivered at his touch and arched against him, her back firmly planted against his chest. His lips found her earlobe and he nibbled softly. "Now this is how it's supposed to be, isn't it?"

Deanna nodded, then shook her head, unable to find the strength to agree or disagree with him. As she closed her eyes she knew there was only one thing she did know at this moment in time. He was her tormentor and her savior. Her life and her death. But he was hers. At least for the moment.

Chapter 21

They were silent for most of the ride back to Manhattan. Deanna was mortified for so many reasons, but especially for wearing an evening gown at two o'clock in the afternoon. She had to prepare for the dreaded Walk of Shame she'd have to take from his car to her apartment. Hopefully he'd find a close spot to park. She didn't even dare to think about everything that had transpired last night and then today.

In the darkness of the Midtown Tunnel Cord spoke first. "Well? Are you going to say anything to me this morning?"

"I wouldn't know where to begin." She softly.

"How's the hangover?" He chuckled.

"Don't even start."

"We should drink champagne more often," he said, reaching out for her hand and giving it a light squeeze. If possible her face grew hotter with his comment.

"You're not funny," she argued, knowing full well what he was implying with "champagne."

"I'm not trying to be funny. A lot of our problems could be solved if we took the time to drink more champagne."

"We've probably had too much champagne for our own good."

"Hmmm. Sure didn't seem like that last night. Or this morning. I think we should have more champagne more often."

"This doesn't change anything, you know. All the champagne in the world with you won't change a thing."

"I thought last night could be a fresh start." He glanced over at her, braking quickly as traffic nearly halted to a near stop then began crawling again.

"Fresh start? No. Last night was . . ."

"Good sex?" He clenched his jaw and stared straight ahead, both hands now on the wheel.

"Yes. That's it. Good sex." She stared out the window, hands clenched in her lap.

"I thought we called a truce?"

"I don't' want a truce. I don't want to have anything to do with you." Somehow the words sounded hollow and meaningless.

They came to the end of the tunnel and Michael glanced at her in the bright sunlight, then focused his gaze on maneuvering through the Sunday traffic.

"Where is this coming from? That's not at all what you said last night."

She cringed, hoping he hadn't heard, or that she had dreamed it. Or that he would not remember.

"Well it's what I'm saying now."

"You little liar."

"You don't know. You don't know anything," she mumbled.

"I know what I know. We made love. And that counts for something."

"It was good sex. That's all. Good sex." Her voice trembled.

"You are wrong. And give me today and I'll prove it. You love me. You know you do. When will you stop fighting me?"

When you tell me you love me. And mean it. Her heart answered him but those words never made it to her lips. "When you realize I won't marry you so you can develop my family's farm."

"I don't need you to do that." He stopped and waited for the light to change.

"You're right. You don't need me. So why are you even bothering?"

He was silent for a moment, then spoke slowly. "I've submitted the change of zone application. And my lawyer has advised me to move forward with my petition to the courts."

A sob escaped Deanna's lips as she once again focused beyond the passenger side window. Buildings, pedestrians, and yellow cabs passed unseen.

"Deanna. It doesn't have to be this way."

"Yes it does. Your way or else."

"It would be good."

"Don't you get it? I want more! I don't want it to be good! I want it to be great!"

"It was great! We are great together!"

"Don't play with me. How can you joke? I'm not talking about sex. I'm talking about love. Trust, honesty, consideration. Sharing hopes and dreams. Raising a family."

"I can give you all that."

"But for all the wrong reasons!" She groaned in frustration. "Don't you get it? You can't buy me. You want the farm, take it. But you're not going to take me with it."

"We would be so good together, if you'd trust me."

She shook her head. "I can't trust you."

"Why not?" He parked the car half a block from her apartment.

"I don't know."

"There's nothing to be afraid of." He hit the emergency brake and shut the car off.

Deanna watched through veiled eyes as she bent her head to study her hands twisting nervously in her lap. "What are you doing?"

"Parking."

She shook her head.

"Okay, then. What am I doing?"

"No. Don't park."

"Can I at least use your bathroom? If not, tell me where the nearest McDonald's is."

She sighed in frustration. "Okay. Use it. But that's all. Then I want you out. Got it?"

"Yeah, sure."

~ ~ ~

After donning her customary Sunday garb of sweat pants and tee shirt, Deanna emerged from her bedroom to find the living room and kitchen empty. Her heart sank with disappointment as she cast a quick glance in the direction of the bathroom, its door open and the overhead light off. She sighed and walked into the kitchen, questioning her sanity. He was gone. She told him he couldn't stay and he respected her boundary. But he hadn't even said goodbye, she realized running tap water to make a pot of coffee. Half a pot. How could she miss him already? What was wrong with her? Her apartment suddenly felt so, so vacant. Filling the coffee basket with gourmet coffee—the one she saved for when she had her period or company—the swoosh of the sliding doors leading to the patio sounded behind her. She suppressed a smile, then scolded herself once more for her fickle heart. Whoever heard of rejoicing the company of the man you vowed to hate. *One cup of coffee. That's it. Then he's got to go.*

She waited at the counter one more second after she flipped the coffee maker on, expecting him to come up behind her and touch her like he always did. Something about Cord and kitchens, she mused with a smile, which faded within a moment as she heard him moving about the living room. *Stop. It.* She turned around to join him, her face a blank mask.

Cord was standing by the couch leafing through the latest edition of *The New Yorker*. She watched his actions still as she walked toward him, but he did not acknowledge her. Not until she came to stand by his side.

"I left some things here I guess I should collect." He also wore an unreadable expression. "Maybe I can change out of this monkey suit."

"Sure. Your things are in here." Deanna nodded toward the bedroom, a lump forming in her throat. He followed her until he reached the doorway, then halted as she walked across the darkened bedroom to the closet where, after she had washed and dried them, Deanna had hung the slacks and shirt he'd worn the day it had rained. Turning, taking great care not to trip or bump into anything beneath his scrutiny, she laid them on her bed, then walked to her dresser, where she pulled out his socks and underwear. She struggled not to hug his boxers to her chest, conflicted with the finality of her actions. "You need to shower or anything?"

"With you?" He raised an eyebrow as he leaned casually against the doorjamb.

"Of course not!" she snapped, now aware of how stupid she sounded.

"No thanks, then. We showered on the boat, once last night, if I recollect correctly. And twice this morning not more than, what, two hours ago?" He smiled at her then. "I'll just get changed, thanks."

She blushed once again then headed toward the living room, carefully sidestepping Cord as she did so. Her hands trembled as moments later she set out two blue coffee mugs. She felt, rather than heard, him behind her, and called out, "Can you stay for a cup of coffee?"

He said nothing as she turned and came toward him into the living room, a mug in each hand. Setting them both down on the table she sat on the edge of her green checked easy chair. Cord continued to stand, eyeing her. "Why the change of heart?"

She shook her head. "I'm trying to be friendly."

"What a novel idea," he remarked dryly, bending to pick up the steaming mug.

"Yes, well." She glanced down at her hands laying in her lap. "Have you, uh, seen Trish lately?"

Cord eyed her with a guarded expression shadowing his eyes. He nodded and sipped his coffee, then sat on the end of the couch facing Deanna.

"They'll be moving soon. They found a place in Honesdale. Pennsylvania."

"What about the house?"

Cord shrugged. "It'll stay empty."

"Aren't you guys gonna rent it out? Or are you going to tear it down?"

He shook his head. "They took their cut in the place. The house is yours. And mine. It's in the agreement. There will be no tearing down."

"An agreement I didn't sign!"

"You had no need to. Two-thirds."

"I know." She sighed wearily and shrugged as she sunk into the overstuffed chair. "So you're going to let it rot away?"

Cord shrugged.

"You won't rent it?"

"Too much work to fix up for renters. And they'd only trash it again."

"It seemed structurally sound. I mean, there isn't any roof damage, or cracks in the foundation, is there?"

"No."

"Then what's the problem?"

"What's the problem?" He leaned forward, studying her hard. "The problem is, if you came *home* more, you'd know." His voice was barely more than a whisper.

"But I don't, and I'm asking you to tell me." She set her chin stubbornly.

"Why? Why care now, all of a sudden?"

"Because it's my house. I have a right to care, don't I?"

"It's about time."

"What's that supposed to mean?" Little by little, their voices had gotten louder until now Deanna practically shouted, insulted by his assumptions.

"I mean, you haven't come around for years, except for your dad's funeral and then Easter, and *now* you're taking an interest. Just stating a fact, ma'am."

"Yeah, well. I don't like your implications."

"Facts."

"Whatever." She stood up now, and walked to the sliding doors to study her meager garden. "I don't want to see that crumble away, like, like . . ." *Like everything else in my life.*

"Deanna, I've got too many other things to do. Like I said, it's not completely my responsibility. Do something."

"Yeah, like what? Snap my fingers. Poof. House repaired. Poof. Tenants found."

"Yeah. Poof." He drained his mug and set it down hard on the coffee table. "I'll do my share, if you do yours." He stood up.

"I don't want to do my share. I don't want to share anything with you," she cried, jumping up to stand beside him.

"Too bad. Deal with it." He walked to the door.

"Wait."

Her words halted him, but he didn't turn around until a good minute of silence passed. "What?"

"I—" She shook her head, not knowing how to keep him a little longer without groveling.

"Deanna. I'm not laying out any more money. I'm tired of being used. First your family, then you—"

"I'm not like them!"

"No? You're right. You're worse. They needed my money, but at least they trusted me. You don't give a damn about what I want. Well, Deanna. You're going to have to settle for good sex," he taunted, throwing her earlier words back at her. "I can't give any more than that right now."

And with that he was gone.

Chapter 22

Autumn flew by and before Deanna realized, the four-day Thanksgiving holiday was looming one short afternoon away. Wednesday was filled with the decline of numerous Thanksgiving Day dinner offers from friends and co-workers as quitting time neared. More inspired than embarrassed by the invitations, Deanna stopped at the corner grocer on the way home and bought all the trimmings for a turkey dinner . . . for one. Her next stop was the liquor store, where she picked up a large bottle of Renee Junot, the one tradition she'd begun and followed since her mother died. It was the only way to get through the actual holidays, both Thanksgiving and Christmas.

Surprisingly, the bottle remained unopened Thanksgiving Day, with Deanna finding herself sleepy and weepy enough already, and not in the mood to drink herself into oblivion.

Friday morning came and Deanna forced herself to join the throngs who surged through the shops and malls for the traditional Black Friday shopping craze. She found a housewarming/Christmas gift for Sal and Penny, and something for her boss, purchasing both in a heartbeat.

The thought of gifts she found but did not purchase remained constant in her memory Friday evening, and all day Saturday. A navy-blue cotton sweater and an amethyst tie clip for Cord. And a beautiful leather briefcase—something she realized Cord could use as she recalled the beat up one he carried at the town meeting so long ago.

She frowned with the recollection, wondering if he, like she did with familiar possessions, clung to the briefcase as if it were another appendage, an old friend, never noticing the battering it took and its resulting wounds.

Instead of buying that one for Cord, she shopped for a briefcase for herself, planning to wrap it and stick it under the tree. If she decided to put one up.

Trish also came to mind as Deanna browsed through the Cellar at Macy's. Kitchen gadgets, salad bowls, clocks, and cookie jars shaped like English country cottages filled the shelves. What was her sister's new house like? Did she need anything? Would she get a Christmas card from her this year? Should she send one to Trish and Pike? What about Mike and Jane? Cord?

That thought led her to the card shop, where she purchased a box of the latest Christmas line put out by Susan Wheeler, an artist whose career she'd been following for years, ever since Deanna had found a calendar with the little drawings of mice and rabbits and birds dressed like people living beneath trees and within cracks and walls of homes.

She spent Friday night filling out the cards, as was tradition. Cards for the McCords and Trish and Pike were addressed and banded with a few others for mailing. She hoped the Olde Westfield post office would forward Trish and Pike's card to their new address. Deanna also signed one off for Cord, but kept it separate in case she changed her mind.

Saturday morning, Deanna walked down to the post office, mailed her cards, holding Cord's in her pocket, and checked her box. Along with bills and advertisements she found a notice that she needed to sign for a delivery at the desk. Curious, she went to the line, wondering as she waited what it could be.

Moments later, as she stood by the garbage can, she read the public hearing notice clutched within trembling hands. The change of zone hearing was scheduled for the Tuesday before Christmas. The Tuesday before Christmas! How could they? Deanna thought, biting her lower lip and fighting back the tears. *How could they?*

Of course, she would have to go. Or would she? she pondered as she tossed the envelope, junk fliers, and Cord's un-mailed Christmas card into the trash can.

Could she bear it? Being there so close to Christmas? Seeing him? Having to dredge up all those old memories again? She walked in a daze along the crowded sidewalks, as if on automatic pilot as she winded her way home. She knew it was going to happen. She had been wondering when the hearing would be ever since Cord had told her he filed the application. But did it have to happen so close to the holiday?

Memories of that last Christmas before Mom died were bittersweet. It was the first Christmas she and Cord had been broken up. All Deanna had wanted to do was cry, but Mom was tough. She wouldn't let her baby suffer, so she put her to work. Work was always a cure-all for Mom, Deanna thought now with a chuckle.

After reaching her apartment building, Deanna climbed the steps, putting her reminiscing on hold until she reached her apartment. There she found a small sauce pot, filled it with milk, and placed it on the stove. As the milk warmed, Deanna went into her bedroom to shed her coat and clothes and slip into sweats and a tee shirt. Moments later, she sat on her green-checked chair flipping through her mail, sipping her hot cocoa and thinking about Mom. She put down the telephone bill as she recalled her mother's words.

"Deanna! Get up from that bed this instant. I'll not have you wallowing around, moping all day when we've got things to do!"

Deanna recalled with ease that scolding as if it were yesterday. She had tried to ignore her mother's orders without success.

Her mother had ripped the sheets and quilts off her body and bed, then stormed over to the window to yank back the curtains. "We've got baking to do. You've got to run the food baskets over to the church. I need you today. God knows I can't rely on Patricia or your father. Come on, young lady, I've got your eggs on."

Deanna smiled, a solitary tear collecting in the corner of her eye. "Mom." Her whisper echoed in the silence of the apartment. Mom had worked her to death that Christmas Eve. Baking, packing the food baskets, going to the church. Then when Deanna had finished her chores, Mom had her wrapping toys and dropping them off at the local toy collection center for Christmas Eve delivery "for the less fortunate souls," as Mom deemed to refer to the needy.

Not once had she thought about Cord, Deanna remembered with a smile. Mom had been right. As always. Work had been the perfect cure-all. Deanna frowned deeply in thought for a moment, then flipped through her mail searching for the weekly local mailer. Sure enough, it was there. She skimmed through the pages for the Community Column. When she found it, she scanned the print until her eyes came upon the holiday ad she had seen recent weeks.

"'Volunteers wanted,'" she read aloud. "'Santa's run out of elves to wrap and deliver toys to good little boys and girls. For more information . . .'"

Deanna grabbed her cellphone and dialed the number with anticipation. "It's beginning to look a lot like Christmas," she whispered in tune as she counted three rings. When a female voice answered, Deanna's heart skipped a beat. She cleared her throat then spoke hesitantly, "I'm calling about your ad for elves?"

~ ~ ~

The next three weeks flew by in a whirlwind, between Christmas parties given by her co-workers and her volunteer efforts which kept her out four to five nights a week. Not only had she eased the ache in her heart by helping others, she met new friends, many of whom had focused energies on volunteering for reasons similar to her own: to assuage the loneliness.

Sheila was one such comrade. Raised in orphanages ever since she was abandoned by her mother at ten years old, Sheila had often relied on the generosity of others throughout the Christmas holidays. Had it not been for donations each year she would never know the joy of receiving, the joy that had nurtured her desire to give now as an adult. As a result of the absence of a loving mother or father, or siblings for that matter, Sheila was very introverted, protected by self-imposed barriers no adult had been able to penetrate.

Until Deanna came along. Deanna saw her as her personal ward, and being seven years Sheila's senior, Deanna had immediately adopted her as another baby sister. At first Sheila staved off Deanna's attempts at friendship, sticking mainly to checking in deliveries and wrapping presents. But Deanna recognized pain when she saw it, and was determined to make the young woman feel included, needed, and appreciated.

It was less than two weeks until Christmas Eve, and Deanna was standing beside Sheila wrapping the last load of the evening. It was nearly midnight and all the other "elves" were calling out suggestions of where to meet after they closed shop. When a local coffee café was settled on, Deanna turned to Sheila, her often-silent partner but one Deanna could always count on to lend a hand or join her on a delivery.

"You coming?" Deanna waited for Sheila's customary decline.

"Not tonight." Sheila smiled apologetically.

Deanna pursed her lips and frowned.

"What?"

Deanna sighed. "Forget it."

"No. What's wrong? Are you mad at me?" Concern was etched in the young girl's pale blue eyes.

"Of course not. I just feel badly."

"Why? I'm not stopping you."

"No. But everybody else's partner is going and . . . Oh, forget it. It sounds so trite. Never mind."

"Are you going?"

"No. I don't want to." Deanna gathered her purse and slipped her cell phone out to check for messages

"Of course you do. I can see it." Sheila waved a hand at her.

"Yeah, but, not if you don't want to," Deanna said with a shrug.

"It's not that I don't want to. But. Well. They always pick someplace expensive. I can't afford—"

"Is that all?" Deanna smiled warmly. "My treat."

"No. Don't be stupid. I'm not a charity case." Sheila's fair face blushed pink, making her blond hair seem platinum.

"Charity? Honey, you'd be doing me the favor. I don't want to go home to my apartment. It's so lonely. But I'm not going by myself. I don't know too many of the others. I'd have no one to hang with."

Sheila stared wistfully at the team of volunteers now packing away their supplies until next week. "Well. I suppose so. I'm not thirsty, but I'll come to keep you company."

"Great. Let's clean up and get out of here." Deanna smiled again, pleased she and Sheila would be joining the get-together.

The café was small, so it appeared crowded with only six other patrons filling half of the round oak tables for two. There was one long table parallel to the furthest floral-papered wall, which Deanna and Sheila claimed for themselves and the others. The waitress came over, took their orders of two cappuccinos, as well as Deanna's warning of "there's a big crowd coming, get ready," as she nodded to the rest of the table.

As Deanna spoke, Sheila removed a simply wrapped package about the size of a lingerie box from her carry all. It was wrapped in white paper and tied with a red satin ribbon. "For you. I was going to give it to you before we left." She handed it to Deanna with a shrug.

Smiling, Deanna accepted the gift and then reached into the shopping bag by her side. She handed Sheila a small box that was covered in red and green paper designed with Christmas trees in various stages of decorations. It too was tied with a red sash. "Open yours first," Deanna directed unnecessarily, as Sheila untied the bow.

Seconds later, Sheila lifted the box top off with a gasp. She tentatively reached in to retrieve a small porcelain statue swaddled within the tissue paper. Two little mice garbed in dresses fashioned from the late 1800s, sat before a fireplace with a fire burning and a Christmas tree. Around the base of the statue was printed a saying: *Like the Christmas Yule log burning bright, your friendship warms me through the night.*

Eyes bright with unshed tears, Sheila gazed up at Deanna with a timid smile. "You are the first real friend I've ever had. I love it. Thank you."

Embarrassed, Deanna quirked an eyebrow at her. "Can I open mine now?"

Blushing, Sheila nodded, slipping her treasure back into the box. "It's not as nice as yours."

"Are you crazy, Sheila? Anything given from the heart is a gift well received. My mom used to say that." Deanna surprised herself with that bit of information, having forgotten those words until that moment. The white paper came away with a slight tug from the small package as she spoke. Deanna cooed with delight as she removed the lid and folded back the tissue paper. "Sheila! It's beautiful! Where ever did you find this?"

Sheila's faced crimsoned again as she reluctantly admitted. "I did it myself."

An oval-framed oil painting of a white country cottage, complete with front porch, corn fields, and smoke spiraling from the chimney was lifted from the box. "It is beautiful!" Deanna said softly, taking in the detail. In the corner, an orange tabby chased a black cat. On a tree limb, a mother blue bird fed a worm to her young chick cradled in a nest.

"I grew up in the city," Sheila explained. "But you talk about your childhood and your home with such love, such detail, that this is how I imagined it would be."

"It's beautiful," Deanna said, an ache tugging at her heart. Home! It suddenly hit her. Hit her hard. She wanted to go home. "This is the most beautiful Christmas present I've ever received."

"You're just saying that."

Deanna shook her head, tears spilling from her green eyes. "You'll never know, Sheila."

The door of the cafe opened and a blast of cold air filled the small room. The toy drive volunteers poured in laughing and talking and bringing life to the otherwise quiet coffee shop. Greetings were exchanged, coffee's and desserts were ordered, and while they waited, everyone recapped what their holiday plans included.

When it was Deanna's turn, she very hesitantly, very softly shared, "I'm going home." She didn't elaborate that no one would be there to celebrate with, but by telling everyone her plans she was willing herself to commit to this decision.

All too soon, the cappuccinos and hot cocoas were finished and Brad, the crew leader, reminded everyone that deliveries began next Friday evening. That would give them three nights including Christmas Eve to get the presents to the families. Deanna frowned as she slipped into her cloak, recalling that she had set up a Christmas Eve delivery with Brad. Now, as the elves filed out the door arm in arm, Deanna tugged at Brad's sleeve and asked him to wait up.

"I need to change my pickup and delivery date." Her heart was racing with the idea that had come to her as she was opening her present from Sheila.

"You set it for Christmas Eve, didn't you?" Brad held the door open for her and peered at her through his glasses.

"I have to change it to a week earlier—probably Monday night."

He sighed at the news of the schedule change, "What's up?"

"Well." Deanna inhaled, and then let her breath out slowly, steadying her nerves and voice, and told him about the Tuesday evening public hearing that she had to attend. She then added, "So I've decided . . . I'm going home for Christmas."

Chapter 23

The rain was falling hard Tuesday evening as Deanna handed the taxicab driver a twenty and waited for her change. It was already 8 o'clock and she tried to ignore the knot in her stomach, wondering if she'd missed anything. Taking her change from the driver, she reminded him to pick her up at ten o'clock sharp.

"You got it, lady," he said, impatience tinging his words.

"I shouldn't call?"

"Hey? I give ya my word. I'll be here."

Deanna nodded at his wrinkled face in the rearview mirror, lifted the hood of her cloak and grabbed the handle of her garment bag, preparing to hoist it out of the car, wishing she had dropped it off at the house.

Too late now, she chided herself as she made her way in a dash up the stairs and into the lighted corridor that led to the auditorium. A call made to the town clerk's office earlier that day had provided Deanna with a verbal recount of the evening's agenda, which listed the change of zone on her farm as item six out of eight. The secretary had estimated each hearing would last anywhere from 15 minutes to an hour, with most being unquestioned so probably lasting 15 minutes each. They should be getting ready to hear it now, Deanna thought, hurrying to the town hall's back entrance.

She opened the door to find the hallway overflowing with attendees to the hearing, as the auditorium was jammed to nearly standing room only. A respectful hush quieted what should have been an unruly crowd. Deanna recognized a few faces from the previous hearing. Some were old friends of her family, and she assumed they had come out to oppose Cord's plans. As she wove her way through to the center aisle, Deanna nodded to those who acknowledged her, not paying attention to the voice that now boomed authoritatively over the speakers; at least not until she chose an aisle seat halfway toward the front of the room. LaScala, she noticed, had eyed her from the moment she opened the door. She sat down as the supervisor nodded in her direction and Deanna finally focused on the speaker.

"So, in closing, I'd like to invite anyone up here— after the hearing, of course—to review the preliminary site plan on display. The architects and my attorney, as well as myself, will remain behind to answer any questions. Thank you, members of the board, and ladies and gentlemen, members of the community—" Cord turned at that moment to address the crowd, and as if by radar, focused on Deanna. He cleared his throat and continued, the slightest trace of a smile tugging at his lips. "—for your support and for joining me here this evening. I appreciate your efforts."

Deanna watched, with a bit of pride, albeit reluctantly, swelling within her breast. The crowd applauded as he waved at them, and for a brief instant Deanna was confused. These people were smiling. And clapping. Clapping? With a quizzical frown etched above her eyebrows, she nodded as Cord came to stand beside her, his eyes warm and bright.

"To what do I owe this honor?" he murmured as he stepped over her legs to take the seat beside her.

"Honor?" Deanna quirked a finely shaped brow at the man sitting beside her. "Don't flatter yourself. I guess I didn't believe you'd do this."

"I—*we*—have no choice."

"Yes, *we* do. You're being greedy."

"Greedy? I'm willing to split everything with you—geez, marry you—"

"Marry me!" Deanna hissed. "Don't give me that crap. We both know why you wanted to marry me! I'm not stupid."

Cord said nothing, staring straight ahead with his mouth clamped shut. Deanna studied the muscle twitching in his left cheek while he in turn focused on LaScala calling for those favoring the proposal to step forward to the microphone as their names were called. One by one, each speaker listed a multitude of reasons for supporting McCord's proposal.

"Construction jobs . . . affordable housing . . . quality shopping . . . environmental reasons . . . more jobs . . . boost to the economy . . . It will put Olde Westfield on the map . . . Our own Main Street . . . "

And as each speaker stepped up to the microphone, Deanna watched Cord's face soften, felt her own tighten in misery. After an hour of speakers favoring the project, LaScala asked for a show of hands of proponents of the proposal. Deanna fought back a sob as nearly every hand in the room was raised. LaScala thanked the crowd, then asked for a show of hands of those opposing the project, his gaze focused on Deanna as he spoke.

She raised her hand, along with one other person, Mr. Samuel—the same speaker who had played his guitar sitting beside his invalid mother at the last hearing Deanna attended. As she rested her arm she turned to Cord, expecting to find a leer, expecting him to snicker and taunt her. But what she found instead was sympathy—*or was it disappointment?*—awash in his eyes. Deanna swallowed thickly, blinking hard to fight the tears that threatened to spill. She had lost.

When the supervisor invited the opposition to speak, Mr. Samuel stood up. "Oh, no," Deanna murmured to herself. Her face felt flush as Cord chuckled softly beside her, rummaging through his briefcase she never even noticed had been laying on the third seat when she chose to sit here earlier.

"Supervisor LaScala? Members of the board? I find the raping and pillaging of our lands disgusting, demoralizing, and deplorable. Your heartless and obvious support of this modern-day pirate's exploits is inexcusable. And to voice my opposition, my heartfelt support to Miss Drake and all her family heritage and contributions to the Island, I've written a little ditty." He placed a small harmonica to his mouth and blew softly, ignoring the chuckles and snickers sounding around him.

Deanna closed her eyes and shook her head, wishing she had never hopped the LIRR earlier this afternoon.

Clicking the vintage cassette recorder on the table before him, Mr. Samuels waited for the tinny banjo music to begin, then started singing. "Old Mr. Drake had a farm, EIEIO. And on this farm, he tilled the soil, EIEIO. Like his daddy did, his grandad did, and all the Drakes since the 1600s did. Old Mr. Drake had a farm. EIEIO.

"But then one day developers came. EIEIO. And they drew up plans to take it away. EIEIO. With a chop-a-tree here, and a chop-a-tree there, here a chop, there chop, everywhere a chop. Until the land was flat and smooth, EIEIO."

"Mr. Samuel, thank you—" LaScala interjected.

"I'm not done yet." Mr. Samuel's cast a watery glance toward the supervisor and board.

"Let him sing," someone shouted from the audience and the crowd burst into laughter.

"I'm getting out of here." Deanna started to stand, but Cord held her fast with his grasp on her forearm.

"Aren't you going to speak?" The mirth was evident in his eyes.

"Go to hell. And let go of my arm." Deanna attempted to jerk away, but Cord held fast.

"You'll insult the man if you leave now. Come on, Deanna. He may be your only supporter."

"—Soon the roads were crowded full, EIEIO—"

"Mr. Samuel!! You're out of order!"

"—No more pigs, chicks, cows, or bulls. EIEIO."

"Security?" LaScala motioned to the officers at the back of the room.

"No moo moo here, cluck cluck there, only an oink from the pigs who dared—"

"Where the hell is security?" LaScala boomed into the microphone as he glared at the men in uniform who appeared to be enjoying the performance.

"—to rape and pillage Old Drake's Farm. EEEE—IIII—EEEE—IIIIIIIIIIII—OOOOOOOOOOOOO." Mr. Samuel stood up and held out his arms as two security guards dressed in full uniform came to escort him out. The audience booed, cheered, laughed, and applauded as he bowed and took leave peacefully.

The gavel sounded and LaScala called for the next speaker, once again directing his hardened gaze at Deanna.

"Well?" Cord turned to her.

"Well, what?"

"I believe that was a personal invitation from your good friend—"

"He can stick his personal invitation up his—" Deanna stood up this time, her voice echoing in the now silent auditorium. Someone snorted and someone gasped at her suggestion as she stormed out the back door and spied the taxi cab waiting for her.

She ran down the steps and jumped in, telling him to step on it. It was only when they were turning onto Route 112 that Deanna realized a major faux pas. She'd forgotten her suitcase. Well. Let security take it. She'd pick it up tomorrow. All she wanted to do now was go home. Her real home, she realized. Not her apartment. Take a bath. Go to bed. Her body ached. Her heart ached. Her pride ached.

~ ~ ~

The porch light was on, much to Deanna's surprise. And, after she paid the cabbie, walked up the porch steps, and unlocked the door she began to wonder why the electric had not been turned off, and was the water still running? Was there oil in the tank? She hadn't thought about any of this. Much to Deanna's surprise and amazement, after a quick assessment, she realized everything but the telephone was still hooked up.

Thank goodness. All Deanna needed right now was a bit of pampering. And it came in the form of a bath. The water was hot, steaming, and the perfect cure-all for Deanna's bruised spirit. Lacking bubble bath, she improvised and poured shampoo into the running water. Moments later she immersed herself up to her chin in the tub.

As she had expected and hoped, Trish had the forethought—or was it laziness?—to leave the house and possessions completely intact. Towels, sheets. Deanna's room. Everything was left as if someone had been here that day. Only the kitchen had been touched. But even so, most of Mom's pots, all the dishes and glassware, flatware and utensils still filled the drawers and cabinets.

As Deanna sighed and closed her eyes, she realized Trish and Pike must have made a pretty penny from Cord. "Who said blood was thicker than water?" she asked to no one in particular.

As Deanna soaked, head resting against her mother's well-worn, vintage foam bath pillow, she wondered what was going to happen next. Cord was obviously going to get the change of zone. But since she hadn't agreed to anything, hadn't signed a thing, what could happen next? Could he truly petition the courts to get her to agree to sell? Couldn't she sue him for moving forward without her signature? And his site plan still had to be approved. Had it even gone before the planning board yet? She sighed, letting the water ease her aches. Her heavy lids drooped, her head nodded and Deanna succumbed to the hypnotic pull of the relaxing effect of her bath.

~ ~ ~

Cord struggled to keep from chasing after Deanna as she fled the auditorium. He struggled to maintain a calm exterior as people congratulated him, asked questions, and patted him on the back. It was not often both builders and environmentalists approved of the same project. He deserved the praise, he had it coming. Why, then, he questioned himself as he stood there smiling and nodding at remarks made by his supporters, did he feel as if his world was crumbling down around him?

By the time the auditorium had nearly emptied out, LaScala came up to Cord with a toothy grin on his face. "Ya did it, Mikey." LaScala slapped him on the back in camaraderie. "Ya won 'em."

Forcing a smile, Cord nodded at the supervisor, who had spent the last ten minutes speaking with his mom and dad. "Where'd my parents go?"

"They're out in the hall waiting on you. Hey, what'd Drake have to say?"

"Not much." Cord answered as he stared distractedly at the door, wondering if Deanna had returned to the city or to her home. *Their home*, Cord corrected himself. The thought brought the slightest curve to his lips, and yet it was his first real smile all night.

"Did you see her face," LaScala said, "when everyone in the crowd supported you?" His laugh was victorious, his brown eyes dark with satisfaction. "Ha. Old Samuel's enough to turn anyone's opinion around. You haven't been at the recent board meetings he's been at, fighting this thing tooth and nail."

"I read about it." Cord's gaze swept around the room, searching for a reason to leave when he spotted a suitcase sitting against the back wall. His heart thumped with a strange thought. He didn't recognize it, but then again, he'd never seen Deanna's luggage. Could it be? The room was vacant, but for he and the supervisor, whose words were now falling on Cord, then rolling off like water off a rain slicker. "Will you excuse me?"

Cord left him and walked over to the tapestry-covered suitcase. Kneeling, he lifted the tags attached to the black leather handle and smiled as he found his reason to leave scrawled elegantly and encased in plastic. Deanna Drake. Apartment 12 B, Terrace Tower, New York, New York. She wouldn't be going there tonight. Not this late. She was planning on staying at the house. For Christmas? Or only tonight? He stood up and tested the suitcase, and noting its heaviness, he determined she was planning on staying more than one day.

He turned to LaScala who had now joined him and Cord answered his unasked question without delay. "Deanna's."

"Want me to have security lock it up?"

"Nah. I'll take it over to her. I'm sure she's got a few things she wants to say." He chuckled, wondering if God was giving him yet another chance to make things right with Deanna.

"Tell her I didn't appreciate her departure—nor her suggestion—which I imagine was meant for me," LaScala said with a snort.

His words only made Cord's smile deepen, as he recalled Deanna's hasty exit.

"Michael? Are you ready?" Jane popped her head in through the doorway. "Your father's waiting by the car."

"Sure thing, Mom. All right then, Mr. Supervisor, Merry Christmas." He extended a hand to the man standing beside him. They shook hands with a firm, sure grip, then walked to the woman in gray beckoning to her son.

"Michael? What's that?" She nodded toward the luggage. "Is that Deanna's? That was Deanna, wasn't it? We thought so."

Cord nodded, grinning devilishly. "She came."

"Do you think she's home?"

"From the feel of this, she mighta been planning to stay for the holiday." He put his arm around his mother and led her out the door.

"You'd better go over there. She needs you."

"I'm the last person she needs right now."

"Then I'll go over there."

"No, Mom. I'll bring over her suitcase. If she wants to talk, I'll stay. Otherwise I'll give her some space. Trust me."

"Why should I trust you? You've done nothing but hurt the poor dear." Jane set her lips in a grimace as they reached her son's car, where her husband stood waiting patiently. "That *was* Deanna," she told him as they came to his side.

"Ahh. Well, I'll be." He shook his head. "Can't imagine what that young girl musta gone through tonight. You going over there, son?"

"If we ever get out of here, I'd like to." The more they talked, the stronger his guilt grew, along with his misgivings. It was nearly midnight. If Deanna had stayed she was probably sleeping by now. Maybe he'd better wait until morning for the confrontation. Give her some peace, at least for tonight. Cord hit the button on his key fob and unlocked the car doors, opened the passenger side, and helped his mother in.

"Maybe you should wait 'til morning," his mother offered after they were buckled in and Cord had maneuvered the car onto the highway.

"Hmm." Cord eyed the nearly empty road, wondering the same thing. The ride home was silent, except for the soft snores of his father, who had fallen asleep before they even left the parking lot.

The lights were off at the Drake house, he noted as they drove past. Even the porch light, which he'd turned on earlier like he had every night since Trish had moved out, was off. That was a good sign.

"If she's there she may be sleeping," his mother whispered softly as their car turned into the McCord driveway.

"Yeah." He drove up to the house, parked the car, and left it idling. He walked around to the passenger's side and opened the door, wakening his father. "C'mon, Pops. We're home." To his mother he said, "I'm going over."

She climbed out of the car and hugged her son. "You were so grown up tonight. I'm so proud of you. You were good, honey."

"Well. Let's hope I can ace this next presentation as well. Hm?" He chuckled low as he helped his mother up the stairs. "I'll fill ya in in the morning. Night, Pops." His father grunted as he unlocked the front door.

"Good luck, dear." She kissed him soundly on the forehead, then followed her husband into their home.

~ ~ ~

Although the porch was dark, the foyer was dark, the entire house was dark, Cord knew his way around with ease. He'd been coming here every day, every night, since Trish left, walking about the place, sitting in the living room, touching the things Deanna had touched. Even the sight of that old green Tupperware made him smile. God. He missed her. He missed her laugh, her touch, her voice. Her eyes. Her love. Would he ever stop paying for his mistake? Would she ever allow him peace?

He swallowed thickly as he turned the hall light on, making his way up the stairs. Should he wake her? No. He would check in on her, leave her suitcase in the hall outside her room. If she was awake, then he'd stay. Otherwise, he wouldn't bother her. His heart beat loudly in his ears as he reached her door. Slowly he turned the handle. He saw her form huddled beneath the blankets. He heard her soft breaths coming evenly. He couldn't resist. "Deanna?" He whispered, never stepping foot into the room. "Deanna?" Nothing.

He shut the door softly, setting the suitcase in the hall, then turned to make his way downstairs, turning off the hall light when he reached the landing. Rather than leaving, Cord decided at the last minute to sit in the living room, in the darkness, on the old couch he and Deanna had made out on so often, so many years ago. He smiled as he ran his hand over the worn fabric, recalling their eager, fumbling passions. Memory of her angry words marred the thought, the words she'd lashed out at him the last time they saw each other echoing in his mind. The last time they saw each other and fought. *"Good sex. That's all it was."*

Cord sat there, thinking, remembering, for quite a while, until finally, after having tortured himself enough, he stood to leave. He walked silently to the door, picking up his keys from the hall table. As he opened the door he smiled once again as he witnessed the first snowflakes of the season cascade softly, painting the Drake property, his car, with a soft white film. It was going to be a good Christmas. He knew it.

Chapter 24

A blanket of snow covered the naked limbs of the old lumbering oak tree that, come summer, stretched far enough to shade a good portion of the Drake's front yard closest to the house. The sky was gray, the clouds swollen, and snow continued to fall, softly, silently, unrelenting. Deanna sat with her legs drawn up beneath her, wrapped in her peach chenille robe. The robe that had been in her suitcase she left at the town meeting last night. The suitcase she had found by her bedroom door this morning.

She sipped gingerly at the cup of hot black coffee cradled within her hands, hands that would be trembling had they not been anchored around the warm ceramic mug. Her thoughts swirled and shifted, fluttering like the flakes outside the living room bay window.

Although it was nearly 10 a.m. the room was shadowed from the storm outside. Deanna liked it this way. The grayness gave the room an ethereal, timeless feeling. So she left the lights off. In the utter silence, memories of passed days echoed about her, wrapping her as warmly as her robe. Despite last night's meeting, despite the fate of her family's farm, despite the fact the man who had taken her heart, her virginity, her soul, in that order had now taken her heritage away from her as well, Deanna felt an overwhelming sense of peace. It was almost a spiritual feeling, she mused, sighing softly as she took another sip. Maybe it was because she was home. Home for the holidays.

Deanna watched, and waited, wondering what time Cord had come by last night, how he had gotten in, and why he hadn't woken her up. To talk, to gloat, to make love to her? She sighed again, this time the sound turning to a soft gasp as she watched a very familiar hunter green Ford Explorer turn off the highway onto her driveway. It was almost as if her thoughts had beckoned him to her.

Her heart beat rapidly beneath the folds of her robe, but Deanna was determined to appear calm. She watched him park, watched him get out, watched him trudge up the snow-covered walkway and steps. She swallowed thickly as she heard him stomp the snow away from his feet, open the screen, and knock twice. A moment passed and he opened the door, softly calling her name.

"I'm in here," was all she could find the strength to say. Surprisingly her voice was steady.

Clad in his gray London Fog overcoat, wool cap, and leather gloves, Cord could have stepped off a page of GQ, Deanna thought with reluctant admiration. She reflectively tugged at the wisps of hair she knew had fallen out of the knot at her crown and wished she had put on makeup.

"Good morning." His voice was tentative, his gaze steady as he took in the woman curled up in the corner of the overstuffed couch.

"I guess congratulations are in order," she said as she peered over the rim of her coffee mug.

Walking over to her, Cord smiled and ignored the sarcasm in her voice. "You came."

"Did you think I could stay away?"

"I was hoping you wouldn't."

"I meant from the hearing."

"Yes, the hearing. Sorry."

She shook her head. "No, you're not."

He grinned at her. "I see you found your suitcase."

"Thanks." Deanna fought his charm, the easy manner he faced her with. "How did you get in here last night?"

Keys dangled from a ring he now held up before her as he sat beside her on the couch.

"What time did you come by?"

Shrugging off his coat he answered simply, "After midnight."

"I didn't hear you."

"I know."

Deanna blushed, imagining him watching her as she slept. Had she been snoring, or worse, drooling? "Well. That's creepy."

Cord chuckled and leaned back against the couch, stretching his feet and legs out before him so they disappeared beneath the coffee table, his feet coming out the other side. "How long you staying?"

Deanna sipped her coffee. "I don't know."

"Christmas?"

No answer came since she hadn't decided to stay for the holiday or not. Could she handle another holiday alone in the city? Now that she was home, she didn't want to leave. But would the memories be too strong? Would her holiday be nothing but one miserable tear-jerking experience, giving her little reason for joy, and too many for sorrow?

Cord stared at his knees, where they came up to the edge of the coffee table, touching just before his legs dipped below and under.

"Mom would love to have you for Christmas."

She sighed. "I don't know. I may have plans. I'm supposed to, to be in the city." She was always a terrible liar.

"You're a horrible liar."

"Whatever. Besides."

"Yeah?" He looked at her now, a slow smile forming.

"I'm not sure what would be the lesser of the two evils." It was difficult realizing she had no one. Even Trish was gone.

"How's that?"

"Well. Say I didn't have plans."

"Yes?"

Deanna picked at a piece of lint she found on her robe, tearing it apart as she spoke. "I don't know what would be worse, honestly. Spending another holiday alone in the city—"

"Or?"

Letting out a huff, Deanna threw the lint away from her. "Or spending it looking at you."

A deep hearty laughter rang throughout the peaceful room, bringing a wry twist to Deanna's lips. "I'm serious." She hit him with a pillow, nearly spilling her coffee.

"I know you are." He sobered quickly with the realization. "You caught me off guard. I forgot how candid you can be."

Deanna raised her brows and shrugged.

"If you're staying out here there's no way Mom's going to let you spend Christmas Day—or Christmas Eve—alone in this house. She won't hear of it. I'll warn you right now."

"Look, Cord. I love your mom. I love your dad. And I don't blame them for having such a jerk for a son. But I'm not going to suffer through a whole evening with you to make your parents happy." Deanna's voice was melodious, her face angelic as she spoke.

"Two."

"Excuse me?"

"I said two. Christmas Eve and Day."

"See?" Deanna stood up and shook her head. "No. I can't do it. I can't." Her cheeks were hot, her eyes moist. "Go."

"You're not going to get rid of us this easily, you know." Cord stood up, but not to leave as Deanna expected. Rather than reach for his coat, he reached for her, enveloping her in an embrace. She stiffened and tried to step away, but he wrapped his arms around her middle, his hands lightly directing her head toward his body, so that her cheek rested against his chest. And she stayed there, because it was where she wanted to be. Tears ran down her cheeks, splotching the expensive black material of his suit. "Stop fighting us," he whispered as he kissed her hair.

She shook her head, but before she could speak he slipped a lightly closed fist under her chin and nudged her face upwards. His eyes, black as midnight in the shadowed living room, were filled with warmth.

"Please?" His whispered word was her undoing, combined with the touch of his nose against hers as his thumb caressed her cheek.

Her heart skipped a beat, her breath quickened. Deanna closed her eyes and whimpered in acknowledgement of her surrender, hating herself, loving him, hating him. The moment she had dreaded, had anticipated, since she first watched his truck make its way down the drive came then, as wonderful and terrible as she knew it would be.

"I hate you," she whispered as he claimed her lips in a fierce kiss. He probed, she melted. He demanded, she gave. He conquered, she yielded. And then he stopped.

Just like that.

Deanna's eyes flew open in disappointment.

"You little liar," he charged, with amusement dancing

in his eyes before placing one last peck on her nose. Then, releasing his hold on her and turning toward the couch, he said, "I've got to try to get to work. If the roads are too bad, I'm closing for the day. If they're passable, I'll be back by six or so. Don't go out. I'll have someone deliver what you'll need. If you want specific items call ShopRite and tell them to add it to my order. They'll be by before noon." He talked the entire time he donned his coat and hat and now leaned over to give her another kiss. Deanna caught a whiff of his aftershave, its heady, musky scent melting her insides, and she trembled.

"Wait a minute." She finally spoke as he walked onto the porch.

He turned around, pausing by the door. "Deanna—I gotta get going—"

"Sorry, Cord. But I'm not the concubine you think you can keep holed up here—"

"Concubine?" There went that damn lopsided grin of his.

"You can't possibly think I'll stay here and let you keep me."

"Keep you?"

"Yes!"

"Deanna. It's snowing out, for cripes sake. You have no car. It's got to be at the most thirty degrees outside. You want to walk to ShopRite, or better yet, the local deli? Be my guest. But you're being pigheaded."

"I'm not being pigheaded. I don't need your money, or your influence. Or you. I won't be bought." Her green eyes sparked in anger as she faced him, hands on her hips, chin thrust forward in defiance.

"You don't get it, do you?"

"No. And I don't want it, either."

"Fine. Starve then. See if I care. But you explain it to my parents. I'm not doing your dirty work for you." He turned and stomped down the porch stairs to his truck, slamming the door behind him.

~ ~ ~

It was still snowing after Deanna finished her shower and dressed. And, from what she could see through the blizzard, all the stores lining the streets were closed. She had no house phone, no food, and she kept losing cell service. Luckily, she had had the foresight to pack a can of coffee and a box of Oreos. But by noon, the caffeine and sugar was making her jittery and a bit nauseous.

Her weather app on her phone predicted the storm would stall and last at least two days, with another storm front following close behind. The alert warned people to make alternative plans to stay off the roads for the holidays, and that, if they were planning to travel, to leave early to avoid delays.

Now that—thanks to her stubbornness and pride—she had snubbed Cord's hospitality *and* his parents' Christmas invitation, Deanna was sure this was going to be an even worse holiday than originally anticipated. If he hadn't butted in at least she wouldn't have guilt eating at her, which was worse than starving. Her stomach growled with the thought of food, with the thought of no food, and she set her sights on working off her hunger.

Surveying the living room, Deanna wondered if Trish had ever done a major cleaning, had ever rearranged the furniture, had ever done a thing besides take up space. That sounded so angry, but Trish deserved it. She hadn't responded to Deanna's Christmas card, not even by text or phone, and hadn't made any attempt to contact her for Thanksgiving or Christmas.

The living room was laid out the way it had been while Deanna was growing up. The same paintings, now yellowed with age, hung dusty and crooked on the walls.

The couch, the chairs—everything—all smelled musty. The wood end tables were marred with watermark circles, left from Pike's beer cans no doubt. Wrinkling her nose in disgust, Deanna decided the only way to keep from drowning in the refuse of sad memories was to scrub them clean and rearrange them, not to mention vacuum beneath them and around them.

By five o'clock, the paneled walls had been saturated and wiped clean with Murphy Oil Soap, as well as the hardwood floor beneath the worn hook rug that had laid for years in the middle of the living room. The draperies, olive green and frayed, now laid in a rolled-up heap in the hall to be discarded. The metal, thick-slatted blinds were once again a creamy white, as opposed to the nicotine-stained yellow they had been that morning. The furniture had been vacuumed and rearranged, tables polished, and old paintings removed, leaving the walls bare except for Sheila's gift which now adorned the wall dividing the kitchen and living room. A good painting was needed, Deanna thought as she scrutinized with satisfaction the task now completed.

She felt grimy, grungy, and wanted desperately to take a shower. But she would only get dirty again, since she had nothing else to do but clean. Deanna sighed, her stomach growling ferociously as her thoughts strayed to food, and headed toward the hallway to the heap of paintings and curtains.

She carted the paintings up to the attic then poked around a bit to see if there was anything she could use. After a moment, she ceased her efforts, deciding that would take a whole day. On her way back down to the first floor, Deanna imagined how the house would look redecorated, modernized, and filled with her plants and treasures. Although there definitely were pieces she would keep, like the curio cabinet, the dining room set, and Mom's coffee table and end tables, much of it had to go. She smiled, imagining where her favorite chair would go—by the window, with the standing brass lamp behind it—and where her favorite van Gogh print would hang—over the fire place.

Next, she brought the curtains down to the basement, intending to wash them to see how they would turn out once she bought laundry detergent. She tugged the chain on the overhead bulb and froze. *Mom. Oh, Mom.*

There, still lining the shelves against the far wall were jars of peaches, apple butter, beans, tomatoes, okra, potatoes, and strawberry preserves. Behind her, still stacked in the individual pyramids Dad so methodically created were piles and piles of wood. "You never know when we'll need this stuff," Mom and Dad used to say. Deanna laughed as tears filled her eyes and rolled down her cheeks. "You're still taking care of me," she said aloud.

"I miss you so much!" Deanna heard her voice crack as she spoke to her parents, half-expecting them to answer her. Nothing but the hum of the oil burner clicking on sounded in the shadowed cellar. Deanna walked over to the shelves, wondering if any of the stuff was still good. Running her hand over the mason jars she selected one each of the potatoes, beans, apple butter, and strawberry preserves. Laughing with delight while praying they were still safe to eat, Deanna returned upstairs to the well-lit kitchen. She would get wood later to start a fire. Right now, she was eating.

Before even opening the jars, Deanna knew the preserves would be edible. Her mother had told her repeatedly that although the FDA said they'd stay safe for one to two years, she'd been canning all her life, and her mom and granny before her, and that was plain hogwash. Their canned goods would last a lifetime.

"Thanks, Mom," she said, as she dumped the potatoes into a frying pan and the beans into a small pot. While the food warmed, Deanna trekked back downstairs for some wood and old newspapers, making three trips and piling the majority of her collection of logs and kindling on the front porch by the door. She stuffed the fireplace with kindling and wads of newspaper, and set a match to it. When it was flaming nicely, Deanna threw a log on, which caught almost immediately. Satisfied, she headed toward the kitchen to finish dinner.

After sniffing the food warming on the stove, she decided that yes, it was safe to eat, then walked back into the living room, bent over her and her parents' old record album collection, and thumbed through the selection left untouched by her sister. She was so different than Trish. What Deanna deemed irreplaceable, Trish had always viewed as junk. And, apparently, this fact had not changed over the years, as Deanna observed considering all the contents left behind with Trish's move. Nothing, as far as Deanna could tell, had been claimed by Trish. Not one thing.

After selecting Tchaikovsky's "The Nutcracker," in the spirit of Christmas, Deanna went back into the kitchen to check on her feast. Seeing it ready, she realized she couldn't eat yet, as her entire body was caked with dust, dirt, and sweat from her afternoon efforts. She groaned, her stomach echoing with its own growl, and shut off the stove.

It was only after a quick but thorough shower did Deanna finally find herself enjoying her first meal of the day. She ate nearly all the potatoes and beans while compiling a list of things to do around the house. After cleaning the remaining rooms—which included scrubbing floors and walls and windows, tearing up old rugs and carpets, discarding curtains and drapes—she would spackle and paint. Maybe even wall paper.

The living room would be done, of course, in hunter green, like her living room in the apartment. The dining room? Creams and beiges, maybe a splash of cranberry. The kitchen, Deanna drummed her now cracked fingernails against the worn Formica table. White? and yellow, maybe? That would be cheery enough. And yellow had always been Mom's favorite color.

Sunflowers! Now that was a popular design these days. The den, which had only been used as a playroom when the girls were younger, would become Deanna's library and office, she decided, jotting that down in parenthesis. Maybe she could even hire someone to build a wall of bookshelves, she added that word with a question mark.

Deanna stopped suddenly, and stared in disbelief at her list. What was she doing? Who was she kidding? She could never move back here, she thought sadly. Too many memories. Too close to Cord. *I'd go crazy, wondering if he was going to pop over, if he was going to kiss me.*

She sighed and looked at the clock. It was nearly 8 p.m. and she hadn't thought about him all day. She stood up and stretched, walked to the sink, did her dirty dishes and pots and dried her hands. Then, after retrieving the quilt and pillow from her bed, Deanna settled on the couch before the fire, exhausted and contented from her labor. Maybe it wouldn't be so bad moving back here. Other people commute. *So could I. And living here would be so less expensive.*

~ ~ ~

It was all Cord could do to keep from touching Deanna as he stood over her while she slept on the couch.

He had stayed away all day, but memories of her had crowded his every thought. He knew Deanna. She was a trooper. She was also very stubborn. Maybe he had been wrong in assuming she would want his help. That she would want to eat. That she would want to bake him cookies and spend Christmas with him and his family. He grimaced, disgusted with his inability to read her. On the one hand, she responded to him, his touch, his kiss, as if she wanted him. As much as he wanted and desired her. Yet, she showed utter disdain for him at the same time. But he didn't believe her. How could she respond like that then tell him to go to hell in the blink of an eye?

All day he worried about her, but he knew she would be all right. Teach her a lesson, that's why he originally vowed to stay away. Let her starve. But as the day wore on, he remembered the preserves he had spotted in the cellar, and he knew she would find them and she would be all right. And if the pots and dishes and mason jars drying in the drainer were proof, he had been correct.

He looked around now in admiration. She worked her butt off today. The living room didn't look the same at all, even the furniture seemed less bedraggled. The hardwood floor gleamed reflecting the firelight, the walls were bared. It smelled fresh, like pine and lemon rather than nicotine and mildew. She had covered the couch with cream chenille bedspread, rearranged everything, and now reaped her rewards in the form of sleep.

Maybe she was planning on staying?

Cord pushed that hope away. He couldn't figure her out anymore. Why even bother trying? He walked over to the fire and poked at it, sending a shower of sparks flying up the chimney, hoping the noise would wake her up. It didn't.

He went into the kitchen, unpacking the groceries he bought for her. Bread, butter, eggs, milk. Cheese.

Enough food for a few days. Rice, pasta, canned goods, salad fixings, and fresh cut meat from the local butcher now filled the old well-worn refrigerator. He set a pack of batteries and a flashlight he bought on the counter, in case she lost power tonight with the storm blowing in, and turned to leave.

As he walked out of the kitchen he noted the pad and pen on the table, his curiosity urging him to check out the scribbled notes she had made. He scanned the list for a moment, realizing finally what it was, and smiled broadly, pleased with her decorating ideas. Then he took out his smart phone and snapped a picture of the list, slipping his phone back in his pocket. He remembered the van Gogh prints he had picked out for her, intending to surprise her with them as a gift. It seemed like a lifetime ago. Now, he decided that those prints would be wrapped and under the tree for her Christmas morning. They would look great in here.

He walked over to the fireplace, stoking the embers and log once more, then threw another thick piece of wood on top, sure that it would burn until early morning. Then he threw a smaller one on top of that for good measure. Passing by the couch he leaned over and kissed Deanna on her forehead. He thought he noticed a flutter of her lashes, but after studying her for a moment, noting the rhythmic breaths she took, he decided she was truly asleep. He left reluctantly, vowing not to return until she called him.

It was only after Deanna heard the SUV start and head down the driveway, the tires crunching over the snow, did she open her eyes. Sitting up, she took a deep breath, her body achingly awake and taut with the need to be held by Cord. Trembling, she bent her head to rest against her knees and wept.

Chapter 25

The next few days kept Deanna busy–real busy. So busy she hardly thought about Cord at all.

Any dishes, pots, and pans Deanna knew she would never use sat in cardboard boxes by the front door to be donated to Good Will.

The cabinets' maple doors had been scrubbed clean with Murphy Oil Soap and polished to a sleek shine. The shelves had been vacuumed and washed. The countertop and sink had been bleached, the refrigerator washed and disinfected inside and out, and the oven had been soaked in oven cleaner. The kitchen curtains had been removed and thrown away, disintegrating in Deanna's hands as she slipped them from the rusted rod. The inside of the window had been wiped thoroughly, but along with removing dust and insect carcasses, Deanna also wiped away bits of rotted wood and caulking. Like most of the windows she had cleaned over the last few days, these too would need to be replaced.

All of this had been started on Thursday, after a hearty breakfast of eggs, toast, and coffee, thanks to Cord, she noted grimly. She had woken up right after dawn, her stomach a bit queasy. Deanna passed it off as hunger and nerves, then slid out of bed, anxious to finish the rest of the house.

However, her plan to complete this monumental task in one day was interrupted by naps and bouts of sickness. Positive that she was coming down with a flu, Deanna gave into her body's demands and did not push herself.

The dining room and rest of the rooms on the first floor had been cleaned thoroughly and purged of any damaged or unfixable items including lamps, knickknacks, wall décor, throw rugs, and occasional pieces of furniture.

Now, Christmas Eve morning, Deanna paused as she prepared to do the last bit of floor washing and once again acknowledged the unsettled feeling within, wanting to eat something to ease the sensation. However, she still had the remaining floors to sweep and wash, and she was filthy from head to toe. Lunch would have to wait a little bit longer.

The stained scatter rugs laying before the sink and oven, Deanna noted as she picked them up with her thumb and forefinger, covered the well-worn linoleum that revealed the wooden floor below. She made a note that the kitchen floor would have to be replaced also.

It was nearly noon when a knock sounded at the door. Surprised, since it was still snowing and she was expecting no one, Deanna made her way to the door without bothering to lower the stereo, which now belted out The Cranberry's. She opened it to find Jane bundled up before her. Peering over the woman's shoulder Deanna noted Cord's truck idling in the driveway.

"Are you going to let me in or what, young lady?" Jane admonished through the scarf wrapped about the lower half of her face. She wasn't wearing a hat, and the snowflakes rested against her brown and gray-streaked hair.

"Of course," Deanna stammered, bracing for what she knew she going to be the lecture of her life. She glanced back at Cord's truck and saw him waving at her as he beeped three times before driving off. Deanna swallowed thickly as she waved the woman in and shut the door behind them.

"Hi, Jane. Merry Christmas!" Deanna offered too brightly, her heart beating rapidly.

"Don't 'Hi, Jane' me, young lady. Is this your idea of celebrating Christmas? Coming out here and not even bothering to say hello?" She unwrapped her scarf and unbuttoned her coat and laid it across the wooden bannister that needed polishing. "Do you have any coffee? It's freezing out there."

"Of course. Come in." Deanna detoured to the stereo, shutting it off with a click, before heading toward the kitchen. "What are you doing out there in this blizzard?"

"What do you think I'm doing?" Jane sat down at the kitchen table, rubbing her alabaster freckled hands together. "I've got better things to do then come over here and try to talk sense into you, young lady. I've got a house full of people coming tonight, including Father John. It's a good thing I did most of the cooking yesterday. Not to mention the cleaning. Which, I notice, you've been keeping busy at. It's about time someone did it. I swear, Patricia is a sweet thing, but she wasn't one for cleaning. Now. Speaking of which," Jane paused, "where was I?"

"Excuse me, Jane?" Deanna asked. "Milk or sugar?"

"Both. Now, where was I? Oh, yes. Have you heard from your sister?"

"No."

"Me neither. Now, I know I shouldn't be upset, but I can't help it. We are the closest thing to family you two have and you've gone on and forgotten us completely. I don't appreciate being cast aside like a pair of old tennis shoes, you know."

"Here you go." Deanna set a mug of coffee before the woman, who paused long enough to take a sip.

"Now, where was I? Oh, yes. Family. It only stands to reason that I expected you to be spending the holidays at my house rather than cooped up here, cleaning from the looks of things! If you weren't planning on spending it with us, why even bother coming out?"

Although a question was asked, Jane didn't give Deanna a chance to respond. "Naturally I assumed when I saw you at the hearing that you'd be staying with us."

"You were at the hearing?"

"Of course. That's another thing, young lady. Since when did you become so darn pigheaded?" And on and on Jane went, admonishing, chastising, and reprimanding Deanna as if her life depended on it, never giving Deanna the chance to defend herself. She was still ranting half an hour later when the front door opened and Cord walked in, much to Deanna's reluctant relief.

Cord stood in the kitchen entranceway, one broad shoulder resting against the frame, arms folded across his chest, listening intently to his mother's lecture. He nodded and smiled only slightly when Deanna threw him a beseeching glance.

"Has she been doing this since I left?"

Deanna nodded, not knowing whether to cry or laugh.

"Cord, hush. I'm not done."

"Mom. That's enough."

Once again, Cord was coming to her rescue. And once again, Deanna felt her heart tug with gratitude.

"No, it is not enough. You, get in here. Take your coat off and sit down. We're going to clear this up once and for all." Jane turned to glare at her son.

Only when he obeyed her directive and was seated beside Deanna did Jane continue. "You, young man, have got to learn to stop being so bullheaded. Good lord, you're as bossy as your daddy. And you, young lady." She pointed a frail finger at Deanna. "You have got to stop being so pigheaded and so independent. You've got people who care about you, who want to take care of you, who, who"—a sob broke her last chastisement, causing Jane to lose momentum—"who love you. Why don't you let us love you, Deanna?" She sniffled and tears puddled her eyes, causing Deanna to reach over, hugging and weeping with her at the same time.

Cord leaned back, saying nothing.

Jane drew away from Deanna after a moment, allowing Deanna to settle back down in her seat.

"Now, where was I? Oh, yes. I want a truce between you two. At least for the next few days, or better yet, until after the New Year, if you two can't bury the past once and for all. Come on now. I won't take no. It's Christmas. Don't do this to me, to each other. Trust me, you won't regret it." Jane cast a stern glance at them, not unlike the time she'd caught them coloring all over her living room walls. Or the time she'd caught them painting the cat. Or making out in the gazebo.

Deanna and Cord exchanged looks, both apparently struggling to keep a straight face.

"Well?"

Cord shrugged. "I'll call a truce if she will. How about you, Deanna?"

Deanna smiled weakly at Jane, suddenly feeling very queasy. She peeked out from beneath her lashes at Cord, and relented with a nod. "Very well. For Christmas. But I'm only doing this for you, Jane."

Jane hugged Deanna, and smiled triumphantly at her son. Then Jane spoke aloud to Cord, not giving Deanna the chance to argue. "Let's go."

Moments later, as the pair stepped gingerly down the snow-covered steps, Jane waved to Deanna who stood at the front door.

"I'll be back by three," he called out over his shoulder as he helped his mom into the truck.

She nodded and waved once more, waiting until he maneuvered the truck down the drive before she slammed the door shut. Then Deanna sobbed, bringing her thumb knuckle to her teeth and biting hard as she walked up the stairs and into the bathroom. She stared into her reflection, gulping in breaths of air to still the rumbling within her belly. It must be nerves, she thought. Nerves, caffeine, and no lunch. The thought of food made Deanna wonder what Jane would be serving for dinner besides the traditional turkey. Homemade cranberry sauce? Potatoes? Gravy? Suddenly, although she was feeling ravenous, Deanna's body shuddered repulsively and her empty stomach rolled and lurched. Automatically Deanna leaned over the bowl, gasping and choking as her stomach attempted to rid itself of the least little bit of anything she had consumed that day.

The flu, she thought, moments later, brushing her teeth to rid the foul taste in her mouth, only to dismiss the thought. No fever. No chills. No achy body or sore throat or headache.

Food poisoning? No. The preserves tasted too good. But they were nearly five years old. Nah. They were fine.

Deanna stared at her face in the mirror, lost in thought as she tried to figure out the cause of her sickness. A thought came to her from the deep recesses of her mind, but Deanna scowled and shook her head. *Impossible.*

Then her stomach rumbled once more as if protesting her conclusion. "No!" she shouted aloud this time. "No way." But already her subconscious was working hard for proof.

I'm always sleeping lately. I've been keeping late hours.

I'm so emotional. I'm constantly crying. "That doesn't even deserve an answer," she told her reflection. "I'm losing the farm. I've lost my family. And Cord is driving me crazy."

When was my last period?

"Oh, my God." Deanna stared at her reflection, trying to read the truth in her eyes she could see beyond the shock. "It can't be true."

Yes, it can. The bet. What had Cord wished for that night on the yacht?

Deanna's hand flew to her mouth as she moaned aloud, dizzied with the thought. "No, no, no." She left the bathroom, running toward her bedroom where she grabbed her leather pocketbook, ripping the zipper open to find her datebook.

The last date she recorded for her period was in August. Nothing for September, October, or November. And it was the end of December and she didn't recall having a period this month either. How was that possible? Her hands trembled as she scanned the notes and found the entry for the yacht ride. Two weeks prior had been her last period. Now she remembered. Two weeks after her last period she and Cord had made love.

Had they conceived a child?

A child! Oh, God, please no. I'll do anything, anything. I'll go to church every Sunday. I'll make up with Trish. I'll let Cord develop the farm. Please, God. Don't let me be . . . be . . .

But even as Deanna blindly walked back to the bathroom she knew her prayers were unheard. The bet had been lost and Cord's wish apparently had been granted. About four months ago, aboard a yacht cruising out of Hempstead Harbor.

She looked in the bathroom mirror, turning sideways, lifting her tee shirt close to her belly. Nothing. She felt her breasts. Didn't pregnant women always complain of achy breasts? Nothing. She stared into her reflection again, her eyes, green orbs of confusion glittering in the dim bathroom light. It was there. Only, she had never looked before. "Oh, my God." She wept, sinking to the floor in a huddled ball in the corner.

I can't do this, she thought irrationally, not knowing exactly what it was she couldn't do. "I can't go to dinner at the McCord's. I can't face Cord. Or Jane. I cannot have this baby."

Her conscience gave her no argument until she'd finished ranting, and then she came to her senses. She had no choice. She had to go to dinner. She had to face the McCords. She had to have this baby. Who was she fooling? She wanted to have this baby. With or without Michael McCord.

Once she had calmed herself down, she turned on the shower, stripped, and stepped into the tub, the warm water comforting her, nurturing her like an embrace.

This can't be happening, she thought, closing her eyes and letting the water rinse the shampoo from her hair. Too much was happening too quickly. She was losing the farm. She was very possibly pregnant. No, more than likely she *was* pregnant! And now she had to face the McCords for Christmas. And Cord.

Isn't this what she wanted? To spend the holidays with a family? Wasn't that why she came out here?

I won't be able to hide this. He'll know. They'll all know. I can't go there.

She couldn't decide why she desperately needed to avoid the McCords, if it was because she might be pregnant, or because she had lost to Cord. *Face it, Deanna. He won.*

Her mind restated those words, chant-like, the whole time she showered and got ready to celebrate Christmas at the McCords. With little consideration for style or flair, knowing that later this evening the crowd would probably venture out into the cold midnight air to attend midnight mass, Deanna chose a pair of satin-lined winter white wool dress slacks—that did seem a bit more snug than the last time she wore them. She paired the slacks with a cashmere green sweater and her green suede boots for the evening celebration. After knotting her hair into a soft twist at her crown, applying rouge and a bit of eye makeup, she waited by the front door for his truck.

When he arrived, she wrapped her black cloak around her shoulders, ran out and climbed into the passenger side before he even had a chance to unbuckle his seat belt or shut off the engine. "Let's go," she said, clenching the dashboard.

"What's the big hurry? No one's there yet." Cord watched her as she stared out the windshield.

"I want this over with."

"What? It's Christmas. There's nothing to get over. It's supposed to be fun." He shut the car off and turned his body toward her.

His silence as he continued to scrutinize her unnerved Deanna, so she began to pick at the lint on her coat. "Why'd you do that?" she asked.

"We've got time. Maybe if we get cold enough you'll invite me in."

"I don't think so."

"We could go back to my place."

Deanna giggled in disbelief and rolled her eyes. "Hardly."

"I thought we called a truce."

"I don't think a truce means I have to jump into bed with you."

It was Cord's turn to laugh. "Who said anything about bed? Deanna, you've got a one-track mind."

She blushed, finally turning to look at him. He sobered as he saw her tear-filled eyes. "What's wrong?"

Deanna answered with a shake of her head. "The holidays, I guess." She sniffled and sobbed, feeling hysteria mounting. *I just want to stay home.* "Can't I back out of this thing? I'll come over tomorrow."

"Right. Mom would have my hide, then take my keys and come over and get you herself."

Deanna suppressed a grin at the thought of Jane's wrath if she had to leave her kitchen now to retrieve Deanna. Sobering, she said quietly, "I don't want to be there."

"Wrong. You don't want to be with me. And that, Deanna," Cord said gruffly, starting the engine once again, "is your tough luck."

~ ~ ~

Dinner was not a complete failure, but Deanna could not claim it a success either. With Cord sitting beside her, all she managed to do was toy with her shrimp cocktail appetizer, sip a bit of the chicken consommé, spear an olive and cucumber from her salad, and pick apart her filet stuffed with crab meat.

She ignored Cord when he offered to serve her, speaking over him rudely as she would ask Terry a question about Jenna, or one of Cord's cousins about school. Rather than be put off, Cord saw this as a challenge, his blue eyes sparkling with mischief as he sat silently beside her, waiting for the next opportunity to goad her.

Deanna was in the middle of an explanation to Father John about her work with the Toys for Tots volunteers when Cord decided to pay her back for her rude behavior toward him.

"I never saw so many toys before, Father John. It's amazing to see how the holiday spirit can—" Deanna felt a socked foot rub catlike against her left calf. Her heart hammered wildly as she paused and glanced at Cord, who was helping himself to another spoonful of scalloped potatoes.

"Yes, dear?" Father John urged politely.

"—touch people." Deanna felt her cheeks heat as Cord looked at her now and raised a knowing eyebrow, a subtle tug of a grin twitched his lips. She dropped her fork and raised her napkin to wipe her lips, then replaced it back in her lap, keeping her hands there to hide the fact they were trembling.

Almost immediately, Deanna regretted that decision for Cord's hand followed hers, hidden by the folds of tablecloth, and grabbed her hand gently, but firmly, with seemingly no intentions of letting it go soon.

"Our collection baskets are indeed heavier this time of year," Father John began, with the rest of the diners focusing their attention on his explanation as to why people give more at the holidays. However, the words were lost on Deanna, whose head was filled with the pounding of her blood rushing through her temples as Cord's thumb traced circles on the soft cup of her palm. Her senses returned only after Cord claimed his victory with a firm squeeze of her hand before releasing his grip.

"Deanna, honey. Aren't you hungry?" Jane eyed Deanna's flushed face with a raised eyebrow. She looked at her son and gave him the slightest glance, warning him to behave.

"Actually, Jane. I'm not feeling very well. I must be coming down with something," Deanna said, dropping her gaze to her plate, realizing how little she had eaten. She couldn't eat, though. Not when the shrimp brought to mind little baby embryos.

Jane nodded sympathetically. "Well, it *is* flu season. Goodness, I hope you aren't contagious."

It was during dessert that Deanna's eating habits again became the topic of discussion for Jane. "Feeling better?" Jane asked as she watched Deanna down a second piece of Black Forest Cake. She raised an eyebrow, then turned toward her son, who was also watching Deanna.

"Much, thanks," Deanna said. "But even if I wasn't, who could pass this up. You make the best cake."

Locking eyes with Deanna, Jane smiled. "Would you like some wine, dear? This sangria goes well with that cake," Jane offered, passing the bottle to her son and nodding to Deanna's glass.

Deanna put a hand over her glass, and declined, explaining she was stuffed. Jane smiled again, as Cord set the wine down.

~ ~ ~

After dinner, all the McCords helped clear the table, with the women moving immediately to the kitchen to wash dishes and stack the dishwasher. The younger men shuttled back and forth from the dining room table, putting food away and bringing the dishes to the kitchen while Mr. McCord, his brother-in-law, Jack, and Father John retired to the living room.

Jane's sister Deedee, her three teen-aged children, along with Deanna, Terry, Matt, and Cord worked like trained elves until the kitchen was clean and coffee was brewing. Only then did they join the older men in the living room, where Jack and Deedee's daughter, Samantha, offered to play Christmas carols on the piano.

Deanna sat on the floor by the fireplace, her legs tucked beneath her as she fitted together pieces of the Christmas puzzle started on Thanksgiving by Jane.

Father John reclined in a rocker, dozing peacefully. Matt and Terry sat arm in arm on the loveseat, their little daughter, Jenna, asleep on her father's shoulder.

Cord surveyed the scene from the arm of the couch, not ready to join Deanna, but content in watching how the flames reflected in her dark eyes. More than once she would pause in her efforts and glance up at him. At first she appeared angry with his attention, then downright annoyed. But by the fourth or fifth pointed glare at him she cracked, and the merest smile broke her grimace.

He came to sit beside her. Together they worked in silent camaraderie, nearly completing the 3,000-piece puzzle of St. Nick packing out presents beside a Victorian Christmas tree adorned with candles, silver bells, holly berries, and angels. When they brushed hands reaching for the same piece, Cord guided her fingers that held the likeness of a doll's cherubic face to the beheaded form resting under the tree, against a set of carpet-covered stairs. To fit the piece in its place Cord had to lean over the puzzle, inclining his head so his cheek was inches from Deanna.

After gently nudging the puzzle piece into position, he smiled softly as he gazed into her eyes. His pulse quickened when he saw she had been studying his face rather than focusing on the task at hand. He picked up another piece of the puzzle and offered it to her.

~ ~ ~

She returned his smile, then looked away, her cheeks glowing warmly beneath his scrutiny. Settling her sites on the Christmas tree, Deanna sighed wistfully, feeling guilty about the lack of decorations in her own home and her apartment. There hadn't been any need to celebrate before. But now, as she looked at the towering eight-foot evergreen, decked out in ornaments, the Lenox and crystal store bought treasures placed alongside homemade ones given to Jane by her sons when they were little boys, she regretted not hauling down the decorations from the attic. Tinsel glittered gaily, reflecting the blinking orange, yellow, green, red, and blue lights. Strands of popcorn hung from the branches. An angel, all gauzy and soft and loving, looked down from her perch at the top of the tree, a white light hidden beneath her flowing gown.

Tomorrow, Deanna thought, she would dig out the fake tree and put it up. Tomorrow. That would be her gift, her Christmas gift to herself. And her baby, she thought dreamily, unconsciously laying a hand across her belly in the most fleeting of caresses.

Jane, who Deanna observed had been watching she and Cord throughout the day, raised an eyebrow and smiled knowingly. Deanna removed her hand quickly and ignored the McCord matriarch, concentrating on the puzzle without acknowledging Jane's attentions.

It was shortly before 11 p.m. when Father John stood up. "Well. It's been wonderful, but I must be going." He looked at Cord, who had picked him up after dropping off Deanna earlier in the day. "Anyone joining me for midnight mass?" He looked around the room. Deanna stood up and nodded. Cord unfolded his legs and came to stand beside her. The three teenagers rolled their eyes, but Jack and Deedee nodded to Father John in confirmation. Everyone but Matt and Terry bundled up, with Deanna, Cord and the three teenagers piling into the SUV, and the adults loading up Mr. McCord's super cab pickup truck.

Deanna remained silent as she watched Cord maneuver through the snow. How many midnight masses had their families shared? Twenty? At least. And now, after so many years, the Drakes and McCords were once again being united by the tradition. Only things were different, very different this time, Deanna acknowledged thoughtfully.

As if reading her mind, Cord spoke softly, nodding to the giggling youths in the back seat. "Funny how things change and things stay the same, isn't it?"

She nodded.

"Hey!" Billy called from the back seat. "Let's do up a pizza and blow off church."

"Yeah, right," Cord answered dryly.

"How about a snowball fight?" Samantha suggested, and her brothers supported her enthusiastically.

"Yeah, sure." Deanna spoke this time, amused with the role reversal she found herself in. For the first time in her life she felt like the adult. *Weird.*

Cord parked the truck in the snow-covered parking lot filled with cars, and motioned for everyone to enter the church rather than linger in the more-than-tempting snow. Once the McCord crowd was seated, Cord excused himself to check the truck and to make sure he'd shut the headlights off he added as he slid out of the pew. Deanna eyed him suspiciously, sure he had other, less noble, intentions. He returned ten minutes later, his cheeks rosy, his gloves dripping wet. Deanna squirmed for a minute or two, then whispered to him to move, for she had to use the ladies room. He studied her for a second, disbelief in his eyes, then relented. "Hurry. Father John's about to start."

Deanna grinned, knowing she had a good 15 minutes before mass would begin. Fourteen minutes later she entered the vestibule, waved at Father John, who was preparing to lead the processional, and slipped down the aisle to her pew.

"What took you so long?"

"There was a line."

"Yeah, right. Remember where you are, Dean." he gazed heavenward. "God hears and sees everything." He then picked up her wet mittens and hung them next to his, over the pew arm to dry. Deanna giggled softly as she glanced at his knowing frown.

Mass was as beautiful as it had ever been, Deanna recalled, teary-eyed. She recited each prayer with solemn, heartfelt sincerity. She tried to concentrate on the entire homily, even when Father John became sidetracked with one of the points he was attempting to make. When it came time to offer the sign of peace, she turned to shake hands with the tormentor of her heart, but was caught up in a solid embrace, with Cord clutching her to him as if his very life depended on it.

They received communion, sang one last song, and then it was time to leave. Deanna hesitated, wanting to light a candle for her parents, but not wanting to miss the snowball fight that was about to take place outside. She mentally apologized to her mom and dad, then giggled as they filed out the pew and down the center aisle. The choir had chosen to sing a medley of Christmas songs instead of their traditional closing hymn. Their repertoire included "Let It Snow," "Jingle Bells," and "Frosty the Snowman." Her grin was wide and obvious as she stepped lightly through the snow-filled parking lot, detouring off to the left of the truck, behind the lamppost where she had stashed a good dozen firmly packed snowballs. Cord reached his ammunition first, levelling his aim at Samantha, hitting her squarely on the back. The young teen shrieked and scooped up a handful of soft snow— too soft to make a good ball.

"Over here, Sam!" Deanna called, defining sides. As she hollered to Cord's cousin, Deanna hurled a snowball at Chris, Samantha's older brother. Samantha reached

Deanna and immediately hurled one at Billy. Cord threw one at Deanna, hitting her on her right shoulder. Deanna threw one at him and grazed the top of his head.

Other churchgoers joined in the fight and soon the parking lot was filled with snowballs whizzing to and fro. Deanna peered through the mess, clutching her last snow ball to her chest as she searched the crowd for Cord. Suddenly, two arms came around her lifting her off the ground, causing her to shriek in fright. Or was it delight?

"Put me down!"

"Drop it!"

"No!"

"Drop it or I bury you in the snow!"

"Never!" Her giggling turned to peals of laughter as she knew without a doubt he would take her defiance as a dare.

"You asked for it!" He swung her up into his arms and carried her across the lot to the normally grassy area now covered with drifts of powdery snow.

"Don't you dare!"

"Too late!" He huffed and pretended to stagger under her weight as Deanna struggled to break free. A face full of snow was not how she wanted to end this evening.

"Say your prayers!" He held her away from his body, dangling her over a snow drift that came to his waist.

"Wait!" Deanna shrieked one last time.

"Bye-bye!" Cord laughed as he dropped her, and Deanna laughed harder, forgetting her cares immediately as she grabbed the ends of his scarf and tumbled him into the drift alongside her. As he scooped up a palm full of snow she sputtered and laughed, shouting, "I give up!"

"Too late!" He picked up another scoop full and tried to slip it up beneath her coat.

"Stop!" She laughed so hard tears spilled from her eyes. She dug her arm beneath the snow and fanned a wall of the white stuff in Cord's direction.

The more she begged for him to stop the harder they both laughed, laying side by side in the snow bank while chaos whirled around them as snowballs and shrieks fill the air. Their laughter subsided, they both caught their breath, and he leaned down to kiss her. Cold lips captured cold lips, warm breath brushing her skin. Deanna sighed, reveling in his warmth, the clean smell of cold air and snow that clung to him. He kissed her deeper and she murmured something unintelligible as her hand groped in the snow beside her. Lost in the kiss, Cord didn't notice her actions until it was too late. Deanna planted a handful of thick, heavy snow on the back of his head, his neck, down the inside of his coat. He hollered and jumped away from her, yelling something about war. Then he bent down and scooped mounds of snow on her, half-burying her until she was once again laughing uncontrollably.

"S-S-top!" She laughed and gasped and held out her hands, remembering the life budding within her.

"Never! You will pay," he threatened, his eyes twinkling with merriment as he shoveled more snow on top of her.

Mirth shook her body and stole her voice as she giggled and laughed unceasingly. Then he pounced on her, wrestling her deeper into the bank. As he landed deadweight on her Deanna became alarmed at the roughhousing. "I said, stop!" She cried out in a panicked voice, cradling her stomach with her arms. As soon as she spoke she regretted her actions. Deanna opened her eyes to see Cord straddling her, his gloved hands half buried in the snow on either side of her, momentarily frozen.

Slowly, he rose to his knees, resting over her thighs, his mouth gaping.

"What?" Deanna stared at him blankly, catching her breath.

He squinted at her, studying her face as if she was the Christmas jigsaw puzzle they had worked on earlier in the evening, and he was fitting all the pieces together in his mind.

"Cord, are you okay?" She struggled like a turtle on her back, trying to get up. The snow weighing her down, the odd angle, and the bulkiness of her winter garb made it a struggle, so she could only lay there looking up at him.

"What's wrong?" she asked again, unnerved by the look on his face.

"Are you . . . pregnant?" he whispered.

Deanna closed her eyes and sighed. It was too big a burden to bear alone.

"Holy crap," he whispered again, then carefully stood up beside her. He bent over and helped her brush the snow from her body, then hoisted her to her feet. "Let's go." He turned to whistle to the teenagers who were still actively involved in the snowball fight, and motioned to the truck.

Moments later, the kids had been dropped off and Deanna had said goodnight to everyone from the front seat of Cord's SUV. He hadn't said one word the entire ride. She glanced over at him as he concentrated on the road, and noticed the muscle twitching in his jaw.

Finally, he spoke, his voice ragged with emotion. "How far along are you?" he asked.

"I don't know. I think maybe sixteen weeks."

"Sixteen weeks? August."

"Yes. August was my last period," Deanna answered, gazing at her house as they drove closer.

"When are you due?"

"I don't know." They had parked now, and Cord shut off the truck, the lights, and stepped out into the night as she answered. He walked around to her side, opened her door and helped her out, suddenly handling her as if she were a piece of delicate bone china.

"Were you planning on telling me sometime soon?" He guided her up the steps. "Is that why you're home?"

"Well. I only found out myself today."

"Today? You're four months pregnant and you only found out today? C'mon, Deanna. I wasn't born yesterday." He followed her into the house, stripped off his coat, and laid it on top of hers on the bannister.

She went into the kitchen to put on tea water and he went into the living room to build a fire. Deanna started to question his actions, but stopped, realizing the hour of reckoning had come. He'd probably force her to marry him now. For the good of their baby, blah, blah, blah. A hint of a smile twitched on her lips as she mused over the idea and wondered if this was what she wanted after all.

~ ~ ~

Cord was frantic as he built the fire, seeking some release for the hostility, the anger building within. Sal had knocked her up, probably wouldn't marry her since he and Penny had become an item, so now she was crawling back to Cord. Hell. She probably felt he owed it to her. Well. No way. He cared for her, yes, loved her even. Maybe. But he wasn't going to be used as a scapegoat again. Not by anyone, even Deanna.

A sob of anguish caught in his throat as he watched the kindling burn. When it was hot enough, Cord threw a log on then turned to face Deanna, who had walked into the room and now sat on the couch. He joined her there, wondering what she was thinking.

He sat beside her and exhaled slowly. "Well?"

"Well, what?" she answered.

"Well. Have you told Sal yet?"

"Sal?" Deanna stared at him with an incredulous look of horror.

"What, is there an echo in here?"

"Sal? You think Sal did this?"

"Oh, great, here goes. I suppose you're going to tell me I'm the father."

"As a matter of fact, I was. I hope this baby doesn't have your brains, though. I thought you could figure that on your own."

"Cut it out, Deanna. We made love twice. Two times."

"That's usually how a kid is made, Cord."

"You were with Sal in August."

"Sal was my friend, you jerk! I never slept with him!"

"I've been here before." He stood up, disgusted.

"How dare you! Get out. Get out of my house. I don't ever, ever want to see you again!" She didn't move from the couch as she watched him storm away.

"Yeah, right." He walked to the foyer, grabbed his coat, and stalked out the door.

Deanna didn't start crying until she heard his truck tires crunch down the snow-packed driveway.

Chapter 26

The old house creaked and moaned throughout the night, as if it felt Deanna's troubles, and suffered alongside the sleepless woman. It wasn't until early dawn, maybe an hour or so before most families were waking up, getting in their last bit of sleep before children awoke shrieking with glee at the treasures left by Santa beneath their Christmas trees, that Deanna finally fell into a deep, troubled sleep.

~ ~ ~

Cord didn't sleep at all while the moon was high and the skies were dark. He spent the night shoveling a wider walkway around the main house, to the mailbox, garbage pails, and his garage loft entrance way. By 6 a.m. he came into the kitchen, where his mother had just finished fixing a pot of coffee.

She had heard him outside all night shoveling, and knew without a doubt something terrible was bothering her son. Jane had a sixth sense when it came to her children. And besides, the proof was in the circles beneath his eyes. Eyes glistening with anger and unshed tears. His face was dark and in need of a shave. He smelled of sweat and cold air.

"Sit down," she ordered, after giving him a good looking over. Once the coffee maker had been turned on she pulled her robe tighter about her and sat across from her son, who still wore his hat and coat. Jane knew what was wrong. She had guessed correctly last night. "Deanna?"

He nodded, staring straight ahead.

"You two fight *again*? Michael, I don't know what to tell you. You've got to curb that temper, son." Better to play dumb and let him tell her on his own.

It didn't take long. "She's pregnant, Mom."

Her mouth gaped open in shock although she knew in her heart all along. But hearing the words made it seem so much more real. "Pregnant? Are you sure? Is she sure?"

He shrugged and shook his head, scowling. He would not meet his mother's gaze. "I don't know. She thinks she is. She says she only found out yesterday."

"Yesterday? How?"

Again, he shrugged.

"Well. You two were planning on marrying twice now. I guess this cinches it for sure."

"Mom. I'm not marrying her." His voice was deadly quiet.

"What's that supposed to mean? That doesn't sound like you. Surely you can put your differences aside and do the right thing?"

"Mom? Of course, I'd do the right thing if I thought it was my responsibility to do it. I don't think it's my problem. She was seeing someone else. I don't think Deanna's carrying my kid." He sighed, a ragged, defeated sound.

"Whoa!" Matt walked into the kitchen, catching Cord's last statement. "Deanna's knocked up?" He opened the Santa Claus cookie jar and grabbed two Linzer Tart cookies.

"Matthew!" Jane admonished her elder son as she stood up and tied an apron about her robe. She turned toward the pantry, pulled out the flour and lard, and began making biscuits.

"Sorry, Mom. Cord, are you serious?"

"Merry Christmas," Cord answer dryly.

"And it's not yours?" Matt poured himself a cup of coffee as Terry walked into the kitchen carrying Jenna.

"What's not Cord's?"

"Deanna's pregnant," Matt said.

Cord threw his hands up in disgust. "Isn't anything private around here? Why does the whole world have to know?"

"Really, Cord? Is she sure?" Then, before Cord had the chance to answer, Terry smiled. "I thought it was kind of strange how she couldn't eat because of the flu, but man she put away that chocolate cake. That's how I was with Jenna. Congrats, brother." Terry leaned over and planted a kiss on Cord's head.

"It's not his," Matt stated with a grin. "At least that's what she's telling him."

"That's ridiculous! Of course, it's his! Why would she tell you that? True, you *are* fighting, but hey, you guys have fought before. That's not news." Terry rocked her fidgety daughter and handed her one of Matt's cookies.

"She's not telling me that," Cord said in a defeated voice. "I don't want to talk about it anymore."

"Kids, why don't you go inside? I'll finish breakfast in a bit." Jane prodded Matt and Terry gently, then turned to Cord. "Why don't you go over to your place, take a shower, and try to get some rest? You must be exhausted."

"I can't sleep, Mom." Cord's voice was strangled as he spoke. Jane came to him, standing beside him, clutching her son in an embrace, giving him time get it out of his system.

"There, there, Michael. It will be all right. You'll see." She kissed his head, then tilted his face upward and considered his eyes. "You go on to your place and do as I said. We'll open presents later, when you've had some rest."

Cord gave his mom one last hug and turned to go. Only after he'd shut the side door behind him did Jane snatch off her apron, throwing it on the table as she yelled for her husband. "Mike! Get in here! Hurry!"

~ ~ ~

The pounding on the door sounded strange, far off, even though Deanna was curled up in a ball on the couch. Her body ached now, and as the banging summoned her awake she tried to stand and stretch, realizing her legs were still asleep. As she limped toward the door, imagining the angry visitor to be Cord, her stomach rolled and her mouth grew dry. She stumbled toward the door as fast as she could, unlocking it and turning the knob before racing up the stairs into the bathroom. Jane entered the foyer in time to see Deanna fly up the stairs. She clucked her tongue, closing the door behind her.

Peppermint tea was steeping in two olive green ceramic mugs by the time Deanna joined Jane in the kitchen. "Here. I brought you some peppermint tea. It'll sooth your stomach. It always did mine, anyway." She placed a steaming mug before Deanna, who was pale and trembling and curled up tightly on a kitchen chair at the table. Jane sat down across from her, eyeing her the whole while. "So it's true then?"

Deanna blushed and cast her eyes downward as she nodded confirmation. "I'm pretty sure."

"Cord says it's not his."

Two widened green eyes filled with tears of sorrow and then flashed in anger. "Of course it's his," she answered, raking a hand through her tangle of curls. "I couldn't be so lucky."

"He says you were seeing someone else."

Deanna shook her head. "He thinks I was dating this guy, Sal. But we were only friends. I've known him since college. We've never been anything more than friends, Jane."

"He says you were broken up—"

"Yeah. We were broken up all right. But we met at a party and . . . and . . . well." Deanna reddened with the recollection. "Ask your son about the yacht. Ask him if he remembers a certain bet he insisted on collecting." She stood up and paced across the worn linoleum floor. "God. I was so stupid. I should have never—I should have turned the other way when I saw him."

"But you didn't."

Deanna bowed her head. *I love him.* "Jane, he's the only one. Ever."

Jane narrowed her eyes at the girl for a moment, then believing that what she said was the truth, asked simply, "Did you tell him that?"

"Ha! After what he accused me of? If he doesn't realize—"

"Realize what? That you've been faithful to him the whole time you've been split up? That doesn't sound very realistic. If I didn't know you as well as I do, I wouldn't believe it myself."

"But Cord knows me better!"

"But my son is a man. Men don't think like we do, honey."

Deanna sighed. "I don't know what to do."

"Trust me."

Deanna gave a rueful smile. "You're his mother."

"I love you as if you were my own daughter." Jane smiled at Deanna, opening her arms in a beckoning embrace. "And I can't see my son with anyone else but you. C'mon, sweetie, it's Christmas. Let's get this over with and get on with the holiday."

Enfolded in Jane's embrace, Deanna wept. Her torrent of heart-wrenching tears made Jane weep as well. "It wasn't supposed to be like this," Deanna said between sobs. "I don't want to marry him if he doesn't love me."

"If he doesn't love you?" Jane pulled back to stare into the young girl's blotchy tear-streaked face in amused bewilderment. "Where ever did you get that notion?"

"All he wants is my farm." Deanna hiccupped in between sobs.

"Deanna. You listen to me. He's got the farm. Whether you agree or not, he's got the farm. And believe it or not, he did it for you, for your sister, your parents, us."

"Oh, come on now, Jane. He did it for the money. He got that land for a song and he's going to make big bucks from it." Deanna scowled at the woman sitting beside her.

"And you're going to reap the rewards of all his efforts with that project, whether you admit it or not."

"I don't want the stupid money."

"No. You want what's impossible. You want your mother and father back, and you think by holding on to that farm they'll come home. Wake up, Deanna. Face, it, sweetie. They're gone. Nothing is going to bring them back. Not even the farm." Jane's voice had started off angry, harsh, but softened as she went to ease the pain of her words.

Deanna's shoulders sagged with the weight of Jane's words. "You're right," she whispered.

"You would have lost everything to the county, and then at an auction to developers who were only interested in making a quick dollar if Michael hadn't stepped in. And they would have built a mall, or an apartment complex—"

"I know, I know."

"Go on upstairs and get washed up. Dad will be back soon and we'll get going."

"Thanks, Jane."

"You're welcome, dear."

~ ~ ~

Once Deanna was away from Jane's logical, rational reasoning, she grew unsure of coming face to face with Cord. He believed the worst of her, putting her in the same category as Debbie, of all people! Could she forgive him so easily? Should she? Why should she be the one to go over there and apologize? It was up to him. Deanna toweled then blow-dried her hair, put on her makeup, and then got dressed. After checking herself one last time in the full-length mirror hanging on the back of the door, she decided she would tell Jane she had changed her mind. She wasn't going over, not to the McCord house for Christmas, nor to Cord's house to make up. She was a grown woman, she lectured her reflection, and would not be told what to do.

When Deanna descended the stairs clad only in sweatpants and sweatshirt, Jane frowned and pursed her lips. "You are being pigheaded."

Deanna shook her head. "I can't do it, Jane. I can't look at him, face him, knowing what he thinks of me. He's got to have more faith in me."

"As much as you've had in him?" Jane slipped her coat on.

"This is different."

"Well. I did my part. You two are never going to be happy if you don't set things right between you." She walked to the door. "I wish you were coming home with me. I hate to think of you here all alone."

"I'll be fine. I guess I have to stay away from the preserves." Deanna offered a feeble grin.

"It wasn't the preserves that did this to you." Jane hugged the young girl hard. "I love you, Deanna. You've always been like one of my own."

"I know you do. Thanks, Jane. I love you too."

Deanna stood by the door until Mr. McCord's blue pickup drove away. Then she shut the wooden door carefully, retreating into the living room to build a fire. Once Deanna was sure the fire had caught, she went upstairs to raid the library, selecting one of her old romance novels she'd shared and read with her mom and Trish in past days. Curled up on the couch, she fell asleep dreaming about princes and dukes and daring rescues from flaming towers.

When a knock sounded on the door, stirring her from her deep sleep, she jumped and ran to answer it, disappointed when she found herself face to face with Terry and Matt. Terry smiled brightly, saluting Deanna with a tinfoil-covered aluminum baking tray. "Can we use your oven? Mom's got stuff in Cord's and her own and we need this baked ziti heated," Terry said as she let herself in, walking toward the kitchen.

"Sure," Deanna called sarcastically from behind.

She eyed Matt, who had a four-foot-tall evergreen cradled in his arms. "Here. Dad told me to chop one down and bring it over. Since you aren't coming over, Mom wanted to make sure you had your own tree."

"Thanks." Her voice was nothing more than a whisper hoarse with emotion.

"Where should I put this?" He stood in the foyer, looking uncomfortable as she watched him.

Deanna pointed toward the living room. "By the window, I guess."

She closed the door and watched from the foyer as Matt pulled out of his coat pocket two slats of wood, a hammer and two nails, then fashioned a cross and nailed it to the bottom of the tree.

After he set the tree down, he stood up and smiled. "There. Prettiest tree we ever saw."

A smile was all she could offer him by way of thanks, for the lump in her throat made it impossible to speak.

"Dinner's going to be at two today." Terry spoke from the kitchen.

"That's nice." Deanna turned and pushed her way past the young woman. "Can I make you some tea or something?"

"Nah. We're going to head back. Jenna's waiting to open presents. She's probably screaming her little head off right now." Terry hugged Deanna hard. "We'll be back in an hour. Keep it on low so it doesn't burn."

"Yeah. An hour. So, if you change your mind?" Matt spoke over his shoulder as he headed for the door.

"No, but thanks. I'd rather stay here."

"Whatever. C'mon, Ter."

Deanna watched them leave, her heart heavy but her eyes dry. Then, after she watched Matt's truck turn toward the McCord house, Deanna shut the door and turned to study the tree. She smiled, pleased with the gift they had given her.

She made her way slowly up to the attic, a bit excited with the thought of having her own tree. The Christmas boxes were labelled plain as day, although they were dusty from sitting unused over the last few years. Deanna lugged them down carefully, one at a time, aiming to decorate the tree before Terry and Matt came back to show them her appreciation. Slowly, she unpacked the boxes, vaguely recalling previous holidays when the task of decorating the trees had been solely her and her mother's responsibility.

~ ~ ~

"Well?" Jane met Terry and Matt at the door, knowing the answer to her question by the look on her daughter-in-law's face.

"She's not going to come, Mom."

Jane scowled and shook her head. "That stubborn little . . ."

"Don't get upset, Jane. She's gotta do what she's gotta do. I don't blame her, really," Terry offered.

"Terry, don't start," Matt called out as he hung his coat up in the hall closet.

"I'm only saying that if you had reacted like Cord did when I told you I was pregnant . . ."

Cord stepped into the hall from the direction of the kitchen, where he had slipped in through the side door.

"Terry?"

She jumped at the sound of his voice. "Cord! When did you get here?"

"Right about the time you were comparing my brother to me."

"Sorry." She lifted her delicate chin toward her brother-in-law, refusing to be intimidated by his scowl. "But, it's true."

"You don't know the whole story."

"You're right, Cord, she doesn't. Terry? Inside. Now." Matt propelled his wife by the shoulders into the living room despite her protests.

"Go to her, Cord. She won't come over unless you apologize." His mother grimaced at him, her hands set defiantly on her hips.

He shook his head and took his coat off. "Mom. Don't nag. Don't let her fool you. She's not coming over here because she can't face me. It's not mine."

"You are the one being foolish, young man." She turned and walked into the kitchen, leaving her son alone in the hall.

Cord followed his mother into the kitchen.

"C'mon, Mom. How can you say that?" He came to stand beside her as she opened the refrigerator door and began rummaging through its contents of tinfoil-covered dishes. "Here let me help you."

"I can do it myself, Michael." She didn't look at him, and Cord thought her voice was as cold as the air coming from the refrigerator.

"You want me to check on the casserole in my oven?"

"No."

"Well. What can I do then?" He threw his hands up in the air as she turned around carefully balancing four covered dishes and a bowl of fruit.

"You know what you can do." She narrowed her gaze at him before turning her back to her son and walking carefully to the counter.

"Mom?"

She faced him finally, her voice trembling with emotion. "It's Christmas, Michael. And it's breaking my heart to think of that poor little girl over there all by herself. No mother, no father, not even her sister. And now she's giving you the most beautiful gift of all and you don't want it. I'm sorry, Michael, but right now there isn't anything I want of you, except for you to search that heart of yours and go to her. Now, please leave me alone. I have a dinner to prepare." She turned again, mumbling something about how only God knew how she was going to get through this day.

Cord swore softly and stormed out of the kitchen heading toward the living room where Terry and Matt were digging presents out of a stocking for Jenna, who seemed more interested in the gaily-colored wrapping paper than any of the gifts.

"Hey."

Terry refused to look up at him and Matt merely glanced up with a quick scowl.

"Not you, too. Geez." Cord walked over to the stereo and selected a Mitch Miller Christmas CD.

"Here, Jenna," Terry cooed. "Look what Santa brought you, baby." She held up a miniature stuffed reindeer with a red nose and bells within its belly, so it jingled every time Terry shook it before Jenna's chubby outstretched hands.

"Come on, guys." Cord walked over to them, his hands on his waist as he stared down at the family. He chuckled as Jenna fussed with the red Santa cap sitting lopsidedly on her head. He knelt beside his niece and chucked her under the chin. "Hey, Jenna. Got a kiss for Uncle Cord?"

The infant giggled and turned her pursed lips toward Cord's cheek.

"At least somebody loves me."

"To get love you have to give love," Terry offered.

"Terry." Matt cut his wife off before she had the chance to finish reprimanding his brother.

"Spare me, Ter." Cord straightened to scowl down at his sister-in-law.

"Cord, watch it, buddy," Matt said in defense of his wife.

Turning on his heel Cord took off to find his father, who was in his wood shop putting the finishing touches on a set of unstained angel silhouettes. He stood by his father's side watching the older McCord sand the wings of the mirror images of two angels who held between them two hearts that came apart when tugged at gently. He puffed on a pipe, the scent of cherry tobacco filling the workshop. He remained silent until Cord sighed.

"Well," he began, his voice filtering out between his clenched teeth that held the pipe. "Didn't think I'd have this done in time."

"It's good, Pops."

"Yeah. I think she'll like it."

"Mom loves anything you make her."

His father shook his head.

Cord knew then it had been made for Deanna. He grimaced, disappointed that even his father wouldn't stand by him on this issue. "Not you, too?"

"We all make mistakes, son."

Cord was silent as he waited for his father to continue, to preach about how Deanna should be forgiven.

"And sometimes we have to be reminded to be man enough to own up to them."

"What? Wait a minute, Pops."

"Hear me out, boy. She's a fine girl. And I know you love her. She's got the proof, from what I'm hearing."

Cord shook his head. "It's not mine."

"Your mother said Deanna mentioned something about a bet. And a yacht?" His father was always direct, and this time was no different as he sanded away the rough edges of one of the angel's wings. "Now I don't want to hear all the details, but I thought I'd jog that memory of yours in case it wasn't working properly. Maybe you need to do a little calculating."

"She could have been pregnant before then, and she set me up. I seem to be a pretty good target for that." He scowled, surprised that his father would side with Deanna and the rest of his family. He and Pops always stuck together, whether either one was right or wrong. To the end.

"True. But I doubt it. I know Deanna. If it had been Trish, I'd agree. But not Deanna. And if you want to go the distance and wait until she comes to term and has that baby, it might be too late, son."

His words lay heavy in Cord's heart. Still, he said nothing, hoping his father would guide him as he always had in the past.

"So?"

Shaking his head, the elder McCord held the angels up to the light, inspecting his work of art with a critical eye. "That's it."

"What do I do?"

"You're asking me what to do? I'm only a tired old man. You're the business tycoon. You make million-dollar decisions all year. And you're asking me for advice?" He chuckled and placed the angels on the bench. He rummaged through the box of Christmas wrapping paper, tissue paper, and ribbons and bows Jane used to wrap all the presents.

"Yeah, Pops. I am." Cord sat down on a stool beside his father, his voice cracking with emotion.

"I'm sorry, son. I can't tell you what to do. You got to dig deep down inside and find out what's right for you. And Deanna. And that baby." He wrapped the angels in tissue paper, making meticulous folds and taping them carefully, then going through the same motions with the wrapping paper filled with cherubs.

"What if it's not mine?"

"I thought you loved her?"

"I do."

His father raised his bushy brows. "Will you do me a favor, son?"

"Sure." Cord sighed. Obviously, his father was not going to give him the advice he came in here seeking.

Removing the pipe from between his teeth, placing it in the wooden ash tray sitting on his bench, Mr. McCord turned toward his son. "I don't fancy going out in this weather. My bones are too old for this sort of thing. You think you can deliver this to the little lady next door, so she has something under her tree. It would make your mom's day."

His father's knowing gaze reflected a wisdom and love that only years of life experiences could bring. "Sure thing, Pops." Cord stood up and took the package his father handed to him and started to walk away. He'd taken two steps before he stopped and turned back to his father, taking his aging body in a gentle embrace. "Thanks, Pops."

The older man chuckled softly then answered in a husky whisper, "Sure thing, son."

Chapter 27

Andy Williams was wrapping up a moving rendition of "Chestnuts Roasting on an Open Fire" as Deanna placed a gauzy angel at the top of her little Christmas tree. The silence between songs on the old record crackled with age over the stereo speakers as Deanna stepped back to survey her workmanship. She smiled, placing a hand protectively on her belly, still smooth even though the precious life cradled within was already beginning to blossom and grow.

In the forty-five minutes it took to decorate her little tree, Deanna had come to terms with many things. The first and foremost realization was that she now welcomed the precious gift God had made known to her on such a special day.

She also reconciled herself to Cord's response, and knew in her heart that it hadn't been anything more than she should have honestly expected, considering the circumstances. After all, she rationalized, Cord had believed she and Sal were lovers, as foolish as that seemed to Deanna. And, while she knew it only took one time, it seemed Cord and Deanna had indeed made love enough to make a baby. And hadn't Cord been burnt before when wrongfully charged with the responsibility of being the one who had fathered a child? Yes, Deanna graciously allowed that Cord was justified in initially reacting the way he did. And maybe, just maybe, she would give him a second chance. But only on her terms. And after the holiday. No more fights for her this Christmas.

All of this came to Deanna as she hung the handmade angels, wreaths, and sleds, the store-bought balls and the wooden beads on the little evergreen tree. And as she laid eyes on the angel smiling up at her from its four-foot perch, Deanna found peace within her heart, and a new peace surrounding her as well. If Cord didn't want to be a part of her and this baby's life, fine. She would let him develop his magic kingdom. She would sign the contract, let him pay to fix up this house and she would live here, with her baby, offering as much love as her mother had given her. With or without Cord. She smiled devilishly with her last thought. And she would raise her little girl or boy on their daddy's money.

~ ~ ~

It was in the middle of "Jingle Bells" that Deanna heard footsteps stomping off snow on the front porch. Expecting it to be Terry coming to claim the baked ziti, Deanna stood up to greet her with her best smile in place, preparing to fight off any final attempts to get her to join the McCords for Christmas.

The front door opened as Deanna stepped into the darkened foyer, only to come face to face with Cord. Her perfectly-placed smile faltered, her facade crumbled quickly. "What are you doing here?" she asked. *So much for that newfound peace.*

Surprised and apparently annoyed at finding Deanna with a smile on her face, music playing, a fire burning, and a tree all decorated, Cord stepped around her and made his way into the house. "Some damsel in distress you are," he muttered, half to himself, as he surveyed the cheery scene.

"I don't need rescuing, let alone from you." She spoke in a huff, to his back, then noted how his honey brown hair—in desperate need of a trim—curled in disarray about his nape, peeking out from beneath the suede collar of his leather jacket.

He stared pointedly at the Christmas tree and the fire crackling in the fireplace, and then walked over to the stereo, carelessly tossing the package he held in his hands onto the couch. Deanna watched as he knelt and jabbed at the power button with his middle finger, silencing Andy's crooning with one movement.

Riled by the arrogance of his actions, Deanna stalked over to the stereo, aiming to turn it back on. Her efforts were stilted immediately as he grabbed her wrist in a gentle hold.

"Do you mind?" she asked softly, her belly doing flip-flops with his touch.

"Leave it, Deanna." His voice was low. She turned her gaze upward to challenge him and immediately regretted her actions, for in his smoldering eyes there was no masking the pain simmering there. Tears clouded her vision as she realized he was hurting. That was more difficult to deal with than even his accusations from the night before.

"Pops made you something." He let go of her wrist and motioned to the package he'd tossed onto the couch.

Deanna walked over to the package and picked it up, then placed it under the tree. "Tell your father thank you for me."

"You can tell him yourself. Now get dressed."

"What?"

"Get dressed. Please."

"I'm not getting dressed. But I will get your ziti." Deanna tried to walk past him, out of the room since he didn't appear to be leaving any time soon, but he grabbed her once again.

Cord cursed aloud as he touched her, as if doing so singed him. They stood staring at one another, neither budging. "Don't push me, Deanna. I've had it."

"Don't threaten me, Michael McCord. This is my house and I'm telling you to leave." Deanna squared off before him, hands on hips, chest puffed out slightly.

"I don't know what you told them, or why you are doing this to me. But we've got to call a truce. If only for today. Please?" He stood there, not moving.

"I don't know what you're talking about," she muttered, as she walked away and settled down in the corner of the couch.

"My mom. Matt and Terry. They're all pissed off at me. Because of you. I don't care what you do to me, but keep my family out of it. You're ruining my mother's holiday. All she can think about is you suffering all alone over here. Terry won't talk to me, and she and Matt are fighting because every time she does say something to me she goes for my jugular." He held up his hands as Deanna tried to protest.

"Wait, there's more. They send me over here on some crazy errand after making me feel guilty all morning and what do I find? *The Deanna Drake Christmas Special*, complete with musical accompaniment by Andy Williams."

"Now, hold on!"

"Let me finish. I didn't expect all of this. Mom had me believing you're over here crying your eyes out, and I find this. But you're breaking Mom's heart, and it has to stop. So, please get dressed and let's go. Please."

"I don't have to do anything." She folded her arms across her chest and stuck her chin out stubbornly.

Cord walked over to her and knelt down, bringing his face closer to hers with every word. "I know you don't have to. I'm asking you to."

The last thing Deanna wanted was to hurt Jane. Or ruin the McCord family's holiday. She studied the tree lights and said so. "Can't you tell her I'm sick. She'll understand."

"No, she won't." He straightened up and walked into the kitchen.

Deanna chewed her lower lip, and stood up. "I'm doing this for your mom. That's it," she explained as she made her way upstairs.

~ ~ ~

Moments later, she found him in the kitchen, re-wrapping the crinkled tinfoil over a slightly well-done tray of baked ziti. She wore a black velvet jumper with a white turtleneck, giving her a schoolgirl appearance. He considered her for a moment, then went back to covering the ziti.

She was pleased with her appearance, and Deanna saw that same sentiment flash reluctantly in Cord's gaze. She nodded toward the ziti and raised her brows in question.

"Slightly well done. Proof we spent the time making up instead of fighting," he said. Though his face was strained, Deanna understood the implied meaning of his words.

"I'm not going to lie." She turned to get her cloak out of the hall closet. She heard him call out from the kitchen, his tone too pleasant for his mood.

"That's the story, can't we stick with it?" He walked toward her as she shrugged into her cloak. Before she could utter another protest, he caught her up in a gentle, but firm embrace, closing his lips possessively over hers before she even had a chance to breathe deeply. Deanna found herself responding to his kiss as she always did, shamelessly, without conscious thought or the ability to deny what her heart and soul wanted, even if her mind didn't.

With one last brush of his lips against hers, as if he were almost reluctantly leaving them, he began placing soft kisses along her jaw, her cheek, to her ear. He suckled softly on her lobe, whispering her name in a breathless caress.

Deanna shivered as his lips found the tender skin of her neck, nuzzling near the top fold of the turtleneck's collar. Her knees buckled and she would have swooned had Cord's hand not been at the small of her back, pressing her to him intimately.

How could she hate him and love him all at once? She adored him and despised him and reveled in his touch and wanted more. He stepped back and they stared at one another breathlessly, as if both surprised at the intensity of their kiss.

Then the moment was over as her stomach rumbled loudly. Her hand flew to her mouth and she cried out as she ran upstairs to the bathroom.

Her stomach churned and rumbled as Deanna unsuccessfully fought the queasiness, then gave in and bent over the toilet bowl.

Cord had followed her and now came in to check on her. "You drive me crazy. I'm sorry." He rinsed a washcloth with cool water and handed it to her. She took it reluctantly, unable to speak.

He rubbed her back as she shuddered with one last wracking, choking cough, then steadied her as she straightened up beside him. Only after splashing cold water on her paled face did she speak to his reflection in the mirror. "I can't do this."

She brushed her teeth, took a gulp of mouthwash and spit, eyeing him in the mirror the whole time.

He only shook his head, his face a mask. "You have to. One day, that's all I ask. Tomorrow, next week, if you want to hate me, fine. But today we will be the happy couple." He bent his head low and nuzzled her soft, sweet-smelling hair.

She straightened her spine and leaned away from him, still staring at him in the mirror.

"Well? Is it a deal?"

Deanna nodded, her chin tilted proudly. "Yes."

He took her bait graciously. "But?"

"I still hate you."

He chuckled and released her, turning to leave. "If what we do to each other is hate, Deanna, then God as my witness, it might be worth it to settle for that."

Chapter 28

By late afternoon, Cord even had Deanna nearly convinced that things had indeed been worked out between them. He doted on her and hardly ever left her side. His change in personality began almost immediately in his truck, where he spent the few minutes driving back to the McCord home telling Deanna dirty jokes about Santa and his elves and life in the North Pole. The first two Cord told her Deanna had refused to laugh at. Instead, she pursed her lips together and told him he was disgusting. But by the time they had parked and were walking up the shoveled walkway, Deanna was bright red, near tears, and out of breath from laughing so hard. Which is precisely how Cord wanted her when they walked into his parents' house.

~ ~ ~

Jane had been watching from the window, and as she saw the two of them get out of the truck, Cord first, then Deanna after he came around to open her door, her heart leapt with the miracle of love. The two of them were laughing and Cord was talking animatedly, nearly losing the baked ziti more than once since he had a habit of talking with his hands. As they stepped through the front door into the foyer, Jane greeted them and took the ziti from her son, noticing how Cord's hands lingered overly long on Deanna's shoulders when he took her cloak from her. She smiled as she watched him caress

Deanna's cheek with the back of his hand as he slipped her cashmere cap from her head.

Moments later, Jane's good cheer thinned when she took the tinfoil off the well-done baked ziti and hollered at Cord. Cord laughed as he explained the two of them became "preoccupied" in trying to work out their differences. Deanna scowled and shot a not-so-loving glance his way, but Cord held her close and laughed heartily, planting a loud kiss on her petulant mouth. It was worth burning the baked ziti, Jane decided silently.

~ ~ ~

By late afternoon, Mr. McCord's family joined them for Christmas Day dinner, including Granny and Grampa McCord, Mr. McCord's three brothers and their wives, half a dozen of the McCord cousins and their spouses, children, and grandchildren. All in all, Deanna estimated nearly fifty people crowded into the living room, kitchen, formal dining room, playroom, and den. All of whom were laughing, singing, and thoroughly enjoying themselves.

Except for Deanna, who outwardly remained cheery. Inwardly, she died a little with every touch, every caress, every knowing look Cord cast her way. Deanna was having a hard time believing there was any way he could be as miserable as she was throughout the evening. Hell, he truly seemed like he was enjoying himself. And by the time dessert was finished, she had nearly forgotten what it was she was supposed to be so miserable about.

The baby was not mentioned once, although Deanna could see Jane was chomping at the bit to break the news to the family. Only one time did Cord even act like he remembered Deanna was pregnant, when Uncle Ted turned Deanna's wine glass over as dinner was being served. Immediately Cord put his hand out, covering the mouth of the crystal glass, causing a brief hush to fall over the table. Jane raised her brows, but said nothing. Cord turned to Deanna as if he didn't notice something was amiss and asked overly loud, "Are you still taking that antibiotic for your throat, or have you finished it?"

Deanna caught his gaze for a moment, and raised her brow. Then she nodded in support of his lie, and turned to Uncle Ted to explain, "No, thank you, I'm on medication." She avoided catching Jane's eye, knowing full well the matriarch was dying to share the news that she was going to be a grandma again.

Later that evening, when a good portion of the crowd had gathered in the living room to sing Christmas carols, Deanna stood up from the love seat she had been forced to share with Cord in an effort to take a break from this farce he was insisting on carrying out. She had barely taken a step when he grabbed her hand and eased her onto his lap, cradling her close and nudging her head to rest against his chest. She squirmed, but Cord held her fast, unwilling to part with her for the moment.

She sighed, deciding it was time to make him suffer as he had made her do all evening. She snuggled against him, as if trying to burrow deeper into his embrace. She wrapped her arms about his torso and squeezed him hard, her thumbs resting in the one ticklish spot she knew he had, just below and to the back of his armpits. He stiffened and groaned, squeezing his arms tight, nearly cutting off the circulation in her hands. She giggled and relaxed her thumbs and he followed suit soon thereafter. She settled down once again and he held her close.

~ ~ ~

Nearly an hour later, he felt the soft caress of her breath against his neck, signaling she had fallen asleep.

Cord exhaled and let his guard down only then, his hand dropping from where it rested on her hip to her belly. Nonchalantly he laid his hand there, itching to caress, wondering if the child that grew there could honestly be his. For the moment, he pretended it was, and for the first time all evening he felt the Christmas spirit.

~ ~ ~

It was nearly midnight when the last of the guests donned their coats and thanked Jane and Mike for a wonderful holiday. As the final car eased its way down the long driveway, Matt and Terry bid their parents good night and headed upstairs to the guest bedroom where Jenna was now asleep. The older McCords were left behind, wondering what to do with their son and Deanna, both of whom had fallen asleep on the love seat hours earlier.

"I'll bet neither one of them slept well last night," Mike said.

Jane shook her head, her eyes misting. "Michael didn't sleep at all, remember? I sure am glad things are all right again. You think they'll finally get married now?" The two McCords stood in the entrance way to the living room, hugging one another as they whispered a recap of their successful holiday. Deanna was still curled up in Cord's lap, like a little puppy. Cord had tucked his legs up under his body and over the second cushion of the love seat.

"Jane, honey. To tell you the truth, I'd be happy if they made it to the New Year without another fight. C'mon." He chuckled as he extinguished the light on the table next to where they stood. "Let's go to bed."

"Do we leave them there?" Jane allowed her husband to guide her into the hall.

"Don't you remember what it's like to be young? Of course, we leave them there. Hell." Mr. McCord led his wife up the stairs after locking the front door. "He can't do any more damage than he's already done, now, can he?"

Their laughter echoed softly throughout the house as Jane agreed.

~ ~ ~

The grandfather clock struck 12 times, heralding midnight and rousing Deanna from her sleep. Confused, she peered around the darkened room, empty except for one other person, Cord, whom she had obviously been using as a pillow for a good part of the night. She tried to sit up, but found his arms locked around her body, holding her in place. She nudged him with her elbow, surprised to find he was already awake.

"Let me go," she hissed.

"Shush." Cord lifted a hand and pointed lazily to the fire. "Please? Until the fire dies. Okay?"

She swallowed thickly, "We don't have to pretend anymore. I'm surprised you haven't tossed me on the floor." When he did not respond, Deanna settled back down, focusing her gaze on the flickering orange and yellow flames. She remained silent as her mind actively sought something witty and intelligent to say. It eluded her like an ad campaign on the eve of deadline.

"Is that the same log that was burning before I fell asleep?"

"Uh-hm. I guess."

"Wow. That couldn't be pine then, could it? Pine burns too fast, and it pops a lot, no? Is it oak? It must be oak."

"Shhhh."

She remained silent for a moment, the beating of his heart sounding in her ear that was pressed against his firm chest. *Uh-hm. Uh-hm. Uh-hm.*

She chuckled softly, until Cord broke the silence and asked, "Now what is it?"

Deanna giggled, more from nerves than anything, before explaining that his heart was in total agreement with his mind. "That's the sound it makes. *Uh-hm. Uh-hm. Uh-hm.*"

He was silent for a moment, then when he spoke his whisper was filled with amusement. "One question, Drake."

"Yeah, McCord?"

"The only times you're quiet are when you're sleeping or being kissed?"

"You should know." She squirmed, trying to untangle herself from his embrace, but failed.

"I'll let you go when you tell me."

She giggled and squirmed again, her thigh coming in contact with his hardened bulge. She shrieked and almost succeeded in jumping up, but he clasped a hand over her mouth and held her close, back against his chest. He chuckled and whispered softly in her ear, "Shh. You'll wake Mom and Dad."

How many nights had they wrestled on the couch like this so many years ago? How could it only seem like yesterday? How many fires had they made out in front of, right here? Exactly like this?

His warning to be quiet silenced both of them for a moment, those thoughts echoing between them. He bent his head and whispered, "I want you," in her ear before catching her lobe gently with a kiss. Deanna groaned and twisted in his arms, able to do so only because Cord had loosened his hold on her.

She half-heartedly tried to stand.

He held her hands firmly and pulled her back down onto his lap. "Do you truly want to leave? I'll take you home, if that's what you want."

As he nuzzled her neck, she grew silent. His touches led Deanna's mind to a night three months earlier and she shivered with the recollection. It had been so good. So perfect. Too perfect, she thought now considering the result of that night. She tilted her head to provide him better access, and closed her eyes, reveling in the sensations.

He captured her lips against his, claiming her as he searched for the release their love play had been leading them toward.

"When we make love, everything is right in the world," he whispered as he came up for air, his voice ragged with desire.

"I know. You drive me crazy. I can't live with you. I can't live without you." She kissed him back as ferociously, tasting his sweetness, wanting more.

"So what do we do?" He lifted his head and squinted at her in the darkness. His voice was hoarse and tentative.

Deanna looked up and studied his shadowed face in the firelight, noting how sexy he was with his sleepy eyes filled with love. He had a fine nose, and perfect lips, she mused with a smile.

"Well?"

She swallowed thickly, then blinked slowly, preparing for her confession. He could believe her or he could think it was another game. The magic would become reality, or the magic would end.

Her eyes shined warmly, "You know." She gulped loudly as she plunged head-on into a full explanation. "This can't be Sal's baby. Or anyone's baby but yours."

He raised his head up now, and she searched his eyes, her cheeks warmed as she prepared for her confession. She caught her lower lip between her teeth as she chewed nervously.

"What do you mean?" His voice cracked with her implication.

"It's only been me and you."

"Ever?"

Nodding, Deanna suddenly found herself at a loss for words.

"Ever," he repeated, seeking clarification.

Again, she nodded. "That's how come I know you're—only you—"

He contemplated her expression for a moment, then closed his eyes, his voice ragged. "Really? Is it true, Dean? Really? We're going to have a baby?" He sat her away from him, his face a mask of amazement, disbelief, and awe.

She nodded, tears trickling slowly from her eyes. "Yes. Really. I promise."

He shook his head and swallowed. "It's really mine."

"Yes. I wouldn't do that to you. I could never lie." Deanna stopped speaking as she watched Cord lean over, bending over her until his head rested against her belly. He buried his face there, kissing the place that cradled the life they had made.

After a moment, he lifted his head, his eyes filled with pain. He spoke and his voice was filled with anguish. "I am so sorry. I've hurt you so much."

Placing a finger on his lips Deanna silenced him. "Don't. We both did and said hurtful things. I was wrong. And pigheaded. I didn't want to give up anything. I didn't want to make any sacrifices. I was so angry."

Cord sat up now and pulled her into the cocoon of

his embrace, both mesmerized by the dying fire. "Me too. All I could think about was you and Sal."

"There never was a me and Sal."

"So you said. We've lost so much time." Again, Cord's voice was wrought with emotion.

Deanna hugged him hard.

He turned to study her face in the last bit of firelight. He locked on her tear-filled gaze and caught her chin with his hand. She gulped deeply and turned her face toward him, parting her lips in anticipation. Her eyes closed briefly, then opened again when he failed to deliver what his actions were promising.

As he studied her in the shadows, he spoke. "That night playing pool? And on the yacht. This was my wish. You. Me. Together. Not only for those nights, but forever," he said, his voice strained with emotion.

"Ten bucks and a wish," she said softly as she kissed his cheek, his chin, and then his lips, her hand moved gently, caressing his chest, his belly, and finally even lower as she searched his eyes as they crinkled with a warm, knowing glint.

"Haven't I done enough damage already?" he asked, recalling his father's words earlier on.

"I wouldn't call it damage now. Reconstruction, perhaps." She smiled.

"Foundation?"

"That's good too," she whispered.

"So what happens now?" He kissed her forehead and held her close.

"Now? Right n*ow,* or long-term now?"

Cord laughed at her. "Whatever."

"Well. I suppose I can start wearing that ring again."

"You still got it?"

Deanna smiled. "Then I guess I'll have to put an ad in the paper."

He frowned in confusion.

"To sublet my apartment," she continued matter-of-factly. "I'll have to hire a moving company. Give my notice. Find a dress. Call Trish."

"Okay, okay." He laughed again. "Are you proposing to me?"

"It depends. Will you say yes if I do?"

"I don't know. Will it be a marriage in name only? Or will it be a real marriage, you know, marital rights and everything?"

"Marital rights! You had your marital rights." She laughed and pointed to her belly.

"And I plan on exercising them again tonight, so please make this quick."

"Make what quick?"

"Hurry up and ask me to marry you."

She began to speak, then ever so slightly shook her head. "I started. You finish." She nudged him away from her but he captured her up in another embrace.

"Is this really happening? Are we really getting another chance?" He held her close against his chest and rested a cheek on her head.

"It feels so weird."

"We're doing it all backwards."

"At least we're doing it."

"We are, aren't we?"

"I will. If you will."

"Well, then. Deanna? Will you marry me?"

She lifted her head up to study his features in the darkness. "Honestly? One time we thought we would marry for love. That was so long ago, we were kids. Then we were going to marry as part of a business deal. Now why are we doing this? For the baby? Because we're caught up in the holiday spirit? For your mom? Why?"

Concern etched across her brows, clouded her eyes as she searched his face for an answer.

"You should know." He threw her words back at her with a grin.

Deanna shook her head and nuzzled her nose against his neck. "Tell me," she whispered.

He groaned aloud, her breath on his skin, her lips tickling him, driving him to distraction. "No problem." He leaned back and captured her face between his hands. "I love you, Deanna Drake. I always have and always will. When you moved away I lost all hope I'd ever be able to mend what I broke. Every day I thought about calling you or finding you, but the longer you stayed away, the longer I knew I'd lost you forever to the city. All the dreams and promises we shared, the memories we made . . . You were my rock and my best friend and my first love and I lost you just like that. All I've ever hoped for since then was to show you how much I still loved you. And that I was so sorry I hurt you."

"You should have come looking for me."

"I know," he said and laughed again. "But that wasn't exactly the response I was hoping for."

"No?" She threw him a smirk, her response evident in the glow of her eyes.

"Am I going to have to torture it out of you? I'm very good at that you know." He repositioned himself so that he was now kneeling beside her on the couch, gently nudging her onto her back.

Deanna sighed contentedly and rested her head against a throw pillow as she opened her arms in a beckoning gesture. As he came to rest on top of her, Cord hesitated.

"Am I too heavy?"

"I don't think so." Deanna lifted her lips upwards.

"Kiss me." She clutched his shoulders and moved against him.

"No. Come on. The fire's out. Let's go."

"Go?" Deanna groaned. "Go where?"

He stood up before answering her, then as he held out his hand he spoke.

"We're going home."

She took his hand and stood beside him, stretching and yawning all at once. "Cord?"

He smiled down at her, a broad grin that lit up his entire face.

"I love you too. I've been so angry with you for so long, I forgot how much I loved you. You were the only one who ever was strong enough to stand up to me, to respect and understand me. Every good memory I have of growing up is connected to you. Then, when . . . *that* . . . happened . . . then Mom died, I had nothing to stay here for. So all I could do was run."

"I know."

"I love you so much." She hugged him so hard her arms ached.

"I know," he said again, holding her tight.

"You're a beast." She raised her head and captured his lips.

"I know," he murmured against her lips. "Merry Christmas, baby."

"Merry Christmas, Cord."

As the two lovers locked in an embrace, the last of the fire had finally died, and another fire was already burning brightly, deep within their souls. A fire that they would never, ever let burn out again.

Janina Grey:

Janina Grey has been writing since she could hold a crayon, and there has been no stopping her since. Journaling, short stories, poetry, newsletters, news, feature, columns, Op/Eds, and press releases have kept her busy her whole life. But it was the sweet romances she read in her downtime that stayed forever in her heart and gave her the inspiration to write her own.

Growing up on Long Island and living periodically in Tennessee as a youth has given her the opportunity to meet many different types of people and experience many different lifestyles. After moving from Long Island to settle in upstate New York with her family, she found the support needed to pursue her writing endeavors.

When Janina is not writing, she may be marching for women's rights, kayaking, camping, drumming, or dancing around the fire.

With her two children grown, she and her husband, David, share their 110-year-old Mohawk Valley farm house homestead with a few resident spirits and a very squawky murder of crows.

Made in the USA
Middletown, DE
10 August 2024

58398340R00205